RAVENBOURNE SLAVERY

THE RAVENBOURNE TRILOGY: BOOK 1

Benjamin H. Barnette

ECHO BOOKS

ECHO BOOKS

1390 N Heritage LN #4
Tahlequah, OK 74464
Published in the United States in 2025

Map of Achaean Empire:
Original Draft by Benjamin H. Barnette
Graphic Design by Laura Smith, Tahlequah, Oklahoma

Photographs by Shutterstock:
Cover Contributor: DM7
Chapter Heading Silhouettes Contributor: Vladimir Ceresnak
Interior Silhouette Contributor: KHIUS

Library of Congress Control Number: 2023922552

Hardcover ISBN 979-8-9856948-2-6
Paperback ISBN 979-8-9856948-0-2
eBook ISBN 979-8-9856948-1-9

Printed in the United States of America.

Praise for

RAVENBOURNE SLAVERY

"*Ravenbourne Slavery* by Benjamin H. Barnette is a stimulating, mature book with vivid sexual scenes, heart-racing action, and wonderful supernatural undertones."

—*San Francisco Book Review* (star rating 5/5)

"The book's strength lay in its well-developed characters with thought-provoking histories... There is little to dislike in *Ravenbourne Slavery* by Benjamin H. Barnette, which makes it an excellent read for fans of fantasy fiction infused with plenty of hardcore romance."

—*Tulsa Book Review* (star rating 4/5)

"What will happen when fates collide? Tear open a copy of *Ravenbourne Slavery* to find out. Pages upon pages of love, horrors, sex, and punishment await you. Here, the reader is surrounded by a world of fear, hope, and beautiful women."

—*Independent Book Review*

"*Ravenbourne Slavery* is a thrilling and mystical adventure that lovers of early pre-history fantasy will adore.... For the first book in a trilogy, this story does what a first book should do; it introduces and develops interesting characters, dynamic tension, and a future story arc, leaving the reader thirsty for more and looking forward to the next iteration in this trilogy."

—*Readers Favorite* (star rating 5)

"Libraries and readers seeking an exceptionally vivid story of romance, power, and slavery's challenges will find *Ravenbourne Slavery* a heady read packed with opportunities for book club discussions about the kinds of relationships and power struggles that evolve between slaves, warriors, and ordinary men and women."

—*Midwest Book Review*
Diane Donovan, Senior Reviewer

"*Ravenbourne Slavery*, which takes place in a brutal fictionalized ancient civilization, is best described as a picaresque novel. The main characters pass through a series of often harrowing experiences that are connected via an underling story arc."

—*The BookLife Prize*

"In the intricate fantasy novel *Ravenbourne Slavery*, a warrior and an intelligent girl meet in a kingdom marked by slavery and class divisions.... The worldbuilding is lush and sensuous."

—*Foreword Clarion Review*

Acknowledgments

I owe sincere thanks to the following people who read and edited the unfinished manuscript and offered excellent advice and words of encouragement. Relationship banker, Beth Spicer; tennis partner, Carl Rossetti; fellow author Amy Campbell (*Dreaming of a Daughter*); Doug Sims, Ph.D., College of Southern Nevada.

Ravenbourne Slavery is dedicated to archeologist, Natasha R. Nelson (April 10, 1985—May 8, 2021) who lived and worked in twenty-five states but called Milwaukie, Oregon her hometown. We worked together on a large archeology crew, during the long summer of 2010, completing a three-hundred-mile pipeline project in south-central Alaska. She inspired the character Natasha in the novel and read and edited the first fourteen chapters. We enjoyed many hours of conversation while I was writing the novel. I miss her very much—I always will.

Contents

Ravenbourne Trilogy Introduction

One of the goals and purpose of this novel trilogy is to accurately depict the inhumanity of slavery, which clawed its way into human history during the first civilizations of Sumer in southern Mesopotamia, some 5,000 years ago, and sadly long before, reaching back into the age of stone tools. Slaves were captured in war or taken by force—children were sold by their parents or exchanged for profit—some were condemned into slavery because they were criminals or had fallen into debt—and the children of slaves were slaves.

Historically, Classical Athens, Greece is recognized by the world to be the seat of democracy. Nonetheless, one-half of the Athenian population were slaves and the vast majority of those slaves were women. Female slaves were desired and required for household labor.

In mythology, found in Homer's epic *Iliad*, when the Greek army stormed through the open gates of Troy, they slaughtered all the men… threw the babies from the walls of Troy…took the women as slaves… and ransacked the city. Fallen Troy was then set ablaze. The fires lasted for seven years.

The inhumanity of slavery has been in America since its European discovery. The Spanish brought slaves in the early 1500's and slaves came to the English colonies in the early 1600's. The conclusion of the Civil War in 1865 promised to end slavery in America—but it has not. Slavery continues today in a horrible form.

Innocent children, mostly girls, are kidnapped and brought from around the world across America's southern border to be sex slaves. I have heard it stated on National News the horrid trafficking of children as sex slaves is a "billion-dollar business."

America cannot be a free, a humane, or a compassionate nation if this inhumane slavery continues. When enough American citizens become enraged and decide to stand up and demand an end to this horrible condition—only then will the politicians and the governments bring a halt to the sex trafficking of children in America. Politicians appear daily on the news channels and condemn America as a racist nation and yet not one, that I have heard, condemns the sex trafficking of children. Become one of the citizens that do.

A final note: No ages are given in this novel trilogy. It is mentioned that children were slaves, but there is no discussion, dialogue, or story line covering children as slaves. There are sexual relationships between characters (some described to be young or conversely mature) . . . but there are no sexual relationships with children. . . .

The Fall of Opar

No one living within the great city of Opar believed that its army could be defeated by an army of the Emperor. Opar's ranks were filled with the bravest warriors in the Zhana region and throughout the known world. Oparian warriors trained from childhood in the singular occupation of protecting their city and its people. All of them would freely give their lives, and much more, in the service of their people, their city, their country, and their home. One free warrior of Opar, defending his people, was equal in strength, skill, and courage to seven paid soldiers of the Achaean Empire.

Conversely, the soldiers of the Emperor fought for wages, wealth taken in blood from a ransacked city—wealth in the form of loot and slaves. The most coveted merchandise throughout the Empire was bright, red dye or red material; cold bronze, especially weapons and armor; and warm female-slaves, young and healthy. These commodities brought wealth, prestige, and preponderance.

Powerful, ruthless, omnipotent, invincible: the supremacy of the Achaean Empire extended from the western coast of the Outer Ocean eastward to the formidable Hindu-Cush Mountain Range and from the Outer Ocean's northern coast southward to the Great Inner Sea.

The Council of Elders of Opar believed the Emperor's army would be defeated on the plains near the city. They reckoned the Emperor would come to realize that the price required to conquer Opar was too high, and he would withdraw his army, perhaps to return another day, or perhaps not. Conceivably, he might offer some sort of truce or alliance, or perhaps not.

The Council of Elders of the magnificent city of Opar believed they could defeat the Empire of the Emperor. Of equal mind, the citizens throughout the wondrous city of Opar likewise believed they could defeat the powerful Achaean Empire. They all were wrong.

The courageous army of Opar was vanquished and their warriors annihilated—only the very young and the very old of the male population remained. The Council was forced to relinquish the city's wealth and its female population, its children, and the few remaining older men into slavery. It remained the only alternative to save their glorious city from complete destruction.

The soldiers of Opar fought bravely. They did not surrender, nor did they retreat. The vast majority were killed in the battle lines— some were wounded—some taken captive. The warriors of Opar worshipped the 'God of War' who forbids suicide, with the cause of mercy being the exception. The War God would take a warrior when he desired. Death was not of the warriors' choosing. Likewise, the people of Opar believed that suicide was akin to cowardice and self-service. It was far better for a soldier to be taken alive and endure forced labor, slavery, and torture rather than taking his own life. It was better to live and to fight for Opar on another day. There was no shame in a warrior of Opar being taken as a captive of war.

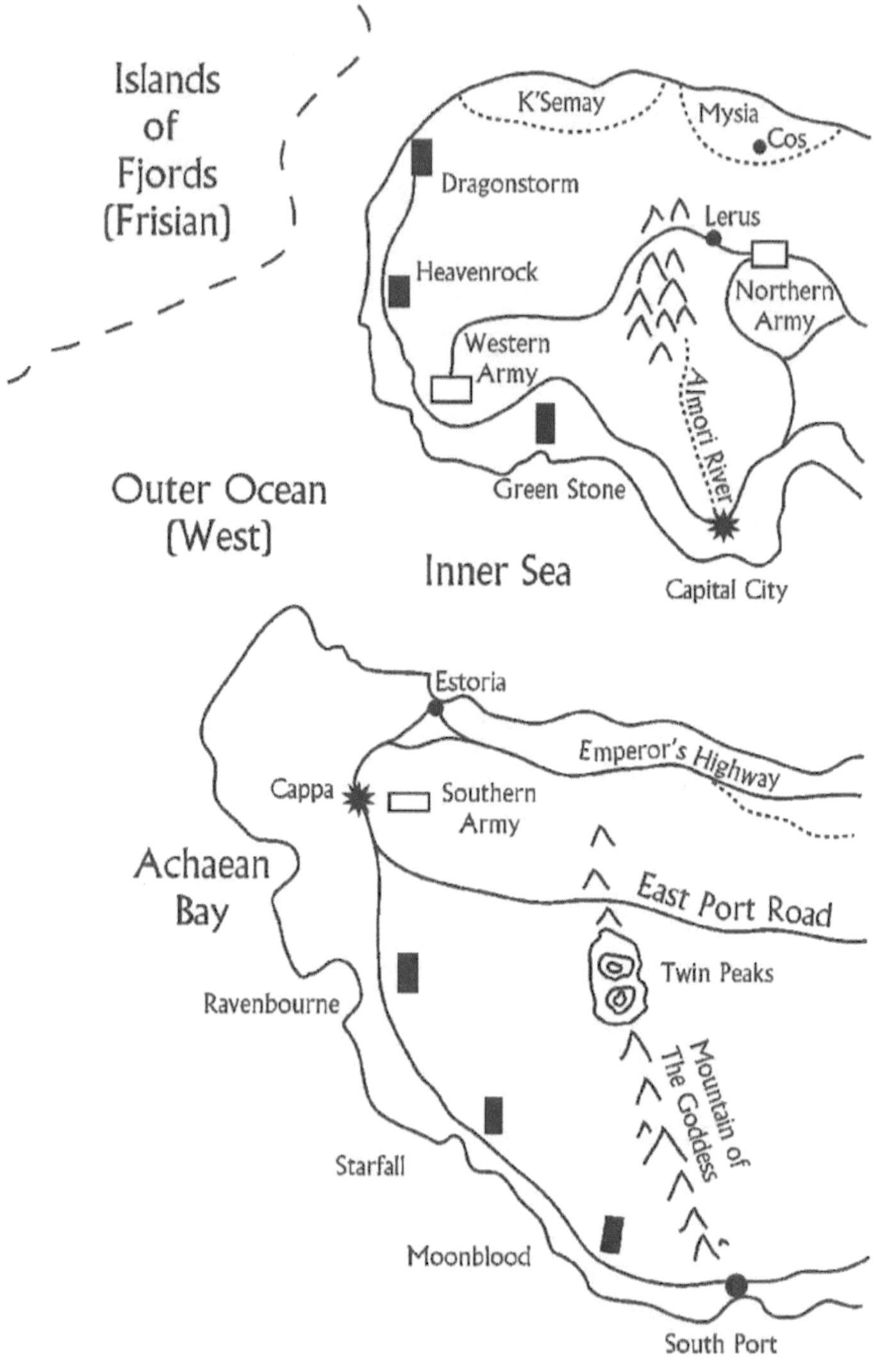

Islands
of
Fjords
(Frisian)
Outer Ocean
(West)
K'Semay
Mysia
Cos
Dragonstorm
Lerus
Heavenrock
Northern
Army
Western
Army
Almori River
Green Stone
Inner Sea
Capital City
Estoria
Emperor's Highway
Cappa
Southern
Army
Achaean
Bay
East Port Road
Twin Peaks
Ravenbourne
Mountain of
The Goddess
Starfall
Moonblood
South Port

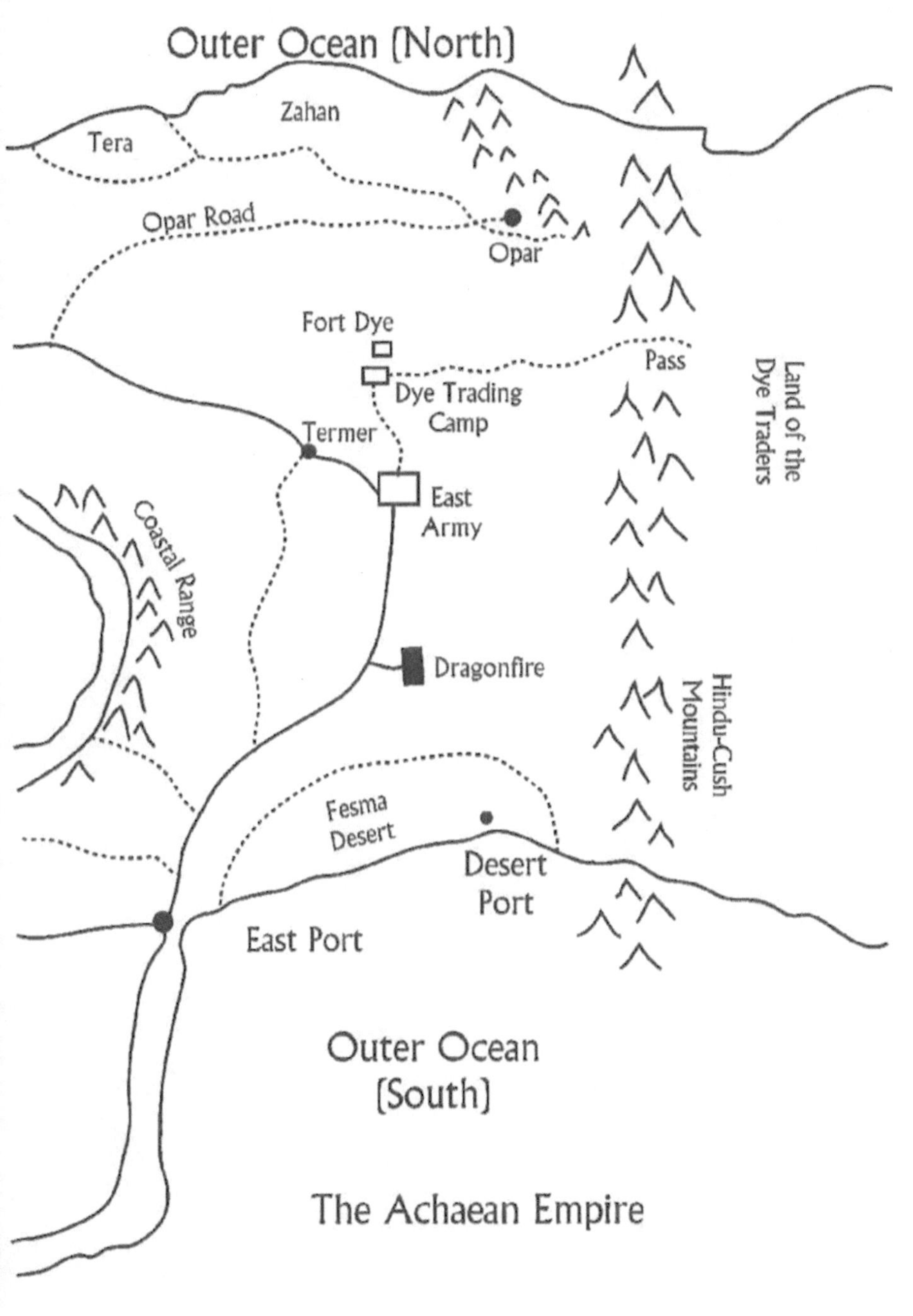

Outer Ocean (North)
Tera
Zahan
Opar Road
Opar
Fort Dye
Dye Trading Camp
Pass
Land of the Dye Traders
Termer
East Army
Coastal Range
Dragonfire
Hindu-Cush Mountains
Fesma Desert
Desert Port
East Port
Outer Ocean (South)
The Achaean Empire

Kaelin: Captive of War

"Why the hell did we get stuck with this goddess-damn work?" complained a man with a deep, husky voice as he picked up a shield and tossed it onto a stack of other weapons and armor. "Stripping bodies of armor! Weapons collection! Burial detail! What the hell, I thought I was a fokken soldier, not a wretched slave."

"You whine like a bitch in heat," growled another man with a rough voice who likewise threw an arm-full of swords onto the stack.

"Why don't the captives or slaves from the city do these goddess-damn nasty jobs instead of soldiers from the Empire? Huh—why?"

"General de Camp wants all the captives and a large number of pal-lakes—taken as slaves from the city—sold today, now! Not clearing bodies or armor from the battlefield!" spouted the rough voice in a loud, disgusted manner. "Our unit waited in reserve; we didn't taste blood. You'll get your pay and share from the sale of captives and slaves. Stop your whore bitching," growled the man as he pulled another breast plate off a dead, bloody soldier and carried it to the pile of armor and weapons.

Opening eyes—one eyelid sealed shut with dried blood or perhaps blinded. One opens. Light—pallid light, bouncing, reflects as though piercing through dark, yet moving, sinister shadows. Pain—extends through the whole body; difficult to move; relentless, agonizing pounding in the head. Pungency—nauseating stench of death saturates the thick air and nostrils. Sound—endless prattle filling every nerve of the auditory senses. This ubiquitous clamor must be interpreted as the sound of war—frantic voices of men laced with fear and bravery, shouts of encouragement, cries of pain and trepidation, screams of death—intermingled, yet each sound distinctive. No, the voices are loud but not screaming and not the groans and moans of wounded, dying men.

Movement—all but impossible, the concentrated weight of bodies lay piled on and all around; movement of legs impossible. The weight recognized—the cold embrace of bronze shields and icy bodies. Bodies in armor; bodies soaked in blood, sweat, and urine; bodies frozen and stiff. Death hovers over!

Voice—another voice. Not the rough, hard voice of men. Soft and soothing, the warm voice of a woman, a whisper in the ear as if a gentle, summer breeze.

"Move your arms up, my sweet love. Yes, it is hard and painful, but you can do it. Push through."

Breathing—hard, very hard. Only a few breaths left—only a few. Death is here!

Voice—again, the warm, soft, mellifluous female voice in the ear.

"Death is not here, my sweet love. It is not your moment. Push your arms up."

Obeying—slowly moving arms up; arms wet with sweat and blood.

Other voices—now close, standing over, speaking the Emperor's words. That loutish tongue is understood. Hear the brutish chatting, in hateful, obnoxious singing.

Again, the sounds of armor striking armor—shields striking the ground—bodies striking against other bodies. Voices—still speaking the same uncouth tongue of the Empire, the same voices. "Will they not cease?"

"Hey, look here! This one is still alive! Help me pull theses bodies off him and get his armor off. We'll take him to a captive wagon."

"Why bother? Just strip his armor, slit his throat, and throw his body on the pile with the rest of the dead."

"You are a butcher, you heathen bastard. These Opar soldiers fought bravely, just as we all believed they would. They did not retreat; they did not surrender; they held their ground, fighting to the death! Have you noticed that all the Opar soldiers taken captive are wounded? They are as brave and dedicated as any Ravenbourne Warrior. So, if one of these Opar soldiers has a chance for a life, even a slave's life, I'm going to give it to him. Look at his bloody face, he's just a boy."

"All right, all right," moaned the other soldier while they began to pull the bodies off the wounded combatant of Opar. Next, they carefully removed his armor.

"He doesn't seem to have any bad blood wounds but a good blow to the head. Blood from that cut covers most of his face, but looks like it stopped bleeding. Their armor is sure made good, especially those helmets and shields. His helmet probably saved his heathen life. Look! There's a captive wagon over there. Pick up his legs we'll carry him toward it and wave it down."

"Goddess damn," groaned the ill-tempered soldier, picking up the wounded soldier's sandaled feet. "May I fokken the goddess in her little cherry ass . . . he's good size and muscular. Weighs as much as a god-dess-damn horse!"

Highly valued merchandise throughout the vast Achaean Empire, slaves were known in the merchandising markets as both the fortune and curse and the boon and bane to many a merchant and trader. Worth nearly her weight in bronze, a young—attractive—healthy—pallake could bring riches and affluence to an enterprising slave trader. A beautiful girl, hale and hearty, might command a small fortune if sold to a wealthy satyriasis, but likewise financial disaster if she were to die before being brought to market. High reward merits high risk.

Slave caravans headed out to any virulent location of war and conflict, with the intention of purchasing slaves at a low price. A recently fallen city was most desirable because it provided the whole range of stock, including strong men for hard labor in the form of soldiers taken as captives of war; attractive young women from the city's civilian population; and children, who were easy to control and transport. Most often, a group of merchants or entrepreneur investors would fund the enterprise as partners so that if it failed, the loss was spread among them, but so, too, was the profit. A slave trader would be contracted thus equipped with wagons, mules and horses, guards, drivers, interpreters, and foremen.

At the scene of a battle, especially a fallen city, military commanders were eager to sell battle captives and citizens as slaves, rather than attempting to transport them back to an Empire city, where they would command a much higher price. After a war, the general of an Empire army had all he could handle in seeing to the care of his battle-worn and wounded soldiers, taking over a new territory, and dealing with an anomic conquered population and its anguished leaders. He could turn a quick profit by selling the captives to slave traders in the field.

The unfortunate strong men, mostly captive soldiers, destined for short, miserable lives of hard labor and lash in the mines, stone quarries, timber mills, and agricultural fields, were generally purchased directly from the slave traders by those industry owners. All soldiers, and often other mature men, did not make good household slaves. They were defiant, stubborn, and disobedient, but most alarming, they were lethal. They constantly plotted escape, and if given the opportunity, they would take the life of their master before they fled. Consequently, guarded forced labor was the only way to handle captive soldiers, veterans, and other mature men. But even though their lives were short and their value low, if taken in large numbers, they could still provide profit.

Women, destined for more specialized servitude, were sold to an assortment of various slave houses, depending. Slave houses, which in turn supplied houses of prostitution or domestic slaves, purchased young, pretty girls. A slave house would then invest its efforts and money to improve the overall appearance and health of the girls. They were washed, cleaned, examined, indoctrinated, and subdued, thus preparing them for a lifetime of servitude. Additionally, a certain amount of training might be required, particularly in language. A slave needed to learn the language of the Achaean Empire to at least be able to say, "Yes Master" or Yes Mistress." Afterward, they could be readily sold directly to a new owner or auctioned off in public, both for a lofty profit.

A few slave houses concentrated on the purchase of the most attractive sylphid girls, specializing and investing in the cream of the crop. Such beautiful, gamine maidens, who were seemingly educated and submissive without question, would be sold to opulent households and aristocratic mistresses to serve as handmaidens and exotic lovers. This type of specialization produced high profits but equally high risks.

Other slave houses might specialize in older women or boys as domestic or household slaves. Nearly every household across the Achaean Empire had at least one female-slave, young or mature, to help with the never-ending household chores. Also, slaves with skills or high education could likewise turn a high profit. Older, educated women, yet still healthy and attractive, were highly sought after by wealthy households to be teachers and nursemaids for their children. And there were some slave houses that might acquire only children from the slave traders. Various craftsmen or shopkeepers were eager to purchase children, especially boys, to provide labor for their small enterprises.

The two soldiers of the Achaean Empire carefully but hurriedly carried the adolescent combatant of Opar to the captive wagon while he drifted in and out of consciousness. They called out and waved their arms. The mule-drawn wagon came to a creeping halt. The Imperial soldiers escorting the wagon came to help carry the unconscious soldier. Two other Opar soldiers, sitting on the wagon and even though wounded, slid off to help load their comrade as best they could. Meanwhile, the rough old driver stood and turned to address his load of survivors. Some would understand his common, slang use of the otherwise sophisticated yet equally uncouth language of the Empire, some would not.

"All yous listen to me! They're settin' up hospitals 'round some small town down by the river up north somewhere. We're headed there. More like holding pens than hospitals, just some blankets thrown out on the ground by the river. Yous captives best. . .." He paused to turn his head and spit on the ground. "Best start takin' care of each other. It'll be a long while before yous get any real doctor's attention . . . if ever. There're jugs of water in the wagon—use 'em. If yous live, you'll be sold as slaves. Them slave buyers and traders are already here. If yous wanted a different life, should have deserted or run to another country or died on the battle field."

With that, the curmudgeon driver spat over his shoulder, then wiped his mouth with his dirty shirt-sleeve. He sat down and snapped the mules forward. The wooden wagon groaned, and the wheels creaked— rolling on toward the river.

The wagonload of wounded captives managed as best they could for themselves and for one another. Using their tunics or any other material they could find and water from the jugs, they washed, cleaned, and bandaged their wounds. They drank the water as well. The youthful soldier with the head wound lay with his head in the lap of another, who did what he could, albeit it was very little. He was also severely wounded in his side, but even so, he managed to pull up the young warrior's tunic so that he might wash any wounds. The blow to the junior soldier's head left an ugly gash reaching past his hairline to his forehead. Luckily, the wound spewed little blood, but the crimson life-liquid had run down his forehead, over his left eye and the left side of his face, sealing his left eye shut when it dried.

Otherwise, the vernal soldier carried only the minor cuts and bruises gained by all soldiers in battle. Providing his lap as a pillow for the wounded soldier's head was probably the best help the other captive could offer. The youngster stirred, moaned, and slowly awoke. He attempted to open his eyes, but the left remained sealed shut with dried blood.

His companion used a piece of cloth, ripped from an adjacent dead warrior's tunic and soaked in water from the wagon jug, to refresh and clean the blood from his face. He noticed his beardless comrade also carried old marks of battle, especially an ugly wound on his right side and a small but deep scar on the left side of his cheek. He thus surmised his comrade was not as callow as he appeared and his experiences reached deeper than his age would indicate. With the blood washed from his sealed eye and most of his face, the younger warrior could now see, and he looked up at his helpful companion. The older warrior struggled to talk but spoke to him in a pensive tone.

"My name, Loaz, warrior," he said, holding back the pain and holding his bloody side. "As you, an Opar warrior taken captive. We're in a captive death wagon going to some holding area. What's your name?" he asked with a grimaced cough.

The young warrior breathed heavily but answered in a dry, rough voice. "Kaelin, my name is Kaelin."

"Well, Kaelin," continued Loaz with difficulty, "my experience, hard to know head-impact wounds like yours. You blackout again, may wake up in a moment—few days—no after effects. On the other hand. . .." Again, he grimaced, holding his side, fighting the pain that would not assuage while blood eased through his fingers. "You may wake up blind, dumb, or crazy the rest of your life. Good chance you'll not wake at all."

Kaelin looked at his companion, managing a halfhearted, caustic smile, and again spoke in a dry voice. "Why so cheerful and optimistic?"

His companion, Loaz, also managed a weak smile. "We have two choices, Kaelin—death or slavery. I'll die before we reach the fokken river—think you'll live. You'll go to Empire mines or quarries. There, slaves don't live out a year, two at best."

Loaz grimaced in pain continuing to grip his wounded, bloody side. "Tell anyone from Opar I fought bravely, if not well. Died best I could." He made a deep groaning sound while he slowly fell over to lie on his side.

Kaelin's head remained in his lap. He took a deep breath, as though to answer that he understood, and swallowed hard. He then drifted back into unconsciousness.

Natasha: Vision

APPROACHING EARLY DAWN, THE FULL moon still aglow, Natasha left the Ravenbourne Village. She first considered following the Ravenbourne Road, which led from the grand Ravenbourne Villa down to the main peninsula road, the Emperor's Highway. Then she would follow the peninsula road to the enormous Great Stone Bridge across the Tyner River. Immense, pulchritudinous trees—ancient as the goddess Asa herself—lined the Ravenbourne Road. Natasha's mother told her the trees along that wonderous road were not as old as the magnificent trees of the Primeval Grove, near the ancient ruins, but they were still majestic. Some say the first Lord of Ravenbourne placed the trees in the ground along the road, although others held that the ancient people who had built the structures that now lay in ruin, planted them along this prehistoric roadway, which also led to the ruins. In addition to the huge trees that line it, the Ravenbourne Road was paved with large, flat stones inlaid with mortar. Consequently, the road presented an enchanting scene, winding its way from the villa, over and through ancient, black lava flows, to the Emperor's Highway.

After second thought, Natasha decided to trail the village creek to the main Emperor's Highway, then to the bridge. She stopped along the creek at a familiar location where steep cliffs and rocks formed a deep pool in the stream. Village children often came here to swim, but this early morning found her alone, sitting on a large rock by the edge of the clear pool. The woods seemed especially quiet, and the pool so calm and still, it created a mood of enchantment. She gazed into the water.

The pool was a mirror, reflecting her image even better than a bronze mirror. She could see her fire-red hair, streaked with strands of flaxen gold, and her deep, verdant eyes. Her mother told Natasha that she was beautiful, very beautiful. But of course, that was a mother's biased opinion, although she had heard others say she was pretty, and plenty of boys teased her. Still, she did not think she was beautiful, but she did not think she was ugly, either. She gazed up at the full, blue sky. The morning sun shone brightly over the tops of the trees as she took a deep, long breath, feeling lucky that she was not obliged to work today.

She'd begged her father for a day or two free of work. He was a stern man, ex-military but certainly not implacable, although reluctant. Nonetheless, he finally gave into his pleading daughter, understanding that she was emotionally saddened. She wanted an opportunity to be alone, an opportunity to think. It had been hard for Natasha since the recent death of her mother, who had been not only her parent but also her friend and companion. She struggled to leave grief behind. When she and her mother had worked in the garden or doing other chores around their cottage, they had talked and laughed. It was fun—enjoyable.

Reaching up, Natasha retied the drawstring on her left shoulder and, by habit, looked over to check the ties on her right. Something else that brought a warm but now sad memory of her mother: her frock. She and her mother had cut the flax from the extensive Ravenbourne fields that stretched, as far as could be seen, to the horizon. Lord Ravenbourne's Law allowed villagers to cut flax for their own use. Flax was the material common people used for clothing. Wealthier households often kept a female-slave to help with household work such as weaving thread into material. They were not wealthy and she and her mother had woven the fine thread into the prized linen material. Her mother was an expert seamstress. And even though her frock was plain, without pleats, beads, or trimming, it fit perfectly.

Once, her father had gone with the army to the far northeast area, maybe with the Eastern Army, and stayed at the Red Dye Trader Camp and Fort Dye. He watched the Nak'la-Sat traders, who had just come over the Hindu-Cush Pass, bring their caravan into the Dye Trader Camp. They traded their red dye for bronze weapons.

"You would not believe the Nak' la-Sat traders," he said with excitement. "They dress in animal skins and have brown skin and black hair. Their language is very strange," he said, laughing.

From that journey, he brought home some red dye kernels and some expensive material. The same material Ravenbourne Warriors used as capes. She and her mother had dyed the material and sold it for a nice profit. They also kept some of the material and made expensive undergarments for themselves. This was not long before her mother died.

Nearly everything around her reminded Natasha of her mother. And worse, working alone in the garden or at other household tasks now just seemed to be hard, dirty work. She hated her life.

Perhaps *hate* was too strong of a word, but nonetheless, she was very dissatisfied with her life, even though she knew she shouldn't have been. They weren't poor—better off than most families in the village, certainly better off than slaves or landless peasants. Her father received a military pension from his long service in the army. He had served bravely, was decorated by the Emperor, and had also been given a "Request" by Lord Ravenbourne himself. He asked for a good house on one acre of land. They were very lucky because only a chosen few owned any land within the vast Ravenbourne Estate, other than the Lord of Ravenbourne. The house wasn't fancy or lavish, but it was solid and well-made of stone, brick, and timber.

Also, her father made spear shafts of ash wood that he cut from the mountains, and the quartermaster at the Ravenbourne Corps bought each one, always offering a good price. A few summers ago, he and two other village veterans had planted an ash-tree plantation in the mountains. Soon, they would return and spend several weeks harvesting their trees, then earn a healthy profit.

No, they weren't wealthy but well-off, considering. They ate well, wore good clothes, and had a solid roof over their heads. Nonetheless, Natasha remained wistful—far from content.

She reached into her shoulder bag, taking out her most prized possession—her anodyne—a book. Her mother taught her to read from this very book. She knew it by heart, and she could recite the complete volume. She recalled reading to her mother from the book and her mother correcting and teaching her as she learned. Not so long ago, her mother had purposely misread a passage to see if Natasha would catch it and correct the passage by memory, like a game. She missed her mother, so very much.

She also fondly recalled that her father was somehow able to borrow two other books and had brought them home. She and her mother read each one together, separately, and to each other over and over. Books were extremely rare and expensive and this was the only one Natasha owned. It brought her the utmost joy and comfort.

Books also made her think of when her Aunt Elbe lived with them; it had been a blissful period. Aunt Elbe had once served Lady Ravenbourne as a teacher. Natasha's mother told her that Elbe came to stay during those long occasions when her father was stationed in some far-away land of the Empire. Aunt Elbe taught her mother before Natasha was born, and Natasha could remember her aunt teaching both her and her mother.

Natasha exhaled noisily. *Oh, it would be wonderful to have another book to read.* Her aunt had told her that Ann Y'Sloic, Lady of Ravenbourne, owned many books, used by the teachers to educate the children of Lord Ravenbourne. This was one example of why she was so dissatisfied with life.

Why couldn't she have books? She did not necessarily need to own them; she'd happily borrow them to read and then return them to their owner. She had only read three books in her whole life. *I wish I had another book to read,* she thought. She longed for books about far away, exotic places and daring people who went on dangerous and exciting adventures. In the story in her book a poor peasant girl married the son of a rich aristocrat.

Analogous to the girl in her book, she was an adult and old enough for marriage. She nearly had sex with one of the village boys. He was handsome and popular. Everyone in the village liked him, but it had not been an enjoyable experience for Natasha. It had been awkward and frightening for both of them. When she told Melissa, her friend was proud of her.

"I'm happy for you, Natasha," she said with a big smile. "He's very good-looking, but he's just a boy. You should find a young man for yourself, one of the Ravenbourne Warriors. They're exciting. If you're nice to him, and you're so pretty, he will give you things, maybe even a dagger." Melissa laughed and hugged her.

Melissa was probably correct. Perhaps if the boy had more maturity, the outcome of the experience would have been different. Her only pleasure was derived from doing something illicit. Also, she had been afraid her father would discover her iconoclastic deed and remained fearful of what he might do. She wondered if he would give her a child's hand-slapping punishment or even a strapping. Her father had skelped her once before when she was a young girl. She recalled the incident vividly. Now, it seemed humorous, but anxious at the occurrence. Additionally, as part of the incident, she thought a Ravenbourne Warrior might punish her. Again, she was lucky because he released her with a warning. He did, nonetheless, give her and her mother a kiss. It was a real kiss, not a child's kiss on the forehead but an adult kiss on the lips. Some of what Melissa advised must be true, she thought, because it was exciting when it occurred; in fact, it still was. Kissed by a Ravenbourne Warrior, a sergeant! Well, she was safe from her father's anger. The boy in question would never tell, she told herself as she reached into her bag for a red apple.

The Ravenbourne Villa supported extensive orchards of apples, along with other fruits, especially cherries. Near the mountains, where the air was cooler, grew vast groves of cherry trees. The estate wineries produced the exotic Ravenbourne cherry wine. So renowned were the Ravenbourne cherries, the word *cherry* was used in the Empire's language in various sexual and generally vulgar situations. She smiled, taking a nibble of the apple.

She and her father had two apple trees on their land. They were lucky, but the apples did not last long because they shared the bounty with the village children. It did give her a warm feeling, watching the village children eating the apples and hearing their laughter. She and her father enjoyed the delicious fruit as well. Natasha fondly recalled sun-drying sliced apples with her mother. When combined with dried wild grapes and tree nuts, the savory mix provided a tasty morsel during the off-seasons. She searched through her bag and pulled out her knife to slice the apple.

It wasn't really a knife, just a broken blade end. She wrapped a piece of cloth around the broken end of the blade, then cut slices of apple. She took one into her mouth. "Mmm," she said out loud with a smile, "this one is very sweet." But her smile did not last long.

Natasha wished she had a real knife, a real dagger with a handle. Her best friend, Melissa, owned an army dagger with a wooden handle and a sheath. She proudly carried it on her belt, a rare leather, army belt. Melissa told her that two friendly soldiers had given her the belt and the dagger. Melissa was considerably more daring than Natasha when it came to men. Natasha's father had an army dagger from his days in the military. Army daggers were strong, well made, the best daggers in the Empire, but she was not allowed to touch his, much less use it. It would be so wonderful to have her own dagger to wear on her belt—an army dagger. Or better yet, a Ravenbourne Army dagger.

Ravenbourne Warriors were issued special daggers, the most coveted knives throughout the whole realm. The blades were strong, rigid, sharp, and polished to a resplendent shine, reflecting as if a mirror. The handles were carved from bone and occasionally ivory. The Ravenbourne crest was embedded into the blade at the hilt. They once had a neighbor woman, who had a Ravenbourne dagger. Natasha presumed a Ravenbourne Warrior protected her. On one occasion, she allowed Natasha to hold it. It was exciting just to handle it. The daggers were beautiful indeed.

The neighbor woman told Natasha how the renowned knives had become ingrained into the common lore and language in much the same manner as the terms *cherry or tea-rose*. She had whispered to Natasha.

"Occasionally, Natasha, you might overhear older women talk and gossip, especially at the village well, making references to men and their penises. Such as, 'I bet that handsome young man is as hard as a Ravenbourne dagger,' or 'The other night he pushed so deep into me, clear to the hilt, as if he had a Ravenbourne dagger between his legs.' Then they will all laugh."

Yes, that would be wonderful, to own her own dagger. Natasha sighed, another sad moan. She reached again into her bag.

Fumbling around, she pulled a bundle of small willow sticks and a flat homemade paddle brush from her bag and began to brush her hair. Long and red in color, with brilliant streaks of gold that flashed in sun, her hair fell on her shoulders. Since she was a little girl, her mother had brushed her hair every day, telling her she had the prettiest hair of all the girls in the village.

It was no secret that Natasha's mother was a Hyacinth Gatherer with brilliant red hair, and Natasha inherited her red hair from her mother.

Natasha's father, as a soldier, once protected her mother's Gathering during their movement from the mountains with their precious hyacinth oil, intending to sell the oil to the Priestess at the Sacred Temple of the goddess Asa. Her father had taken her mother's hand from Natasha's grandfather and brought his bride to the Ravenbourne Village.

Her mother spoke the Hyacinth Gatherer's secret language as she brushed Natasha's hair. They only spoke the language when they were alone, strictly alone. They never spoke the secret language in front of anyone, not even her father or her aunt.

"Nearly all of us Hyacinth Gatherers have red hair," her mother explained. "But very special girls of the Hyacinth Gatherers, like you, Natasha, have streaks of gold in their red hair. We Hyacinth Gatherers are a very special people to the goddess Asa. Therefore, she put streaks of gold, the same color as the melted lava stone from deep inside the earth, in the hair of favored girls. This will remind all Hyacinth Gatherers of our singular relationship with the goddess."

Her mother would say her hair was prettier than that of the aristocratic women who spent a fortune on their hair and owned slaves to brush it for them. Natasha could still hear her mother's sweet yet resolute voice:

"Wash your hair with hair soap Natasha, dry it in the sun, brush it every day, and you will have the fairest hair in the realm." Her mother used this same stick bundle and the homemade paddle brush of boar bristles.

On occasion, she braided Natasha's hair, especially a length of flaxen gold on the side of her head in a thin, tight braid, occasionally attaching a bead or a shell from the coast. Once, she recalled, they'd found a beautiful bead while digging in the garden. It must have belonged to a woman of some means, and how it came to be in their garden, they did not know, likely long ago. On the day she died, her mother had braided Natasha's hair, attaching this favorite bead. It was her mother's last gift to her. Natasha swore she would keep this braid in her hair, as a token of her mother's memory. Reaching up, she felt the braid and bead, then began to brush her hair with the paddle brush.

Her father had killed a boar at the base of the mountains. They baked the meat in a rock-lined pit all day and night—it was extremely delicious. He used the boar's bristle to make the brush. He first carved a split piece of wood into a brush-size paddle and sanded it smooth with sandstone. He drilled holes into a flat side, then attached the coarse, tough bristles. Her father was no craftsman, but he worked hard on the bush, and in the end, it worked well. She and her mother were grateful. Still, Natasha wished she had a real craftsman-made brush. Other women in the village owned such brushes.

Her mother once told her that she watched a young handmaid brush the hair of her wealthy owner with a beautiful craftsman-made brush. She was not sure how it was made, but it was beautiful, she said—inlaid with precious stones even though it was still made from boar bristles.

Her frugal mother cautioned, "A well-made willow-stick bundle, Natasha, and a homemade boar-bristle brush work just as well as a fine, expensive, craftsman-made brush."

She lectured, pulling the sharp ends of the bundle through Natasha's locks. "It's a matter of female arrogance, not function. It is the same . . . demonstrated, by the amount of money a wealthy woman will spend on hair soap. An expensive soap doesn't make aristocratic hair any cleaner."

Natasha smiled, remembering her mother's voice. She recalled making a batch of hair soap with her mother just before she died. She now wished she had been more attentive to the process. The root of an aromatic herb gave the soap a magnificent fragrance. She was not sure she could recognize the plant. She still had an ample supply of the hair soap; besides, surely other women in the village would identify the herb for her.

All of this was, in part, the source of Natasha's melancholy mood— no, more than melancholy: depression. Her dissatisfaction with her life and her life's probable future, as it appeared on her horizon, gave her little hope of happiness. She did not want to marry a village boy, even if he was handsome and good to her. She did not want to live in a village hut, even a good, sound house like her father's. She did not want to have village children, taking the deadly risk of a long, painful labor simply to bring forth a village baby. She wanted to have a lover, a husband, a partner, but not a village boy. She had always wanted to travel, see other places, and go on adventures similar to those described in her book. Her mother had been content to live in the village and enjoyed the woman's work of a housewife. Natasha was not opposed to that life—quite the contrary: she was exceedingly grateful she had her mother when growing up.

But she also knew her mother was not a native village girl. Born a Hyacinth Gatherer, she enjoyed experiences and adventures beyond the village. It had been fun to listen, while her mother taught her the ways of that mysterious, mystical culture, including their enchanting, clandestine language.

Similarly, Natasha remained grateful to her father, who provided well for them, but as a professional soldier, he was frequently gone. In fact, before he retired, he was gone much more than he was at home. He experienced a full soldier's life and visited every corner of the Empire. It was not an easy profession. He had borne hardships most people could hardly entertain. He endured several battles and had been severely wounded in his hip. He was battle scarred from cranium to pedis.

But he also told exciting stories of faraway places he had seen. Tales of strange people with strange customs and beliefs, such as the Nak'la-Sat Dye Traders, and extraordinary gods and goddesses.

He had been to the great Capital City. He was decorated on the steps of the huge capital building by the Emperor himself. He went to the colossus arena in the company of the Emperor's entourage and sat with a whole group of aristocrats in the Emperor's special booth.

He described the phenomenal Great Temple to the goddess Asa at the Capital City.

"You should see the Great Temple of the goddess Asa!" he called out loudly, holding up his mug of beer, as though offering a proud toast, then downed a hardy drink. "It is larger than many of the small towns along the coast. Many hundreds—no, thousands—of women pray, worship, and offer gifts of sacrifice to the goddess each and every day."

Natasha and her mother had sat wide-eyed and excited, listening to his tales. He lowered his head close to theirs, pretending to tell a secret and whispered, "You would not believe the things I heard that went on in that temple!" Then he moved back with a hardy laugh, and they all laughed together.

Not long before her father retired, he became the First Spear of the 13th Legion of the Southern Army. General Y'Sloic is the Southern Army Commander and he is also the Lord of Ravenbourne. All the soldiers of the 13th Legion vote to select the First spear and they voted for her father, Thoas. It is perhaps a greatest honor a soldier can receive.

She was not looking down on her parents or other people in the village, certainly not—how could she? But she also wanted more than a village existence. Natasha loved her mother, so very much, but she was not like her. She was more like her father. She wanted adventure: she wanted the things normally denied to a villager because of the cost or rarity—books, for instance. There must be a better life, a better way, but how?

Natasha was not naive or gullible; she knew she would never become an aristocrat because noble men married upper-class women or at least wealthy women. Maybe not always, but on most occasions. At least, that is what she thought. Besides, she was aware she had the reputation of an ill-tempered girl. She was abrasive to nearly all the boys and young men in the village, including the nice boy she almost had sex with. She threw rocks at the soldiers whenever they came through the village. As Natasha thought about it, she laughed to herself. Sometimes they chased her, but they couldn't catch her.

Even if they did, she knew the Ravenbourne Warriors would not hurt her because they were sworn not to harm any villager. Except in the olden days—she'd read in her book—when the village soldiers meted out punishment, upholding the Lord's law and justice. By tradition, the punishment took the form of a public strapping. There was an old saying she had heard the village women say: "Men are punished above the waist and women below." She put her hand on her book, taking a deep breath, remembering her mother.

In the story told in her book, a young woman, one of the protagonists, offered a sacrifice to the goddess Asa. Many women in the village were votaries of Asa. She and her mother were not members of the cult, but her mother told her various aspects about the goddess, including several of the ceremonial and worship practices. Natasha knew that the loyal followers gathered each year at a small temple on the coast, but her mother had told her that soon there would be a One Hundred Years Ceremony, and women would come to Ravenbourne from all around the Empire. That would be exhilarating. Most importantly, her mother taught her that Asa was the goddess of women and children and that she could assist mortal women in their searches for happy, content, productive lives. Most of the followers made sacrifices and prayers to the goddess, seeking her support.

Natasha had given this idea of sacrifice and prayer considerable consideration. It was an important matter not to be taken lightly. She had decided she was ready to make an offering to Asa. But she did not know what to offer the goddess—or how to go about it.

From her mother's teachings, Natasha knew women would pray and drop objects of offerings into pools of water sacred to the goddess. She did not know which pools were or were not sacred or if it mattered. Her mother had said, "Deep, lucid, still pools are revered by the goddess, Natasha, and hot-water pools. . . well, those are especially hallowed." She now sat beside one of the deepest, clearest pools of water she was aware of. Certainly, if any pools were sacred, this one must be, as it possessed such a magical aura. Children played and swam in this pool and the goddess protected children—perhaps it was sacred. But what was there to sacrifice?

Her book was her most precious possession. It had belonged to her mother and now her. She treasured all the memories the book held for her. She could not part with it. Losing her book would be akin to losing the memories of her mother. A sacrifice was equally a gift, and all gifts come from the heart. The goddess, or any worthy deity, would not desire a sacrifice offered in regret and remorse, wrapped in lament.

Suddenly, Natasha felt something burning inside her, deep inside. She knew what she must offer. She took the broken knife blade, rewrapping the broken end. Reaching up to her hair, she found the lone small braid—her mother's last gift—and cut the braid off. She looked into the pool, at her own reflection, and took a deep breath.

"Goddess Asa," she whispered while a feeling of anxiety rose from deep inside her. She paused, taking another breath.

"I wish I could find a better life for myself, but how can I—how?"

Slowly, reaching out her hand, she again saw her own reflection shimmering in the deep pool. She dropped her mother's braid, with the attached bead, into the still water. Tears began to run down her cheek. She sat back, crying, watching the braid float on the tranquil, silent water as though she was dreaming.

Natasha's attention drifted off, and she was not sure where her thoughts had drifted to or how long she was gone. Suddenly, she heard a strange but familiar sound that startled her from her daydream. Wiping her eyes, she looked up to see a solitary raven perched in a nearby tree. She had not noticed the bird before. Fluffing its ebony feathers, it made a strange clucking sound. She often marveled at the odd calls and puzzling behavior of the large, black, mysterious birds. They frequently remained quiet as the silent night, but on other occasions, they were loud, even obnoxious. The raven looked at her and made another weird call. Suddenly, it took to the air. Natasha thought she saw a flash of purple color when the raven spread its wings, reflecting the sun. She was certain she saw a beautiful purple color, but only a flash. She watched while the raven flew away the along stream.

Her eyes were now dry and she looked back at the pool. The braid was gone. The pool was completely still, mystically still, as though somehow frozen by the breath of the goddess. She did not think it could have float away so quickly. She leaned over to look into the tranquil water to see her reflection—she froze. She wanted to take a deep breath but could not. She wanted to call out, but her voice was gone. The reflection was not hers.

The face of a man, a young, beardless man with short flaxen-colored hair, reflected from the calm pool. Natasha saw a young but serious face. His deep, piercing brown eyes silently spoke of experience far beyond his years, and all that experience had not been welcomed. He bore a scar on the side of his face and another on his forehead, extending back past his hairline.

She recognized the deep, thin blemishes—painful battle scars. The hair along the scar on the front of his head had turned white creating, a furtive, thin line of white among the flaxen strands. The healed wounds, however, did not distort his face. In fact, he appeared very handsome to Natasha—dangerously handsome.

Natasha quickly looked around, expecting to see the young man standing behind her. No one—she remained alone. She frantically looked around. There must be someone, someone close behind her. She saw no one.

She looked back into the water at the reflection of the scar-faced, attractive boy. As she began to look for more details in his young, solemn face, her own image, suddenly and magically, reappeared in the calm water.

She swiftly rose up. Fear—more fear than she had ever known— fell upon her. She was now very much afraid of the ominous vision. Hastily, she gathered up her belongings, stuffed them into her bag, and hurriedly made her way toward the main road. She traveled along the well-beaten path, following the stream, and returned to the village. She would visit the bridge another day.

General Y'Sloic: Starfall Villa

GENERAL SOL Y'SLOIC REINED HIS mount to a vivacious halt. His puissant snow-white stallion tossed his head up and down, snorting and pawing the ground. The General's coveted thoroughbred sire was of a rare variety, bred by the Ravenbourne stables to enhance speed and endurance. White emerged the unique, dominant color—although not exclusively—nor was it intentional. Primarily, the horses were employed as mounts for the extensive Ravenbourne courier system, but they were also ridden by other warriors of noted distinction.

The long, noisy colonnade following behind General Y'Sloic likewise halted. He seldom gave gestured commands anymore, such as raising his hand in a clenched fist to command the trailing unit to halt. He simply acted, and the trailing unit followed.

The assorted column he led along the Emperor's Highway included his personal Ravenbourne Equestrian Guard, a unit of his Southern Army Cavalry, and also a file of the Imperial Guard, which normally patrolled the palace and the streets of Capital City. This mixed command also included civilian construction inspectors and engineers, along with numerous slow wagons loaded with supplies, equipment, and civilians who could not ride and slowed the column—a mild aggravation to the Lord of Ravenbourne. Still, each member of this mixed body had his own assignment and duty.

By command of the Emperor, General Y'Sloic had left the head-quarters of the Southern Army, just outside the city of Cappa, on a mission to inspect the progress and condition of the deepwater port under construction along the coast of the peninsula near the villa of Starfall. The whole Southern Peninsula supported but two ports. One was located at the southern tip of the peninsula, at the town of South Port, and the other on the eastern side, which likewise maintained the small community of East Port. Both were shallow-water ports and unable to accommodate large cargo vessels. Consequently, the mass volume of trade flowing to and especially out of the peninsula was largely transported overland. Several years ago, the Imperial treasury found itself in a solid condition, accordingly; the Emperor had ordered the construction of a port on the peninsula.

The commander of the Ravenbourne Equestrian Guard, Captain Aaragon; second officer Lieutenant Rin Rohan; and First Sergeant Twilsua rode up to either side of their General who gazed down the entry road leading to the Starfall Villa. It emanated a hoary presence. Older than any other villa on the peninsula, it was constructed in the ancient manner to be a stone fortress lacking, landscaping, gardens, and other luxuries that adorned the more contemporary villas. Still, General Y'Sloic admitted to himself, if he were ever obligated to defend a villa against overwhelming odds, he would choose Starfall, even before Ravenbourne. Yet it remained a gloomy ominous fortress, constructed from rough-cut stone, and hewed timber. He turned to Captain Aaragon.

"Captain, send a courier ahead to announce our arrival and order the commander of the Imperial Guard forward!"

"Sir," answered Aaragon, who then turned to deliver the same order to Lieutenant Rohan. However, Lieutenant Rohan quickly responded.

"I'll deliver that message, Captain."

Aaragon looked to Sergeant Twilsua, but Rohan promptly spoke again. "It will be my honor as well as my duty, Sir."

"Understood Lieutenant Rohan. "Ride out!" ordered Captain Aaragon.

Again, Aaragon looked to Sergeant Twilsua. The hard-cut sergeant reined his horse back toward the awaiting column. Promptly, Lieutenant Rohan galloped, down the road, toward the distant fortress, his red cloak flowed behind him, reminding General Y'Sloic of the waves on the Inner Sea. A single imperial soldier rode up alongside Captain Aaragon, astride a rambunctious mount that could not remain halted. He awaited General Y'Sloic's orders.

"Commander, escort your command and the civilian inspectors to the construction zone. Remind the inspectors and engineers I want a complete, detailed inspection and a full report. Advise them not to hasten their work. We are all prepared to bivouac, as long as necessary. The day after tomorrow Commander. . .." General Y'Sloic paused, allowing his command to sink in. "I'll inspect the port construction myself."

"Understood, Lord Ravenbourne!" called out the Imperial Commander, who reined his horse back to the column.

General Y'Sloic, the Lord of Ravenbourne, softly chuckled to himself. Imperial soldiers always use imperial title before military rank. But of course, they are stationed at the Capital City and obliged to imperial, political correctness. He turned to the Commander of his Ravenbourne Equestrian Guard, the most politically, incorrect Ravenbourne Warrior known to this date.

"What do you make of Starfall, Aaragon?" spoke General Y'Sloic, looking toward the villa.

"The villa appears old, cold, yet durable, General," replied Captain Aaragon. "You must have explored the fortress before, General, on calls in the past."

"Without doubt," nodded the General. "I've walked through most of it, but it has been numerous years, since my last visit." The General now turned to look at Aaragon. "However, Aaragon, regardless of the rustic appearance of Starfall, Lady Y'Liory, bears the reputation as a generous host. Let us see if that standing remains true." Kicking his anxious mount into an easy gate, General Y'Sloic rode down the gravel road, toward the Starfall fortress villa, the column followed.

Lizabeth Y'Liory, Lady of Starfall, prepared a gracious, lavish fête for her noted guests, setting a praiseworthy table overflowing with strong drink, succulent meats, spicy wild fowl, sweet fruits, marble-white feta, breads, honey, and olives. The sturdy, rough-hewn table, however, was a short-legged construction, necessitating that her guests sit on the floor in a barbarous fashion, comforted against the hard-stone flooring by thick fur rugs and stuffed pillows. The personal handmaid of Lady Y'Liory, who quietly sat some three or four paces behind her lifelong mistress, took the only chair in the whole dining hall. The table was wide enough to accommodate two guests across from each other. Lady Y'Liory and General Y'Sloic sat at the head.

The dining hall was an open courtyard, allowing the bright sunlight to dance across the rough wood table and seated guests. Huge timbers, laid across stone pillars, supported the roof. The wood for the table and the support timbers was cut from the ancient primeval forest of Ravenbourne, a gift from Lord Ravenbourne's father to the old Lord of Starfall.

Hoping to impress the General, Lady Y'Liory had arranged fare of conspicuous consumption, having the intention of persuading him toward her goals. Slaves, mostly pallakes, women captured in war, but a few boys as well, carefully maneuvered around the table, holding oinochoes of sweet red wine, strong beer, and cool water, and plates of delicious food. They wore only a miniature chain around one ankle, with an attached copper bell, secured to a small plate inscribed with Lady Y'Liory's name and the Starfall crest. The plate would identify any run a way to be her property.

It remained a rare opportunity for soldiers to receive such royal treatment, including the Ravenbourne Warriors. Thus, they took full advantage of the extraordinary situation, and the boisterous men relaxed around the table enjoying, the festive atmosphere.

The scheming Lady of Starfall Villa sensed the General to be in a receptive mood now that he'd consumed a generous amount of food and drink. He was relaxed—much at ease. Calculating the mood of powerful men was the Lady's stock and trade, and she applied the art with an expert amount of cunning.

"The Port of Starfall is nearly complete, General Y'Sloic. How many years now has it been under construction?"

General Y'Sloic looked at his hostess's face with raised brows. "There is no need to be so formal, Lizabeth; we have known each other for many years."

Lady Y'Liory reached over and gently laid the palm of her hand on the back of General Y'Sloic's hand which rested on the table. She purposely looked into his face, smiling. "Of course, you're right, Sol."

Taking a long drink of beer, General Y'Sloic looked at the dark-haired beauty across from him. "I'm confident you know the exact years and days, Lizabeth, but I only know it has been several years now."

Lady Y'Liory thought to herself before she answered. *The General of the Southern Army and the Lord of Ravenbourne, a man whose wealth and power are surpassed only by the Emperor himself, drinks strong beer and plain water— liquid fare of a common soldier. How to maneuver such a man?*

"I owe you at least a small token of gratitude for recommending the bay at Starfall as the site for the Emperor's new port." She spoke with a smile, removing her hand from his and reaching for her glass of wine.

General Y'Sloic chuckled. "Everyone knows, Lizabeth, that there were few choices to consider, because there are just four deep water bays on the Southern Peninsula, suitable for accommodating large vessels. The Achaean Bay is isolated, lacking road access. Construction of a road over that rough terrain simply to reach the bay would be a labor-intensive, difficult task itself."

"The Moonblood Estate lies on the coast of the Moonblood Bay. The Lord and Lady of Moonblood resent the idea of a harbor constructed on their coastline and the town that would certainly emerge, engulfing their ancestral estate. They have on several occasions voiced their opposition to the Emperor."

"Yes," she replied, drawing out the word. "The choice was narrow, leaving only two suitable deep-water bays on the peninsula, one near Ravenbourne and the other near Starfall. And everyone knows the followers of the goddess Asa hold Ravenbourne Bay as a holy place and the location of the Annual Rites and worship ceremonies. It is a sacred place of pilgrimage. Thus, there really remained no question."

Lady Y'Liory took a sip of wine. "This Ravenbourne cherry wine is delicious." She glanced at the Lord of Ravenbourne, pausing before she spoke again.

"The whole Empire knows that you and you alone rule at Ravenbourne, Sol, but Lady Ravenbourne would have never forgiven you if the port had been constructed in her sacred bay."

"The bay is sacred to all the women followers of Asa," stated General Y'Sloic.

"Yes, of course, Sol, but you are not concerned with the opinion of all the women followers of goddess Asa. You care only about one."

"I chose the Starfall Bay, much to your delight, Lizabeth. You have long desired a port here. The prestige and wealth derived from a nearby port, and the town that will most certainly develop near the port, will be substantial. I am confident the Mistress of Starfall has already realized a fortune in the sale of construction stone from her quarry."

"Most certainly, Sol. The Emperor paid a good price for the stone from Starfall's quarry to construct the port. And. . . ." She paused with a sincere smile. "That is why I am so grateful."

General Y'Sloic quietly recalled when Lady Y'Liory first arrived at Starfall—the child bride to his friend and neighbor Lord Starfall, who also served the Empire as the General of the Eastern Army before his sudden and seemingly mysterious death. Then, she was a flat-breasted, radiant, beautiful child, certainly not the Mistress of Starfall, yet she still seemed to maneuver the old General with whispers and spiderous smiles. Drako de Camp, the Duke of Dragonfire, replaced Lord Starfall as General of the Eastern Army. The Emperor's son had persuaded his father to appoint de Camp to the position. General Y'Sloic did not trust General Drako de Camp.

Also, Lady Ravenbourne had mentioned to her husband, on more than one occasion, that Lady Y'Liory seemed to display, at least to her, ulterior motives. Nonetheless, General Y'Sloic concluded it was just a young female aristocrat's manner of achieving her own way. She remained, however, a mysterious, radiant beauty, only now, a mature woman.

"Do you remember, Sol, when my husband was alive, he periodically camped a corps of his troops here at the Starfall Villa to patrol the area for the purpose of eliminating the bandits who take refuge in the mountains?"

"Yes, I recall the garrisons," answered Lord Ravenbourne. "I sent a contingent of my soldiers to augment his efforts."

Lady Y'Liory reached over. She again gently laid her hand on the top of Lord Ravenbourne's hand. "You will similarly recall, Sol, how outlaws attacked and harassed the caravans that supply the villas and all the settlements throughout the peninsula. Lord Starfall always wanted a permanent garrison here at the villa, but he feared the Emperor might advise that such a move would appear to show favoritism. Consequently, once the criminal element was removed and the supply caravans again traveled in safety, he withdrew the garrison. There always seemed to be the need for soldiers elsewhere in the Empire."

Smiling, Lady Y'Liory gently massaged his hand with her fingertips. "The bandits have returned and the problem is worse than ever before, Sol. Not only do their numbers seem higher, but they are bolder than in the past—brazen, in fact."

Taking a deep breath, General Y'Sloic slowly exhaled. "Yes, I, too, have heard complaints of the bandit problem. It seems to come up every so many years. I have considered a solution."

"Sol." She waited until the General met her gaze. "Will you allow me to establish my own garrison here at Starfall and an outpost at the new port? A garrison of my own selection that will rid this area of the peninsula of these brigands and protect the new Port of Starfall? We both know the law. Only a general or the Emperor himself may grant permission to establish a permanent garrison. Will you?"

General Y'Sloic could hear the sincerity in her voice and see it in her face. "The need for a permanent garrison at Starfall was always a borderline situation but by no reckoning a frivolous endeavor. Perhaps the port changes the conditions. I will give the matter serious consideration, Lizabeth. That is all I can promise for now."

Squeezing his hand, Lady Y'Liory smiled, content with that answer. *I believe that means yes,* she thought to herself. She took a sip of wine while looking out over the feasting men at her table.

My dining hall filled with Ravenbourne Warriors, large and powerful, several strikingly handsome. The most feared warriors throughout the Empire, all frighteningly lethal. That Aaragon appears especially handsome—jet-black hair, sky-blue eyes, dark and coarsen skin—a rugged handsome man. And judging by the size of his hands, I'd surmise he is built as large as a stallion—a rough, wild stallion. Very sexually stimulating. Finding herself becoming moist, she squeezed her legs together.

The festive mood continued. The boisterous men ate and drank with rich enthusiasm. Meanwhile, firm, petite breasts; white, round behinds; and soft, little penises bounced and wiggled as the nude slaves scurried about the table of their mistress and scampered back and forth from the adjacent kitchen, carrying trays of food and oinochoes of drink. The tinkle of the slight brass chains with attached copper bells, fixed around their ankles, could be heard, if any listened closely for the unique sound.

"Aaragon?" asked Sergeant Twilsua, seated between Lieutenant Rohan and Captain Aaragon, his friend. "If a slave-girl you owned, fokken naked you keep her, hair cut short, as Lady Y'Liory does her pallakes? Yay, or no?"

Captain Aaragon leaned forward to look past Twilsua toward Rohan and chuckled loudly. "Now what could be wrong with a naked slave-girl, Twilsua? Besides, clothing costs money, and short hair is more easily managed. The hair of all slaves, well, nearly all, is cropped short, including the slaves of Ravenbourne. But look closer, Sergeant Twilsua." Aaragon again leaned forward to address Lieutenant Rohan. "And you as well, young Rohan. Learn a little culture. The hair of the slave-girls surrounding you here is not haphazardly cropped off with a knife as if some poor field slave. Rather, it is purposely, with patience and care, cut short with a pair of sharp shears held by a skilled barber or hair dresser. Notice, the hair on the slave-boys is equally trimmed short, much in the same manner as ours."

Sergeant Twilsua had been looking around at the slave-girls as Aaragon spoke. Reaching across the table, he grabbed a slice of game fowl, tossing it into his mouth. He chewed the morsel while he questioned Captain Aaragon.

"Will slave-girls from fallen Opar, Lady Ravenbourne buy? You reckon, Captain, or no? One month's pay, I bet, to Ravenbourne, Opar slave-girls will be coming."

"Would not surprise me, Sergeant. Most of the women of Opar will be sold as slaves. I've heard that hundreds, no, thousands of beautiful slave-girls, young and virgin, are being taken from Opar, first to Capital City and then to the smaller cities throughout the Empire. Not to worry, Twilsua, neither of us, including Lieutenant Rohan, will ever have enough wealth to own a slave-girl, especially one as beautiful as any one of these girls. Unless we are willing to give up a year's wages to buy a Ravenbourne slave-girl to wife. So we best take advantage of this opportunity while we can."

Captain Aaragon raised his mug and, looking over his shoulder, called out, "Beer!"

A timid slave-girl with deep-black hair, standing behind the two men, carefully approached. She slowly went down on her knees between the two soldiers, carefully keeping both hands on her oinochoe. A slave could be disciplined for spilling food or drink, especially if a ceramic oinochoe was dropped and broken. Reaching between them, she cautiously took the Captain's mug to refill it.

While she was pouring, Aaragon reached up, wearing a mischievous grin, and cupped her breast, then gently massaged her. "This one is especially pretty. Don't you agree, Sergeant Twilsua?"

Twilsua looked up at her face. She grimaced, attempting to continue to pour the beer, avoiding any spillage. He rubbed the back of his hand over his thick, gray beard. "Very pretty, this one, no doubt, Captain. Dark, black hair——sapphire eyes! Reminds me, she does, of maidens in our high homeland mountain."

The coarse Sergeant looked down and moved his head and face to her groin, taking in a deep breath. He straightened back up, looking at Aaragon with a mischievous grin. "Yay, Captain! Black kunt hair—favorite color of mine. Love the smell of a young kunt, I do, having black, soft hair. Buys slave-girls from our homeland, does Lady Y' Liory, reckon you, Aaragon?"

"I have heard she sends her slave buyers to our aurochs ranges on the eastern flanks of the Mountains of the Goddess," answered Aaragon, looking at both Twilsua and Lieutenant Rohan, "but I've not seen it myself."

When the anxious girl placed his mug back down on the table, Captain Aaragon reached up, taking a handful of the hair on the back of her head. He did not pull her short tresses or hurt her—he only kept her still. He kept the palm of his hand on the floor to maintain balance then he rose to his knees and kissed the timid girl on her inviting lips. She dared not move. She carefully clutched her oinochoe with both hands, all the while her young, timid face frowned with apprehension.

"Lady Y'Liory!" called out the bold Aaragon. "May I take one of your slave-girls?"

Lady Y'Liory glanced over to Aaragon and smiled with an air of dignity. She also looked to General Y'Sloic. "Why, yes, you may, Captain." She now spoke in a louder tone, intending to address all the Ravenbourne Warriors at the table.

"All the naked slaves, girls or boys, in this room are bed-slaves and provided for your pleasure, with a certain understanding. They will not be abused, Captain. And keep in mind, they are not whores. They are willing and obedient, but they will be equally frightened. You are Ravenbourne Warriors, both frightening and exciting to all females, slave or not. Consequently, if you possess 'male skills' and know how to calm a timid bed-slave and not abuse her, then take your pleasure with any slaves . . . girl or boy . . . within this hall."

She paused with intended purpose, then looked to General Y'Sloic. "General Y'Sloic and I maintain a long-standing agreement, correct, General?"

Understanding her subtle meaning, General Y'Sloic spoke calmly—without emotion—but at the same moment gave a rigid order in reply. "My men understand the courteousness of hospitality. The same law applies at Ravenbourne."

"Most surely, General Y'Sloic! My husband adopted this law from a very young Lady Ravenbourne," said the Mistress of Starfall in a loud voice, intending for all to hear.

The Ravenbourne Warriors now looked around the table at each other. Sergeant Twilsua tossed another slice of fowl into his mouth and looked at his comrade, Lieutenant Rohan, seated next to him. "Single-minded our, Captain," he spoke again with a mouth-full of game fowl. "Like his old Sergeant!"

The two warriors laughed while the clamor returned to the dining hall. The Ravenbourne Warriors now studied the naked slaves with a new interest. Captain Aaragon took the oinochoe of beer from the slave-girl's hands and set it on the table, then rose, taking her hand. She looked up at him, timid and anxious, her sapphire eyes open wide and her beautiful face apprehensive.

"Don't be afraid," he said in a calm, confident manner, "I won't hurt you—come along." His commanding voice reassured the nervous girl, and after all, he was a Ravenbourne Warrior.

He gently pulled on her hand, she rose, and he led her away from the tables. He stopped, turning his head back to look at her. Smiling, she stepped up to him, placing her hands on his shoulders, and kissed him on the neck—her bare breasts rubbed against his back. Keeping her hand, Aaragon led her off to the walls of the hall, dimly lit by long-burning torches. Pillows and fur rugs were laid out in the same manner as around the table, obviously to provide a more private setting. Soon, the other men boldly approached other naked slaves within the great Feasting Hall, with Sergeant Twilsua and Lieutenant Rohan in the lead.

"Your young Captain jumps first at an opportunity," Lady Y'Liory said chuckling.

"That is why he is the captain," answered General Y'Sloic, wearing his usual commanding smile.

CHAPTER 4

Calea: Sack of Opar

IN WARFARE JARGON, OPAR ESCAPED sack. Following the city's surrender, it was systematically pillaged of its wealth. No, more than its wealth, its treasure. Nearly all its male population, as soldiers, were killed in battle, consequently; majority of the remaining male populace was elderly. What would have been the city's next generation, the young women and girls of Opar, would be led away into slavery. Calea, a scholar of languages, found it difficult to distinguish, in warfare terminology, the differences between *sack and pillage*. Now, it mattered not.

During the first several days of plunder, all females between the ages of ten and forty were ordered into the streets and plaza centers. The helpless babies of female slaves were ripped from their mothers' arms and slaughtered. The buyer and new master of a pallake slave-girl did not want her saddled with a child so that all her efforts could be devoted to him and his family. Besides, if she was impregnated, he wanted the child to be his.

Anyone caught concealing young women of that age was put to death on the spot. Executions were swift, merciless, and bloody. The egregious offenders were dealt with more aggressively. A man caught hiding a roomful of maidens was dragged through the streets, tied to a post, stripped naked, and whipped or beaten to near death. It was rumored that the soldiers who carried whips for the Eastern Army knew the exact number of lashes a man could endure before dying. He might be left hanging on the post to die a slow death or a large bronze spike was hammered through his mouth, impaling him to the stake. For good measure, his balls and penis were cut off and left at his bloody feet. After the first days of cruel street executions, few dared disobey the order.

With the streets, plazas, and city squares filled with young females, aggressive slave buyers combed the city resembling scavenger curs, seizing young girls and women to fill the quotas of their prospective slave houses. The unfortunate chosen beauties were stripped—examined without dignity—collared—and then transported back to an Empire city.

An accurate accounting was kept. Following their selection, the slave buyers presented their merchandise to the Emperor's administrators and accountants, who maintained guarded stations at the city gates. Once the slave buyers purchased the slaves, they were presented with bills of sale. Few slave buyers, even the most audacious, would risk an attempt to sneak out of the city without paying for their spoils. Any man caught by the guards in possession of slaves from Opar and lacking bills of sale faced certain death from sword or spear . . . if they were lucky.

More often, they suffered a penalty similar to the the men who attempted to hide females. They were first whipped without pity. Next, nailed to crosses at the city gates to hang naked and screaming until their throats dried up and they could no longer make any cacophonous sound other than gasping for air. Death came as the only mercy. It remained a dire crime to steal from the Emperor.

A record of each slave was kept by name, gender, age, price, and purchaser. Slaves were transported back to the cities, with the majority delivered to Capitol City. It could be a long, hard trip. Absent proper planning and supplies, slaves could die enroute, especially children, with resulting loss of fortunes.

Calea had lost her beloved husband and her dear son Kaelin to battle. Word from the battlefield brought heart breaking reality. Few

Opar soldiers were taken captive, and those who were captured were wounded. That was expected. Very few, if any, Opar soldiers would surrender. Most wounded Opar soldiers would die. Those able to survive would be sold to the mines or stone quarries or some other camp of misery, usually succumbing to hard labor and starvation in less than a year. Calea prayed to her goddess that the two men she loved and held most dear to her heart died quickly and did not suffer. She knew they had died bravely. War hardens all hearts, and there was little opportunity for tears. She must act swiftly and boldly.

Her daughter, Susanna, was a young virgin, exceedingly beautiful and healthy. In horrible times, such as war, beauty can be a curse. Susanna would certainly be thrown on the first wagons of young pallakes to leave the city. What if she were eventually sold to a prostitution house? Her virginity would be peddled to the highest bidder, and she would endure a cruel life of daily thrashings and rape by vile, drunken men. Calea could not bear that grim future for her daughter.

And her own future held equally little hope. Even though she was nearly thirty years older than her adored daughter, she knew she was still attractive. More importantly, she was a daughter of the Empire and well educated. Her knowledge of the languages of both Opar and the Achaean Empire could render her invaluable. The possibility remained high that she would also find herself tied to a pallake slave wagon, bound for an Empire city.

Yet she knew she could not fight the inevitable destiny—she must embrace it and render the best outcome possible. Now was the moment for boldness and cunning. The slave buyers were heartless men. Still, they were men, nonetheless, and she could manipulate men. Even though she fell in love with and chose to marry a common man of Opar, Calea was trained in the art of aristocratic male manipulation.

In the aftermath of Opar's surrender and the occupation of the conquering army of the Empire, Calea was able to steal into the home of a very wealthy family, and there she liberated the clothes and fineries of an affluent woman—an elegant white chiton trimmed in red; a translucent red palla; sandals trimmed in gold leaf; and brooches, necklaces, bracelets, and other jeweled adornments. She also found a women's coin belt, concealing small silver coins, which she likewise kept. The wealthy family had fled, leaving a full household of humble servants who remained afraid and stayed inside, hiding. Calea dressed herself, as best she could, to appear to be a suave, noble-woman of the Achaean Empire. Only aristocrats of the Empire dressed in fine red or red-trimmed clothes far, too expensive for the working middle-class. The soldiers would immediately recognize her as a noble-woman of the Empire and most likely leave her alone. For those few who might approach, her commanding voice and use of the Empire language, spoken loudly in the manner of an aristocratic woman, would most certainly cause them to turn away.

Calea also undressed her beautiful daughter and examined her, knowing all along the crescent-shaped sepal of Susanna's virginity remained intact, but she wanted to be able to say she had done so. She slowly slid her hand down Susanna's back and over her perfect round buttocks. Gently, she touched two small blue dots at the base of Susanna's spine, just above her behind and below the two adorable dimples on each side of her spine. She gently kissed each numinous dot and clothing young Susanna to be a servant girl.

Lifting the pale, ragged palla, Calea gently laid it over her Susanna's head. She then fussed with the material just as any mother would, keeping her trepidation hidden. She had to remain calm, disciplined. The wife and mother of two brave, daring soldiers knew that fear was a killer.

"I am so afraid, Mother," cried Susanna as she wept bitter tears.

Calea reached out a tender hand and gently stroked her daughter's cheek. "I know, sweet child, but we must be brave."

"Mother, are you sure Father and Kaelin have been killed?"

"Yes, Susanna, I am."

"Are you sure, Mother. . .." She paused, taking a hard swallow. They will take us into slavery? Maybe we could hide."

Calea cupped her daughter's distressed but beautiful face with loving hands. "I am sure they will take us, Susanna. If we are caught hiding, we will be punished. Empire soldiers discipline females by whipping their behinds with an evil leather strap they call the Dragon's Tongue. It is a humiliating, terrible punishment. Most likely, we would also be raped, although your virginity has value. Remember, my sweet love, how brave Father and Kaelin were marching through the streets with the other brave men of the Opar Army.

"Yes, Mother, I do," whispered a gently crying Susanna.

"Therefore, we, too, must be brave. We must use all our cunning and wits to ensure we acquire the best slave positions and situation we can. You remember how we've talked and planned?"

Susanna nodded a tearful yes.

"Are you ready to go?"

Again, there was a tearful nod.

"Stay close behind me. Walk humbly, with your head bowed and covered."

"I'm afraid all I will do, is cry, Mother."

Calea smiled and kissed her tearful daughter. "Cry if you must, but do so softly. Remain quiet. Do not attract attention to yourself. Our survival hinges on that. Understand?"

"Yes, Mother," whimpered Susanna, "I will try my very, very best."

"That's my good girl. Now here we go. May the goddess be with us."

The plaza near Calea's home bustled—resembling a busy market—because it was now a slave market. Crying, sobbing young women and girls filled the streets, along with slave buyers, their company, and soldiers dressed in blue capes, falling from the shoulders to the back of the knees—soldiers of the Eastern Army. Daring Calea strolled along the streets with her head held high, as though she owned the lanes and plaza. Daughter Susanna followed along close behind. Occasionally, Calea reached back and placed her hand on the small of her back, and Susanna took her hand, following in silence with bowed head.

They passed the gruesome sight of a naked man, his outstretched wrists nailed to a mansion door and a large spike driven through his mouth to hold him in place. His bloody genitals lay at his feet while his grotesque face and sunken eyes stared out into the street. Blood still ran down his arms, from his mouth onto his chin and chest, and from his groin down the large wooden door. Calea recognized the unfortunate wealthy fellow. He kept horses at their stables and had the reputation of being a greedy sort. She stared at the grisly site to remind herself. Akin to fear, greed likewise was a killer.

Suddenly, two soldiers approached. Calea stopped, raising her head, and looked at them as if to say, '*How dare you approach a noble woman?*' That was all it took. The soldiers, being soldiers, decided it best to leave the noble woman alone and went on about their business. She next approached a trio of soldiers who were blocking her path. Two carried vicious whips that only malicious men with rancorous hearts would employ. She stopped and looked upon them with disdain.

"Step aside!" she ordered—her aristocratic voice telling them they would be stripped naked, tied to a post, and whipped with a cane if they dared disobey. Given an order from a woman of the aristocracy, in the stern language of the Achaean Empire, the prudent soldiers obeyed.

A slave buyer approached, with the same results—he left her and Susanna alone. In fact, he paid Susanna no attention. Her brave daughter was playing her part well—so far, so good. Suddenly, she saw what she was seeking, a prominent slave buyer.

He appeared balding and overweight, dressed in a nobleman's attire. A large entourage followed him, including his guards, paid employees, and servants. With humble Susanna in tow, Calea boldly strolled up to the man, as close as she dared. The goddess was with her.

A tall, well-dressed middle-aged man was standing next to the slave buyer, who was examining a whimpering young girl. The slave buyer questioned the girl, and the well-dressed man interpreted between the language of the Empire and that of Opar. Calea overheard the conversation.

"Yes, Master Smyth," said the interpreter. "The girl states that she is a virgin."

Now was Calea's opportunity—now!

"That is not what the girl said!" Calea interrupted, boldly and with a loud, polemic voice.

A long, silent pause followed. Both men, Master Smyth and the well-dressed interpreter, looked toward Calea. The interpreter frowned.

"I beg to differ, woman!" the interpreter blurted in an angry, snobbish voice. "And even though you appear noble, just who do you presume…"

Master Smyth raised his chubby hand to silence the interpreter. He gave Calea a serious frown, as he looked her up and down. "Tell me, what did the girl say, noble woman?"

"Your interpreter has misunderstood two related words—*virgin* and *pregnant*. Each holds a very different meaning, but in the language of Opar, they are uniquely similar."

Another quiet pause ensued. "The girl said she was not pregnant, not that she was a virgin," said a bold, calm Calea.

Master Smyth turned and looked at his interpreter, who blurted out. "She doesn't know what she's talking about, Master Smyth. She wants to cause trouble or take the girl for herself."

Turning back to Calea, Master Smyth spoke in a loud, frustrated voice, "Ask this girl if she has ever been fokkened or not and if she maintains a sweet, delicate little hymen."

Calea nodded to Master Smyth. She stepped over to the girl and spoke to her in a soft, pleasant voice. The timid girl also spoke. Calea gently put her hand under the girl's chin and lifted her head. She continued to calmly speak with the girl in the poetic language of Opar and listen to her responses. She then addressed Master Smyth.

"The girl says she is not a virgin, Master. She has had several sexual encounters with her young male lover. But she also says she is not now, nor has she ever been, with child. She speaks the truth, Master. Although an alluring nereid, she is too young and ignorant to realize how much better off she would be if taken by you, as a virgin, as opposed to being taken by a slave buyer representing a house of prostitution. I could, nonetheless, examine her here, where we stand, and tell you with certainty if she is virgin or not."

Again, Master Smyth looked to his interpreter, who now stood speechless, looking straight ahead. A final brief but silent pause ensued. "Very impressive," declared Master Smyth. "Now this is the information I want."

He stared straight into Calea's face. "You appear to have more than fair command of the Emperor's language and the language of Opar. Explain!"

"I am a woman of both Opar and the Achaean Empire, Master. I was raised on the Greenstone Estates, on the northern coast of the Inner Sea, and educated with Lord Philemon's many offspring. I married a man of Opar when I became an adult."

"You were reared at the Greenstone Villa?

"Yes, Master . . . a child ward of Lord Philemon and Lady Baucis."

"Where is your husband?" asked Master Smyth.

"Killed in battle, Master."

Calea took a deep, silent breath before striking her final blow. "This is what you seek, Master." Calea moved to her daughter Susanna, and removed her head cover.

"Your servant girl?" asked Master Smith.

"No, Master, my daughter. You will not find a fairer maiden in the city. She has not engaged in sexual intercourse, and her delicate innocence remains intact. A mother knows the sexual behavior of her daughter; nonetheless, I examined her myself this morning. I would not dare to offer you damaged goods or a girl that has been—fokkened."

Calea smiled to herself at her use of the vulgar word, *fokken*. It was really the obscene word *fuck* from the Opar language, used to mean sexual intercourse void of love or affection. Borrowed and bastardized into the Empire language, it was commonly used by rough men and soldiers in bars and brothels—most certainly never used by ladies of status and dignity.

"Yes!" declared Master Smyth, drawing out the word and looking upon Susanna's face for the first time. "Now this may be what I am after."

Boldly, he stepped in front of the frightened Susanna. Reaching out his chubby hands, he grasped the sides of her head. Susanna closed her eyes and whimpered.

"Do not be afraid, girl," said Master Smyth.

"Yes, my Lord," murmured Susanna in a frightened voice.

Master Smyth smiled. "I am a Master, child, not a Lord."

"Yes, my Master," whispered Susanna.

"Open your mouth," ordered Master Smyth.

Calea quickly spoke the command in the Opar language. Susanna obeyed. Master Smyth looked toward Calea, then raised his eyebrows in approval. He now looked into her mouth and smelled her breath. Putting his hand to the back of her head, he took a taste of her in the form of a hard kiss. He then proceeded with a hasty examination.

First taking her shoulders, Master Smyth next grasped and

massaged her breasts. He ran his plump hands down her trunk, and then reached them around her narrow waist. Turning her around, he massaged her buttocks and delivered a smart spank to each delicate cheek. Susanna responded with a delightful jerk, raising up on her toes with each swat, and looked back over her shoulder, smiling—an adorable, frightened smile. He turned her back around. Taking her chin in one hand, he slid the other hand between her legs, cupping her virgin flower. Susanna responded with two high-pitched whispered "Ohs" in the sweet voice of a young girl. Seemingly pleased, Master Smyth slid his hand up from between her legs to her stomach and once more reached up and grasped her shoulders. Susanna looked into his eyes and offered another adorable, frightened smile. She licked her lips and breathed quietly, yet hard—frightened and timid—extremely desirable.

Calea remained calm yet anxious, watching Susanna's examination. Whether a superb actress or a sincerely frightened child, Susanna was playing her part without flaw. She was sealing the deal.

"Now this is what I am fokken looking for," called out Master Smyth, as though delivering an announcement.

He released his grasp on Susanna's shoulders, looked over to the officer of his guard, and called out a one-word order: "Collars!"

Instantly, a soldier stepped forward with several leather collars in hand. Calea now recognized that all the soldiers of Master Smyth's guard were Imperial soldiers from Capital City. This one was a sergeant, and she noticed a well-used Dragon's Tongue attached to his waist. She also noted that each collar buckled with bronze fittings and had a bronze plate, inscribed with a symbol, attached.

Ever cunning, Calea reacted. She took one of the collars and stepped to Susanna, attaching the collar around Susanna's neck. In so doing, she recognized the collar's symbol was the Imperial insignia of the royal family. She nearly jumped for joy but remained nonchalant.

This could not be going any better. Surely, the goddess was with her and Susanna.

She spoke softly to her daughter and comforted her. "Do not fear, my dearest. Stay calm. All will be well."

"You have certainly impressed me, woman," stated an energetic Master Smyth. "What is your name?"

"Calea, Master. My name is Calea."

"Well, Calea. I seek some ten or twelve beautiful, young virgin girls and other handsome women of various skills. The wife of the Emperor's son contracts me. I serve the royal family. Do you know what that means?"

"Yes, my Master, I do."

"What do you want, Calea?" asked Master Smyth in a demanding tone.

Calea took a deep breath and swallowed hard but remained focused. This was her opportunity for deliverance—an opportunity offered by the goddess. "I want to remain with my daughter. I do not want her or myself beaten, raped, or abused."

Master Smyth folded his chubby arms over his fat chest and looked into Calea's eyes, tilting his head in thought. The guard with the collars continued to stand nearby. Calea thought to herself, *One final daring act.*

She stepped over to the guard and took a collar from his hand. She attached it around her neck, looking into Master Smyth's eyes—and lowered her hands—offering him just the proper smile.

Master Smyth turned to his silent interpreter. "You are dismissed."

He now turned to Calea. "You will serve as my interpreter."

"Gladly, Master Smyth," she responded.

"Now then, Calea. I want virgin daughters, yes, but I don't want flat-chested, skinny-legged girls. I want small, firm tits or budding nipples, curved hips, gorgeous butts, beautiful faces, and smiles. But most of all, I want that sweet smell of a young virgin kunt. Learned physicians will examine each tight little kunt and must declare her a ripe virgin." Master Smyth paused, but Calea's knowledge of men told her he was not finished. She remained calm, listening.

"Every wealthy woman in Capital City hopes to own a virgin slave-girls if she can." Calea knew his discussion was now drawing to an end. She could now close the final pact. She thought to herself.

Entice him and use both elegant and vulgar language. Then, he will be yours.

"I understand, Master." Calea moved in front of Master Smyth and looked up into his eyes. "The girls will be more forthcoming with me, a woman from Opar, about their sexual condition than they would be with a man from the Empire. Also, I already have several girls I know who are certainly very striking, and I also believe they have not yet experienced a sexual *recontre*. I am most assured the petals of their little flower kunts in front and the tight, tiny 'ass cherries' between the cheeks of their soft, petite behinds remain intact. I am confident and certain I can hasten your selection of prized girls before other slave buy-ers secure the cream of the virgin crop."

"Yes," answered Master Smyth with a pleased smile, "I am convinced you will." He enjoyed the manner in which she spoke, using both so-phisticated and vulgar language, but he certainly didn't realize it was all part of her calculating plan and purpose.

"And much more, Master," continued the ever-cunning Calea, mis-tress of male manipulation. "I now see you are an intelligent, adventur-ous man. Such men possess complex desires. You may, for instance, crave the delights of a young . . . tight . . . submissive . . . frightened, girl in the morning but desire a more educated, mature. . . ." She paused and tilted her head, slightly to the side. "Let' us say, a much bolder woman in the evening."

Calea moved even closer to Master Smyth. Slowly, she reached up and laid her hand on his fat, soft, chest. Leaning into him, she gazed into his eyes and drew so close that he might smell her breath while she spoke.

"Such intricate men as yourself, my Master, may pull a naughty, naked slave-girl over his lap to administer a hard lesson of obedience and enjoy her cherry-red buttocks just spanked into submission in the dawn's early morning. Later, however, in the afternoon, he may relish the pleasures of a more, say, experienced woman, who straddles his lap and rides him as if he were an untamed stallion." She now smiled knowingly; her hand gently squeezed his chest.

Master Smyth gazed at Calea. He grinned. "You are a very intelligent, beautiful, and daring woman, Calea. You will serve me well."

"Yes, Master," answered a confident yet obedient Calea.

"Captain!" called out Master Smyth.

"Sir!" replied the blue-cloaked officer.

"Have our first young virgin escorted back to our quarters. Should any misfortune befall her, Captain, I'll first have your balls and next your life."

"Sir!" called out the captain.

"Now, Calea. Let us locate beautiful, young, healthy, submissive virgins. I will realize a small fortune from each one."

"Yes, my Master," answered a coy Calea, "as you wish. I know an abandoned villa, my Master. The wealthy lord of the villa fled the city with his wife and children, leaving everything else behind—food, slaves, wine—everything. It will serve us well as an excellent headquarters."

"Very well, Calea," replied Master Smyth, taking her by the back of the neck with his chubby fingers. "Lead on."

CHAPTER 5

Kaelin: Slave March

DEATH REMAINED THE ONLY VIABLE escape. The long procession of male slaves staggered and stumbled as they rambled their way along the rough, dusty road toward the sprawling Empire city of Cappa, the capital of the Southern Peninsula. Secured by long lengths of leather rope, fastened to their necks, the ragged chattels marched in two lengthy files, one on each side of the road. The slaves were linked together in groups of roughly ten or so. The ardent sun showed little mercy. Sweat, blood, and urine dripped from their filthy bodies, moistening the packed dirt of the highway as would a short summer rain. Mule-drawn wagons carried supplies down the center of the road while armed guards, some mounted, some afoot, secured the pitiful columns of hopeless men.

Kaelin struggled, second in a ragged line of chattels, not knowing if being tied first or last in line was of any benefit or disadvantage. The poor wretch in front of him continued to groan—deep, gurgling sounds of looming death—while he staggered and strained with all his might to keep from falling to his knees. A filthy piece of cloth was tied around his waist, and his sweat and blood, from many whip lashes, glistened in the zealous sun. Suddenly, the suffering wretch fell to his knees, calling out in a rasping moan.

The line stopped. Kaelin halted, along with those struggling in line behind him. A guard stepped up to Kaelin and cut the rope line

51

near his neck. With the help of another guard, they dragged the fallen slave to the side of the road. One of the guards slit his throat. They left him on the edge of the road—dead if the gods were merciful, half-dead if not.

Occasionally, a slave might somehow free himself of his bonds and attempt a futile running escape, only to be hit in the back by a javelin or run down and trampled by a mounted guard. No, it was more than futile; it was a desperate act of a frantic man, driven to near insanity by starvation and hopelessness. It was not really a failed attempt at escape; it was a final act of suicide.

Several guards carried whips, using the bloody bite of the lash to keep the nearly naked chattels moving. They applied the lash more for their own enjoyment of cruelty rather than any need. The circumstances provided enough incentive.

Kaelin fought with inner strength, keeping himself alive through each day's torturous, endless march. Strenuously, reaching deep inside, he made certain he did not swagger or stumble. A single lash from a guard's whip would add agonizing pain throughout the day, enduring into the night. And, a continuous, painful reminder of death by whipping.

He had watched more than one ill-fated slave be whipped to death. The bare thrall, writhing in the dust on the side of the road, his tortured body covered with bloody lashes and his throat too raw and dry to cry out. The guards would halt their flogging to witness the blood-spattered slave's last agonizing groans. The cruel men enjoyed watching their victim's final breath as he sucked in the dust of the road through his nose and mouth, then died with an excruciating expression on his dirty, bloodstained face.

Deviant slaves who had offered any form of resistance usually met the fate of a pitiless whipping death. Some slaves were flogged simply because the gods withheld mercy. Kaelin bore several lashes.

Although numerous slaves were doomed, the pitiful columns were watered and fed. The guards were obliged to deliver a respectable number of live specimens to the quarries, and the more they delivered, the more they were paid. Nonetheless, the dawn-to-dark march was torturously exhausting, and slaves fell daily.

The leather rope around Kaelin's neck was loose, allowing him to grasp the noose with both hands. He was not sure if this was a blessing or a curse. There was much he was not sure of. He was, however, certain of one thing. He would not die a slow death in the mines. But once chained to a gang of slaves, his chances of escape would be nonexistent. He knew he had to attempt his escape before they reached the mines, and he would have only one stab of a sword, one throw of a spear. The result would be success or his death.

Kaelin's nine-man line staggered behind and to the side of one of the mule-drawn wagons, which was of no benefit. Three boys were attached to the wagon—called "Cherry Boys" by the guards. He was not sure why the guards of the Achaean Empire used the term *Cherry Boys*. He did recall, as a youngster, when he and his mother sojourned at the impressive villa of Greenstone, located somewhere in the northern area of the Empire, near the coast. His mother was a daughter of the Empire and had been raised in this villa. They all talked about the exquisite cherry wine from Ravenbourne.

Naked, the unfortunate Cherry Boy slaves were used by several of the foul guards as sex-slaves. They were spared whippings and beatings but did not escape harsh punishment. They were often hand-slapped until their buttocks were inflamed, bringing laughter and joyful comments from the sadistic guards. Occasionally their backsides were beaten with a heavy leather strap the guards called a Dragon Tongue.

Their humiliating situation was in some ways more miserable than that of the rest of the wretched slaves, although the Cherry Boys were often thrown into the wagon and allowed to ride rather than walk and given ample food and water. Occasionally, they were also bathed. A cruel-trade off because riding in the wagon most likely kept them from death, but they paid a high price.

When dusk neared, the caravan would stop for the night. The slaves were fed, watered, and bedded down, and the caravan was secured. Several guards would drag or carry the Cherry Boys off to the edge of the camp, where they were beaten, sodomized, and forced to commit other vile sexual acts. Several ceramic urns, swung from leather thongs, were attached to the side of the wagon as a constant reminder. The urns contained attar that a guard would use to lubricate his stimulated phallus before penetrating his helpless catch.

Occasionally, a guard would tie a slave boy's hands and feet, sleeping with him all night. The guards were experts with knots. A Cherry Boy could be bound in such a manner as to avoid cutting off the circulation, thus keeping him safely tied all night. On many evenings, Kaelin watched off-duty guards carry tied boys to their beds and keep them all night, where they endured rough sex. He could hear the boys in the night, groaning and whimpering for the guards to stop. Kaelin truly had empathy for the pitiful boys, but as a struggling slave himself, he could do nothing except try to sleep.

Today's march was harder still. This morning, a guard on horseback meted out three bloody lashes across Kaelin's buttocks. The gods had smiled on the guard on this day, because on the fourth lash, Kaelin was prepared to drag the guard from his mount, kill him, and attempt a horseback escape. He could still feel the blood soaking into his tunic, and walking was now more difficult.

Kaelin's father had worshipped the God of War, as most men of Opar did. He had followed his father's reverence, mostly to please him.

Kaelin did not care to worship any god or goddess, but on this day, he swore an oath to the God of War that the next guard who laid a whip on him would meet a certain death, and he would attempt an equestrian escape. Perhaps that moment was at hand.

A mounted guard rode up next to Kaelin, walking his mount alongside. All the mounted guards were officers. Kaelin continued to walk, his eyes focused straight ahead, as though marching in a rigid column of soldiers. He could feel the vibrations of the horse's hooves and hear its heavy clomps on the dusty road, along with its loud, blowing snorts. The strong aroma of the magnificent, sweating animal filled his nostrils. It reminded him of his father's stables and the long rides he took as a youth, on sunny afternoons, to exercise the horses out in the lush green meadows adjacent to the back walls of Opar.

Finally, the mounted soldier spoke in a loud, hoarse voice.

"Your ragged tunic's tellin' me you are an Opar warrior, slave! You speak the Emperor's language?"

Kaelin continued his marching pace. He did not look up at the soldier but gazed straight ahead with a poignant expression. "I do," he answered in a calm, soft-spoken voice.

"Many pallakes from the fallen Opar city speak the good language of the Emperor," remarked the uncouth guard, as though the two were lifting jugs of beer in a favorite brothel. Kaelin surmised the guard was up to something, but he was not sure just what. It could be malice or benevolence—his chance for freedom or a trap.

Suddenly, the column halted. Periodically, the march was stopped for some reason, usually a broken-down wagon. The other slaves in Kaelin's line quickly sat down on the road. Kaelin remained standing.

The guard pulled up on the reins of his mount and spoke again.

"You know slave, you're young and pretty enough that those guards who like fokken young boys might have taken you as one of their Cherry Boys. You'd be forced to kiss and suck them smelly men, sleep with'em—butt spanked—cherry fokkened sore every night. You've seen them poor little Cherry Boys in the wagon in front of you—crying and beggin'!"

The guard laughed to himself. "Now, what if I was to tell them guards to take you as a Cherry Boy? What would you do about that?" he asked with a sneer.

Filled with unyielding temerity, Kaelin's first impulse was to ignore the guard or tell him to fuck off. Suddenly, that same mysterious phenomenon occurred. A warm, gentle breeze blew against the side of his face, reminding him of a woman blowing into his ear. It was as though an unseen female being was standing next to him—placing her warm, gentle hand on his forearm—lifting up on her toes—speaking soft and warm into his ear.

"Play along and maintain a solemn temper," said the pleasant female voice.

It was the same mysterious voice that had spoken to him on the battlefield. Had he not pushed his hands and arms through the bodies that lay on top of him, the Empire soldiers would have passed him by, leaving him to die on the battlefield.

Although mystified and perplexed, Kaelin followed the advice of the unknown voice. He looked up into the face of the guard and responded, though his throat was painfully dry.

"I would see it as an opportunity to escape." He spoke as clearly as his parched throat allowed. "The vermin who would drag me off to the side of the road, expecting an easy fokken, would be deadly surprised when I cut off his cock and escaped on foot, leaving him to die a slow, painful, bloody death. Witness to such mutilation, other guards may think twice about following me. Conversely, I would hope a mounted guard, such as you, would pursue, giving me an opportunity to secure a horse."

Now the mounted guard laughed out loud. "Them vermin guards, as you call' em, know your tunic and you as a soldier of Opar, just as

I do. Them cowards wouldn't dare try fokken you or any other Opar soldier, no matter his age. Maybe some of them brave or stupid ones might give you a few whip lashes, but that would be it."

Kaelin did not reply, and the guard continued.

"Cause you are a soldier, a warrior, and also young, I figured you'd cause trouble or somehow try to slow up this slave march. I thought you would at least try to escape, givin' me the chance of killin' you."

Remaining calm, Kaelin now turned to look up at the guard. "Sorry to disappoint you," he replied without emotion, but he swallowed hard before continuing. "I presumed you were watching me closely, so I remained on my best behavior, hoping you would ease your caution. That would provide me an enhanced opportunity to pull you off your horse, cut the rope from my neck, and ride off on a desperate mounted chase, taking your life with me."

At first, the guard paused, a worried expression covering his face. Following the silence, he threw his head back to laugh, even louder than before. "You got guts, slave, real guts. What better chance you got to kill me and make your getaway than now?"

Kaelin wanted to smile but remained stoic, and he was again forced to swallow to be able to talk. Once more, the warm voice spoke into his ear. Still a soothing female voice.

"*Solemn temper, my young love. Solemn temper.*"

Kaelin took a deep breath and spoke as clearly, as he could, "You did not ride up alongside and address me by chance. Another mounted horseman has come up just behind us. And up ahead, another turns around, watching behind. You're anticipating I'll attempt an escape now. When I do, I will take you unaware."

"Very sharp-eyed, young warrior," the guard said, smiling. "You're much smarter than the average foot soldier, I'll give you this. Quarry slaves don't live long. But once in a while, them slave buyers come from the Feohtan colleges to buy slaves from the quarry mines. They train them to fight and die in the arenas—entertains the citizens of Cappa. Especially that buyer from the Heart Blood College. He says if a slave can stay alive on the slave march, he should be able to stay alive in the arena. If that happens, do something to get his attention. Better than a slow death in the quarry. He'll be a fat man, dressed rich red. Likes to eat." With that, the guard reined his mount around and rode back down the column.

Occasions had come and gone where Kaelin judged he had a chance, no matter how slim, to cut free, pull a guard from his mount, and flee on horseback. He reasoned, other mounted guards might or might not follow. Kaelin was prepared, in mind and skill, to ride a horse to its death. Perhaps, his pursuers would not go to that extreme. If they didn't overtake him at the beginning of the chase, and once they realized that he would stay mounted on a running horse to the end, they might not choose to follow. A good horse had more value than a hopeless quarry slave. Even so, if the guards did not follow him, what would he do next?

What chance would a naked fugitive slave have, albeit on horseback, with no money, no allies, in a foreign land and not sure where he was? Well, he knew the answer. He would most likely be reduced to thievery and joining a band of brigands. He would not call that life freedom, and most certainly, he would never learn the fate of his beloved family—his mother, sister, and father, although it was all but certain his father was dead.

For better or worse, Kaelin resolved to take the mounted officer's advice, and attempt to be taken by the fat man, or any slave buyer from the arenas, as a fighting slave. He could not explain the female voice he heard whispering into his ear. Did a goddess speak to him? He was not certain, but the voice had saved him twice.

If the fat slave buyer or any other was not at the quarry mine, he would still have the opportunity to attempt a horseback escape. Perhaps a better chance since the guards would be focused on turning the slaves over to the mine and collecting their pay. Also, he suspected more would be dismounted at the mine than on the caravan road.

He was only certain of one aspect of his future: he would not be chained to a line of quarry slaves. He would act, no matter how desperate, before he was chained. Once permanently attached by bronze links, there would be no escape. He rested assured that if nothing else, he could force the guards to kill him.

The nearly full moon appeared clear and bright, casting long, dark shadows across an open landscape, wondrously still and quiet. Normally, the pitiful slaves groaned and moaned throughout most of the night in painful, broken sleep. Tonight was different.

The caravan had the fortune of stopping early in the day at a clear, cold, shallow stream, taking the opportunity to recoup and refit. The concern was for the mules, drivers, and guards, nonetheless; the slaves also benefited. They were allowed to bathe and soak in the stream, which greatly soothed their battered bodies. They were fed nutritious food—thick stew with meat and vegetables—and all the water they could hold.

A blanket of thick grass covered the ground from the edge of the road to the steam, and the whole company spread out across the field, as if it were a soft bed. A welcomed luxury for the slaves, sleeping on a bed of comfortable grass rather than the dust, dirt, and rocks of the road edge. Unexpectedly, the peace was interrupted by slapping and crying.

Kaelin rose to his elbows. Not far away, he could see the dusk-clear figure of a guard on his blanket and bed. Casting a long moon shadow, the guard was on one knee, with a Cherry Boy over his raised knee. He was spanking the young slave, who squirmed, cried, begged, and soon promised to be a good "fokken boy."

Kaelin cursed to himself. Why didn't the wretched guard take his pitiful boy away from earshot to abuse him? Suddenly, the clamor stopped.

The guard let the boy up. He ran toward the wagon near Kaelin, using short, hopping steps, rubbing himself. He stopped at the wagon on the bright-moon side, giving Kaelin a clear view of the hapless boy only a few paces away. He was small and thin. Kaelin could even see the painful abuse of his buttocks, given the brightness of the moon. Unfortunately for him, he was handsome and callipygian, just the type the guards desired.

The youngster removed the urn of oil from the wagon. He turned to look at Kaelin with such a sorrowful expression, as though asking for help. Still crying, he ran back to his guard.

For the next half turn of the hour-glass, the stillness remained broken with the grunting of the guard and the deep gurgling and crying of the boy as the guard abused him. Eventually, the guard's hateful lust waned. He curled the boy against him and slept. The calm returned to an otherwise beautiful night.

Kaelin felt sorry for the boy. A slave himself, what could he do? As peace returned, Kaelin also drifted off into a much-needed, restful sleep. This extra attention and care for the slaves told Kaelin they had to be near the quarries.

CHAPTER 6

Ann Y'Sloic: Lady of Ravenbourne

SEATED COMFORTABLY IN A LARGE low-backed chair, the Mistress of Ravenbourne gracefully rested her arms on the intricately carved sides— the seat, soothingly padded with thick, soft fur. Skilled craftsmen had sculpted the rough wood, producing a wondrous work of art from an ancient tree, over three thousand summers in age. A single tree had been sacrificed to provide wood, for use as elegant decoration and furniture, for the Ravenbourne Villa. The remaining prehistoric giants in the Primeval Grove were left standing near the ancient ruins of a city, protected by Lord Ravenbourne's Law. The rings of the one fallen tree provided the age of the grove and, by extension, the age of the ancient city and adjacent temple ruins. In addition to Lady Ravenbourne's chair, two luxurious pieces of furniture had also been carved from the ancient wood: two throne-like, regal chairs for the Lord and Lady of Ravenbourne, which were placed on the stone stage in the Receiving Hall.

Another tree from the ancient primeval forest had been felled many seasons ago by Lord Ravenbourne's father, DeMond Y'Sloic. That dying giant was called Maladarwin and said to have been the oldest living creature in the Achaean Empire. Huge, valuable slabs of the tree remained stored in a great underground cave. DeMond Y'Sloic, the Lord of Ravenbourne, had presented several slabs as a gift to his friend and neighbor the Lord of Starfall.

Five females served as the constant companions of Lady Ravenbourne. First and foremost was her lifelong nanny, who had been called Old Nanny for nearly all her long life. Next, her personal bodyguard, Ginal, a well-trained warrior—the only female Ravenbourne Warrior. And finally, three lovely handmaidens who attended their mistress.

Young and beautiful—more than beautiful, radiant—the three handmaidens remained naked as the day they were born. Aside from special "Receiving Days," the only attire the handmaidens were allowed were menstruation pads worn during their moon cycle of the goddesses Asa. The hair of most slave-girls was cropped short for ease of care. Lady Ravenbourne, to the contrary, allowed her handmaids to grow long strands of beautiful hair. A sufficient period was allotted each day for the three girl-slaves to attend to each other's extraordinary locks.

The first handmaid, and the oldest, stood behind her mistress, brushing Lady Ravenbourne's long amber hair. Her name was Kasena, and she was sired by an unusual group of people who called themselves the *Vratzan*. They live in large, crowded communities within the more populated Empire cities, such as Capital City and Cappa, earning a living as small shop-keepers, craftsmen, and laborers for the aristocracy and other wealthy citizens. Their unique language remained a mystery to Imperial scholars. Kasena's people were a handsome population, small, yet gracefully muscular, sporting well-formed, slender physiques.

General Y'Sloic, the Lord of Ravenbourne, commander of the Southern Army, provided a corps of highly trained, skilled soldiers to serve as a police force to guard, protect, and maintain law and order in the city of Cappa. It was a huge expense, borne by General Y'Sloic, that would otherwise require collections in the form of taxes from the citizens of Cappa. The citizens and the governor of the city very much appreciated the General's generosity.

The police corps included a specialized unit that patrolled the Vratzan community. Men were recruited from the Vratzan population, along with any others having a special relationship with that community, such as those who had married into the populace. The commander of the specialized Vratzan force met regularly with the Vratzan Elders to ensure continued corporation. To demonstrate their total gratitude to General Y'Sloic, the fairest maiden, from the community at large, was chosen and offered to the Lord and Lady of Ravenbourne as a servant. Kasena now served Lady Ravenbourne as a duty and service for her people.

She was an extraordinary example of Vratzan beauty. Her full, long, flowing hair just reached her petite nipples and reflected an astonishing two shades of color, which was a remarkable feature of Vratzan elegance. Near her head, her hair reflected a bright-gold shade, kissed by the sun. The ends, however, about a hand's length, were a darker russet color. The second extraordinary Vratzan feature was her bright, golden eyes, certainly touched by the goddess. The Lord of Ravenbourne had offered his protection to the Vratzan race to insure they were not exploited and thus obliged into a life of servitude for the wealthy. Only unusual circumstances, such as those that befell Kasena, would justify the enslavement of these remarkable people.

Malia stood next to Kasena, likewise brushing her mistress's hair. She represented a large group of pallakes who were enslaved after the conquest of K'semya. Their unusual, stunning appearance of black hair, cream-colored skin, and blue eyes made them highly desirable throughout the Empire. They might be seen anywhere throughout the realm, but generally, their unique combination of hair, eye, and skin color allowed that only those with wealth and influence were able to obtain any of these rare beauties.

The youngest handmaid of Lady Ravenbourne drifted on the edge of maturity. Sitting at her mistress's feet, preparing her nails, Aleah's nudity revealed that she was a rare blooming dryad of conspicuous beauty. Spun from threads of gold, her brilliant hair cascaded past her shoulders and onto her back, loosely tied into a tail with narrow strips of purple lace. Long, thin braids fell on each side of her head over her ears. Her flamed sienna eyes were as clear as a glass mirror, seeming to glow in the bright sunlight.

The goddess Asa had certainly smiled on young Aleah and ostensibly protected her. Her father had sold her into slavery. She had stood at auction on a public slave stage in Cappa, along with an assortment of pallake slaves. Most likely, they all would have been purchased by a brothel, destined for a hard life of abuse. By chance, the governor of Cappa had strolled by. He saw the beauty, hidden by unwashed, dirty bodies and unkempt hair, and purchased the whole lot of girls, then graciously presented Aleah to Lord Ravenbourne as a gift. Lord Ravenbourne, in turn, sent her on to his wife. Aleah now attends Lady Ravenbourne. When she reaches adulthood, she will be freed and allowed to go her own way.

A singular example of Taolian strength and beauty, Ginal was a rarity indeed. She was tall, strong, and beautiful—uniquely beautiful. Her skin was soft, smooth, and a very pleasing shade of pale, parchment white. And although she was a creature of the sun, as were all the women of the Taolian race, its warming rays did not cause her to tan or darken her complexion. Somehow, as if touched by the goddess, her skin remained light in tone—the result of a strange natural pigmentation. The hair of all her race was a striking, salient black and straight, void of curves or waves. Still, the most exotic feature of Ginal, and the entire Taolian race, was her remarkable eyes. An inexplicable mauve color that shined like rare glass jars used to contain cosmetics, only the wealthiest of women could afford.

A rare beauty, yes, but a beautiful rose that concealed her sharp thorns. Ginal protected her mistress with the lethal skills of a Ravenbourne Warrior. She could kill in an instant, without hesitation or remorse. General Y'Sloic's finest Ravenbourne Warriors had taught and trained Ginal, from a young age, in the art of war and the deadly cunning of a warrior. She learned, practiced, and studied with enduring enthusiasm, and continued to do so.

The goddess-like hair of Lady Ravenbourne emanated long and full, falling down her back, past her buttocks to the back of her legs, just past her calves. It was meticulously groomed daily, with careful caution, by her handmaids. Pure auburn in color, it flowed with the gentle breezes as she walked, giving her a mystical yet unintimidating appearance when she approached. Many would say her hair and beauty, charm, grace, and wit were the gifts of the goddess. They would, most certainly, be incorrect.

Lady Ravenbourne was born the product of several generations of selected breeding intended to capture beauty, health, and intelligence. Her great-great-grandfather, the cantankerous old Lord of Heavenrock, family name Y'Arle, ruled the rugged coastal lands of the Northwest Territories, adjacent to the country of K'semya. On one rare, beautiful morn, as the usually rough seas lay still and calm and the sun shone brightly through a cloudless blue sky, the Lord of Heavenrock experienced inspiration, as though in a vision from the goddess.

With careful forethought, he decided he would wed the healthiest, most beautiful, and most intelligent girl he could find from throughout the Empire. He could not have cared less about her family background, her family's wealth, or her social status in life.

The crabby Lord of Heavenrock was quoted as having said. "The vapid lords and wealthy men of the Empire will spend a fortune educating their dim-witted daughters so as to make them appear to be intelligent. I, on the other hand, will find the most intelligent, prettiest, and healthiest girl that my family fortune and political influence will allow.

I don't give a fokken how rich or poor her father is. I will educate her, and her little kunt will bear me as many babies as she might. And given the goddess's nature of fokken and birthing, my offspring will also be beautiful and intelligent and equally healthy."

And so it was he brought into his employment the most renowned scholars he could entice to come to the Heavenrock Villa Estates. In particular, he employed one young teacher who had devised a battery of tests that he said could define someone's "intelligential capacity" even though they were illiterate. The test was primarily oral but also utilized pictures and geometric patterns as well.

In legend, it is said that the tetchy old lord interviewed, examined, and investigated several thousand girls and young women from across the Empire. The tests revealed, as the old lord had asserted, that educated girls from wealthy families were not necessarily intelligent. To the contrary, uneducated girls from poor families might very well be, especially girls from middle-class working people. He finally settled on a young auburn-haired beauty from a poor community whose father was a hardworking carpenter. He married her and made her Mistress Y'Arle, Lady of Heavenrock. Although she could not read or write, in due course, his scholars and teachers provided her with the finest formal education. Just as the young teacher who had devised the intelligence tests predicted, she was bright, sharp, and easily taught. When she physically matured, she presented her lord with several healthy, beautiful babies. But it didn't end there.

The sons of this steadfast Lord of Heavenrock followed the same procedure as did their father, and more so did his oldest boy, who took his father's title. This heir apparent to his father's title searched the land to find the prettiest and smartest auburn-haired maid his wealth could secure. Auburn hair, glowing cerise sienna in the sun, was his only mandate. The next few generations continued this practice, and in due course, the maidens of Y'Arle were highly sought by the most powerful lords, across the Empire. It was whispered throughout Capital City that the Emperor himself considered taking the hand of a Y'Arle maiden of Heavenrock.

Rumors, from the halls of Heavenrock, stated that Lady Ravenbourne, when a very young Ann Y'Arle, could read and write at age three, and when she reached ten summers of age, a glance of her beauty alone would bring tears to the eyes of old men.

Although now a mature age, Lady Ravenbourne remained an exotic beauty. She was old enough to have raised two grown children. Her two beloved boys had both followed the Y'Sloic military tradition and, as young officers, had been killed in battle. Those around her were not sure if she would ever emotionally recover from the loss. Lord Ravenbourne, hardened warrior to his core, publicly showed little remorse. Privately, however, it was whispered that he wept with deep sorrow when alone with his beloved wife. They were, if ever a husband and wife were, bound together by heart and soul.

Old Nanny always dressed in a plain grey frock with a rope around her waist as a belt. She always carried a sharp dagger, attached to the belt, and now, as for many years, a Ravenbourne dagger. One might think a Ravenbourne Warrior protected her, but in fact, they all did. When Lady Ravenbourne's mother, the elegant Mistress of Heavenrock, was a but a baby girl, Old Nanny had served as her nanny, even though she was only some ten summers older. Twenty summers latter and both women—the child bride of Heavenrock and her loyal Old Nanny— were ripe and full with the offspring of Lord Heavenrock; after all, he was the lord of the land. They shared each other's term of pregnancy, believed to be beneficial for both expecting mothers.

Fortune did not smile on the infant child of Old Nanny; it succumbed to weakness. With the birth of Lady Heavenrock's child, Old Nanny accepted her duty as nursemaid and guardian. With the loss of her own infant, she suckled the baby girl who would become the Mistress of Ravenbourne and raised her as a child of Heavenrock. The stern Lord of Heavenrock demanded that all children in his household be raised with strict discipline, something the beautiful, intelligent, yet gentle Lady of Heavenrock could not provide. Old Nanny reared the extraordinary child of Heavenrock with unending devotion and love, infinite patience, and unbending discipline.

Angry Nanny stood with her hands on her hips and a stern expression on her face, as her cold, steel-grey eyes all but glared. The youthful Lady of Heavenrock reached down and gently touched the face of her daughter, nine summers of age. The young maid of Heavenrock stood defiantly with arms folded and a glare that matched her strict nanny's.

"I want Father to punish me," she said with as stern of a voice she as could find. "I don't want Nanny to spank me!"

Lady Heavenrock was caught off guard by her daughter's request. "I will need to ask your father, my dear, and I will. For now, Nanny is your disciplinarian. I'm sorry, Ann." Hanna Y'Arle turned and left the bedroom sanctuary of Heavenrock through tall wooden doors and found a bench in the hallway.

Nanny stepped up to her defiant charge and undressed her with rough purpose. She then took her hand, pulled the girl to a padded stool, sat down, and took her over her lap.

"Naughty slave-girls are punished naked and thus humiliated, and so will you be, Ann!" scolded the stern Nanny as her strong hand rose high above her head and delivered a just spanking.

Nervously waiting in the bedroom hallway, the tender Lady of Heavenrock could not punish her mischievous daughter herself, nor could she watch. The echoing sound of the punishing hand made her cringe. Finally, she could hear when the ordeal ended, along her daughter's crying. She returned to the bedroom.

Her maiden stood naked as a helpless retainer, rubbing her pink behind. "Now go tell your mother that you are sorry and beg for her forgiveness!" ordered the firm, and still angry Nanny. She clapped her hands together loudly. "March, young lady!"

The only girl child of Heavenrock ran to her mother in tears and threw her arms around her waist. "I'm sorry, Mother, I'll not do that again. You promised to ask Father."

Lady Heavenrock cupped her daughter's wet, red face and kissed her. "All's forgiven now, my love—all is forgiven. I will talk with your father," she softly replied, nearly in tears herself.

Suddenly, without warning, Aron Y'Arle, Lord of Heavenrock, stormed into the private bed-chamber and, with commanding steps, advanced toward his wife. The naked, timid maid of Heavenrock sneaked to hide behind her mother's chiton. The lord took his lady in an embrace and kissed her long with more than a hint of passion.

"My lord," she sighed softly with a shy smile. He moved close and whispered into her ear.

"The Lord of Ravenbourne sends an advisory, my love. The confirmed bachelor now looks to his future progeny, and it seems rumors of our maiden have motivated his interest."

The Lady of Heavenrock found a delicate smile. "Oh my! Really, Aron. How fascinating." Leaning forward, she likewise whispered into his ear. "Very fascinating!"

Lord Heavenrock now reached down and, cupping his daughter's face, quickly kissed her forehead, then rubbed his hand across the top of her shining auburn hair. "Now you behave, Ann!" he ordered.

"Yes, Father," replied the girl, still hiding behind her mother's chiton as best she could.

The lord now stepped to Nanny, also taking her into his arms for a fervent embrace. "Continue your duty," he said with a matter-of-fact tone.

"Yes, my lord," replied Nanny, bowing her head.

The lord turned and left the bed chamber with the same commanding steps he used to enter.

Lady Heavenrock covered her mouth with the fingertips of both hands, looking at Nanny as though she might burst with excitement.

"What is it? What is it?" asked Nanny in a loud whisper, both seeming to forget they were still in the middle of discipline.

CHAPTER 7

Natasha: Hyacinth Gatherers

REACHING THE EMPEROR'S HIGHWAY, NATASHA headed northward to the Tyner River and the Great Stone Bridge. Accommodating travel throughout the Empire, the Emperor's Highway was built and maintained by the Emperor, and thus so named. It allowed all the north-south travel on the Southern Peninsula, especially the caravans that supplied all the estates, including Ravenbourne and Cappa, the capital city of the southern Peninsula.

Spanning the Tyner River, the Great Stone Bridge was one of Natasha's favorite places, and she came here often with her best friend Melissa. Natasha was hoping she could find the courage to tell Melissa about her vision. She remained, however, in a quandary—a dichotomy where on one side, she was afraid to tell Melissa, and on the other, afraid not to. She would just need to find the courage to tell her best friend, asking for her advice. She knew she must. Today, however, Melissa was working in the dining hall for the Ravenbourne Warriors; consequently, she would attempt to put it aside for now. *Working for the Ravenbourne Warriors.* Natasha smiled, thinking of her friend. Melissa was always lucky with men, and even though she was only a summer or two older than Natasha, she had garnered extensive knowledge concerning sex. Melissa displayed a carefree attitude about working in the dining hall, but it seemed thrilling yet frightening to the uncertain Natasha to be surrounded by a room full of Ravenbourne Warriors.

"You should come and work with me in the dining hall, Natasha," Melissa had encouraged. "It's fun and exciting, and you could earn money. All you need do is ask. They'll for sure hire a pretty girl like you."

"I'm not sure," responded Natasha. "The idea scares me. Besides, all my clothes are plain, similar to this simple frock." She lifted the hem up with a thoughtful expression. "It's well sewn from linen and my favorite because it is the last one my mother made me, but it's not similar to anything you wear. Conversely, your clothes are elaborate, eclectic, and decorated with pleats, beads, and trimmed in colored material, not to mention revealing."

Melissa laughed out loud. "Oh, Natasha! You're so adorable. Men don't care what clothes a girl puts on! They only care about what clothes she takes off."

Without warning, Melissa reached up and placed her right hand under Natasha's chin so that her fingers were on one cheek and her thumb on the other. Her left hand took Natasha by the back of the neck. Holding her best friend still, Melissa moved to Natasha, giving her mouth a full, deep, warm kiss. She moved slightly back so that her lips were nearly touching Natasha's.

"Think about it, sweet girl. You'll earn money and also have fun!"

Natasha swallowed hard and found a partial smile. "Your very adroit, Melissa, in the manner you manipulate me. Yes! I'll consider it, but I remain apprehensive."

Melissa smiled. Natasha used such big words, including Opar words. She took Natasha's shoulders and moved back.

"Good girl!" she said with a wide grin. "I'm going to finish teaching you how to kiss this afternoon, young lady, so pay attention." She then gave her best friend five light taps on her face with her finger-tips, becoming an approving mother.

"Just relax, Nati, don't be so stiff. He's not going to hurt you or slap you. If he was going to slap you, he would pull you over his knees and spank your bare behind."

Moving her fingertips, Melissa now touched the corners of Natasha's mouth with her thumb and middle fingers and gently massaged her. "Relax. Just relax," she whispered.

She then cupped Natasha's neck and gently pulled her close, giving her a warm, deep kiss—slowly inserting her tongue into Natasha's tender mouth. After the kiss ended, Melissa moved her lips to whisper into her dear friend's ear.

"You know sweetie, men don't care if a girl has another girl lover. Most men like that because they think they can take both of them to bed. There's a fancy word for three fokken together in bed, usually two girls and one man."

Natasha now turned to whisper into Melissa's ear. "It's called *ménage a' trois*. It's an Opar word."

Smiling, Melissa again cupped Natasha's neck. "I should have known you would know. Now I'm going to kiss you again. Move into him, sweetie, and kiss him back. And close your eyes."

"I will," responded Natasha, closing her eyes as Melissa moved closer. Amused, Melissa gently tapped Natasha's lips with her fingertips. "Relax, sweet girl, relax."

Sitting on the sidewall of the bridge, Natasha enjoyed one of the small loaves of bread, she had baked yesterday, while she patiently read her book. Across the highway, in the clearing, camped an Uncle Group of some forty Hyacinth Gatherers, probably seven or eight families, busying themselves around the camp. They all seemed to be in a light hearted mood. The gathering season had ended, and they had journeyed from the mountains down to Cappa to sell their precious oil. Or possibly the Priestess of the Temple of Asa at Ravenbourne bought their oil. Maybe they intended to stay for the flax-harvest season.

Two soldiers were also with them. Natasha could see they were not Ravenbourne Warriors. Possibly and mostly likely, they were soldiers of the Southern Army.

Suddenly, to her great surprise, one of the Hyacinth Gatherers approached her, crossing the highway. Hyacinth Gatherers were notoriously taciturn toward outsiders and generally avoided them, but this one continued on toward her with a quickened pace. She recognized the figure as a chubby-faced girl about her age, perhaps a summer or so younger.

Natasha also noticed that the girl wore breeches, usually worn by men, but also by anyone who worked in agricultural fields or, especially, in the thick forest undergrowth. The front legs of the breeches, extending from the thighs to just below the knees, were padded with leather. The pants were homemade but well-crafted by an expert seamstress. Her long-sleeved tunic was likewise homemade, from rough, undyed flax, sporting double layers at the elbows. Her high leather boots, however, were manufactured by a leather craftsman. A rope, tied around her waist, held a pair of leather gloves and an army dagger.

Once she saw the army dagger, Natasha felt a bit of jealousy. How was it this poor peasant Hyacinth Gatherer could obtain a valuable army dagger and she could not? As the girl drew near, Natasha saw her thick, matted russet-red hair—common to Hyacinth Gatherers, including herself—dark freckles and a sun-tanned face. She wore a friendly smile on an amiable cherubic face. Pleasantly attractive, in a wild, natural way, the girl stepped up close to Natasha.

"Hello! My name Lois. I am Hyacinth Gatherer. You from village?"

Natasha looked up and smiled. "Yes," she answered but did not offer her name.

"I still learn Empire language. Mother, our uncle speak good Empire language. Girl, boy our group still learn. You have beautiful book, wonderful bread. I not see book."

Again, Natasha smiled. The girl had such a pleasant voice. Natasha recalled her mother's teachings and warnings.

"Never! Natasha, never! Never speak the secret language of the Hyacinth Gatherers in front of anyone except a Hyacinth Gatherer. It is more than naughty—more than bad—it is a sin. To do so jeopardizes the lives of all Hyacinth Gatherers."

Natasha and her mother did not speak the secret language in front of anyone, even her father. It was very difficult not to speak the language with Father in the same house, but they managed to follow the Hyacinth Gatherers' law. She had not uttered a word of the secret, magical language since her mother's death, and she longed to do so. It would not break the sacred oath to speak now because Lois was a Hyacinth Gatherer.

"Hello," said Natasha in the clandestine tongue.

The young girl opened her mouth and sucked in a great gulp of air. Her big eyes opened wide, and she brought her hands to her breast. She appeared startled and afraid.

"Do not fear," said Natasha in a calming voice. "My mother was a Hyacinth Gatherer. My origin is no secret. All the village people know, and as you see, I have hair the same color as yours. I have not spoken our magic language for so long. It warms my heart to do so."

The two girls smiled at each other. They both gently reached up to cup each other's faces, then softly pressed their lips together in the manner that female Hyacinth Gatherers used to greet one another.

"Would you like to see the book?" asked Natasha.

"Oh, yes, very much! I may?"

Closing her book, Natasha handed it to the young Hyacinth Gatherer. Reluctant at first, the girl slowly reached out and accepted Natasha's prized possession. Her face lit up as she took the book in hand. "Oh, it is so heavy," she declared, carefully moving the book up and down, as though weighing it. "I had not realized a book was so hefty. I may look inside?" asked the forward Lois. She was polite but far from humble.

Natasha smiled at Lois' use of the words *I and may* in the style of their secret language. But also, thinking to herself, she had not considered a book to have an inside and an outside as though it were a box. "Certainly, you may look inside."

Carefully, Lois sat down on the bridge, holding the book in her lap. She turned the pages, examining each one. She gently laid her fingers on a page and looked up at Natasha, beaming.

Such a precocious girl, thought Natasha as she watched Lois examine her book, *and she has such a beautiful smile.*

The girl was washed and clean, but her hair was completely matted. Natasha was tempted to take out her brush and apply it to the poor girl's tangled curls.

Continuing to inspect the book, Lois spoke in a forlorn tone, "I know I will not learn to read." She paused, looking up at Natasha. "You can read?"

"Yes, I can," answered Natasha, "my mother taught me."

Lois took a heavy sigh. "I also know I may never have a book. At least I got to touch one."

Lois diligently examined the thick tome, including smelling some of the pages with a deep inhalation. Periodically, she glanced up at Natasha with a thankful smile. Finally, she stood and returned the book to Natasha.

"I am very much thankful," said Lois with a serious expression, which turned into a curious one, followed by another question.

"You have small loaves of bread?"

"Yes," Natasha answered, "I baked them yesterday."

"I wish I may buy a loaf from you. But as your mother probably told you, we are forbidden to spend money. My father would punish me if he found out." Lois reached both of her hands behind her, rubbing her backside, and forming a painful expression. "He has such a hard hand, and he can skelp very hard and fast!"

Natasha understood Lois's painful meaning but snickered at her comical expression.

"Does your father skelp you?" asked Lois in a sincere tone.

"He did when I was younger," answered Natasha.

"Did he pull your clothes off and expose your behind?"

"Yes," whispered Natasha.

"Only three or four days ago, I did something very wrong, and my father pulled all my clothes off, every thread, and he skelped me harder than ever. The two soldiers watched.

I was so embarrassed. They saw all of my red, burning bottom and me naked. But I will tell you."

Looking around as though someone might hear, Lois moved close to Natasha and whispered, "Later that night, they both wanted to sleep with me. And to have my affection and sex."

The thought of sex placed a joyful grin on her face, but it soon quelled, and Lois made a deep sigh. "My father says he will skelp my behind until he marries me off to a man as husband. After that, it will be his task."

Natasha realized Lois must have suffered a dreaded camp-fire punishment. Her mother had explained it to her. She wanted to change the subject of the conversation.

"If you can't spend money, how did you buy that dagger?" asked Natasha, pointing to Lois's dagger.

Lois reached over her lap and touched the weapon. "I am so very lucky to have a dagger, but I did not buy it. I traded for it. We are allowed to trade. The two soldiers in our Gathering, well, you must know, they travel with us and protect us from thieves. We do not pay them. The girls in our Gathering sleep with them. Your mother must have told you."

Nodding her head, Natasha agreed, "Yes, she did."

"Did your mother's Gathering have soldiers travel with them for protection? Did she sleep with them and give them affection and sex?"

"Yes," answered Natasha, "she said she did. It was part of her duty, but she also enjoyed it."

"Some nights, I sleep with one soldier; he is young and handsome. I like him. He gave me this dagger in trade for affection. He may have sex with me."

Lois leaned over to Natasha and moved her hand to the side of her mouth, once more whispering as though someone else might hear.

"I like the way he gives me sex. And he is—you know—large and very hard. Soldiers are the best to have sex and affection with."

Lois moved back and looked at Natasha with a tilt of her head. "You must see Ravenbourne Warriors?"

"Oh yes!" Replied Natasha with a chuckle, "nearly every day."

"Our Gathering had Ravenbourne Warriors protect us when I small," said Lois with an informing tone, "but my Mother and our Uncle would not let me have sex, because I was too young. My Mother said she slept with a very young Ravenbourne Warrior when she was a girl and he protected us. She always smiles when she talks about him. I hope I may have sex and affection with a Ravenbourne Warrior someday."

Reaching her hand into her bag, Natasha took out the other small loaf of bread. "You may have this loaf. It is an extra one."

As she looked at the loaf, Lois's eyes opened wide, lighting up. But she formed a gloomy face. "We may not take food for free. It is the same as begging, and we may not beg." Suddenly, her voice turned to a happier tone and her face again to a smile:

"But I may trade for the loaf."

"Trade?" questioned Natasha.

"Yes, but the only thing I have to trade is a kiss."

"A kiss," replied Natasha with a smile of curiosity.

"Yes," answered a now jubilant Lois. "I may trade a kiss for your loaf of bread."

Natasha pondered the proposal. Lois gazed into Natasha's eyes and smiled. "I think you may want to kiss a girl."

Swallowing hard, Natasha replied, "Yes, we made trade."

A delighted grin filled Lois' face. She cautiously stepped between Natasha's knees and slowly moved her chubby face close to Natasha's. Then, ever so gently, she pressed her lips to Natasha's closed mouth, and at that tender moment, she slowly drew a deep breath in through her nose.

Lois leisurely drew her head back and gazed deep into Natasha's eyes. Natasha gazed back. She now noticed Lois's eyes were a deep, beautiful sienna-brown color.

Now with more confidence, Lois reached up with both hands, cupping Natasha's face. Natasha watched as Lois slowly moistened her lips with her tongue. Gently, she pulled Natasha to her as she leaned toward Natasha at the same moment. Softly, Lois kissed her, full on the mouth. Natasha could hear Lois's hard breathing through her nose as they shared a long embrace. The kiss ended. Lois moved back but remained close to Natasha's face, gazing into her radiant verdant eyes, wearing a furtive smile.

"I may not be finished with you, little girl," she whispered in a calm yet commanding voice.

Again, Lois moved close to Natasha but also reached her hand up so that her thumb rested on Natasha's chin. She pushed down, bidding Natasha to open her mouth. She obeyed. Once more, Lois kissed Natasha full on her lips—a warm, passionate kiss—inserting her tongue deep into Natasha's mouth. The kiss ended, and Natasha could hear herself breathing hard.

"Place your hands behind your back," ordered Lois.

Natasha obeyed.

Now, Lois moved her left hand to the back of Natasha's neck, holding her, not allowing her beautiful captive to escape. She slowly moved her right hand from Natasha's chin down to the front of Natasha's frock.

"Stay still, little girl," repeated Lois, using that same whispered but commanding—captivating—voice.

Her nimble fingers untied the drawstrings at the neck of Natasha's frock and loosened the collar, pulling it open. Sliding her strong little hand down the front of Natasha's frock, she cupped one of her small breasts. Gazing into Natasha's eyes, Lois's strong hand, gently massaged and squeezed Natasha's breast. Natasha began to feel a strange yet wonderful sensation running through her veins—her nipple turned hard. Lois now pulled Natasha to her and kissed her with a passion she had never felt before.

The fervent kiss ended as once again Lois moved back, remaining close. Natasha could hear her own breathing, slow and heavy. Lois now slowly slipped her hand out from Natasha's frock and reaching up, took a firm grip on the back of her neck. She leaned forward, allowing her lips to gently touch Natasha's ear.

"Thank you," she whispered. "You know you are a special girl from the goddess Asa. She put beautiful streaks of gold in your hair so that all would know you are a special love-girl.

Suddenly, taking Natasha by surprise, Lois reached her other hand up Natasha's frock and, sliding it up between her thighs, firmly cupped her virgin flower, secretly hidden behind her red undergarments.

"I wish I may spend the night with you, a tender, special girl, and teach you Asa's affection," said Lois in such a manner that it kept Natasha spell-bound. "I would take you into the woods, and we would spend the night alone, where no one could hear us. You would be my tender little girl, and I would be the same as a man, teaching you to be my special love-girl. I would skelp your bottom until you begged to be my love-girl. I would skelp you until you begged me to sex you. I would cause your little girl innocence to wet like never before. I think your girl innocence has never wetted. I think your little innocence still has a tiny petal. I would make your tight—little—innocence—squirt. You would never forget."

Quietly panting, Lois released her hold on Natasha's neck and slowly removed her cupped hand from her maiden flower. She leaned back but continued her gaze into Natasha's eyes, a pleased-with-herself look on her face. Natasha could not respond. She swallowed hard and sat in silence, staring into Lois' face. Lois smiled, a beautiful but mischievous smile, both seductive and petulant.

Reaching down, Lois patiently removed the loaf of bread from Natasha's hand. She took a nibble of the bread as she gazed into Natasha's eyes, then slowly leaned forward, placing a light kiss on her lips. She suddenly turned, stood up, and ran across the Emperor's Highway, back toward her Gathering.

CHAPTER 8

Calea: Pallake Acquisition

THE LONG LINE OF MULE-DRAWN wagons of Master Smyth's military convoy came completely fitted to endure the long trip from Capital City to fallen Opar and a return expedition. This was the largest and most complex slave-buying venture Master Smyth had ever attempted to organize, but the challenge promised exceptional rewards. The Imperial soldiers and officers under his authority were highly trained and well-armed, though some would argue they were better suited for defending a city rather than a battle in open country. Nonetheless, each bivouac camp seemed appropriately positioned and well-guarded to Master Smyth.

He bore in mind they did not carry the wealth on their journey to Opar, but they would on the return trip. Any large force of brigands seeking to ambush a convoy would certainly wait until it departed vanquished Opar, loaded with wealth and slaves. The most dangerous segment of the whole enterprise would be the return trip from Opar to the capital city. The continued health of his pallake slave-girls on that dangerous journey was likewise of equal importance.

He was thinking too far ahead, much too far into the future. First, he must secure a covey of bona fide pallake virgins. Next, he had to ensure none were pregnant before the return journey, and he believed the number ten was too ideal. He now reckoned he could take a risk

83

with one or two girls, perhaps three. But he needed to have at least ten unpregnant virgin maidens before he started the return trip. Any less would not bring him the profit he desired. He remained sanguine that Calea would be invaluable in this maiden search. However, she still had to prove herself.

Calea directed Master Smyth and his entourage to the abandoned villa she had successfully utilized to disguise herself. She was familiar with the villa, as the wealthy owner had been a patron of her husband's stable and boarded several fine horses with him. Seemingly, the wise master of the mansion had taken his family—along with gold, silver, and precious stones—and fled, dressed as peasants, if he were wiser still, and leaving all else. Calea searched the jewelry boxes in the master's bedroom; each had been opened and quickly discarded to the floor, as though the mistress of the manor hurriedly collected the most valuable items, tossing the rest aside.

"Take possession of this villa, Captain, and everyone in it," ordered Master Smyth as he looked around the imposing estate, standing in the impressive courtyard just inside the main gate. Calea stood alongside him.

"Have the whole company relocate here," continued the authoritative Master Smyth. "And look after our first virgin, Captain. You've been warned that your life depends on her safety."

"Understood, Sir!" replied the Captain of the Imperial force assigned to Master Smyth's enterprise.

Gently taking hold of Master Smyth's arm with both of her hands, Calea looked into his eyes. She had already confirmed he enjoyed being touched, common of most men. "Master, my brave husband owned and operated a stable. It provided us a good life. Most of our patrons were wealthy men. My husband worked in the stable daily, but I also helped by handling the books. Over the years, I have come to know many wealthy families in the city of Opar, and if they have daughters or not, including where they live."

She briefly paused, allowing this information to be absorbed, then continued, "Lord Talcrane, Master, kept impressive horses at our stable. He was a very wealthy man with a lovely wife and two beautiful daughters. I can guarantee, my Master, they are virgin. For reasons unknown, he led an unusually modest life, perhaps for religious purposes."

"We should leave now, Master Smyth," continued Calea in earnest and becoming bolder as she lightly squeezed his arm, "and hasten to his neighborhood and his house with enough soldiers to keep others, slave buyers and soldiers, at bay."

Master Smyth gently patted Calea's hand with an unusual smile. Again, he directed an order to his company commander. "Captain, my new interpreter and I will take two squads, the collaring crew, and an officer out to find more treasure. Prepare the force to leave immediately."

"Understood Master Smyth!" answered the captain. He began to shout out orders and names, as the force quickly assembled.

Susanna ran to Calea, seeking a reassuring hug from her mother. Calea embraced and kissed Susanna, now her only offspring. "All will be well, my love—all will be well," assured Calea with a mother's warming voice.

"Yes, Mother," replied a whimpering Susanna, who remained frightened but comforted.

Master Smyth and Calea stepped briskly, followed by two squads of Imperial soldiers and the collaring crew, through the crowded streets and plazas of Opar, filled with women, slave buyers, and soldiers of the Eastern Army. Two Imperial soldiers led the way and cleared a path through the throngs of people.

They stopped in a plaza on the edge of a lower-class neighborhood, in front of a large wall and gate. The plaza was filled with anxious women and solemn slave buyers. A few Eastern Army soldiers, as security guards, stood away from the plaza but prepared to maintain peace and order, if necessary.

"This is it, Master Smyth," confirmed Calea with an urgent tone. "Have your soldiers move in, circle the whole crowd, and take control. Force all the slave buyers to leave and the women to stay."

Master Smyth agreed and barked out the order. Immediately, the Imperial soldiers quick-marched in formation, spears and shields in hand, and surrounded the crowd in the plaza. Calea remained in place as Master Smyth hurriedly stepped into the crowd.

"I claim all these women for the Imperial house!" called out Master Smyth. "All you slave buyers, step away!"

"Who the fokken do you think you are, fat man?" yelled out one arrogant slave buyer.

"Shut that son-of-a-whore up!" yelled a now-angry Master Smyth. He looked at a nearby soldier and pointed at the slave buyer. "Drag him out of the plaza."

Immediately, an Imperial soldier stepped up to the unwise slave buyer and struck him on the side of his head with a swipe of his shield. He fell limp to the brick floor of the plaza. Two more soldiers each gripped an ankle and dragged the unconscious, bleeding man past the circle of soldiers.

Again, Master Smyth yelled out an order. "Lieutenant, execute every slave buyer who remains in this circle of soldiers."

Before the lieutenant could initiate the order, every slave buyer ran out of the circle of Imperial soldiers. Some hurriedly went to a pair of nearby Northern Army soldiers to voice a complaint, shouting, waving their arms, and pointing. The Eastern Army soldiers did not respond.

Calea ran quickly to the side of an Imperial soldier forming the circle. "May I enter, soldier?" she asked with urgency.

Looking over his shoulder and recognizing her, his answer was to step aside. Calea quickly stepped up next to Master Smyth. The crowd of twenty or so frightened females shuffled about, nervously squeezing their hands or elbows, and crying.

Using the loudest voice she could find, Calea called out in the language of Opar, "All of you, keep quiet! Quiet, I said! Fall to your knees and remain silent or you will all be punished!" The women obeyed and were somewhat hushed, but they remained anxious and apprehensive.

Master Smyth looked to his new interpreter, pleasantly surprised. "I'm beginning to think you are my best find, Calea." Wearing a bold grin, he reached up, taking her by the back of the neck and pulling her to him for a public kiss.

Calea, wisely, went to her master, reaching up to touch his neck and moving her face to him. She leisurely, however, turned her head so that she put her cheek against his lips and kissed the side of his cheek. Calea had nonchalantly avoided a lips-to-lips kiss but continued to be warm and affectionate. Master Smyth remained pleased.

Clever Calea then changed the mood by offering more than an intimate kiss.

"There, my Master." Calea pointed. "That *svelte* beauty is named Ciri and next to her is her sister, Alexa. Two of the loveliest virgins in Opar and daughters of wealthy Lord Talcrane, who maintained a modest existence. That high wall surrounds his villa."

Master Smyth looked over to the two kneeling maidens. "Impressive, Calea! You continue to please me." He now turned to his officer.

"Lieutenant!" shouted Master Smyth. "Collar them all and secure them with ropes. Order your rough men to be gentle and try not to scare them any more than they already are. We'll take them back to the villa."

"Sir!" responded the lieutenant.

Master Smyth now put his chubby hands behind his back and, with his protruding stomach leading the way, began to walk around the group of kneeling females. He wore a pleasant smile. Most were young, a few middle-aged. He thought to himself,

It is true what legend holds. The women of Opar are beautiful.

Suddenly, a mature woman rose to her feet and slowly walked to Calea, who recognized the daring woman as the wife of Lord Talcrane. She stepped up to Calea.

"So, Calea," quipped the woman in a snobbish tone. "I see you have joined the side of our enemy."

Calea turned and stared at her, wearing a face of scorn. "That is unquestionably correct, Lady Talcrane—lady of poverty," Calea said in anger. "I just saved your two innocent daughters from a horrible life in a filthy Empire brothel. There, you could watch them be stripped na-ked, bent over a pommel horse, abused, beaten, and raped by vile men nearly every day. If you possessed any tenacity, wisdom, or courage, you would have done the same yourself."

Calea turned her back on Lady Talcrane and moved through the small crowd of kneeling females, talking and calming them. The Lady of Talcrane stood in silence. She realized Calea was right. How could she have been such a foolish coward? Her husband was away from the city on a business trip, but he was now, as was she, a slave of the Empire. He would need to remain in hiding until somehow pardoned by the Emperor or the Commander of the Eastern Army.

She now quickly stepped to the soldier with the bag of collars and, with her limited knowledge of the Empire language, asked to be col-lared. The soldier complied. Armed with a new purpose, she, too, followed Calea's example. She first went to her daughters to reassure them as best she could. Next, she began to talk and calm the women as soldiers buckled collars around each female's neck, attaching lengths of strong rope to the collars.

CHAPTER 9

Kaelin: Quarries

SLOWLY, THE MISERABLE PROCESSION OF slaves advanced upon the gated entrance of the quarry area. Toward the back of the entrance, in the near distance, Kaelin could see a large cliff face—an outcrop of white stone. Several guarded buildings lay on each side of the road, which widened as the procession approached the gate. Off to one side, large, rough stones formed a sturdy wall border, creating a sizable, circular holding area. Guards lined the holding area with, some standing in front of the stones and others positioned on top. Other buildings, tents, and shelters dotted the quarry district. The mortal convoy proceeded into the holding area to be further organized. Kaelin began building strength, inner strength. He staggered and groaned, pretending to be near death—most of the other hapless slaves actually were.

Suddenly, the whole area enclosed by the large stones became alive with activity and shouting. Slaves were counted while they were herded around, orders were called out, and the leather bonds and ropes were cut then the slaves were dragged away to be chained together. The cold sound of hammers striking metal echoed off the distant cliff face.

Perhaps Kaelin's end had not come, or maybe some unknown deity smiled on him. Possibly it was a female deity that spoke to his inner self and now offered help. Or it could be, he was just lucky. His file of slaves, most nearly dead, was pulled to the front of the whole pack of groaning slaves. Suddenly, a well-clothed fat man strolled in front of him with a following of guards, bickering assistants, and others. He wore blue garments trimmed in red, obviously a man of wealth. Just then, a guard approached.

Kaelin's ruse of pretending to be nearly dead had worked. Paying no attention to him, the guard cut the leather rope with a sword, freeing the slave adjacent to Kaelin, and began to pull the slave away. Now was his chance. Now!

Kaelin grabbed the guard's hand that was holding the sword, and in the same instant, he brought his forearm against the side of the guard's head. The guard fell. Kaelin took the sword, cut the bonds from his neck, and ran into the open, calling out as loud as he could.

"Buyer of fighting slaves! Take me—take me!"

Quickly, a guard stepped forward, casting a spear at Kaelin, head-on. Kaelin saw the flash of the spear and easily ducked it. The spear flew over his back. He stood with both his arms stretched out at his sides, his right hand holding the sword, inviting the guards to attack him.

Without warning, the fat man stepped out into the open and, raising his arms up, called out in a loud, deep voice. "All of you, halt! No guard hurt this slave!" Abruptly, all was quiet—hauntingly—frighteningly—quiet. Several guards stepped into the area, with drawn swords and spears poised to cast.

Once more, Kaelin called out with his throat dry and his voice rough. "I am a soldier of Opar, slave buyer! I can fight in your arena!" He doubted if another shout remained in his rasping throat.

The slave buyer, although fat and wealthy, had little fear. He stepped straight toward Kaelin, stopping in front of him. He called out in the brawling voice of a first sergeant.

"I see you are a soldier of Opar, slave. Why were you not killed in battle, at the fall of your city? Only cowards of Opar surrender."

"I am not pretentious, slave buyer. I was wounded . . . knocked unconscious," replied Kaelin. He spoke as plain as he could, but he heard his own voice rasping, in a loud whisper. He could scarcely swallow.

"So, you seek death or freedom from the quarry?"

"Yes," Kaelin shouted, still hearing his own voice in a yelled whisper.

"And if I order the guards to kill you?" asked the fat man.

"Then it's death," replied Kaelin. "I intend to take many guards with me to the other side. . . ." He paused and swallowed hard. "Perhaps your guards."

"Why don't you kill me?" asked the fat slave buyer—wearing a sarcastic smile on his stout lips—his arms raised—palms up.

"I gain nothing by your death. I want you to take me to your college."

"What if I lie to you?" questioned the plump buyer, still with a smile. "And entice you to give up your sword then allow the guards to drag you away and nail your hands and feet to a post, where you will die a slow, miserable death?"

"I doubt I would last long," answered Kaelin. He knew his next words meant his life or death. He was a poor orator, and his dry voice was hoarse. The words came from inside him—unrehearsed—in a loud whisper.

"Most of us stand at the gates of Hades. Besides, how would you profit from my death, slow or otherwise? You are here to buy fighting men, Feohtans for the arena. The best buy of the day, perhaps for the year, stands before you. Once I have killed men in the arena, they will come to you, coin in hand, asking you to find more men as skilled as I."

The slave buyer looked at Kaelin appearing to be in deep thought. Kaelin could hear his own harsh breathing and his own heart beating. The overweight slave buyer called out.

"Done! Go to that wagon over there." He pointed. "There is food and water in the wagon." He held out his hand.

Kaelin flipped the sword over and caught the tip. He stepped forward, staring into the fat man's round face, and believed him to be sincere. He placed the sword's handle in his pudgy hand. He looked toward the wagon, turned, and walked toward it. He heard the obese slave buyer shout out.

"That slave belongs to me. I'll have the balls of any guard who harms him!"

Walking away, Kaelin heard all the noise of the quarry return, as suddenly as it had stopped. Men's voices called out orders, others haggling words, and the dreaded sound of pounding metal began again. Kaelin passed a frightened group of eight to ten naked Cherry Boys and several of the slave caravan guards, who were talking and bartering with guards of the quarry. He saw the same mounted officer who had advised him of the Feohtan slave buyer. He was thankful. Heading toward the wagon, he could hear that the poor Cherry Boys were being sold to the quarry guards, continuing their miserable sex service. Better, he thought, than being a chained quarry slave, although he doubted any would last long as a sex-slave. Nonetheless, at least as sex-slaves to the quarry guards, they held some chance for life and freedom.

Approaching the wagon, he stopped and turned around. He took a last glance behind him. He saw the fat slave buyer walking toward the group of Cherry Boys and haggling guards.

He stopped at the uncovered wagon, which had board rail guards on the sides and front. Four riding horses were tied to a nearby hitching post, with an armed guard standing by them. The man seated in the driver's seat of the rough-hewn wagon turned to look at him, along with another guard, who was standing by the wagon mules, holding a lead rope. The driver made a long hacking sound and spit his phlegm to the ground while the guard took a drink from a water pouch, then also spit on the ground. They both turned away, unimpressed.

Kaelin climbed into the back of the wagon. He was still not certain how or what female voice had spoken to him. Only a god or a goddess could do such a thing. He was too exhausted to ponder it now, but he was grateful—very grateful. Crawling to the front of the wagon, he sat with his back against the side boards. Water and food pouches hung from the boards, and rough, folded blankets lay stacked in the corner. He lifted a blanket from the stack, laid it on the floor, and sat on it. Lifting the water pouch, he took a long drink, allowing the water to run down his chin and onto his tattered, dirty tunic. Resting his head back against the side boards, he closed his eyes.

Nearly dreaming, he heard a whimpering sound and felt the movement of the wagon. He opened his eyes and was surprised to see a naked Cherry Boy climb into the wagon. It was the same handsome boy who had been abused just nights ago along the creek bank. He struggled to crawl into the wagon and lay at Kaelin's feet, shaking and crying, emitting low moaning sobs. Kaelin now had a clear, daylight view of the young slave. He appeared to be going into shock.

Reaching out, Kaelin gently touched the poor boy's shoulder. He jumped and cried out, "No! No!"

Don't be afraid," said Kaelin, his throat still hoarse, in the calmest voice he could muster, gently rubbing his shoulder. "I won't hurt you."

The boy looked up at Kaelin with red, swollen eyes and seemed to recognize him. He swallowed hard. "Will you be my master?"

Kaelin did the best he could to smile. "I cannot be your master. We are both slaves, but I will be your friend."

"I've not ever had a friend," spoke the boy in such a heart-breaking tone.

"You have one now," said Kaelin, holding out his arms. "Come— have some water."

Kaelin helped the weakened boy crawl nearly into his lap—his head resting against his left arm. He held the water pouch to the boy's mouth, who instinctively grasped Kaelin's hand and the pouch, taking a long drink with water running down the sides of his mouth. Kaelin stopped and the boy gasped, just as a young child does when given a long drink by his mother.

The boy swallowed hard. Kaelin offered more. "Drink as much as you can." The boy obeyed.

When the youngster seemed sated, Kaelin sat him up and reached over to pull the top blanket from the stack, then laid it on his lap. He maneuvered the boy so that he lay with his head on the blanket as a pillow.

"Rest now and eat later," said Kaelin in a soft yet still-rasping voice.

"Yes Sir," he answered in the voice of a frightened child. The sad boy curled up and put his thumb in his mouth, sucking on it.

Kaelin pulled another rough blanket from the stack, unfolded it, and draped it over the boy's hips and his bruised buttocks. He squirmed to reposition himself because his own buttocks remained in pain from the whip lashes. Gently, he petted the boy's head, who whimpered but was otherwise calm and soon fell asleep.

Again, the wagon rocked back and forth, causing Kaelin to look up as another slave crawled in. He was a burly man with hairy arms and chest. He crawled his way to the front and sat against the front guard wall. Kaelin picked up the water pouch and stretched out his arm, handing it to the new arrival.

Taking the pouch, the man barked out, "Thanks!" in a deep, hoarse voice. He lifted the pouch with his large, hairy arms and took the longest drink Kaelin had ever witnessed. He emptied the pouch, ending out of breath.

"My name is Ox," said the large man in a rasping voice after he wiped his mouth with his forearm. "You an Opar warrior?"

"Yes," Kaelin replied, "My name is Kaelin."

Ox nodded, allowing this was all the introduction needed. He looked at the sleeping boy, then reached out his large, hairy hand and patted his ankle. "Poor boy. Well, where ever we're goin', it's better than here."

Kaelin did not reply, because their fat Master now stood at the wagon with two dismounted guards, holding the reins of their mounts. "Eat, drink, and rest the best you can," ordered the Master. "We are on our way to my camp by a clear spring. There, you can rest and recover. Don't cause any trouble or I'll have my guards leather-strap the goddess' piss out of you."

Kaelin spoke out still with a rasping voice and struggling to speak. "We owe you our lives, Master, and grateful you saved us. We won't cause any trouble. I ask that you don't abuse this boy."

The Master paused, looking at Kaelin and then Ox. He then looked at the helpless boy asleep on Kaelin's lap, sucking his thumb. He tilted his head to the side. "Done! No one will harm or touch him. Help him recover. But I want no trouble from you two!"

"Yes, Master," replied Kaelin. "Thank you." Ox likewise responded.

The Master walked to the front of the wagon, and the two guards mounted. The wagon shook side to side with the weight of the Master climbing aboard. The wicked sound of leather on bare skin broke the silence, and the driver called out to the mules. Soon the wagon jerked, creaked, and rolled on, trailed by the two mounted guards.

CHAPTER 10

General Y'Sloic: Nefarian Gift

"I HAVE SOMETHING I WOULD like to show you, Sol. Will you come with me?" asked Lady Y'Liory while she and General Y'Sloic, Lord of Ravenbourne, sat comfortably at the end of her feasting table. The festive mood continued, although somewhat subdued, allowing that several of the Ravenbourne Warriors, following Captain Aaragon's lead, had taken a naked pallake to a dimly lit corner to taste and enjoy her enticing female favors.

"Certainly," replied General Y'Sloic. He rose from the table.

Lady Y'Liory remained seated. She held up her hand, displaying a smile and a slight tilt of her head. Reaching out and taking her hand, General Y'Sloic also smiled as helping her rise from the table, as any lord of grace and manners would do.

"Thank you, my Lord," stated the Ladyship in a tone that suggested she had expected his assistances all along.

As Lady Y'Liory stood to leave, her handmaid also rose to follow, but the Lady turned to her. "Stay and watch the girls." The mature slave-woman bowed her head, understanding her instructions, and returned to her chair. General Y'Sloic noticed she wore a dagger in her belt. It was common for a lady's personal handmaid or matron to carry a small weapon. He had not noticed it before and reminded himself to pay more attention to his surroundings.

Wrapping both of her arms around General Y'Sloic's arm, Lady Y'Liory led him out of the Feasting Hall and down the wide corridor. "Your servant woman is very dedicated. I'm impressed," remarked General Y'Sloic. "I understand she has been with you since you were a girl."

"Yes, that is true, my Lord. She has offered a life of devotion and served as my nanny and personal maidservant since I was a baby. More of a mother than maid." Lady Y'Liory softly chuckled. "I remember she tanned my behind once or twice, very hard, mind you, when I was a disobedient child—with the approval of my father, of course." General Y'Sloic also chortled as they walked down the corridor. The footsteps of their sandals echoed off the stone floor.

At the end of the corridor rested a sturdy closed door where a single soldier stood guard. As the two approached the wooden door, the guard opened it and stepped aside. They entered the room and the guard pulled the heavy door shut behind them.

General Y'Sloic glanced around the large, lavishly decorated chamber, which appeared to serve as Lady Y'Liory's bedroom or perhaps a guest room reserved for aristocracy. An open balcony allowed the warm summer breeze to gently blow in, lifting the sheer, white curtains, while the bright setting sun lit the room in a mystical glow. Tapestries and other heavy curtains bedecked the stone walls, adding both color and soft warmth. A sunken bathing pool, elaborately decorated with colorful ceramic tiles, was filled with warm water. General Y'Sloic could see the steam quietly lifting off the clear, still water. A large bed stood toward the wall, nestled against a great colorful tapestry. Pillows and sheer coverings adorned the bed.

Lady Y'Liory led General Y'Sloic past the foot of the bed and out onto the balcony. The view was breathtaking, the Outer Ocean in sight. General Y'Sloic scanned the horizon, then closely observed the ornate stone banister. He stepped to it and rested his hand on top. His host followed. He observed the banister, the outside wall, and the extensive distance to the far ground below, then gazed out once more to the ocean's horizon.

"My lord husband would stand here in silent thought for what seemed to be at least one turn of the hour-glass," recalled Lady Y'Liory. "I can only imagine how long he would have tarried had I not taken his hand and led him to bed."

In like manner, she took General Y'Sloic's hand and turned around so that the whole of the majestic bedroom came into view. He followed. She smiled up at General Y'Sloic as though she were about to reveal a great mystery. He looked back at her with a hint of puzzlement. Looking across the room, she spoke in a soft yet commanding voice, "LinDar!"

A figure slowly rose from the bed—a female figure. General Y'Sloic had not noticed her silently hidden among the bed pillows. Unclothed, the female form gracefully approached, stepping onto the balcony and into the still, bright sunlight. She stopped about two paces from the noble pair with a bowed head.

"Mistress," she answered in a submissive, childish voice with a soft accent, not familiar to General Y'Sloic. He was surprised and taken aback by her but remained stoic, not revealing any emotion to Lady Y'Liory.

The unadorned female standing before them was one of the most striking beauties General Y'Sloic had ever cast his eyes on. He was a high lord, the general of a powerful army, an aristocrat of supreme influence and wealth; consequently, he had experienced the rarest beauties throughout the Empire. His own wife, Lady Ann Y'Sloic, was one such rare beauty. But this one was most certainly the daughter of a goddess. The rarest female within the entire Achaean Empire—a Nefarian.

She was petite, having not experienced many summers. She raised her head, seemingly on cue, with an alluring smile for the General—a perfect, ivory-white smile—then submissively lowered her head again. Her form was flawlessly sculpted, as if by the hands of a skilled craftsman. Muscular yet slender shoulders; a flat, narrow stomach; curved, tapered hips; and small, firm breasts, although she had reached full female maturity. The sun reflected off the porcelain pallor of her skin, and seemingly void of blemish, she appeared to glow like the snow-covered Twin Peaks of the Goddess's Mountain.

Ebony eyes held mystery and were dark enough to hide her pupils, distinguished only by specks of reflected sunlight. Her full lips could lure any man with the promise of a cherry sweetness, and once drawn to her, a perfect smile could melt his heart.

Yet, her most tantalizing feature must certainly be her onyx-blue hair. Full, long, and trimmed in front, across her forehead, virtually concealing her ebony eyebrows. It was as if her wonderous blue hair, woven in long, thick tendrils and punctuated by marvelous strands of white sunlight, had been softly spun by the maidens of the goddess. Unlike the other common slave-girls owned by Lady Y'Liory, this one's hair reached down to her waist, touching the tops of her round buttocks, falling from thick ocean waves on each side of her head. Long locks of her onyx-blue hair delicately fell on her breasts and shoulders.

Slaves throughout the kingdom sported ankle bracelets and copper bells, but this one wore a small gold chain around her narrow waist. Instead of a thin plate engraved with the crest of the Starfall Villa to identify this precious slave-girl, should she be lost or stolen, the chain held a small locket etched with the Starfall crest. The smiths and jewelers must have taken acute care not to injure such smooth, lovely skin when they affixed the chain. General Y'Sloic briefly wondered why the locket rather than a plate, but he then turned his attention to her femininity.

The folds of her young womanhood stirred the lord's mature blood.

Rather than appearing coarse, her pubic hair showed a thin, soft texture, as soft as the fur of a rabbit. The small, triangular patch mirrored the same blue color of her wonderous hair, and in a similar enchanting fashion, when the sun struck at a certain angle, it reflected thin wisps of white, aurora sunlight.

Suddenly, to General Y'Sloic's surprise, another female figure approached the rare Nefarian from behind. He recognized her as a slave-matron. She stood, head bowed, hands folded in front.

Lady Y'Liory spoke in a foreign tongue. General Y'Sloic recognized the language of the Frisians. A rough, guttural, language at best. He knew there was a long connection between Lady Y'Liory's family and the Frisians, who resided within the Islands of the Fjords. Still, it surprised him to hear her speak the barbaric tongue, a soft-spoken lady using such a rough, little-known language.

The young matron raised her head and answered, seemingly in only one or two words of the crude patois. She bowed, turned, and walked to the tall door. She slapped the door twice with the palm of her hand, giving a signal. The guard opened the door. The matron passed through, and the door was closed behind her.

Turning to his hostess, General Y'Sloic said in a calm voice, "A Nefarian, I am impressed. Such a rarity and difficult, if not impossible, to acquire." General Y'Sloic played naive, if not innocent. He was well knowledgeable of the Frisian kingdom and its rare Nefarian inhabitants.

Nefarians originated on the Islands of the Fjords, a kingdom of extensive, innumerable islands laid out in such a maze, only the Frisians could find their way through to reach their homelands. For hundreds, if not a thousand of years, the Frisians had raided the Empire's shores, small towns, and hamlets, taking wealth and women back to the Fjords. Throughout this lengthy period, they evolved into a raiding, waring culture. Growing bold, they landed an army on the Imperial shores with the hopes of permanent occupation. They were defeated.

The Emperor and the Frisian king sealed a treaty between them. The Frisians would no longer raid the seaside towns and villages of the Achaean Empire but would instead trade. Imperial war-ships would no longer attack Frisian ships, which were now free to sail throughout the kingdom, filled with valuable merchandise. Trade replaced war. It was beneficial to both nations.

Lady Y'Liory's deceased husband, the Lord of Starfall and former General of the Eastern Army, had played an important role during the treaty negotiations. Moreover, Lady Y'Liory's family was one of the few noble families of the Empire that were on friendly terms with the Frisians. Her father, the Lord of the Dragon Storm Estates, located on the rugged coast of the Northwest Territories, held fast to a long-lasting relationship with the Frisian King Horic. It was also rumored Lady Y'Liory had dwelled, for several lengthy periods, in the households of the Frisian hierarchy.

"Have you had the opportunity to meet a Nefarian, Sol?" asked Lady Y'Liory, knowing full well he had.

"Certainly," answered General Y'Sloic with an impatient response. "I accompanied my father, who introduced me to the most powerful lords throughout the kingdom, including the Emperor. But I will confess, my contact with a Nefarian was only on one or two rare occasions and always at a distance—never close—surely not intimate."

"Rare occasions do present themselves, Sol," offered the sly Lady Y'Liory. "Her name is LinDar. An incredible figure of exotic beauty, wouldn't you say?" she inquired. She paused slightly then continued, not expecting the lord to respond.

"She was a gift from King Horic to my late husband, thanking him for his role in the tense treaty negotiations between the Achaean Empire and the Frisian Kingdom."

Lady Y'Liory continued, "The Frisians speak in such a harsh tone, both men and women, regardless of the language. Conversely, a

Nefarian speaks in a soft, almost child-like voice. LinDar is far from fluent in the Achaean language, but we have taught her a considerable vocabulary."

Lady Y'Liory looked up at him with a tempting smile. "What do you think of her, Sol?" She paused, knowing the answer. "Perhaps you should see more?"

"Come closer, my sweet." As Lady Y'Liory spoke, the graceful Nefarian took a small step or two, now standing only a pace in front of the General. She put her hands behind her back, gently tilted her head, and looked up into General Y'Sloic's eyes. She then smiled a warm, adorable smile.

"LinDar," said Lady Y'Liory, nearly in a whisper. As she spoke, she made a circular motion with her index finger, maintaining a confident manner.

The young Nefarian elegantly turned around to present her alluring backside and, looking back over her shoulder, smiled again. General Y'Sloic's eyes followed her from neck to ankle.

She is perfectly sculptured, he thought. *The women followers of the goddess Asa say that she has daughters. If so, surely this must be one.* His eyes could not help but focus on her buttocks.

"Doesn't she have the sweetest, little, bottom you have seen, General?" offered Lady Y'Liory, in a tone that was both a joking and serious at the same moment. Again, she addressed her uncommon gift: "Bend, my sweet! Be graceful."

Elegantly, the rare prize bent over, placing her hands on slightly bended knees. With her feet spread about shoulder-width apart, she again looked back over her shoulder at General Y'Sloic. Her face glowed bright with a blush. With her thighs, buttocks, and golden innocence so displayed, the General could feel his old warrior blood stir, as though he were filled with the ardor of a young recruit marching to his first battle or into his first bedroom.

The beautiful 'mistress of manipulation titled her head and smiled, thinking to herself.

I sense I have touched some nerves. He beams as if a teenage boy who has just first milked himself.

Delicately wrapping her arms around Lord Ravenbourne's left arm, Lady Y'Liory spoke in a warm whisper. "Will you have a seat with me Sol?" Lord Ravenbourne did not respond but simply walked with his host back inside the luxurious chamber. LinDar followed behind and then quietly stood two or three paces nearby.

They sat on a comfortable, well-padded bench. The old Lord of Starfall was a warrior and accustomed to a warrior's tastes. This sanctuary was built with protection in mind. With the light from the balcony and the opening over the warm pool, the chamber was well lit and in good view. It was certainly not this well adorned when he last saw it, many seasons ago.

"LinDar!" said the Lady of Starfall. "Bring us each a glass of wine and beer."

"Yes, Mistress!" The obedient servant quickly stepped to a serving table and poured the requested drinks. Returning to them, she handed each a glass.

As they sat side by side on the comfortable bench, a warm, gentle breeze blew in from the balcony, lightly stirring the sheer curtains. Somewhat to General Y'Sloic's surprise, the Nefarian elegantly sat on the floor next to him, cushioned by a pillow. She gently placed her head against his knee. She looked up at him, smiling, and as if by impulse, softly caressed his calf. He glanced over to Lady Y'Liory, who returned his glance with a smile.

"Nefarians are instinctively affectionate, General—it is born into them. Oh, she has certainly been trained in the art of erotic love and seduction, but nonetheless, her warm, loving behavior and passive manner cannot be taught; it is the way she is—the way they all are."

Another calm breeze drifted from the balcony, quietly wafting the sheer curtains. Its tepid kiss felt good, gently raising the Nefarian's onyx-blue hair. Picking up her glass, Lady Y'Liory took a seductive sip as she watched General Y'Sloic with an alluring smile.

Perhaps a small demonstration will lure him!

She looked down at LinDar, seated on the floor against the General's legs. "Come, sweet love, come kiss your mistress," she ordered in a pleasant whisper.

With a girlish simper, LinDar crawled around General Y'Sloic, placing her small hands on her mistress's knees. Slowly, she stretched upward, her inviting mouth slightly open. As they tenderly kissed, General Y'Sloic could faintly hear the soft moaning of the affectionate Nefarian. Once the embrace ended, the beautiful nymphet returned to General Y'Sloic's side, remaining on her hands and knees.

If Lady Y'Liory intended to arouse me, thought General Y'Sloic, *her ploy has been successful.*

Lady Y'Liory paused, watching for any signs in General Y'Sloic's unemotional face while taking a leisurely sip of the rare cherry wine. General Y'Sloic did the same, although he drank several large gulps. She kept a pleasant expression, thinking to herself.

Men never seem to sip or savor any drink. They all seem to guzzle whether it be water or a rare, aromatic wine. I think I have his attention, and if he kisses her, the permanent garrisons at the villa and the port will be mine.

Reaching down, General Y'Sloic gently caressed the soft, spun hair lightly falling on the side of LinDar's head. She looked up beaming slowly moving her head in such a way, responding to the caress of his hand. Once more, he marveled at the amazing blue hue of her hair, reflecting the sun as she tenderly moved her head. Slowly, he leaned down to kiss her, and yet again, as if by some magical instinct, she rose to meet his lips with her sweet, warm mouth, gently placing her small fingers on the side of his cheek. A man of extensive sexual experience, Lord Ravenbourne could feel that the delicate Nefarian enjoyed offering her sweet tenderness and affection to him, as though it was all pleasantly natural. This was no act; General Y'Sloic genuinely believed her warm affection toward him was real, and he was rarely deceived.

Now, the moment is now! surmised Lady Y'Liory. "I would be extremely pleased, even honored, my Lord Ravenbourne, if you would accept LinDar as a night's gift of infrequent pleasure." Lady Y'Liory lightly laid her hand on the hand of her powerful guest and looked seriously into his eyes. She felt him respond inwardly, but outwardly he remained silent.

Silence means yes!

Lady Y'Liory was pleased. "I'm going to take my leave now, Sol." She paused briefly, as planned, then continued. "At sunset, I'll send servant girls with refreshments and to light the lamps and fires. Enjoy a pleasant evening. I bid you farewell until the morrow, my Lord."

Employing the grace of a well-rehearsed aristocrat, Lady Y'Liory rose and, with her palms together in front of her, slightly bowed, turned, and graciously made her way across the lavish chamber to the door. She tapped her palm twice on the thick door to be opened, which was quickly closed by the guard after she tactfully passed through.

Lord Ravenbourne now stood and walked to the door then bolted it shut. He'd visited this chamber before with his friend, the old Lord of Starfall, before he wed the young daughter of Lord Baron of Dragonstone, a royal maiden of the ancient Dardanus family. Then, it was the old lord's private sanctuary, built for security and virtually impenetrable. Once bolted, the solid door would require a small force, and a battering ram, to break through. The doors remained unbreachable if the heavy bronze portcullis was employed. It was still functional, ready to slide into position once the stop was disengaged.

Also, the sheer walls of the balcony reached such a height, it could not be scaled unless aided by a long rope or rope ladder attached to the banister. The old lord took precautions to ensure that a large force of assassins would be denied entry. To breach his sanctuary would require an army siege.

In the presence of his unsuspecting hostess, Lord Ravenbourne had inspected the balcony banister, looking for a rope or ladder, and saw none. Consequently, the doors remained the only entry. If bolted, he would be secure and unreachable.

Although he bolted the doors, he would not employ the portcullis. The Lady of Starfall needed him alive, at least until the construction of her port was completed. And without his permission, she could not form a garrison at Starfall or at her port. No, his life was safe at Starfall, at least for the present.

I reflect too much and ignore the reason I am in this luxurious sanctuary. The untasted charms of the rare, exotic Nefarian.

Lord Ravenbourne approached LinDar who still sat on the floor. He cupped his hands to her face—she rose to him—pressing her lips to his. The rapt passion of her kiss beckoned his warm blood to flow into a male hardness of an intensity he had not experienced for a lengthy period. Her warm, soft lips remained close to his as the kiss ended, and she panted her hot, sweet breath against his mouth. She whispered, "My Lord," over and over, as though she were weeping.

He swept the rare prize up off the tile floor and carried her to the awaiting bed. The battle-worn warrior still retained unusual strength in his mature arms. Continuing to pant, LinDar kissed his ear, the side of his face, and his neck.

After gently laying her down on the bed, she quickly came to him on her knees. Reaching out she unfastened the leather military belt around his waist with skilled fingers. Grasping the helm of his Ravenbourne tunic, she lifted it up, taking it over his head and raised arms.

As the morning sun crested the peaks of the Mountain of the Goddess, its golden rays danced over the waves of the Outer Ocean, while a warm breeze gently blew through the elegant bed chamber. Young LinDar stretched, arching her back and reaching her arms out, smiling as she sighed. Next, she snuggled into Lord Ravenbourne's armpit, gently rubbing the side of her mouth against his ribs, as does a female lynx to the side of her favorite clawing log. Taking a deep breath, she drew in the aroma of his male scent, prompting her to sigh again. Growing more daring, she said in a whisper, "I hear something, Lord. I am much curious to know it true."

Lord Ravenbourne smiled. She was both quiet and polite. "You may ask."

She rose on her elbows and looked at him, moving close to his face. "I may ask question?"

She was so close to his face when she spoke, he could smell her breath. It was warm and sweet. And she requested to ask a question. Both pleased him. "Yes, ask your question."

She glowed as she spoke. "I hear female animal, ready, become with baby, she has strong scent only male, same her, can smell. When male smell, no can stay away. Male run to her, he want sex her. Is true?"

Lord Ravenbourne chuckled. "Yes, I have witnessed such behaviors in the animal kingdom."

Growing more playful and daring, she posed another question. "My lord! You think women have same scent; men like. They want sex her, but they not know?"

"I suppose that's seemingly possible," answered the lord. "It is most certainly true that some women appear to possess a strange allure to men, who are drawn to them, apparently unaware."

Continuing to gaze into Lord Ravenbourne's eyes, LinDar took a slow breath but also swallowed hard. Becoming slightly bolder still, she reached her hand down to the warmth of her inner thighs, adjacent to her pubic hair, and gently rubbed the moist area. She slowly brought her hand up to her face and softly inhaled her own aroma lingering on her fingertips. Lord Ravenbourne watched with a curious expression.

Slowly, she reached over and gently touched his lips with her fingertips. "You think I have nice scent, Lord?" Her voice remained pleasingly innocent yet equally serious.

A smiling Lord Ravenbourne drew in a deep breath. "Your scent is most alluring, pleasant beyond description."

Glowing with excitement, the exotic Nefarian leaned down and softly kissed her lord's lips. Slowly, she pulled back to see his face and smiled sweetly. Lying back down, she again snuggled up under his arm pit.

CHAPTER 11

Lady Ravenbourne: Marriage

"MY LADY," STATED OLD NANNY in the same tone she had used when Lady Ravenbourne was a girl and in trouble, only then she often called her *young lady*. "Do you recall the day Lord Ravenbourne arrived at our Heavenrock Villa to take your hand in marriage?"

"Most vividly, Nanny. You, Mother, and I watched from my bedroom window while Sol led the Ravenbourne Equestrian Guard past us below, followed by a long train of supply wagons. I think all our female hearts skipped a beat or two. I know mine did."

"Yes," Nanny agreed. "It was our first occasion to see Sol and the Ravenbourne Warriors. They were certainly magnificent. Afterwards your mother took you to your bed and set you down, and I stood by. Her hands cupped your young, innocent face, and she told you three truths to never forget."

There was a pause, and then Old Nanny cupped Lady Ravenbourne's face. "Repeat the truths."

"I remember them well, Nanny," declared Ann Y'Sloic with an acerbic tone.

Without warning, Old Nanny delivered a quick but stinging slap to the cheek of her lifelong charge.

"Repeat!" she ordered.

111

Somewhat surprised, Lady Ravenbourne went momentarily wide-eyed, but she swallowed hard and obeyed.

"The first: The Lord of Ravenbourne is first and foremost a warrior, as were his father and his father before him. He does not order his men into battle; he leads them without fear for his own life or limb."

"The second: he is the most generous man; I will ever know."

"Finally, and most importantly: he, and he alone, rules Ravenbourne."

Old Nanny pulled the Lady of Ravenbourne to her, giving her a tender embrace. Holding her, she recalled suckling the beautiful infant child. She wished she could do it again, if only for a short while. She silently wept.

Old Nanny wondered with some concern, about the future of Ravenbourne. Who would be the next lord and lady? She had grown to love this mystical land of the goddess, as did her mistress. She was not devoted to the worship of the goddess Asa but participated to appease her lifelong charge. She knew Lady Ravenbourne would never leave Ravenbourne and would continue her devotion and worship of the goddess Asa.

The tragic death of both sons of Lord and Lady Ravenbourne left no true heir to the lands, the estate, and the title. Certainly, there were children of Lord Ravenbourne—all girls, to the best of her knowledge—some being reared and nurtured in the Ravenbourne Sanctuary. Seemingly, Lord Ravenbourne sired only girls and partially that purpose was in concurrence with the worship of Asa. Old Nanny did not know or understand all that was happening during these important days with the worship of goddess Asa.

She did know there was not a son being raised and prepared by of the Lord and Lady of Ravenbourne to inherit the Ravenbourne Estate.

No heir prepared to meet the challenges and sacrifices required to be Lord of Ravenbourne, as had been done for hundreds of years. This situation disturbed her.

Thus far, Old Nanny had not voiced her concerns to Lady Ravenbourne, and categorically, she would not dare approach Lord Ravenbourne. To do so would break her lifelong confidence with Lady Ravenbourne, and—she remained unashamed to admit—she would not approach him out of fear. But she would certainly confide in Ann Y'Sloic, whom she had helped bring into this world, nursed as an infant girl, and tanned on more than one occasion. Nonetheless, she likewise had to keep in mind that her lifelong charge was also the Lady of Ravenbourne, perhaps the most powerful woman in the Achaean Empire.

The marriage of Ann Y'Arle, a maiden of Heavenrock, and Sol Y'Sloic, Lord of Ravenbourne, came to pass on the rugged coastline of the Northwest Territories at the Heavenrock Estates at the behest of her father, Aron Y'Arle, Lord of Heavenrock. The custom of the day declared that the marriage and its consummation were appropriately accomplished in the domain of the groom. Lord Ravenbourne, however, was more than accommodating. It was far from a lavish affair, at least as the elite society of the aristocracy viewed the world; nonetheless, the uniting of the Y'Arle and Y'Sloic families rose to the level of extremely significant in the Achaean world of power and wealth.

The Emperor did not attend, as he never left the palace, but his son, Prince Kaius Y'Capis, did thus adding a royal touch to the affair. Ann Y'Arle remained unimpressed with the prince, yet she realized there remained a long relationship between the family of her husband-to- be and the royal family. Therefore, she was more congenial and pleasant with the heir apparent to the throne than her young, female feelings urged her to be. A continuing relationship of respect with the royal family would be of infinite benefit to both the Y'Sloic and Y'Arle families.

The prominent guest, however, who would alter Ann Y'Arle's view of the world, and her mother's as well, was the High Priestess from the Sacred Temple of Ravenbourne—the High Priestess of the goddess Asa. Ann, Lady Heavenrock, and to a lesser degree, Nanny, were worshippers of the goddess Asa. Many women throughout the kingdom were followers of the goddess, but tended to be most prominent in the Capital City and the cities of Cappa and Estoria in the Southern Peninsula.

Ancient in age, the High Priestess would not have attempted the long, rugged journey for any soul, aristocrat or slave, including the Emperor himself, save one—the Lord of Ravenbourne. The Y'Sloic family and the Lords of Ravenbourne had been generous supporters of the worship of Asa and the Sacred Temple at Ravenbourne for hundreds of years. Nothing compelled or obligated them to do so.

It required an untold number of days to comfortably transport the elderly Priestess along the rough route from Ravenbourne to Heavenrock. The journey was made more difficult because the High Priestess would not travel over water; consequently, the easier route across the Inner Sea could not be taken. Not to mention the extraordinary planning that was required. The journey must have been initiated long before the terms of the marriage were agreed to. The Lord of Ravenbourne planned far into the future—a proven man of unique confidence.

A surprising number of temple acolytes accompanied the Priestess and assisted her throughout the ancient marriage ritual. The ceremony was more touching than anyone, especially the young maiden of Heavenrock, could have imagined. That afternoon, high waves on the rugged coastal shore of Heavenrock provided a distant, poignant background. The blue flames of the ceremonial fire, laced with precious hyacinth oil, and the haunting liturgical songs, voiced by the temple acolytes, provided a stirring ceremony—seldom experienced.

Perhaps the most inspiring moment was the homily given by the Priestess in the arcane temple language that only the priestess, acolytes, and other chosen women throughout the worshipping sphere of the goddess Asa could understand. The moving marriage ceremony touched everyone present and was forever etched into the heart and memory of Ann Y'Sloic. On that day, Sol Y'Sloic had endeared himself to his young bride.

Although it was difficult and short-lived, Ann Y'Sloic, with unyielding patience, managed to find a moment alone with the Priestess, and the two stepped to a far wall. She offered her sincere thanks for coming, her young eyes filled with tears. "May I know your name?" asked the new bride.

The elder lady smiled. "I have no name child, but allow me to ask you, Lady Ravenbourne. Are you a true believer and follower of the goddess Asa?"

"Yes, High Priestess," answered a surprised Ann Y'Sloic. "I am. I truly am."

"Then there is something you may do for me." The Priestess looked out over the room and raised her hand.

To Ann's surprise, one of the acolytes walked up to the two of them. Ann had noticed this one. She was older than most of the acolytes and a few years older than Ann. The other temple assistants wore a common frock of pale-yellow flax, but to signify her status, this one wore a black chiton, complementary to the attire worn by the Priestess.

"Lady Ravenbourne," began the High Priestess in her enchanting voice. "This is Ish-Bel. When the goddess calls me to return or I become too feeble to perform my duties, Ish-Bel will take my place as the High Priestess. The last and final century of the last thousand years, named the Dragon, comes to an end. The new century of the Raven will begin. Will you talk with and learn the way of the goddess from Ish-Bel?"

Ann Y'Sloic looked first to Ish-Bel, then back to the Priestess. "Yes, I will," she responded. "I sincerely will."

"Wonderful!" exclaimed the ancient High Priestess. "All will be well."

The indisputable safest route for the newlywed, Lady of Ravenbourne, to reach her new home was by way of a great sailing vessel. Departing the Heavenrock Villa, the ship would sail the coast, southward and eastward, into the Inner Sea to the Capital City, then cross the Inner Sea to the north shore of the Southern Peninsula at Estoria. From there, a short but pleasant journey along the Emperor's Highway through the city of Cappa, and arriving at the Ravenbourne Estate.

The adventurous Ann Y'Sloic, however, wanted to journey by land and follow the coast of the Inner Sea along the Emperor's Highway, camping along the route. Consequently, a colorful, impressive army departed Heavenrock after a bittersweet farewell between Aron and Hanna, Lord and Lady Y'Arle, and their precious daughter.

The young Lady of Ravenbourne was perhaps the most protected bride in history. A full legion of Ravenbourne Warriors, both mounted and afoot, provided the heart of the corps which included a contingency of the First Strike Force of the Southern Army and an unnumbered force of supply wagons. Lady Y'Arle presented her daughter with her personal handmaiden, and Lord Y'Arle provided her with the family's luxurious wagon. Ann Y'Sloic, however, preferred to ride her palfrey she had galloped throughout the Heavenrock lands since she was old enough to ride. Well sired and patiently trained by the Heavenrock stables, the horse would be desirable by any lady of the aristocracy. Lady Ravenbourne rode alongside her husband in front of the Ravenbourne Equestrian Corps. Old Nanny and the handmaiden were delighted to absorb the journey from within the luxurious wagon.

At the behest of the Emperor's son, Kaius Y'Capis, Lord and Lady Ravenbourne spent one night at Capital City in the palace. It would have fallen short of aristocratic and royal etiquette not to do so. Both Sol and Ann Y'Sloic had stayed at the palace on numerous occasions, and the Emperor was a long acquaintance of each of the newlyweds and both of their families. He congratulated the couple and they briefly talked. That evening, they dined with Prince Y'Capis, and were on the road again the following morning.

The youthful Lady Ravenbourne had not traveled far to the east, past Capital City, and was most eager to follow the rugged terrain between the Coastal Mountains and the Inner Sea shoreline. Consequently, today's trek was difficult yet exciting. The narrow highway was flanked by a steep mountain wall on the east and a sheer cliff, dropping to the sea, on the west. It was more challenging to set up camp for the army that escorted the Lady of Ravenbourne, and the sheer size of the camp—horses, men, wagons, and tents, all spread along the narrow highway—was exhilarating. An experience she would long remember.

Additionally, a rough pass had been chiseled through the mountains, interconnecting the western and eastern segments of the Emperor's Highway. The coarse corridor was primarily a military road. Lady Ravenbourne, seeking more adventure, wanted to take the pass. The possibility of seeing the Fesma Desert, which lay along the eastern section of the highway, added more stimulus. Relaxing at the campfire late that afternoon, she queried her new husband about this idea and was jolted by his response.

"No, Ann. We will not take the pass. It is too rough and dangerous."

Lady Ravenbourne was taken aback. There was no discussion or attempt at appeasement. Lord Ravenbourne said no, then walked off to check on the army's encampment. The surprised Ann Y'Sloic realized several realities that afternoon.

She had married into a military kingdom. She was not familiar with the military way of life. Certainly, there were soldiers and guards at Heavenrock, but she had not been associated with any. They were simply men who worked on the estate. Her father was not a military man. Men-at-arms had always been mostly fictional or romantic characters to Ann, found in a book or a childhood story told by Old Nanny. She was now surrounded by more soldiers than she had ever seen or imagined she would ever see—a thousand Ravenbourne Warriors, the most feared and lethal warriors in the Achaean Empire. Every one of them would fight and sacrifice his life to protect her. And yet, not even one would obey her. She likewise learned she would not always have her way.

Sitting on a driftwood log, arms wrapped around each other, Sol and Ann Y'Sloic watched the sun dip into the other side of the Inner Sea, filling the sky with a fast array of color. Every sunset was different, and each one beautiful.

"You'll be able to watch the sun every evening at Ravenbourne, Ann," offered Sol in a quiet voice.

"It sounds wonderful, Sol," she responded. "I look forward to the warm, gentle coast of the Southern Peninsula, as opposed to the rough shores of the Northwest Territories."

Ann Y'Sloic yawned and smiled at her husband. "I realize it is still early, Sol, but I can just keep awake. Unless you raise objections, my

Lord, I would enjoy spending the night in the wagon with Nanny and my handmaiden." Looking into his eyes, she inadvertently smiled, then blushed. "You are certainly welcome to join us, my husband."

Lord Ravenbourne similarly smiled gazing at his bride's face. "No, you go alone. I think you have been too many nights with soldiers and campfires."

Reaching out, Lord Ravenbourne gently took his young bride's face in his hands and brought her to him. She eagerly came for a goodnight kiss—tender and heartfelt—in the manner of newlyweds in love.

"Until the morrow, my Lady," whispered Sol Y'Sloic.

"Yes, my Lord," said Ann Y'Sloic with a smile as she turned and walked toward the luxury wagon.

The Lord of Ravenbourne watched her dignified yet youthful gait—her long auburn hair and curved hips swaying—in graceful, flowing movement. He was a lucky man, and he knew it. He turned back to watch the sunset a while longer.

The following morning, before the sun broke over the peaks of the Coastal Mountains, the escort corps was striking the camp and preparing to move out. Ann Y'Sloic led her beautiful grulla mare to the front of the column, bringing smiles and salutes from each warrior she passed. She wore a pair of tight-fitting cotton pants. . . as sable in color as the legs and neck of her palfrey mount . . . and a pair of military sandals, custom-made to fit her petite feet.

More eye-catching, she wore a Ravenbourne military tunic, altered by a skilled seamstress to fit her slender frame. In addition, a Ravenbourne red cape, likewise altered into a woman's cloak with a hood, lay on her shoulders and back. Her hair, brushed and tied into a horse's tail, swung with her sprightly gait. When she released her horse's reins, her colorful palfrey walked to make muzzle and neck contact with her husband's white destrier. Meanwhile, she embraced Lord Ravenbourne with a long good-morning kiss.

"Ready for today's journey?" asked an energetic Lord Ravenbourne. "The coastal lane is breathtaking for the next several miles."

"I am, my Lord," answered Lady Ravenbourne, likewise in a feisty mood. She then took on a serious expression.

"I am anxious to see Ravenbourne, my Lord, but may we sojourn a night at Estoria. I have wanted to pray and make an offering to the goddess at the Estoria temple since childhood. And I would dearly love to meet and talk with the priestess of the temple. She is just a child, but a remarkable child … blessed by the goddess."

"Excellent suggestion, my Lady," responded Sol Y'Sloic. "It is an excellent location to camp an army, and the coastline is stunning."

The escort corps camped for two nights at Estoria. The draft animals required a long rest, after the difficult trek along the steep coastal highway. In stark contrast to the eastern coastline, the southern coast of the Inner Sea lay flat, with wide, sandy beaches and a blue, calm sea. Sol and Ann Y'Sloic walked hand in hand along the sun-kissed beach, as private as it could be. Five hand-selected Ravenbourne Warriors followed along behind at a safe distance, yet allowing privacy.

"It's so lovely my Lord," marveled Ann. "The sun does not fill the sky this much at Heavenrock. I never realized the sea could be so blue and waves could turn turquoise at midday, kissed by the sun."

Inspired by her speaking the word *kiss*, Sol took Ann's face in his hands and gently caressed her. His thumbs traced the feathery arch of her perfect auburn eyebrows. He kissed her tempting lips as she wrapped her arms around his waist, pulling herself to him. They parted but remained face to face, looking into each other's eyes. It was a wonderful moment, silently ended as Ann looked toward their guards out of the corner of her eye.

"Sol," said Ann in a near whisper. "I don't think I can make love with you with the guards watching." Sol smiled and lightly chuckled.

"We can be alone in our bedroom, Ann, if we desire. But they will always be nearby."

"I suppose," Ann sighed with a shallow breath. Her excitement quickly returned, and she stepped back, holding his hands.

"How many more days to Ravenbourne, my Lord? I have now become anxious to see it."

"Four," answered Lord Ravenbourne.

"Would it be possible to accomplish it in three, without creating burden or stress on the Warrior Corps?"

"Perhaps," he answered. "There are occasions when a Warrior Corps readily accepts a challenge."

Ann Y'Sloic smiled. She wrapped her arms around Sol Y'Sloic's waist and hugged him with her head against his chest. All around, it was peaceful and quiet, and she could faintly hear his heart beating.

CHAPTER 12

Kaelin: Heart Blood College

SITTING ON THE FLOOR, THE three slaves once again found themselves in a mule-drawn wagon on their way from the fat Master's stream-side camp to the sprawling city of Cappa. They occupied the lead wagon with the Master, followed by supply wagons, other wagons filled with male- slaves, and a small corps of mounted guards. They each wore a well-made tunic, trimmed in red, something only people of wealth could afford to wear, including a red symbol of a heart painted on the front. The burly Ox leaned against the front rail guards, and Kaelin, the side. The young and handsome Cherry Boy, whose name was Coe, lay on the floor with his head in Kaelin's lap.

Ox amused himself by gazing skyward, looking for birds. He might spot a large soaring bird and most likely could identify it. Kaelin watched the mounted guards—change positions; a scout sent out ahead of the procession; the commander moving around the caravan, checking on the forward and trailing units. It reminded him of his two years of service in the Equestrian Corps of Opar during their campaign against the mountain marauders. Both Ox and Kaelin remained quiet.

Young Coe, however, was talkative, perhaps from anxiety and fear about going to the Heart Blood College, a new, unknown place. "I'm so glad you helped me remember my name Kaelin," said Coe, his voice trembling as he looked up into Kaelin's face.

123

"Coe is a good name," replied Kaelin. "It fits you well."

"You're the first friend I've ever had, Kaelin." He turned his head toward Ox. "And you're my second. I hope we can be friends forever." The two men smiled and nodded but did not speak.

"No man in our large Master's camp abused me, beat my behind, or fokkened me because of you, Kaelin. You saved me. Even the Master did not fokken me, and I heard the guards say he liked boys."

"We were all treated well in the Master's camp. We three did our part, not causing any trouble," added Kaelin as he reached down to pet Coe's hair to ease his tension.

"I could of stayed there forever," spoke up Ox, "but they didn't have enough beer and no women. Can't live without women or girls to fokken."

"I wish I could belong to you, Kaelin," confessed Coe, becoming emotional and beginning to sob. "And we could all stay at that camp by the stream, and build a house, and be friends. I could be your lover."

Kaelin smiled. "We three are lucky to be in this wagon and not on a chain gang at the quarry, Coe," said Kaelin. "Remember all those poor men who were on the slave caravan with us."

"I know, but still, I wish we could," whined Coe.

"I do love you, Coe," said Kaelin. "As I would a younger brother or even a son. But not as a lover."

Coe sat up, looking at Kaelin. "I know," he said in a dejected voice.

Kaelin reached out and cupped the boy's face. He pulled him close and held him in his strong, rough hands. He kissed him on the mouth.

Coe smiled, sniffed, and wiped the tears from his eyes. "Thank you, Kaelin."

"Lay your head back down and listen to me," ordered Kaelin. Coe obeyed.

"When we reach the college, we will be separated. Ox and I will become slave-fighters, and you will be a sex-slave. Fighting will be our path to freedom. If we fight well and win, we may have a chance to be free."

"If you don't win," sniveled Coe, "then you will both be killed." Young Coe began to cry.

"Yes," answered Kaelin, petting Coe's head. "Death will be our freedom, but your path to freedom is sex. I don't think the men at the Heart Blood College will be brutal. Not like the slave caravan guards. Be a good sex-slave, Coe. Give them what they want. Perhaps you can become persuasive and find your way to freedom. Our fat Master told me the Master of the Heart Blood College and his wife enjoy handsome boys as house boys. They are not abused or punished if they are obedient and please them."

Kaelin stopped and allowed this to sink in. He continued, "In Opar, slaves can be given their freedom for faithful service. A wealthy man or a lord may buy a beautiful young slave-girl as a sex slave, sharing her with his wife. She is well treated, and if she does her part and serves her master and mistress well, she may be given her freedom by a grateful master. The same thing occurs with boys."

"It happens, too, in Cappa," interjected Ox. "I know. I'm from there."

There was a long silence as the wagon jerked and the wheels rolled on a rough section of the road. The driver snapped the reins and called out to his mules. Similarly, the mounted guard commander shouted out an order, and one of the trailing guards rode past the wagon, heading toward the front.

"All right," sighed Coe, still sniffling, but accepting his fate. "I'll do my best."

The singular procession of mule-drawn wagons and mounted guards approached the large gates of Cappa, the capital city of the Southern

Peninsula, and came to an uneasy halt. Kaelin, Ox, and Coe came to their feet from the wagon floor to find a corner and grasped a side rail. These types of wagons were railed cages to ensure that a foolish slave did not attempt an escape once they were within the crowded city of Cappa. Men in the trailing wagons also stood, grasping the wagon rails.

The very large, hairy Ox stood next to Kaelin, who was a tall, strapping youth. Yet Ox was a head taller than Kaelin and appeared to be nearly twice Kaelin's weight. He had bragged all along that he was from Cappa, and how he had ended up returning to the city in a slave wagon on this hot mid-summer day kept him in a state of welter. It remained a mystery that he could not "figger-out."

Coe snuck under Kaelin's arm pit and reached his arm around his waist. In turn, Coe was the size of a woman, and head and shoulders smaller than Kaelin. Kaelin wrapped his arm around Coe's shoulder.

Kaelin looked out over the horizon. The blue sky was clear, clear enough to see forever, perhaps into the future. Off in the distance, magnificent snow-covered mountains peaked on the horizon.

Ox put his large, hairy hand on Kaelin's shoulder. Kaelin still did not appreciate Ox touching him. He permitted it because Ox was good-hearted and had been a loyal friend. He would need friends, and so would Ox. Besides, Ox meant no harm. He was more akin to Coe in behavior, a large, immature boy rather than a man about to be trained in the art of killing. Ox pointed to the mountains.

"Twin Peaks, those, Kaelin. The breasts of the goddess Asa. Can see those peaks any place in the peninsula on clear days. Those mountains separate the peninsula. They make an east side and west side. The whole fokken world can suck on the tits of the goddess." Ox paused to chuckle at his own joke. "Do you worship a god or goddess, Kaelin?"

"My father worshipped the God of War," offered Kaelin as he continued to gaze at the mountains. "Most Opar soldiers do. I respect all but worship none."

"Good idea, Kaelin!" barked Ox in his often-humorous, boy-like voice. "I worship the goddess of fokken." He took his hand from Kaelin's shoulder to reach down and grab his groin. "And I'm just about ready for a white, soft, tight little cherry butt, girl or boy."

Then Ox reached over Kaelin's chest and rubbed Coe's head. "I would never fokken you, Coe, or ever hurt you. I will fight to protect you if I can."

Coe looked around Kaelin's chest. "Thank you, Ox, very much."

Ox again massaged his own groin, laughing at his joke, as a guard officer rode to the center wagons. He called out a loud order.

"This is Cappa! Stay in the wagons. As we roll through the streets, citizens might approach the wagons—ask questions. Wagonloads of new Feohtans sometimes cause a stir. Do not speak to them!"

The guard reined his mount toward the lead wagon and called out, "Forward!" The wagon drivers snapped the wide leather reins on the rumps of the mules, and the creaking wagons rolled through the massive gates of Cappa, with the mounted guards on each side of the procession. The still air erupted with the noise of the busy city.

Standing, Kaelin gazed out over the city and noted the buildings and population to be mixed and diverse. The paved streets were lined with an assortment of structures, including both grand stone buildings sporting tall columns and small brick shops with open, wooden front ends. Wealthy citizens, clad in expensive red garments or at least trimmed in red, intermingled with poor folks clothed in plain, flaxen garb.

The wagons rolled to a wide crossroads. Ox tapped Kaelin on the shoulder. Kaelin turned, and Ox pointed down the side road. "The Great Arena," he revealed. "There, we fight."

Kaelin nodded in response. He was only allowed a glimpse of the arena as the wagons rolled on through the intersection. The walls were round and enormous. At Opar, large stone buildings dotted the urban landscape, but nothing to equal what he witnessed here in Cappa. The largest structure in Opar was the theater, but it was dug out of a hill, and the natural hillside remained on the back section of the theater. Adults attended a play or a community meeting, sitting in the arc-shaped theater seats; meanwhile, children played on the back of the grass-covered hillside. No, Opar was far humbler.

Thus far drawing little or no attention, the wagon caravan clambered past another colossal building. It was raised high on a massive stone platform with lengthy steps leading up to huge pillars—all constructed from white stone blocks.

Pointing, Kaelin inquired of his companion. "What building is that, Ox?"

Ox began to laugh and slapped Kaelin on the back. "You want to get fokkened? Then try to go there! The temple of the goddess Asa. On worship days, packed with women, young and old, rich and poor, kunts by the thousands. They like to masturbate each other's little kunts as they pray." Again, Ox laughed out loud, causing Kaelin to smile. "Imperial guards watch the temple on worship days. They won't let any swingin' cocks in."

The wagons rolled on. Once more, Ox grasped Kaelin on the shoulder and pointed. "Look!" he shouted. "Ravenbourne Warriors!"

Kaelin turned to see two mounted soldiers, side by side, astride two magnificent horses. They were identical, with bronze helmets and leather breast-armor jerkins with shining bronze attached. Long, bright-red capes fell from their shoulders to lie on the rumps of their mounts. Each held a spear in the right hand, straight up, with the butt end fitted into the right saddle stirrup. A sword lay on their left side, and a bronze shield with a black symbol in the center, was attached to the left flank of the horses. Kaelin was impressed, along with the citizens of Cappa.

Numerous people stopped, waved, and cheered as the Ravenbourne Warriors passed. The Warriors responded similarly. Kaelin saw two young girls run to the side of the street, kiss the palms of their hands, and throw the kisses to the passing pair. The mounted Ravenbourne Warriors saw the girls and reacted. They each dropped the reins in their left hands to the necks of the horses and reached out, pretending to catch the kiss. Next, they kissed their own palms, as though kissing the girls. They made a saluting gesture to the girls, who laughed and clapped their hands while jumping up and down.

"Oh my!" called out Coe's high-pitched voice. "They are both handsome and frightening." Kaelin looked to Coe. He was glad to see him smiling and pointing.

Once more, Kaelin's large companion spoke up. "Not usual seeing them so far from Ravenbourne. They are the best warriors in the Empire and fight for Lord Ravenbourne and his lands and villa to the south. Only a rich lord like Lord Ravenbourne could afford red dye for those capes. Those heathen Dye Traders bring red dye over the Hindu-Cush Mountains and trade for weapons. You know of Ravenbourne Warriors, Kaelin?"

"Most people of Opar know of Ravenbourne Warriors, Ox. They are held in high regard by Opar soldiers. I met several once when I was about ten summers old. One of them trained me in fighting skills for a short but well remembered period."

Ox looked at Kaelin with a rare serious expression. "You surprise me. Then you should know to stay away from a fight with a Ravenbourne Warrior, young Kaelin. Stay clear if you can." They continued through the busy streets of Cappa.

The wagons stopped again, before a massive wooden gate blocking the entrance to a tall wall of rough-cut stone. Men stood guard on each side of the gate. Slowly, the gates swung open, and the wagons rolled through into the courtyard of Heart Blood College.

The Feohtan training center appeared to be a military fort to Kaelin. Men trained in combat skills in a central courtyard. Barracks, a chow hall, and an open kitchen lined the edge of the yard. The wagons halted in front of a large wooden platform. The guards unlocked the doors. The guard commander remained mounted and loudly ordered the slaves to fallout of the wagons and line up in front of the platform. They obeyed.

The slaves stood in a line, quietly staring up at a gruesome sight. A cross, constructed of a wood post and a thick board, formed part of the platform structure. An unfortunate naked wretch was nailed to the cross, his legs straddling a wooden peg in the post. Dried blood covered most of his broken body. His head lay on one shoulder, his mouth gaping open. He desperately breathed, a horrible, gasping sound.

Suddenly, a man dressed in the fashion of the wealthy walked up to the platform. In arrogant demeanor, with two guards following him, he climbed the stairs. He turned to the line of slaves below him and rested his hands on the top rail. Though he was dressed in red-trimmed wealth, his manner was not aristocratic. He was hard-cut. More akin to a rough merchant, accustomed to risky business. All became silent. He pointed to the blood-soaked, dying man on the cross and called out in a lurid, abrasive voice.

"He tried to escape! He failed! I usually cut out their tongues before their tortured bodies are nailed to this cross. But on this occasion, I let him scream until he was hoarse and could scream no more. He has been there two days now. Heed my warning. If you attempt to escape, kill yourself before my guards capture you and return you to me. I am the proprietor of the Heart Blood College. And to you, my name is Master." He paused and looked down at the line of men, all dressed in the same type of white tunic, all with eyes fixed on him.

"All of you are slaves! At my discretion, you can be punished or executed in the cruelest of fashions." Once more, he pointed to the hanging, tortured soul. "Bear witness. Some of you, unfortunately, will meet this destiny. Many of you were soldiers or criminals, and some of you sold yourself into slavery, finding your own purpose. Whatever your prior life was—*does*—*not*—*matter*. All of you have one thing in common. I saved your wretched souls from a short-lived life of misery and hard labor. I did not do so because I am a man of compassion. I did it to make a profit from you." He paused, looking out over the silent, small corps of men before continuing.

"You will be trained as a Feohtan—a warrior, a fighter—and you will fight in the arena to bring enjoyment to the citizens of Cappa and the Empire. Most of you will be killed in the arena or die a slow death from bloody wounds, caused by your fighting matches. But if you are successful in defeating your opponents, you may also be rewarded. You may even be granted freedom."

"The path to freedom is not easy!" he shouted. He paused again, then continued in the same loud voice. "Few complete that journey, but it does lie within your grasp. Obey all the rules, train harder than you are required to, fight harder than your opponents, and with luck from the gods, you might gain your freedom.

"Here in this college, you will train hard every day, but you will also eat well, sleep well, and you will bathe every day. The night before you fight in the arena, you may be given a woman, and on other occasions, as circumstances allow, I might give any of you a woman for the night. I can guarantee you, the slave-girls I give you will be prettier and sweeter than any girl you have fokkened in your entire wretched, miserable life." Smiles and chuckles came from the men as they looked around at each other. The patient Master waited for silence, then continued.

"When my grandfather ruled the Heart Blood College, the crowds clamored to watch mounted horsemen fight in the Great Arena. In my father's day, foot soldiers with sword and shield drew the loudest applause. In today's world of bloody pleasure, the Emperor, the governor, the aristocracy, and the wealth of Cappa pay the highest price to those who train men to die in a spearman's duel.

"The Achaean Empire is a cruel world. The Great Arena a cruel creation. And I am a cruel Master. But I am also a Master of mercy." The Master pointed to a guard, then at the tormented man on the cross. The guard walked over to the cross, drew his dagger, and in one fatal swipe, cut the man's throat. He scarcely moved. Fresh blood flowed down his chest. In a short moment, he hung limp.

The Master again put his weight on the top rail of the platform. He looked out over the small group of male-slaves, who stood in silence. With a rock-carved stern face, the arrogant Master pointed to a guard.

"Take the boy to my private quarters," he barked. He turned and slowly made his way down the stairs of the platform and passed the line of slaves.

Daring Coe ran over to the Master and fell to his knees in front of him. "Master, please, can I say goodbye to my friends? Please, Master."

The Master reached out with one hand, cupped the side of Coe's head, and looked down at his frightened face. He looked up to the guard standing by, then over to the line of slaves. "All right, but make it quick."

"Thank you, Master," responded Coe, then he quickly rose, running to Kaelin.

Coe stopped in front of Kaelin and threw his arms around him in tears. "I'm going to miss you so much, Kaelin. Thank you for taking care of me and being my friend."

Kaelin cupped Coe's head and kissed his hair. "All will be well, Coe. I know it will."

Ox stepped up next to Kaelin, and Coe reached out, wrapping his small arms around the big man's waist. Ox grasped Coe's shoulder.

"Remember how we talked," cautioned Kaelin in the calmest voice he could find.

"Yes, sir, I remember. I'll do what you said. Coe's heart ached, and he was in tears as he looked up at Kaelin's face.

"Bye, Kaelin." He looked to Ox. "Bye, Ox."

"I will see you again Coe—remember that," assured Kaelin with sincerity.

"This true," said Ox. We will both see you again."

Coe dropped his arms from his two friends and ran back to the guard. The guard put his hand on the back of Coe's neck and walked him off toward the buildings at the end of the yard.

Kaelin and Ox heard the blistering sound of a whip crack. They quickly turned their heads, along with all the slaves in the line. A large guard wound the whip up.

"Follow me!" he barked in a deep, rasping voice. He turned and walked away. The line of slaves followed.

CHAPTER 13

Calea: Virgin Innocence

"Sɪᴛ ᴏɴ ᴛʜᴇ ᴇᴅɢᴇ ᴏғ the table, Ciri," said Calea in a serious tone. The nude, timid girl did as she was told. Lifting her bare feet off the cool tile floor, she lowered her bottom onto the heavy wooden table covered with a thick blanket. Master Smyth and Calea stood by at the end of the table.

"Now, lay your head back on the stack of pillows," continued Calea. "Lift your feet to the edge of the table and scoot down just a little." Again, the timid girl, slightly whimpering, complied.

"This will be our first test, Master, with the first girl we have taken from the streets. I knew my daughter, Susanna, was a virgin with an intact sepal. You watched as we examined her. But this girl, Ciri, and her sister, Alexa, will be our first real test. Daughters of the former Lady Talcrane, Master. I am fully confident each will prove to be a *bonafide* virgin.

Smiling, Master Smyth did not realize *bonafide* was an Opar word until Calea pronounced it correctly in the elegant Opar language. He was beginning to enjoy her poetic manner of speaking.

"Proceed, Calea," answered Master Smyth, holding his palm up in a gesture to continue.

"Yes, my Master."

"Ciri," explained Calea in a confident yet motherly voice, "I am

135

going to examine you, my love, but I'm not going to hurt you. Master Smyth will look on. Certainly, your mother, your nanny, and a physician have examined you before, have they not?"

"Yes, Mistress Calea," answered Ciri with a timorous yet obedient voice.

"Did they hurt you?" Calea paused, then asked again. "Did they?"

"No, Mistress Calea."

"It will be the same with me, my sweet," assured Calea in a calm voice of authority, rubbing her hands together to warm them. "And when I have finished with you, I will also examine your sister, Alexa."

She gently laid the palm of her hand over the girl's small pubic area, acclimating the young examinee. "How does that feel, Ciri?" asked Calea, keeping her motherly attitude.

"It feels good, Mistress Calea."

"Good. I'm going to proceed. Remain still and calm, and simply relax. Remember, I will not hurt you."

Calea lifted her hand, leaving her finger-tips in place. She looked to Master Smyth. "This, my Master, is the top of our golden prize. Her *mont de V`enus* or pubic mound. This is where her pubic hair begins to grow."

Gently and slowly running her fingers down, she calmy continued, "And these are the outer folds of her flower, concealing her precious female delights."

With two fingers, Calea gently parted the upper area of her outer folds. "Here, Master! This is the small, very sensitive hidden organ, the seat of female sexual pleasure. If you wet your fingertips, or employ the tip of your tongue, and softly caress this secret organ of any female, young or old, she will release her passion. Accordingly, she will belong to you." Master Smyth looked on but did not speak.

With experienced fingers, Calea now gently exposed the inner petal folds of Ciri's innocence. The girl remained timid, almost frightened, but remained still. "Here, Master, just below her secret organ is where she urinates."

"And just below where she urinates, Master, what all men crave and desire, her vagina. The opening of her virtue. And our success or our failure."

Calea's skilled fingers moved delicately. "In place here, Master—the hymen membrane."

Master Smyth looked up to Calea, smiling, and she returned his smile. "Success, Master, our first. The goddess continues to smile on us, and more to come."

Master Smith leaned over and softly kissed Calea's lips. Accordingly, she kissed him back. A short but tender kiss.

Calea continued, using a soft, pleasing voice.

"The crescent-shaped sepal of Ciri's virginity, Master. The precious little hymen of most virgins commonly appears as Ciri's does—one-half of the moon's full form."

Calea paused. Master Smyth looked up, asking her to continue without speaking. She obeyed. "But not always, Master. On occasion, the hymen membrane will cover nearly the whole vaginal opening, leaving only a small hole that will later allow her menstrual blood to flow out during her moon cycles. Also, occasionally, the hymen membrane will show two side-by-side elongated narrow openings. Physicians will refer to this condition as a 'septate hymen,' Master. And finally, on more rare instances, the hymen may cover the whole vaginal opening and must be carefully cut, creating a small hole to allow menstrual blood to flow."

"I did not know that," stated Master Smyth.

"Of course not, Master, one of many female secrets. Only those who attend a baby's birth would know. Usually, an experienced midwife or nanny, sometimes even the mother, will complete the surgery, leaving nearly all of the vagina entry covered. On occasion, a physician-surgeon will be summoned to complete the delicate operation, especially among the wealthy. They also keep this secret."

"I always knew physicians could not be trusted," scoffed Master Smyth.

"Now, Master, we are certain her virgin innocence remains intact. One more observation."

Calea looked up at Ciri's face. "Pull your knees up, my sweet. All the way, touching your nipples. That's my good girl." As Calea spoke, she reached over, taking a tiny alabastron from a small round table-top adjacent to the examination table.

"Observe, Master. Is this not a lovely virgin tea-rose? Most certainly, never penetrated. And similar with all brown-haired females, a beautiful pink-sienna hue."

Calea took a drop of the scented oil from the alabastron onto her first finger and once more looked into Ciri's face. "Remain still, my love. I will not hurt you." She then tenderly massaged Ciri's small anus but did not penetrate her.

She looked to Master Smyth with a satisfied smile. "Deliciously tight, my Master. What man could resist her?"

When Calea surmised, he was ready, she asked, "Have we seen enough, my Master?"

"Yes, Calea. I am content," said a calm and seemingly pleased Master Smyth.

"Very good girl, Ciri," praised Calea. "You may get up, dress, and return to the others. Without speaking, Ciri did as she was told.

"This is where, and how, we must decide, Master. Is this what we are looking for?" Calea now spoke in a rare, serious voice. She included herself, as though she and Master Smyth were partners, by using the words *our* and *we*. Subtle manipulation does not end.

"Will we present this girl to the royal family and their physicians?" She paused, a planned pause. She continued. "What if the royal family is not pleased and rejects our virgin?"

"That will not happen!" stated Master Smyth, as though he was stating a direct order or a command.

"Certainly not, my Master. We will take every precaution, and more, before we present our maidens to the royal family."

Following a short pause, Calea asked, "Will you allow me to explain the entire situation, Master?"

Master Smyth nodded in agreement.

Calea smiled, then continued speaking in a teacher's tone.

"The middle class and the poor do not care or hold virginity in high regard. Girls of the lower classes work hard. They will most likely lose, or tear their hymens by doing so. It does not mean they have forfeited their virginity, only their little half-moon of innocence."

Master Smyth listened intently. He did not indicate or reveal in his expression if he was aware of this information or not. He simply bid Calea to continue with a simple gesture.

"The lower classes do not care if the bride in question has bedded men or not. In fact, if she is a normal, healthy young woman, it is presumed she has slipped out with other young men in her community. What the lower classes respect and demand, Master, is pregnancy—or rather, its absence—and fatherhood. If it becomes known that an intended bride is pregnant, it could be a disaster. If there is any doubt that the soon-to-be husband is not the father of his expecting wife, another disaster. Conversely, if he is satisfied that he is the father of any and all children, all will be forever well."

"The wealthy hold virginity in high esteem—*bona fide*—virginity. To them, it is profit. It is proof, whether real or imagined, that the maiden in question has never had sex or has not been penetrated."

"Although we could find virginity among the lower classes, we must seek the affluent neighborhoods and daughters of the aristocracy. The wealthy may have had the means and power to escape Opar, taking their families. The Lord who owned this charming villa was apparently able to do so."

"Also, it is quite possible for a girl to have sex, be deeply penetrated, and retain her hymen. But as long as she is not pregnant, we do not care. Most girls are naive. They can be easily persuaded and cajoled into revealing their sexual encounters. Nonetheless, we must retain them long enough for their moon cycles to be completed. It may only require a few weeks. This is our life or death. I suggest we wait at least two moon cycles. We must ensure they are not pregnant. The royal family, who will spend a fortune on a verified virgin, will not touch her until she has a moon cycle, proving she is or is not with child."

Pausing, Calea took a silent breath. She placed the palm of her hand on Master Smyth's chest and patted him, smiling into his face. She continued.

"The virginity of the elite is guarded day and night, as though their sweet, little kunts were made of gold, and in their minds, they are. A wealthy virgin will be married into an affluent family, giving each father access and roads to more wealth. That is what they each desire."

"How have you come by all of this information, Calea?" asked Master Smyth.

"Do you recall, Master, I mentioned to you I was a ward of Lord Philemon and Lady Baucis of Greenstone Estates?"

"I do Calea, now that you have stirred my memory."

"Do you know Lord Philemon of Greenstone, my Master?"

"I know of him, but I have not met him," answered Master Smyth. "Only the ignorant peasants and slaves of the Achaean Empire do not know of Lord Philemon."

"I know I am your slave Master Smyth, and I serve you and your enterprise. I tell you this about myself so that you will have knowledge of me. I hope you will also think of me as a partner, at least in some minor capacity."

Master Smyth nodded approvingly. "Continue, Calea."

"I was an orphan, my Master, abandoned in the streets of Opar the day

Lord Philemon, the formal General of the Western Army, came to Opar. He had commercial business with the Opar Army. Upon seeing me in the streets, he befriended me. He took me in, and I returned with him to his magnificent villa, the Greenstone Estates, located westward of Capital City. We traveled in a military caravan, along Opar Road, to the Northern Army. We continued north to Mysia, then south to Capital City, finally arriving at the Greenstone Villa. It was a wonderful adventure."

"The Lord's family and his lovely wife, Lady Baucis, raised and employed me. I was not a slave but a servant girl, working as a nanny's helper for the Lord's many children, sired from many virgins. Lord Philemon and his family were very kind to a waif of Opar. I was treated more comparable to a daughter than a servant. I cared for the younger children of the Lord but was also educated along with them. I received all the benefits, including education, as would any daughter of the aristocracy. Over those several years, I was also present at the examination of the sundry virgins who would bear Lord Philemon's numerous offspring."

"I'm impressed, Calea," stated Master Smyth. "You have been to the country of Mysia?"

"Yes, my Master. Lord Philemon had an old military friend who was from Mysia. We stayed at his villa in Cos."

"You must tell me about Mysia, Calea, on some cheerful evening," suggested Master Smyth.

"Gladly, my Master. Lord Philemon discussed Mysia often."

Master Smyth reached out and laid his chubby hand on her cheek. Calea rubbed her cheek against his hand and sighed. Smiling, she waited, with purposeful anticipation, for him to speak.

"This is the manner we will proceed, Calea. We will retain all twenty-two females from that lower-class neighborhood. I am confident each will provide a valuable service, especially those I make bed-slaves. The three young pallakes who were left here in the villa would be hard-pressed, and sore, to satisfy the loins of my hundred soldiers and the other men in my company. We are also lacking in kitchen help," noted Master Smyth.

Certain Master Smyth had completed his thoughts, Calea spoke. "If I might be so audacious, Master, and speak openly?" With a nod from her Master, she continued. "I noticed, Master, that you have already tasted the favors of the former Lady Talcrane."

"Very little escapes you, Calea."

"Yes, Master."

"I find Talcrane attractive, Calea. I think I'll have her join us for a night or two."

"That sounds exciting, Master, adding her to your *répertoire* of sexual delight. Little doubt, a high-born woman of Opar would know how to please both men and women and actively enjoy *ménage a` trois.*"

Master Smyth lightly chuckled. He did not realize that the word for a threesome was an Opar word until Calea pronounced it correctly in the Opar language. Calea continued.

"I also think she would make an excellent nanny, Master. She appears to have been a matron and leader in her neighborhood. I've noticed that all the females you selected from her area look up to her."

"Good idea, Calea. Nanny Talcrane and Old Nanny will make a faithful nanny pair to our valuable maidens."

"May I offer another suggestion, Master?" asked Calea, retaining her soft, submissive voice.

Master Smyth, looked at Calea with a pleasant expression. "You may always interject your opinion without permission, Calea," he said.

"Thank you, Master. I think we should complete the examination of Ciri's sister, Alexa, and the pre-pubescent girl I pointed out to you in the plaza. I also recommend you consider sending soldiers to my husband's stables and claim any horses, should any remain."

"Wise suggestions, Calea," said Master Smyth, rubbing his small, chubby hands together. "Let us proceed."

CHAPTER 14

Coe: Following Advice

CUPPING COE'S FACE, THE MISTRESS of the Heart Blood College gently pulled him toward her to tenderly kiss his mouth, making several sighing sounds. "Mmm!" she purred taking a deep breath, her lips gently touching his. "Such a honey-soft mouth on a pretty male face."

"Yes, Mistress," answered Coe in a high-pitched, submissive voice.

She lightly glided her hand down his back in slow, gentle circles while they lay nude together in a large, comfortable bed. Sliding her hand farther down, she rubbed and caressed his buttocks. "You have such a soft bottom. Don't you, Coe?" she asked, her voice still in a whisper as she moved her index finger between his buttocks' cheeks and gently massaging his anus. "And such a honied, tiny tea-rose. Hmmm! You're going to be our sweet boy, aren't you, Coe?"

"Yes, Mistress," he answered, maintaining a high-pitched mewl. "I belong to you and Master."

Coe lay snuggled between Mistress and Master . . . wife and husband . . . of the Heart Blood College. The stern Master likewise enjoyed massaging and fondling Coe's girlish buttocks. His hand rubbed over his wife's hand and Coe's buttocks simultaneously then he leaned over Coe to kiss her with a growing passion.

The three lay on a hefty wooden bed, cornered by large carved posts. Soft blue pillows, fringed in brilliant red, lay along the tall headboard, which was also elegantly carved. Cool cotton slips and thick wool blankets adorned the bed. Graceful tapestries lined the solid rock walls, and the bright sun-light reached through the balcony doors and onto the bed, filling the entire luxurious bedroom with dancing brightness. Set on each side of the headboard, side tables were decked with containers of liquid refreshment. More importantly, where lovers are concerned, a large hyacinth-oil lamp burned on each table, engulfing the room with the aphroditic fragrance from the burning aromatic, mythical herb, filling each occupant with a delightful sense of amorousness.

"Slide down now, Coe, and pleasure our Master," whispered the Mistress into Coe's ear. Coe obeyed, and the Mistress slid with him, continuing to whisper, licking his ear. "Gently caress the Master's large, heavy balls. That's it! Now, take him into your mouth, just the way I showed you. Yes, slow, and gentle." She now moved back up to find her Master's mouth with hers. He lay panting—eyes closed.

Sliding back down to Coe, the Mistress now slowly moved him to his side while he continued to pleasure their Master. Her hand slid down Coe's stomach, caressing his testicles and penis.

"Soft, baby-size balls, drawn up tight, and such a hard, little penis," she panted in a whisper, maneuvering to kiss him again. "Come on, my boy. Come on, Coe, come to Mistress."

Coe rose just enough to climb between her legs. She wrapped her left arm around his neck and reaching down took his small erection in hand. Guiding him—it easily slid into her.

The mature Mistress now locked her ankles over the back of his knees and held him in place. With both hands, she lifted his head off her breast and kissed him again. "Open your little, honey mouth," she ordered. Coe obeyed. She kissed him with unfathomable hunger, vigorously pushing her tongue deep into his mouth. Meanwhile, the Master rose and moved behind Coe.

The kissed ended and Coe began to pule. "I'm afraid, Mistress."

"Oh, my little Coe. Don't be afraid. I know those horrid guards abused you on that abominable slave march. But have we ever punished you?"

"No, my Mistress," he sniveled.

"Have we ever spanked you, figged you, or made you spend the day standing on a stool or in a corner? You know the Master has a very large and very strong guard called Calloused because the palms of his hands are so very hard. He is an expert spanker of slaves. You have watched him take all disobedient slaves, male and female, over his knees and discipline them. Even the Feohtan fighters dread being sent to him for slave-punishment. Have we ever sent you to Calloused?"

"No, my Mistress," answered Coe's distressed voice.

"Master is not going to hurt you, Coe. He will be. . .." She paused and once more whispered in his ear. "Oh, so very gentle. We want to keep you tight and innocent, and we are both loosened with hyacinth oil. It will be a wonderful pleasure. You will see. Now, just relax. Relax your bottom and your little tea-rose in the manner I taught you."

"Yes, Mistress," answered Coe, still frightened but trying to obey and relax.

The Master now fondled Coe's oiled behind, gently inserting his index finger into his secret opening. Quiet whimpers escaped from the frightened Coe. Taking his large erection in hand, the Master guided it between Coe's buttock cheeks. Soft, quiet cries and moans escaped from Coe as the large hardness slowly penetrated.

Bracing himself on both hands, the Master now lowered himself down on top of Coe's buttocks and back. Turning his head, he kissed and bit the back of Coe's neck. Moving upward, he passionately kissed his Mistress-wife, whose head was elevated on a soft pillow.

"Ride with us, Coe!" ordered the now-gasping Mistress. "Ride with us, sweet boy! That's it—in and out! The Master is an expert with fledgling boys. He won't hurt you. You'll enjoy it like never before. That's it! He won't go hard or deep."

Coe obeyed his Mistress and easily thrust in and out of her while his Master equally moved in and out of him. The three rode together, locked in an embrace of *ménage a` trois* affection. The experienced Mistress kept Coe pinned—her ankles still held the back of his knees—she wrapped her arms around his back and neck—holding him against her.

The inexperienced Coe could not hold out long. He grasped both her shoulders and raised his head high off her large breast. He emptied into her with gasping exhaustion.

"Oh, yes, my boy! Oh, yes, Coe! Squirt for Mistress. Squirt!" Coe lay his head on her breast, spent. But his Master was far from finished.

He continued to ride Coe. His thrusts were fast and steady, but he maintained his placidness, without full or hard penetration. Finally, he groaned out loud with release.

"That's it, my Master! Fill our boy! Fill him up!" gasped the Mistress as the Master collapsed on Coe. All three of them lay exhausted—softly panting—unable to move.

Eventually, the Mistress said in a rasping voice, "Please, Master. May we roll to our sides? There is so much weight."

The Master complied and rolled to his side, taking Coe with him. The three lovers lay, spent and snuggled, with Coe remaining between his Master and Mistress. They kissed, embraced, and fell into a sleep.

Shadows in the large bed chamber slowly moved unseen, as would phantom spirits, across the carpet-laid floor and the rough stone walls adorned with elegant tapestries. A slight breeze blew in through the balcony doors, causing the flames from the hyacinth-oil lamps to flicker. The alluring, stimulating aroma lifted unseen from the lamps, continuing to fill the room with the mystical scent—the scent of passion—the scent of the goddess.

Outside the bed-chamber doors, Lucas, the chief trainer, waited with fortitude in the wide hallway. His employment by the Master and the Heart Blood College had endured for at least a score of years. What he waited to show the Master was important, but he knew it could also wait until the morrow.

The Master rose, gently rolling out of bed. His wife opened her eyes. With ease, he crawled back in and kissed her. Coe remained undisturbed.

"Go back to sleep, wife. The chief trainer awaits. There is something of importance he must show me."

He kissed her again, Coe as well, and once more climbed out of the large bed. He wrapped a white robe, trimmed in red, around his naked frame and stepped out into the hall. He closed the heavy doors behind him.

"Will you follow me to the training yard balcony, Master?" asked ChiefTrainer Lucas. The Master nodded, and the two headed down the wide hall.

They stood on the balcony overlooking the extensive training yard. Kaelin and another trainer waited just below. Trainer Lucas pointed to a man-size target located a far distance away, toward the opposite end of the field.

"The distance from here to the target, Master, is great. Few men, if any, no matter how well trained, could cast a spear that distance, much less strike the mark."

"Yes, I see that," answered the Master, leaning both hands on the railing.

ChiefTrainer Lucas signaled. Kaelin raised up his hand, armed with a spear. He balanced himself, preparing to throw. With three running paces, he cast the spear toward the distant target. It flew in a low arc, and within only a few blinks of an eye, it struck the target. With another few blinks of the eye, the noise the spear made as it hit the target returned to the Master and the chief trainer. The sound of silence followed. An eerie calm because the training yard was always a place of unending noise during the day, with the only tranquility falling on the yard at night. The chief trainer broke the unsettling stillness.

"He can do it nearly every throw, Master. All my years in the army and my many years here, I have never seen a spear cast such a distance with such accuracy. If I were told this, I would not believe it. I still find it hard to believe, even seeing it."

"Yes, I see what you mean, Lucas," agreed the Master, lifting his hands from the railing and wearing a large grin on his face. "Simply stated, it is remarkable."

"He lacks some conditioning, Master," explained Lucas, "and detailed instruction in the Feohtan spearman contest, but he is very young, and condition will be easily gained. He endured a slave march." Trainer Lucas shook his head, wearing a sour frown on his face. "I find it hard to believe such a skilled warrior was on a slave march, but he is otherwise ready for the arena."

Trainer Lucas waited for the Master to speak, but he remained in deep thought. He seemed to be calculating, perhaps scheming. Lucas again broke the quiet calm.

"May I make a suggestion, Master?"

"By all means, Lucas."

"Keep his skill a secret. Guard it well. Let all believe he is a young, green recruit. He certainly looks the part. Try to match him with a veteran fighter, one with a reputation. The other colleges will think they have an easy victory. But when the veteran is killed, coin will come your way. The aristocracy loves surprises. After that, let the word out about Kaelin. A warrior of Opar—taken captive—endured a slave march before finally coming into your hands. Kaelin's reputation will rise with more kills. I'd say you'll be asked to bring him to Capital City, to fight before the Emperor, in a very short period. If you are smart with this young warrior, Master, and with a little luck, success and wealth, by the fokken goddess, await you."

"Well stated, Lucas." The Master beamed with a smile. "That is exactly what we will do."

"I also advise, Master," continued Lucas, "reward that fat Master slave buyer. Tell him Kaelin and that large Ox were good buys but require a lot of training before they are ready for the arena. But also tell him you're much pleased with the boy."

"Well thought-out, Chief Trainer Lucas. I will certainly do just that. And you deserve some compensation as well. Is there a slave-girl on the compound you have a fancy for?"

"There is Master," admitted Lucas with a seldom-seen grin. "A new, fresh girl just arrived. Soft little quail with beautiful tail feathers. I think she comes from Opar."

"Well then, Lucas, she will be yours. I'll have her set aside for your pleasure alone."

"Thank you, Master."

The sound of bare feet and the tinkle of a slave ankle bracelet caught their attention. They both turned to the balcony doors. Allowed to wear a waist wrap, Coe ran up to his Master, who lifted his arm. Coe threw his arms around his Master and hugged him under his arm-pit. He looked up smiling and spoke a single word, "Master."

The Master bent down and kissed him just as the Mistress walked up, embracing them both. Coe looked down into the yard and saw Kaelin. "It's Kaelin, Master," he said, his childish voice now filled with excitement. "Can I wave and say hello?"

"You may," replied the Master.

Coe placed his hand to the side of his mouth and called out, "Kaelin! Kaelin!"

Kaelin looked up while Coe waved his hand back and forth, all smiles.

"Hello, Kaelin! Hello!" called out Coe.

Kaelin recognized Coe. He smiled and instantly waved back. "Hello, Coe! Hello!"

Wise Kaelin then looked into the Master's eyes. He raised a closed fist in a military "spear salute." The Master acknowledged his salutation with a raised hand.

"Oh my!" interrupted the Mistress. "What a handsome, young man."

She looked to her husband and Master wearing an excited expression. "Do you suppose, Master, you would allow me to have him for a night or two?"

The Master chuckled. "Yes, he is handsome, my wife, and also a very lethal warrior."

"Dear me," the Mistress said laughing. "More exciting still."

They all looked down to see Kaelin following the trainer toward the other end of the training field. Coe had another question.

"Master, can I ask how Ox is?"

The Master looked and nodded to Chief Trainer Lucas, who responded. "Ox is well young Coe. He trains with the sword and shield section."

"Thank you," Coe replied.

"That reminds me, Lucas," stated the Master. "Arrange for Kaelin to have an attractive slave-girl the night before he fights. Give him a little something extra to fight for."

"I know several of the Imperial Guards at the arena," answered Lucas. "Consider it done, Master."

"Good!" replied the Master. The small group left the balcony.

CHAPTER 15

Kaelin: Arena Holding Cell

LATE IN THE AFTERNOON, KAELIN walked in the middle of a single file of near-naked Feohtans, clad only in loincloths and high, laced military sandals, down the hallway of the Great Arena of Cappa on their way to the holding cells. All the Feohtans in the file were from Heart Blood College, trained and destined to fight in the spearman's duel. Imperial Guards led the solemn procession, also following behind it.

Aligned along the outer wall of the arena, the individual holding compartments were not intended as prison cells, although each could serve in that capacity, being constructed of thick stone walls with bronze-barred windows and doors. Oil lamps and torches, fixed to the walls, provided light in the hallway. The torches could be easily removed and carried by the guards, if necessary. Centuries of combat wisdom dictated that Feohtans were individually separated the night before facing death in front of the roaring crowd in the arena. An old, rough sergeant led the procession. He stopped, opening the cell door for the Feohtan first in line. Kaelin ascertained the sergeant had been on duty for a considerable tour, as he knew the names of several of the Feohtans.

"I'm considering placing a bet on you, Hessa. How do you feel?" inquired the veteran sergeant. The burley Hessa looked at the guard with a strange grin. "Good," he replied, quietly entering the cell. One by one, the Sergeant of the Guard opened the cells, allowing each Feohtan to step in.

The strong-barred windows in each of the rectangular stone cells were set in the center of the back wall, the outside wall of the arena, allowing outside light into each cell. An equally strong-barred cell door was placed at the end of each front wall of the cell, rather than the center, thus providing a corner of the cell with a measure of privacy. As the sergeant opened his cell door, Kaelin stepped in and stood in the center of the room. He remained still and listened. The small, rock-solid chamber emanated a strange presence, something not tangible—not of this world. Within the eerie silence, Kaelin could sense a small element of the spirits of the thousands of men who had spent their last night in this cell, subsequently dying in the arena. Somehow, their spirits seemed to linger within the walls. He glanced around the stone partition.

It did not flash a hint of luxury but at least appeared clean and moderately comfortable.

A covered ceramic and mortar chamber toilet was fixed to the floor, about knee-high, near the back wall. It emptied into the underground sewage system that controlled waste for the whole Great Arena. A bucket of wash water sat in the far corner, while an oil lamp burned on the end wall of the cell. The lamps from the hall also provided light. A straw mattress lay on the floor in the more private corner. It was made of a single large piece of strong, rough flax, folded over, with the sides stitched, leaving the end open, thus stuffed with straw. What appeared to be a clean section of flax cloth, a bedcover, lay folded on the straw mattress—a smaller piece of cloth also lay on the bed. A low, wooden bench, set near the bed, was topped with food and drink. Not an aristocrat's cuisine, but still a hardy last meal of cooked meat, two loaves of bread, two apples, a small block of white feta, a baked vegetable tuber, and a leather flask each of beer and water.

Kaelin stepped over to the bench of food. He picked up the flask of beer, pulled the top, smelled it, and took a deep drink. "Very good," he said quietly to himself, somewhat surprised at the quality. "Very good beer." He took another drink, replaced the flask on the bench, and tore off a section of the bread. He walked to the window as he ate the bread. Unexpectedly, he heard the heavy hallway doors open and close, followed by footsteps down the hall.

He turned around to see a file of naked women pass his cell door and stop, standing quietly in the hall. He heard several low whistles, moans, and groans from his Feohtan cellmates as each cell door was opened and closed. Abruptly, the sergeant opened his cell door and roughly pushed in a naked woman. She first stumbled, then stood quiet, with her head bowed. The old sergeant spoke in a low, forceful voice.

"If death comes for you tomorrow, Feohtan. . . ." He paused, placing his fist on his hips, then continued. "Will be loud with the roar of the crowd, same you were in a battle. Feohtans here appreciate peace and quiet for their last mortal night. Hear me! Don't slap or hurt this woman, causing her to yell and scream. Keep her calm! Fokken her all night long . . . if you can. But I want it quiet! She'll do what you say. If she don't, alert the guards, and we'll take her outside and lay a few strap licks across her sweet, little butt. After that, she'll beg you and do anything you want. You understand?"

Kaelin did not speak. He looked at the guard with a stern expression and nodded that he understood.

"She's a foreigner," continued the guard. "Like you she's new. Many say she's the prettiest little kunt we have here in the holding cells. You're a lucky man. Might be she'll bring you luck tomorrow." The guard abruptly left, closing the cell door.

Standing in the hall, he yelled out. "I want all of you to keep it quiet in those cells!" His loud footsteps echoed down the hallway as he left.

The woman remained motionless in the center of the cell. Her hands covered her pubic area, her head bowed. She shook, nearly in tears, obviously and understandably in anxious fear. Kaelin slowly walked up to the woman to have a closer look. She was slender, well built, with ample breasts but unusual in color. Her skin was a soft, light-cream color, and her short-cropped hair a was deep charcoal black. She wore an attractive but frightened face. Suddenly, to his surprise, she spoke.

"Please, please, no hit," she said in a whimpering, nearly tearful, strange foreign voice.

Kaelin had heard this unusual but pleasing accent before, when he was still a youth in Opar. Exotic Salomi had spoken in a similar manner. She was a stunning, mature woman he would not forget.

Kaelin stepped closer in front of her. She was shaking like a small, captured animal. He well knew such fear. "Don't be afraid," he whispered. "I am not going to hurt you."

She kept her head bowed and her eyes closed tight, as though anticipating a slap. Her voice trembled while she spoke. "You speak. I do. I fokken. Please, no hit."

Kaelin slowly reached up, gently touching her chin with his fingers. Three little "ohs" softly escaped from her trembling lips. "I'm not going to hit you or hurt you. Raise your head and open your eyes." Carefully, the timid woman complied. She seemed to understand but remained frightened.

Kaelin stepped back, giving her space. She looked around with slow caution.

"We are both slaves in a stone cell. Why would I hit you?"

"Man hit slave. Her obey. He fokken her."

"I won't hurt you," assured Kaelin, speaking in a soft voice.

She looked at his face, searching for sincerity. When she found it, a small sigh of relief escaped her lips. Her eyes were a deep, beautiful blue color. Salomi was the only other person Kaelin had ever seen with black hair and blue eyes. As she glanced around the room, her eyes stopped when she saw the bench topped with food, growing wide with reflexive excitement. Kaelin noticed her reaction.

"Are you hungry?"

She looked back at him. "Guards strap, steal food. No want strap."

"It's not stealing if I give it to you." Kaelin smiled. "Are you hungry?"

She continued to look at him—swallowed hard—and slowly nodded her head yes. Kaelin walked toward the bench, motioning for her to follow. "Come."

She took careful steps toward the bench. Kaelin picked up the loaf of bread, broke off a piece, and handed it to her. Cautiously, she took the bread, glancing once more into his face to ensure his sincerity. Then, with a partial smile, she began to eat the bread with sudden enthusiasm.

"You are hungry," Kaelin said with a chuckled. He broke off another piece of bread and sat down on the straw bed, motioning for her to join him. Maintaining caution, she complied. Her eyes lit up again as Kaelin picked up the block of feta, took a bite, and handed it to her. Eagerly, she accepted, and she visibly became more relaxed. Together, they began to consume and enjoy the cold yet hardy meal.

"What is your name?" he asked.

At first, she looked at him with a puzzled face, then seemed pleased he would ask for her name. "Gaelin," she replied with a cheerful expression and a mouthful of food, "name Gaelin." Kaelin repeated her name.

She wiped her mouth with her hand. "You?" she asked, pointing.

"Kaelin," he answered. Gaelin repeated his name several times to herself, storing it in her memory. Then she smiled. She had a beautiful smile.

"Name you—I—same," she said still smiling.

Kaelin likewise grinned. "Yes, our names are very similar."

"Where are you from?" he queried, although he was reasonably certain he knew the answer.

She thought for a moment, making sure she understood his question and searching for the words to respond. "Mother, father, K'semya," she answered. "Empire soldiers come, kill men, take women, children, slaves. Mother slave. I born slave, same."

Kaelin well recognized the littoral country. It lay far to the northwest, along a rugged coast. *So that was where beautiful Salomi was from,* he thought to himself.

Kaelin continued to hand food to Gaelin, and as she ate, she became more comfortable. He held a chunk of the cold meat in his fingers, feeding it to her as if she were a baby bird, causing her to laugh. Her laugh was pleasant to hear and prompted Kaelin to laugh.

"You Empire?" she asked.

"No, I am from Opar," offered Kaelin. "Empire soldiers did the same to my country as they did to yours."

"I hear Opar," responded Gaelin. "Empire soldiers war Opar?" she asked.

"Yes," replied Kaelin.

"I sorry for Opar. Opar brave warriors."

A short pause ensued. Gaelin began to relax and open up. "You speak Empire speak?" she asked.

"Yes," Kaelin replied, "I can speak the Empire language."

"I no speak Empire speak," remarked Gaelin in a wishful tone but wearing an adorable expression, with raised eyebrows and slightly shrugged shoulders.

"You will learn," predicted Kaelin. He took the leather flask of beer. "Do you like beer?"

She looked at him with that same adorable expression. "No speak beer."

He pulled the top off and handed her the flask. She carefully smelled. The pungent odor prompted her to form a sour facial expression. "Man drink. I no like."

Laughing, Kaelin took the beer flask, and handed her the rawhide flagon of water. Pulling the top, she again smelled but now reacted with a cheerful response. "Yes, yes, good!" She drank the contents in large gulps, and in her enthusiasm, the warm liquid ran down the sides of her mouth. Laughing again, she wiped her face with her hand. Unexpectedly, she paused, looking at Kaelin. She formed a strange expression, pointing to her pubic area, before pointing to the waste toilet.

"I go?" she asked.

Kaelin understood. "Yes," he replied, "certainly."

Sporting a forced smile, Gaelin got up and cautiously stepped to the toilet. She took off the lid and slowly began to squat, then glanced at Kaelin with a sorrowful expression.

"Oh," said Kaelin, smiling and turning his back. "I won't watch."

"Thank you," she said tenderly as she sat down over the toilet. Strangely, she whimpered as she urinated. When she finished, she replaced the lid and took a handful of water from the nearby water bucket, washing her vulva with her hand. Again, she softly whimpered, making a painful face.

Kaelin got up. He took the small piece of cloth from the bed and walked over to her. He dipped the cloth into the water bucket and handed it to Gaelin.

"I wash?" she asked.

"Yes," he answered, "wash."

Eagerly, she took the wet cloth and began to wipe herself down, occasionally dipping the cloth back into the bucket. As she was washing, Kaelin went back to the straw bed and returned with the bed cover. He stood by as she quicky bathed.

Reaching around, Gaelin washed her buttocks and between her cheeks. The light from the oil lamp reflected off her wet skin.

Kaelin thought to himself.

She is very attractive. Light, cream-colored skin and large blue eyes. She has a beautiful shape, large yet firm breasts, and short black hair, hurriedly sheared short without care.

He also saw that cruel leather strap marks covered her well-formed buttocks and the back of her shapely legs.

Unexpectedly, he noticed two strange, small blue dots at the top of each beautiful cheek, near the spine, side by side, about the size of a raindrop. Kaelin was taken aback. He had seen these same marks on the behind of his baby sister. His mother told him they were just unusual birthmarks. He had not reflected on them since all those years ago.

Uncanny, he thought. *How could there be rare or extraordinary marks from birth on one child's behind but then the same marks on a second, and both being girls?*

More important matters were at hand. He might consider it another day, if there was another day. He returned to Gaelin.

When finished, she laid the wet washing cloth over the edge of the water bucket. Kaelin stretched the blanket out with both hands. She understood. He wrapped the cover around her as she held her arms up. "I wear?" she asked. Kaelin nodded yes.

With smiling enthusiasm, she took the cloth, fixing it around her and securing it by tucking it in at the front of her chest. It was nearly as though she was wearing clothes. Being allowed to wash and cover herself with a garment made Gaelin feel nearly human again. She had not felt any joy for so long. She reached out, taking Kaelin's hand.

"Thank you, Kaelin," she said, with tears forming in her eyes. She began to weep softly.

"You're welcome," he replied. Taking her hand, Kaelin led her back to the straw bed and bench. "Eat more," he offered.

She nodded her head yes, smiling a teary-eyed smile. They quietly sat back down on the bed to finish the meal. They talked and laughed.

Despite the language barrier, together, they escaped their reality. Both were slaves, locked in a stone gaol—one destined for lethal combat, the other to endure forced sexual servitude. Their futures seemed bleak, and the path to liberty, all but out of reach. But for a short period, a single night, they enjoyed each other and a slight taste of freedom. The oil lamp on the cell wall slowly flickered out, allowing the moonlight to shine through the barred window, painting their confine in a strange glow of light and shadows across the stone floor.

As they sat together on the straw mattress, Gaelin reached her hand up to Kaelin's face, then slowly leaned into him. She tenderly kissed him. Once more, tears swelled in her beautiful, blue eyes. She placed her other hand on her groin and pressed her thighs together. "Kaelin, hurt. Man fokken, hurt."

Kaelin understood. "Is that why you cried when you wet and washed?"

Still tenderly sobbing, Gaelin nodded yes.

Kaelin kissed one teary eye and then the other. "No fokken," he said quietly. "We sleep. I hold you and you hold me. We can sleep, with peace." They lay down together on the straw bed.

Gaelin smiled a warm, glowing smile. Reaching out, she untied Kaelin's loincloth and carefully pulled it from his waist. She removed the bed cover from herself and draped it over them both as they lay on the straw bed, wrapped in each other's arms. They shared a tender kiss, their warmth, softness, and their human scent.

They slept—a single long night of peace together. They slept deep and long. Gaelin had not slept so well since her capture, so long ago, it seemed to be another lifetime.

Duplicating the moonlight, the morning sun peeked into the barred window, casting the same pattern of shadows across the cell floor. They awoke to the sound of distant doors opening and closing and the heavy footsteps of military sandals on the stone hallway floor.

"What do?" asked Gaelin in a whisper as they lay face to face.

"Use toilet, drink water, take food," answered Kaelin hurriedly.

"Yes, yes," she answered with a still, soft voice while she quickly rose and hurried to urinate on the cold toilet. It was not as painful as before. Kaelin also rose, picking up the water flask.

"Get up, bitches, get up!" ordered the guard, clambering down the hallway and past their cell. Gaelin quickly rose from the toilet and washed herself with her hands. Kaelin handed her the leather water flagon.

"Drink," he said. She took the flagon and quickly drank, washing out her mouth and swallowing.

They heard cell doors opening as the guard called out, "come out, bitches—line up!" They also heard loud, resounding slaps and high-pitched female yelps. Kaelin picked up the remaining apple, handing it to Gaelin. She took the apple and his hand at the same time.

"Thank you, Kaelin, thank you. You kind me. You warrior. You true warrior. I pray goddess you, I pray day and day, Asa protect you."

Kaelin did not say anything, but he would not forget her. He simply smiled. Gaelin touched the side of his face and kissed him. The guard opened their cell door.

"Come out, bitch!" As Gaelin walked past the guard, he raised his hand, bringing it down in a hard-spanking slap across her buttocks. She jumped with the force of the slap and hurried to stand in line with the other women in the hall. Kaelin walked to the bars and looked down the hall. All the naked slave-women held food, bread, or an apple, and busied themselves eating. Gaelin quickly did likewise.

"Walk out, bitches! Keep in line!" ordered the guard. Gaelin turned to Kaelin smiling and kissed her fingers to again offer him thanks as she walked out with the file of naked women down the stone hallway, illuminated by the brightness of the early-morning sun.

CHAPTER 16

Natasha: Tanning Stories

RECOMMENDED BY HER FATHER, NATASHA secured a position as a "server" in the dining hall for the 1ˢᵗ Company of the Ravenbourne Corps, albeit, an attractive, young girl was never denied employment. Her dear friend Melissa also worked as a server for the elite 1ˢᵗ Company. On many occasions, Melissa had encouraged Natasha to ask for a job at the dining hall. She finally broke down and inquired.

Only a few summers older than Natasha, Melissa was far more experienced in the "ways of the world" and had traveled through and lived in several regions of the Achaean Empire. Although most of the main roads of the Empire were patrolled by soldiers, it remained unsafe to travel alone, especially for a young mistress. But Melissa learned early on that she could safely travel in the company of soldiers, who were delighted to have a playful, attractive girl join them.

Melissa reminded Natasha of her father—full of stories and adventure. She had once worked as a server in the dining halls of the Eastern Army, and she often revealed tales with boundless enthusiasm.

"It's so much harder, Natasha, working for the Eastern Army. They are strict, maybe brutal, the way they treat common people, even those who work for them. General Y'Sloic's Southern Army is so much better, but the best is the Ravenbourne Army. We are both lucky to live and work here at Ravenbourne."

Melissa lived with her aunt, who owned a comfortable cottage near Natasha and her father's house. The girls often slept over at each other's homes, especially since the death of Natasha's mother, and more so now that they both worked as servers for the 1st Company. They did not seem to tire of each other's company.

Last night, Melissa had spent the night at her aunt's; consequently, Natasha walked to work alone. She thought it would be interesting to arrive at work before anyone else was there. Entering the building, she walked down the side of the hall where the guest rooms were, noticing that one of the guest room doors was open. Light from the room filled the corridor when two figures stepped out of the room. Instinctively, Natasha backed into the doorway of the adjacent room, out of sight. The figures, a man and a woman, embraced and passionately kissed. The man whispered into the woman's ear, prompting her to laugh. To Natasha's surprise, it was Melissa. The man was a Ravenbourne Warrior. He turned and walked at a hurried pace down the corridor.

Stepping out from the doorway, Natasha advanced to her friend. "Melissa, were you having sex with that Warrior?" she scolded.

"Of course, I was, sweetie," confessed Melissa with a laugh. "That's Sergeant Derick. Isn't he handsome? He'll be an officer one day."

Holding up a silver coin, Melissa placed it in front of one eye, smiling.

"Did he give you that money?" inquired Natasha in amazement.

"He sure did, Nati." She laughed, turning in a circle with her other hand on her hip. "And I'm going to share with you and we can buy something really fun."

Melissa stepped to her friend and gave her a quick kiss. Reaching up, she gently pinched Natasha's nose, pleased with herself. She turned and scampered off toward the kitchen.

Grasping the rope handles of a heavy wooden box, Natasha struggled as she carried a load of empty beer mugs to a dining hall table. She softly moaned, lifting the heavy container to the table-top. Taking a mug from the box, she began to set the table when suddenly, a commotion surprised her, prompting her to turn around.

Wearing an angry expression, First Sergeant Klause walked down the side wall of the dining hall toward the company stage, up the stage steps, and to the pommel horse.

Suddenly, Sergeant Klause turned and looked over to Natasha. Unexpectedly, he stepped with a brisk stride, descended the stage steps, and walked toward her. She quickly returned to setting the beer mugs on the table. She thought she could tell by his loud steps that he was angry, and her heart, filled with anxiety, began to beat rapidly. Sergeant Klaus stepped up to her.

"How has the work been going for you, Natasha?" he asked in an unusually mild tone.

"It goes well, First Sergeant," answered Natasha in an uneasy, frightened voice as she swallowed hard and looked up into his indifferent face, attempting to smile.

"They tell me you're a hard worker, Natasha." His voice remained mild, putting her at ease. "I think you'll do well here."

"Thank you, First Sergeant," Natasha answered in a frightened voice still attempting to be as pleasant as she could be.

"I served with your father in the Frisian Wars," confessed Sergeant Klause, completely surprising Natasha.

"Oh!" was the only response she could find.

"He was a good soldier and leader, your father. He inspired us all." Sergeant Klause continued, showing a rare grin. "I bet he can tell some good stories."

Natasha suddenly found her trepidation vanish. She smiled, looking up at his face, and laughed. "Oh yes, Sergeant! Very exciting! He can tell wonderful stories through several turns of the hour-glass."

Natasha now heard Sergeant Klaus laugh for the first occasion. Then, surprisingly, he reached out and laid his hand on top of her hand, where it rested on the table. He then rubbed and gently patted her hand.

"You'll do well, Natasha," he said in a rare cheerful voice. He turned and walked away in rigid Ravenbourne Warrior fashion. Natasha swallowed hard, but she felt good about the encounter. She returned to laying out the beer mugs on the table. Suddenly, a strident bang surprised her, causing her to look up.

It was Melissa. She had just walked up and loudly dropped a wooden box of ceramic ware on the table. Natasha looked over to her friend, who smiled back.

Melissa paused and took a deep breath. "Every so often, I wish a Ravenbourne Warrior to protected me." She sighed.

"What about Sergeant Derick, the warrior I saw you with?" asked Natasha.

"Oh, he's just for fun, Nati. Besides, protection is very serious, and it's both good and bad. Still, I think it might be wonderful," continued Melissa, "especially a young, handsome one. Like the one who is Captain of the Ravenbourne Guards, who rides horses and protects Lord Ravenbourne. I don't know his name, but I saw him more than once when I worked for the Southern Army at Cappa."

"Oh yes, I know," added Natasha. "I've seen mounted Ravenbourne Warriors on the Tyner Bridge. It's very exciting. Maybe on our next no-work day, we'll go to the bridge and I'll show you all my secret hiding places."

"That will be fun, Nati," responded Melissa. But as she spoke, she saw a serious expression fall across her friend's face. She waited for Natasha to speak.

"Something else, Melissa. I have something very important to tell you, but we must be *incognito*."

Melissa usually smiled when Natasha used Opar words, but she could also tell her friend was serious and anxious. "I understand, Natasha. And if that Opar word means 'alone,' we will have a serious talk, alone, just you and me, the very next chance we can, when we have a no-work day."

"That sounds wonderful, Melissa." Natasha felt a large portion of her anxiety leave her. Melissa was now wearing a mischievous smile. Natasha knew she had just thought of a way to place them both in jeopardy and big trouble.

"Let's sneak off and go today, Nati! Doesn't that sound fun?"

"No, Melissa! Absolutely not! I'm not sneaking off, and neither are you, young lady! Do you hear me?"

"If you say so, momma Nati," Melissa joked laughing. "We'll wait till our next no-work day."

Looking around, Natasha believed no one was watching, and the dining hall appeared empty. She stood by the pommel horse, next to the wall, on the stage. She stared at the leather strap hanging from the wall. It was about the length of a man's arm and wide as a man's hand. The smooth strap was fixed to a sword like handle at one end. The other end was rounded. She remained too cautious to dare take the dreaded Dragon's Tongue down from its wall peg. Instead, she lifted the end and delicately rubbed her fingers along the flat, cold surface.

Without warning, Melissa stepped behind her and put her hand on her shoulder. Natasha jumped and let out a caught-in-throat-yelp and quickly turned around.

"Melissa, you scared me nearly to death!"

Smiling, Melissa kept her hand on Natasha's shoulder and spoke softly into her ear.

"Aren't you afraid to touch it?" she asked.

"Yes," answered Natasha, remaining startled and looking back over her shoulder, "but I am somehow compelled to."

"My aunt says that men are strapped above the waist, and women and boys, below," whispered Melissa, who cautiously looked around to ensure they were alone, then pulled a slice of bread, topped with honey, from behind her back, taking a hefty bite.

"Melissa, is that stolen?" scolded Natasha.

Her mouth was too full to speak, so Melissa put her hand over her mouth and nodded her head yes, smiling.

"Your capricious behavior will cause you to be in big trouble, young lady, if you don't stop your insatiable habit of stealing honey and bread from the kitchen!"

Melissa pirouetted with her hands over her head. "Want a bite?" she asked, mouth full of bread, snickering and holding up one last portion of the tasty contraband.

"No! I don't want to be in trouble the way you're going to be," warned Natasha.

Melissa quickly finished the last bite, swallowing hard. "I got a Dragon's Tongue lickin' once," said Melissa, still in a whisper, surprising Natasha.

"What?" replied Natasha. "When?"

"Just before you came. It was only three licks. Oh, Natasha, you would not believe how bad it hurt. It stung and burned!"

"What were the circumstances?" asked a now-anxious Natasha.

"Well. . ." Melissa stopped and looked around to see if anyone might be eavesdropping or taking note that they were not working. Satisfied they were alone, she continued.

"The First Sergeant, cranky Sergeant Klause, caught me sneaking out a little honey urn right there in the doorway." She pointed at the kitchen doorway. "One little, tiny urn. He took me by the neck and marched me up the platform steps to the pommel horse. I pleaded and begged, and tried to talk my way out of it, but he was mad and wouldn't listen. I can always talk men out of doing something, but not this occasion!"

"I know," added Natasha. "I'm beginning to believe the First Sergeant is not only stern but, equally, an obdurate man."

"Me too," answered Melissa, not really understanding Natasha's words.

"Take those little undergarments off. Lift your frock up. Bend over the horse! he ordered at me, mad and loud." Melissa pointed her finger at Natasha once for each command.

"Now I was afraid, so I obeyed as fast as I could. He stepped to the wall and took the wicked tongue down. Well, at least he didn't make me strip naked. He swung the tongue through the air. It makes such a scary sound through the air, even though it's not very loud."

"'Lift your feet off the floor and spread those legs!' he growled, just like given an order to a young, new soldier!

"He just wanted to see between my legs, but I was so scared by now I didn't care, and started to cry. I felt him behind me. I knew it was going to be horrible. And then I heard the 'air hiss' of the strap coming. It landed on my right cheek. It took my breath!

"Oh, Natasha! You would not believe how bad it hurt. Just one lick. Now, I really started to cry, with tears running down my face. Next, the second one landed on my left check, and the third across both. We were still alone. The workers in the kitchen were probably too scared to come out. You know, I would have done, anything he said."

"'Are you going to steal any more honey?' he asked in a real scary voice, 'or do you need three more?'

"I begged—I cried—and I promised I would never take any more honey or steal anything from the kitchen ever again. I thought he was going to fokken me, but he ordered me off the horse. He walked over to the wall and hung the tongue back up. He walked back to me as I stood there by the horse, rubbing my butt. He took me by the hair on the back of my head, reached his other hand down, and rubbed my flower. Next, he kissed me long and hard, and I knew I'd better kiss him back, and I did, as good as I could. I still thought he was going to lift me back up, lay me over the horse, and give me a hard fokken. But he told me to put my little undergarments back on, go wash my face, and get back to work.

"'Now you be a good girl,' he warned, 'or next time I'll give you six licks!'

"He let me keep the honey. He said I earned it. I never want another lickin' again. I can't hardly imagine being stripped naked in front of the whole company, being bent over the horse, and taking ten hard licks. I just can't imagine that. Can you?"

"No, I can't," answered Natasha with a stern expression. "Well, why do you continue to steal honey, Melissa? I understand it is not a seditious act, but you're going to be caught, and then you'll be in severe trouble."

"I know," whined Melissa. "But I just keep thinking I won't be caught, and if I do, they really won't strap me. Maybe just spank me with the palm of the hand. That's usually what men do, anyway. Besides, Ravenbourne Warriors won't use a strap on a slave-girl or pallake, so why not me?"

Natasha shook her head with a heavy sigh. She put her hands on her hips. "It's not a law, Melissa, and you're not a slave-girl, and neither am I. We both signed the documents so that we could work and said that we understood the rules. Besides, Melissa, you just told me the First Sergeant has already used the strap on you. Don't you think he will do it again and apply it to me as well?"

Suddenly, a terrifying image flashed through Natasha's head. She saw herself naked, bent over the pommel, with the stern First Sergeant standing behind her with the dreaded tongue in hand.

"I know, I know," Melissa said, pouting. "I'll do better and be more careful. But we're not the same, Natasha. You know no one will punish you because you have a father who is a war hero and Elder. Maybe one day, your father will be the same as a father to me."

Melissa paused and looked at her friend with an unusual expression. "Have you ever had a tongue lickin' Natasha?" asked Melissa.

"No," replied Natasha. "My father had a Maiden's Tongue hanging on our wall, but he did not use it on me."

"Did he spank you?" she asked in a whisper.

Natasha blushed. "Yes, once, with his hand."

"Did he use the Maiden's Tongue on your mom?" continued the nosy Melissa.

"No, but he spanked her with his hand. That's the way of the Hyacinth Gatherers, Melissa, and that form of punishment is prescribed by their law. They call it 'skelping.' According to the Hyacinth Gatherer law, the father—" Natasha stopped. She then leaned close to Melissa and whispered, "The father disciplines everyone in his household, especially the children but also including the mother, his wife. It matters not the age of the children if they are still living at home. Once, my mom told me her father skelped her brother's bare behind until he was married and left the household. He was older, grown, and large."

Both girls began to chuckle, covering their mouths with their hands. "I bet that was funny to watch!" Melissa admitted laughing.

"My mom said it was," replied Natasha, trying not to laugh. "She said her brother was persistently in trouble. On occasion, he was chastised so severely and keenly, he would cry."

Both girls hugged each other, laughing. Then, with a little apprehension, they looked around to see if they were being watched. Seemingly unnoticed, they promptly returned to work.

CHAPTER 17

Lord Ravenbourne: Returning

GENERAL Y'SLOIC'S ESTEEMED ANCESTOR AMASSED a great fortune as a merchant, subsequently finding favor with the first Emperor of the emerging Achaean Empire. This patriarchal grandfather wisely joined with a group of wealthy aristocrats who were instrumental in bringing the Emperor to power. Thus, anointed an ancient lord of the rising Achaean Empire, he was deeded the coveted domain of Ravenbourne. The wondrous, exotic lands of Ravenbourne extended from the snowcapped mountains of the Twin Peaks of the central Southern Peninsula westward to the tropical coastline of the Outer Ocean.

The bountiful landscape abounded in lush natural resources embracing vast stands of timber, expansive meadows of tall grasses, and mountains of outcropping stone perfect for quarries. The lands of Ravenbourne, however, were not an untouched wilderness. This domain had been farmed by ancient peoples for millennia. Productive agriculture fields of fruit and flax stretched to the horizon. It was its breathtaking natural wonders, however, consisting of deep, clear pools, flowing hot springs, and ancient lave flows and lava tubes—that made Ravenbourne magical and wonderous—that made it an enchanted land.

Primeval molten rock that once flowed from the distant mountains to the shores of the Outer Ocean had now hardened into black lava flows, natural walls, and lava tubes. These natural flows were often incorporated into the construction of walls, bridges, gates, and other estate features. Hot-spring water, flushed from deep within the ground through bedrock fissures, formed pools of soothing mineral water. The pooled water then flowed on toward the ocean, eventually to cool, creating sparkling streams, lush with vegetation and woodlands. In some locations, both hot and cold springs glistened in the sun side by side as the warm vapor floated from the hot pools, ascending into the heavens, appearing as though illuminated spirits of immortal beings.

The lands of Ravenbourne remained the most coveted terrain across the entire Southern Peninsula, perhaps the whole Achaean Empire. General Y'Sloic's prosperous ancestor stepped from a merchant class into the elite aristocracy, thus enthroned with the title "Lord of Ravenbourne." General Sol Y'Sloic now bares the coveted title today.

The first Lord of Ravenbourne chose one of the most unique locations throughout the sumptuous Ravenbourne region and the whole Southern Peninsula to construct the luxurious Ravenbourne Villa. Long before mortal memory or mortal life, and before the eons of generations, a pure, unsullied pool of torrid water flowed deep and steaming from within the bowels of the earth. Heated and purified by the sweet breath of the goddess Asa, it gushed to the surface, and once kissed by the sunlight, the sweltering water formed a deep, numinous pool carved into solid rock.

Ancient legend tells of primeval mortals, long ago, who venerated this mystical Goddess Pool, and near-forgotten myths said the beautiful, naked form of the goddess Asa often bathed in this pool. Here, as she relaxed in its luxurious warmth, she could reach her hand out to drink from a clear, cool adjacent pool and look down upon the coast toward her sacred cove, the Bay of Ravenbourne.

Ravenbourne's first lord constructed the original villa, centered around this spiritual pool. The first walls were erected to enclose the immediate area. Later, the villa was expanded, and a second course of outside walls was built. Natural lava flow and walls were incorporated in the wall construction of both the first and second course of walls. The first interior walls and enclosures became a citadel, the last stronghold in the case of a strong, determined attack in which the outside walls were breached. The citadel now served as Lady Ravenbourne's private sanctuary. Although elegantly decorated, it remained a fortress and was soundly supplied with arms and provisions to last a lengthy siege. Over the course of generations, only the royal palace of the Emperor would surpass the majestic Ravenbourne Villa and surrounding estate in splendor.

Few modifications were attempted on the Goddess Pool. Stairs ascending the pool were constructed from the same natural hard stone, and a low, stone wall encircled portions of the pool with flat smooth stones, laid on top, providing seating. Certainly, the area around the Goddess Pool was landscaped with trees and flora, but the natural beauty of the hot-water fissure and surrounding stone, shaped by eons of running water, were left as created.

A fair distance south of the Goddess Pool, ancient peoples had built a great city that now lay in ruins, located well outside the walls of the Ravenbourne Villa. The once-tall columns, wide walls, and monolithic stones had long since collapsed. Ironically, the stone used by the ancient builders appeared to have been quarried from the same quarry currently used by the Ravenbourne stonemasons. Throughout this primeval complex, impressive stone tools, seemingly spear points and knife blades, lay scattered in abundance. Just how a people of stone technology could construct such a complex settlement remained a topic of mystery.

Lord Ravenbourne's Law prohibited trespass onto the ruins for all. Normally, children were exempt from punishment for breaking Lord Ravenbourne's Law. Trespassing and disturbing the ruins, however, the one exception. Curious children caught playing within the ancient grounds by the Ravenbourne Warrior guards could expect their behinds to earn a youngster's punishment.

More important to the worshipers of Asa, the early stone-tool people built a temple, some distance east of the Ravenbourne Villa, toward the Mountain of the Goddess and the Twin Peaks. The temple was constructed around a unique cavern created by lava formations. A deep hot pool lay within the lava floor of the cavern. The ancient temple of the stone-tool people was incorporated into the complex construction of the Sacred Temple of Asa. Here, the high priestess resided and the Sacred Temple served as the center of worship of the goddess Asa.

Following the same route the Equestrian Guard had for hundreds of years, the riders turned off the Emperor's Highway and onto the Ravenbourne Road, toward the Ravenbourne Villa and the Twin Peaks. Maintaining a loping gait, they passed enormous trees, which had been planted by the first Lord of Ravenbourne. Suddenly, to Captain Aaragon's surprise, Lord Ravenbourne slowed his mount to a walking gait. Raising his hand, Aaragon slowed the small column of twenty-three.

A short distance north of the road, a small group of carefree boys were swimming and playing in a warm pool, their clothes hanging from low tree limbs. They had been hunting, as their slings hung adjacent their clothing, along with several quail and rabbits. A campfire burned nearby, waiting to roast the game the boys killed in this day's hunt.

"On occasion, I would enjoy being a boy again, Aaragon," said Lord Ravenbourne, turning to the captain of his guard, then back to the group of laughing youngsters. "Look at them at play, no cares or worries. They have no past and no future—no empire to defend. Only the joy of youth and the fun of today, hunting small game and swimming in a warm pool. I wish I could join them but for a single day, perhaps just one afternoon. Do you ever ponder such thoughts, Captain?"

"On occasion, Sir," answered Captain Aaragon. "I will wish I could return to a certain event in my youth and change it—thus the outcome. I suppose we all do, Sir. I recall my grandfather often spoke of his youth in his waning years."

"You must be correct, Aaragon." Looking back over his shoulder at the group of playful boys, Lord Ravenbourne smiled. "Well, we don't have an empire to save today. At least that we know of." He eased his mount into a canter gait, heading toward the Main Gate of Ravenbourne.

Wild tea-rose flourished along the outer wall of the villa, especially at the Main Gate. The delightful, aromatic sent filled the air and was carried far on the gentle breezes from the ocean. Approaching the Main Gate, the guards sounded three loud horn blasts to announce the arrival of the Ravenbourne Lord, who again slowed the mounted column to a walk.

"I would be pleased if they didn't blast those damn horns and we could ride through the gates in peace," complained Lord Ravenbourne, wiping the sweat from his face and greying hair.

"I understand it is a long tradition, my Lord," remarked Aaragon.

"Yes, it certainly is. My arrogant grandfather initiated that traditional nuisance," Lord Ravenbourne replied, once more wiping sweat from his face and hair.

The Lord of Ravenbourne seldom wore his helmet. If he were leading a charge in battle, he certainly would. Buy at this moment, he was not sure of the location of his helmet. A teenage recruit would certainly feel the sting of a strap if he were to misplace his helmet. He laughed to himself.

The guards saluted as the Equestrian Guard rode through the massive black lava tube that formed the Main Gate entry and passed through the gates constructed of tall, wooden beams. Lord Ravenbourne returned the salutes, as did the officers and the First Sergeant.

Continuing, the mounted guards rode past a stone monument and sculpture of a warrior. The inhabitants and visitors throughout the villa grounds, who were gathered along the road, paid homage to the passing lord with a bow or a salute. There was no law or order to do so, but the people did, out of respect. A respect that SolY'Sloic had earned as a gallant warrior since his days as a young lieutenant and a life of generosity.

The mounted Ravenbourne Warriors returned the homage with greetings, smiles, waves, and salutes. They enjoyed the prestige the Equestrian Guard offered them, especially from the female population, slave and free alike.

"I'm not certain, Captain, if those girls are blowing kisses to you or to me," jested Lieutenant Rohan, riding side by side with Captain Aaragon.

"I'm confident it is me, Rohan," answered Aaragon. "Although I suspect Sergeant Twilsua remains under the delusion that it is him."

Not hearing the officers' conversation, First Sergeant Twilsua turned, spit, and wiped his face as best he could, hidden under his helmet. Both warriors laughed out loud as they continued to catch kisses from villa girls, kiss their own hands, and thus return the kisses to the young senders. The column stopped at the bottom of the steps leading to the portal entrance, lined with tall stone columns, and the main door of Lady Ravenbourne's sanctuary. Dismounting, Lord Ravenbourne took several steps before he stopped, turned, and addressed his mounted guard.

"Ravenbourne Warriors! Take three days of enjoyment. I can tell you with some certainty that pallakes from Opar have come to Ravenbourne. Women of Opar have long held the reputation as being the most beautiful women in the known world. I am confident that many of you, if not all, will confirm or refute that reputation. Dismissed!"

Lord Ravenbourne saluted his guard, who returned his salute with a one-word, unison shout and raised their spears high. Turning, he climbed the steps of the portal entrance leading to the sanctuary gate. The mounted guard reined their horses and followed Captain Aaragon to the headquarters of the Equestrian Corps. As their lord approached the sanctuary doors, the guards called out and acknowledged Lord Ravenbourne, saluted him, and opened the doors. The only man across the whole Achaean Empire who could enter the all-female sanctuary of Lady Ravenbourne, now did so.

The first female the lord of the villa met, walking across the open entry hall, was a slave-girl, who called out his name, as loud as she could, in the manner she had been taught and quickly fell to her knees. He approached, touching the side of her face. Humbly, she took his leg in both hands, laying her forehead on his knee.

Calls and loud cries suddenly echoed throughout the sanctuary, prompting all the female inhabitants to disregard what they were doing and run to greet their lord. Soon, Lord Ravenbourne was surrounded by a multitude of females, young and old, free and slave, all eager to touch and kiss him—those who were so bold. He stood surrounded by his harem.

He greeted and touched as many as he could. All were delighted, laughing and smiling, saying "my Lord," if he might gently lay a hand on them. Unexpectedly, a strange silence suddenly fell across the entry hall, and the wave of females parted, creating a path. At the end of the path stood Ann Y'Sloic, Lady of Ravenbourne.

Ginal stood behind her, on one side, and Old Nanny on the other. Her three handmaidens lined up behind her. Smiling, his face aglow, Lord Ravenbourne walked toward his Lady. She returned his smile, watching his approach.

The youthful enthusiasm of the three handmaidens could not be contained. They ran to Lord Ravenbourne, falling on their knees in front of him. He quickly touched each pretty face without speaking and continued to walk toward Ann.

Warm tears began to fill the eyes of Lady Ravenbourne. Seemingly, she cried and laughed at the same moment, something only women can do. Unable to restrain herself any longer, she ran to him, throwing her arms around him—embracing him, kissing him—as though she would not release him.

Taking the sides of Ann's beautiful face, Sol kissed her tenderly. The kiss ended, and she melted in his arms. He swept her off her feet and carried his Lady, as though a new bride, across the entry hall, through a wide hallway, and up elaborately decorated steps. Finally, he took her through a pair of large wooden doors.

Ann's small entourage slowly followed, as did the whole female crowd, until Ginal stopped. She turned, facing the excited females, and held up her hand. "Our Lord and Lady have this night alone. Tomorrow, he will see as many of you as he can."

Ginal walked to the massive doors and pulled them shut, first one, then the other. She stepped back to the female crowd, who remained gathered in the hall. "Return to your duties," she ordered. "This will be a good evening for prayers and bathing at the Goddess Pool. I encourage all of you to do so." The females slowly dispersed but remained enthusiastic.

Taking Kasena and Malia by the back of their necks on either side of her, Ginal began to escort the two naked handmaidens across the entry hall. "It would seem that you two young beauties will be sleeping with me tonight." Bending slightly forward, they looked across Ginal's Ravenbourne Warrior tunic, smiling at each other. They each stood up on bare toes, playing a game, and gave her a quick caress on each side of her face with their lips.

"Let us wonder over and find out what feast our cooks have prepared tonight," asserted Ginal, keeping her hands on the back of the neck of each young beauty. She walked toward the kitchens. Old Nanny took Aleah by the hand and followed along.

In their private bedroom, the Lord and Lady of the renowned ancient villa, Sol and Ann Y'Sloic, sat comfortably against the headboard of their elegant bed, large enough to sleep seven or more. The four carved bedposts and wide headboard with detailed relief sculptures of wild horses formed the bed's foundation. Leaning against each other, they looked out through the balcony toward the sacred Ravenbourne Bay and the beautiful Outer Ocean.

The first Lord of Ravenbourne had constructed this area of the sanctuary, offering a wonderful view of the ocean, for defense rather than aesthetics, but it served Lady Ravenbourne well. Each evening, she could watch the sun, and the moon, when she cooperated, set in her sacred bay, painting the sky in lovely shades of pink. Every dawn, the breathtaking beauty was repeated as the sun rose over the Twin Peaks of the goddess to cast its color once more across the ocean.

"It's wonderful to have you back, my love," whispered Ann to her lover snuggling against him, under his arm. "I miss you very much. You're away more than you need be."

"I miss you, too, my sweet," replied Sol. Then placing his lips to her ear, he whispered. "This is an important period. The Emperor carries anxieties concerning the new deep water port at Starfall, and you know I'm increasing the size of the Southern Army Cavalry."

Slowly reaching up, Ann delicately brushed his greying hair over his ear. "The commanders of the Engineer Corps and your cavalry could take care of a considerable amount of that responsibility."

He did not answer but offered a light kiss. Taking the sides of his chin with her slender fingertips, Ann smiled after their lips parted. She would move to a simpler discussion.

"How fares Lisabeth Y'Liory these lonely days?" she asked in the tone of a tartly gibe.

"She has a Nefarian," responded Sol with a boyish grin.

"A Nefarian?" retorted Ann in surprise. She lightly laughed. "I react in astonishment, but I shouldn't be surprised." She titled her head to one side. "Need I ask if you slept with her, my sweet?"

"Of course, I did," answered Sol, maintaining a youthful smile. "She was offered, and I accepted."

"Well, now I'm jealous," remarked Ann. "And look at you—teenage boy with a mischievous smirk. I would enjoy owning a Nefarian."

A quiet pause ensued, and they smiled at each other. Ann remained more than delighted to have him back; nonetheless, her expression slowly turned more serious.

"I do not trust Lady Y'Liory, Sol . . . neither should you. Her husband mysteriously dies overnight in bed." Ann swallowed hard, taking a deep breath.

"I know you were dear friends with her husband, my love. But aside from her beauty and wit, there is a hint of evil in her, Sol. And I also do not trust her and her father's long connections with the Frisian king and his son."

"I similarly remain cautious, Ann. I do not completely trust her. I never have."

Ann was satisfied with that statement. "How long can you stay, my sweet?" she asked in a soft, dulcet voice.

"Only a few days. I promised the governor, I would accompany him to the Feohtan fights in the Great Arena, and . . . I must make a report to the Emperor."

"Please tell me you are not going to journey to the Capital City."

"No, I'm not," responded Sol, punctuating each important word. "I'll send a written report."

"Please promise me . . ." Ann paused to ensure he was completely hers. "When you are confident enough to leave some responsibility with the capable men under your command, you will return and spend several . . . if not many, days . . . here at Ravenbourne. And, that you will be present during the Hundred Year Celebration."

Sol had never broken a promise to her. At least, any that she knew of.

"The first I can promise. But I cannot say I will be here during the hundred-year pilgrimage."

Smiling, Ann leaned into him with an affectionate kiss of thanks. After they slowly parted, she thought to herself.

It will be wonderful having him here with me for an extended period. But now I have more to ask and I must not press him.

"Sol." She paused deliberately. "The Priestess continues to worry. Two of the seven Daughters of the Goddess remain unknown. Are you sure, my love, that you cannot offer some hope to her?"

Sol responded with calm reassurance. "I am certain, my sweet. I have no recollection of a sexual encounter with a woman of Opar or of K'semay."

"You journeyed to the far north during the fall of K'semay. There must have been many K'semay pallakes?" asked Ann.

"Yes, most certainly. And even though the conquering of K'semay was different than the fall of Opar, slave-women were abundant—many bought and sold—and I accepted the hospitality of Northwestern lords. Nonetheless, I have no recollection of sexual encounters with either. I have journeyed to Opar with my father when I was a youngster, but I have never visited the fallen city as an adult. I have no more to offer, Ann." He hesitated, momentarily then asked.

"Does the Priestess believe there are always seven daughters for each century? Perhaps there is but five."

"I'm afraid, she does not know," replied Ann. "The Books of the Temple are vague. Only this new Century of the Raven seems to be exact. The Ancient Priestess with no name stated there were seven daughters in the last century. She is the last remaining daughter of the concluding Century of the Dragon." She looked at Sol with a smile.

"Sired by your grandfather."

Sol broke into light laugher. "Arrogant old man, my grandfather. He said they were lovers all along, once she came of age. He relished the taste of her virginity."

He paused, looking at his wife. "Well, my love. If it is important, will not the goddess Asa reveal an answer?"

"Yes, my Lord. You must be correct," responded the Lady of Ravenbourne. Leaning into him, she offered her husband a slight yet tender kiss. Smiling, she whispered into his ear.

"Tell me about the Nefarian."

Chuckling, Sol responded, "Gladly, my sweet." Ann began to take gentle, small bites, just behind Sol's ear.

Rising from her elegant bed, Ann Y'Sloic gracefully swung her auburn hair, allowing her to wrap a thin blanket over her shoulders. Touching the back of her knees, her amazing hair had never been cut throughout her life—only the ends trimmed. It now required her three handmaidens to care for it. She wondered what would occur if she had it cut. Smiling to herself, she knew what her father and Old Nanny would do while her mother waited anxiously in the hall. She pondered. *What would my Lord do?*

She walked out onto the balcony. The moon and the sunlight were just falling on the ocean, another still, beautiful morning. She whispered a prayer to Asa, thanking her for another day. She watched the Equestrian Guard, in a perfect file, ride toward the Main Gate, her Lord in the lead. The air quiet and still, she could easily hear the horses' hooves on the flagstone road.

"Soldiers were always so busy, even early in the morning," she whispered to herself. The Ravenbourne Warriors disappeared through the gate.

Clutching the blanket at her neck, she whispered another prayer. "Asa, goddess of Ravenbourne. Please, bring him back to me."

Turning, she now quickly returned to her bedroom. So much to do and many questions remained unanswered. A single day could not be wasted.

CHAPTER 18

Kaelin: Arena Fight

Patrons of the fighting arenas throughout the Empire could experience many varieties of combat, death, and blood, including—military-like armored Feohtans facing off with sword and shield, in groups or in pairs; mounted warriors with armor and without; and groups of armored men in a melee battle, with the last lucky one standing, the winner.

The favorite crowded-pleasing spectacle of the Great Arena of Cappa, however, was a simple duel between two warriors without the protection of armor. In fact, each stood nearly naked, clothed only in a girded loincloth, and armed merely with a throwing spear and short dagger, held in a leather scabbard tied about the waist. Women were especially enthralled with this naked, bloody, and lethal combat. Usually, only one duo of Feohtans fought, with the pair given the whole arena as a combat stage.

Commonly, the combatants faced each other, separated by some thirty to forty paces. When the signal was given, combat began. Neither the anticipating crowd nor the combatants knew exactly what to expect, as each individual pugilist was afforded several options.

A fighter could run straight toward his opponent in a sudden attack, hoping to catch him off guard and quickly dispatch him with a lethal plunge or a blow. On the contrary, a combatant could run away from his adversary, thus hoping to gain an advantage in so doing. Conversely, he might choose to do nothing but remain still. Once silence fell upon the crowd, he might cast his spear, looking to claim an easy victory if the throw was true, or, once the spear was thrown, charge his rival with a drawn dagger and a blood-curdling scream, intending to shock or confuse a novice combatant. The fighters might also walk to each other and fight with lunges and blows, although a kill made by a throw of the spear was favored by the crowd.

Kaelin prepared for the impending struggle. He preferred some activity rather than just sitting and waiting. He finished the bread and beer, emptied his bowels and bladder, and washed. He was not sure why he bothered to wash, but he did. After securing his loin-cloth, he began some stretching exercises, as though preparing for an athletic contest. A strange feeling fell over him, prompting him to look up.

He was surprised to see the Sergeant of the Guard from yesterday standing at his cell door. He had not heard him approach. Unexpectedly, the guard spoke.

"You are wise to limber up before your contest, young fighter. What is your name?" Kaelin answered.

"Although you're young in age, Kaelin, I recognize a battle-hardened warrior. I have a good feeling about you, Kaelin. I think I'll make a wager on your successful outcome."

Kaelin smirked. "I hope I don't disappoint you, lightening your purse with my death."

The old Sergeant laughed out loud while he opened the cell door. Kaelin proceeded past the Sergeant, who put his hand on Kaelin's chest, causing him to pause.

"As in battle, Kaelin, fear is often the killer."

Kaelin understood, nodded, and stepped to stand in the hall. The guard opened the doors to the other cells, and the file of warriors from the Heart Blood College paced down the hallway. Led by the Sergeant, with Kaelin near the front, the Feohtans made their way along the stone corridors and halls, into a wide-open armory.

All the spearmen duel fighters from one college were together, forming a line. They would not fight each other but would be matched against the Feohtans of a different college. Kaelin thought of his large, hairy friend, Ox. Although large and strong and certainly fearless, Ox was too slow and not agile enough to be a spearman fighter. He was more suited to heavy shield and sword combat and thus separated to train in the sword and shield section. Kaelin hoped he did not ever meet Ox in the arena, although they each shook hands and swore not to hold back if they were ever pitted against each other. To do so would be death for them both. They would fight to kill each other, then meet again as friends on the other side.

Ahead of them walked a row of spearmen fighters from another college. One of them turned around, allowing Kaelin to notice the fighter bore a red, fist-size circle, marked on the right upper front of his chest. Presuming the mark identified his college, Kaelin chuckled to himself. *Perhaps the circle provides a target.*

Casually, without drawing attention to himself, Kaelin managed to look behind, noting there were only two files of spearmen duel fighters, a file from his college and one from another.

Erect guards stood at various locations along the route, with several posted in the armory. One guard, positioned behind a huge, hand-hewn wooden table in front of a wall, was handing out weapons. Behind him, attached to the wall and stacked on the floor, lay a vast assortment of weapons and armor. Kaelin noted a row of spears leaning against the wall were fixed with dull, unpolished points but also held clear, sharp cutting edges. As the line of spearmen duel fighters proceeded past the table, the guard handed each a spear and a dagger, inserted into a leather sheath attached to a length of rope. One of the fighters near the end of the college file in front of Kaelin stopped when the guard handed him a spear and dagger. He was a large man, muscular and powerful. His head was shaved, except for a long tendril of black hair left on the crest of his head, which was tied with some small ornament and knotted at the end.

He pointed toward the wall and growled, "That one!"

"Fokken me dead, Lood," responded the guard. "Makes no difference; all the same. All army weapons, daggers and spears."

Again, Lood barked out, only louder, "That one!"

The guard laughed out loud, then looked around the room, wearing an alacritous grin. "Lood here, from the Moon Blood College, killed many goddess damn opponents in spearmen duel contests!" The enthusiastic guard called out loudly to address the room full of men.

"Has his favorite spear! I like to test his memory. What the hell, Lood, I'll give you your fokken man-killer."

The guard turned and walked to the wall. He removed a spear and, returning to the table, handed it to Lood, who took the spear, grunted, and moved on. Kaelin presumed the grunt was some sort of thanks.

The guard waved his hand, barking out in a disgruntled voice, now that his moment of levity had passed, "Move on! Move on! This is a weapons issue, not a fokken bitch market."

Slow, deliberately, each man took his weapons. The files of fighters continued on through other hallways and passages, finally entering the corridor that led to the open Great Arena.

Two large wooden doors, with barred windows fixed in the center, blocked the corridor to the arena but allowed bright sunlight to strike the corridor floor. The metal bars in the windows cast the same strange shadow pattern Kaelin had noticed on his cell floor. The light seemed to beckon—convoke—calling them to their deaths. An armored guard, stood on each side of the doors. A third man stood in the center.

He was dressed in some type of official "dress of the state," but it was not a military uniform or armor. Kaelin had noticed other men dressed in the same manner. This one was middle-aged, unsympathetic in manner, and held a carved, wooden crozier.

The long role of nearly naked Feohtans now broke, forming two separate files as they lined up on each side of the corridor. The men from Kaelin's Heart Blood College stood on one side, and those from Moon Blood on the other, each with a red circle painted on his chest. Low wooden benches lined the walls. Before they sat down, the men tied the daggers around their waists—many examining their spears. Finally, they all sat with spears in front of them, both hands grasping the shaft. Kaelin did likewise. The man in the state uniform cleared his throat and spoke out in a loud, rough voice.

"Listen to me! It does not matter who your opponent is, just so you are not from the same college. The crowd enjoys watching one college challenge another. You will follow me, a pair at a time, side by side, out into the arena. I will escort you to the front of the governor's dais. It does not matter if the dais is occupied or not. I will announce your name and college. As I do, you will raise your spears in salute to the dais. The crowd will cheer, and you will follow me to a spot in the arena. We will stop. You will turn and face each other. On my command, you will back up until I order you to stop. I will raise my staff. Watch it carefully. The clarions will trumpet in a single blast. The crowd will roar. Next, silence will fall. I will lower my staff. You will begin your fight. If you break the rules or if you are a coward, refusing to fight, you will be executed in the arena." The official stopped and looked up and down the two rows of seated men with a stern expression, absent any pity. He then continued.

"Subsequent your contest, if you have the wherewithal, it is prudent to return to the governor's dais and salute. The aristocratic occupants of the dais have the wealth and power to set you free or have you executed, including the women. Keep that in mind. Finally, make your way toward the pink Kunt Gate and pass through, where you will be reborn." The state arena official spoke with a strange, hypnotic yet commanding voice. The Feohtans sat in silence, listening. The official paused and began again.

"Most of you will die. At least do so with honor and dignity. Your courage and skill will bring a little pleasure to the crowd and to those in the dais, which in turn will bring honor and wealth to your college. Victory over your opponent is your only path to freedom."

Outside, a blast of the clarions echoed throughout the Great Arena, followed by an uproar of the crowd—both summoned the fighters. The state official looked at the first seated man on his left.

"Stand!" he ordered. The man responded.

He looked to his right, repeating his order. Again, the seated Feohtan rose quickly, in a smart, military fashion.

Once more looking to his left, the official called out an order, "Name and college!"

The fighter spoke out, answering in a clear voice, but not a shout.

The man in official attire now looked to the fighter on his right, issuing the same order. The Feohtan answered in a loud, military bark. The state official looked pleased.

The two guards opened the massive doors, allowing light to fill the corridor. Once again, light invited them to their deaths. The two Feohtans followed the state official out into the arena, to meet their fate. The guards closed the doors behind them.

Each man sat quietly, alone with his own thoughts. What did they ponder? Did they consider all the things they wished they had accomplished before now? Did they desire one last final something—now too late? Did they think of that one beautiful girl they wished they could have, or should have, carried naked to bed? Or the one beautiful girl they wished they could have caressed again, just once more? Was there someone they wished they could have seen and talked with before this day?

All the Feohtans sitting on the benches could hear numerous roars from the crowd during the high points of each contest. Finally, there was a singular roar that somehow seemed different. Kaelin could not explain it. He was not sure how that roar was different from the others, nonetheless, it was. He knew, as did the others, the fight was over, and one of the Feohtans had been killed.

The state arena official returned to the entry gate. He escorted the next two Feohtan spearmen out into the arena. This would continue until the final pair had gone out into the open stadium to meet their fate.

Finally next in the file, Kaelin and the man opposite him stood. They did not need to be ordered to report.

"Kaelin, Heart Blood College!"

"Lood, Moon Blood College!"

The two near-naked warriors stood in stark contrast to the royally attired arena official as they followed him out of the gate and across the arena floor, toward the dais.

When the crowd recognized Lood, they began to applaud and cheer the popular spearman. Lood responded. The experienced performer raised his arms to the throngs, turning around and walking backward to show his face to the whole arena crowd.

Kaelin noticed the arena floor was covered with coarse sand, presumably to soak up the blood and eliminate dust. The trio walked on. Kaelin also noticed blood spots on the sand. They stopped in front of the dais, following all the protocols. The crowd roared when the arena official announced Lood's name and conversely, offered mild applause when Kaelin was announced.

Separated by approximately twenty paces, Kaelin and Lood faced each other while the arena official stood poised, his crozier held high in the air. The clarions blasted, and the whole crowd lifted in a vociferous roar. The Sergeant of the Guard back at the holding cells was right; the noise reminded Kaelin of the bellows of war. The crowd slowly hushed to an eerie silence—a strange, dreamlike stillness. The arena official dropped his staff, giving the signal to fight.

Kaelin thought he could hear each attendee packed into the Great Arena breathing—all of them breathing in unison, as though they were the immense inhalation of a god or goddess. Unexpectedly, he felt a refreshing, gentle wind, soft and cool, which might have blown across a wide, still river. Mystically, still unexplained, within the wind, he heard the same soft female voice that he had heard on the battlefield and the slave march.

"Courage, Kaelin, courage my young love," the gentle female voice whispered.

Kaelin watched Lood, his skilled opponent, who remained perfectly still, staring at him as though he might somehow overcome him with an evil look. The red circle on his chest glistened with sweat.

Suddenly, without warning or little wasted motion, Lood cast his spear with deadly skill and accuracy. The sturdy wooden staff, hafted with a lethal bronze projectile, flew toward Kaelin in a streak of silent death—the point flashed in the bright sunlight. Kaelin's eyes had closely followed Lood's every motion. At just the right moment, Kaelin turned to the side from the waist up, his eyes never leaving his opponent. The deadly spear missed its mark, flying past and across his chest. Kaelin felt the path of the spear, and in a flash, he thought the bronze-tipped javelin may have left a cut. There was no opportunity to consider a flesh wound.

The same instant that Lood hurled his spear, he drew his dagger and charged Kaelin, screaming the loudest bellows he could muster. His distorted face grimaced, as if filled with pain and agony. Clever Lood did not charge in a straight path but rather a small, serpentine pattern. Perhaps because of Kaelin's age, Lood was hoping to confuse or startle what he believed to be an inexperienced opponent. Poor, ignorant Lood did not realize he faced a veteran warrior of Opar. Opar soldiers are never confused or startled in battle.

Without hesitation, Kaelin readied his spear. His throw was aimed to match Lood's meandering charge. He cast true; his spear flew with the flashing speed of a lightning bolt. In less than a blink of an eye, the bronze point sank high into Lood's stomach, just below his chest, stopping him in his tracks.

Lood bared his teeth in a rictus of pain, gasping while gurgled blood spewed from his opened mouth, as if he were vomiting. He stared at Kaelin with an expression of incredulity. His dagger fell to the ground. He gripped the spear shaft that impaled him with both hands, dropping to his knees. Lood took one final look at his executioner, wearing a lurid expression of disbelief. Falling forward, the end of the spear shaft struck the ground—momentarily holding him up—and then his momentum carried him to the ground on his shoulder. Even though the bronze spear tip protruded out of the middle of Lood's back, when he hit the ground, he rolled over onto his back. His legs violently kicked, and his whole body convulsed in a spasmodic rhythm. Abruptly, his arms released their grip on the spear shaft and fell motionless at his side, while the heels of his sandals dug into the coarse sand. The arena remained still, quiet, while Lood lay dying and the sand soaked up his life's blood.

Kaelin did not hesitate. Quickly, he drew his dagger and ran to the side of his fallen foe. He knelt, grasping the topknot on Lood's head, and with one fatal swipe, cut his throat with the dagger. He, too, would play the actor, giving the crowd what it wanted—more blood—and it spurted from Lood's gaping neck wound. Kaelin moved his arms, allowing the spraying blood to saturate his arms and chest. He pulled the topknot toward him, lifting Lood's head off the sandy ground, and reached up with his dagger, cutting the topknot ornament off Lood's head. When he did, Lood's head fell back down on the sand, with blood still flowing from the cut in his throat. Kaelin paused momentarily to glance at Lood's distorted face, his bloody mouth and staring eyes, wide open. He felt no sympathy.

Kaelin now stood up with raised arms, gripping his dagger in his right hand and dead Lood's topknot in his left. He yelled to the crowd as loud as he could. The throngs responded with a cheering uproar. They were pleased because he had satisfied their sanguinary bloodlust. He now walked toward the governor's dais, stopping close in front of it. Again, he raised his arms, allowing the thick, crimson blood to run down his forearms and onto his shoulders, then drip off his elbows into the coarse sand. He did not know or care who was in the aristocrat box, but several of the men in the dais entourage stood and applauded.

Still playing the actor, Kaelin threw his dagger, sticking it into the ground. He held up his arms, the palms of his hands up. He wanted to be sure the men in the dais saw that he had no weapon, only the strand of Lood's topknot, now wet and heavy with blood and sweat. In a side-arm movement, he threw the black tendril of hair up and into the dais. Several of the men scurried to retrieve the bloody memento.

Kaelin raised his arms again in a final gesture, provoking another roar from the crowd. He looked around and easily recognized the pink-colored exit, and walked off toward the Kunt Gate. The exodus gate from the arena was called the "Kunt Gate" because of its resemblance to a female vulva. Two rough-hewn wooden doors were rounded on the outside, where each hinged to the opening in the wall, and straight on the inside, met in the middle, forming a dark, perpendicular line shadow. The doors were painted pink. Above the doors, the cross plank and the wall were painted to resemble a woman's pubic hair.

He was not pleased he had killed a man for blood sport, but neither was he remorseful. He was simply glad he was not killed or wounded. The Master of the college may have been speaking the truth. Perhaps success in the arena opened the path to freedom.

CHAPTER 19

Calea: Pallake Discipline

THE VILLA PROVIDED A PERFECT headquarters for Master Smyth and his risky yet lucrative enterprise. Spared from looting, the comfortable villa remained intact and well stocked with food, wine, beer, and water to include clothing and a bathing pool. There were also several servants: four kitchen servants; one kitchen boy; three bed-slaves; and a nanny. Too frightened to leave, the females and the boy had remained, uncertain of their fate, providing Master Smyth with cooks and labor, a nanny, and three pretty pallakes to cool the flames of his soldiers. He learned there had also been male-slaves, but they were more courageous and had fled.

With the addition of the score of females taken from the plaza adjacent to the Talcrane villa, Master Smyth now owned a sufficient slave labor force to keep his operation productive, including Old Nanny and Nanny Talcrane. Calea's knowledge of the wealthy-owned villas, estates, and manors throughout Opar remained invaluable. Every morning, Calea led Master Smyth and his guard escort through fallen Opar to areas where beautiful, healthy virgins might be located. It did not take long to acquire the desired number of thirteen.

Each evening, after most of the household retired, Master Smyth lounged by a fire, sipping wine, and tasting sweet delicacies. Usually, a pallake beauty slept on his lap, giving him a pleasantry to pet. He was also pleased to have Calea and Nanny Talcrane attending him.

197

"Calea," he proffered, although not asking, "tell me more of Mysia."

"Glady, my Master. Mysia was an important subject during the education of Lord Philemon's offspring, to include your humble servant. This is what I recall."

"Over a century ago, the Empire conquered the small, coastal country of Mysia. A treaty was signed. It stands today. Mysia has no army, but a national police force patrols the country. Mysia pays its taxes, provides men for the Imperial Army, and remains at peace. There was once a Mysia language, now nearly dead. A few pockets still speak the language, especially in small farming communities. Mysia is a beautiful country. Cos, the only major city, is equally beautiful. The people are generous, content, and enjoy a good celebration."

"Interesting, Calea. I have been told that the slave market in Mysia might be profitable. I may investigate that aspect in the future."

"It could be a wise decision, Master. My Lord Philemon purchased two Mysia slaves to be mothers of his offspring. I recall each virgin girl, beautiful and fertile."

Calea briskly clapped her hands twice. The distinctive sound of the non-verbal gesture prompted her covey of thirteen virgin charges to quietly, but quickly scurry, forming a single line in front of her. People of the Achaean Empire were often superstitious concerning numbers. Master Smyth believed the number thirteen would bring him luck, and a smile from the goddess, on his risky enterprise.

The thirteen barefoot maidens were dressed in a breast cloth, an undergarment, and a cloth frock-skirt tied around every narrow waist. Their bottoms bounced and their long hair was tossed about the scampering beauties. Within a common household, normally, a slave's hair was cropped short, but the locks of these slave-girls, destined for the

Royal Family, would remain long—brushed and combed daily into a single horse-tail and tied at the back. Additionally, long strands of hair on the side of each pretty head were braided and fell past their shoulders. Their hair was carefully prepared to present an athletic appearance. A permanent chain of small bronze links was secured loosely around every right ankle, with an attached small plate to identify Master Smyth and the Regal House as the youthful pallakes' owners. The tinkling of the chain and the padding of bare feet on the stone floor echoed a unique, strangely pleasing sound.

Each girl stood silent, at attention, in the manner they had been trained to do—their feet a shoulders-width apart, the palms of their hands laid on the side of their thighs, their heads bowed. Old Nanny and Nanny Talcrane stood adjacent to Calea.

Master Smyth sat nearby, sipping morning wine, pleased with what he saw. Each unblemished, white, virgin behind would garner him a small fortune. He was not naïve enough to count his gold just yet, but he was on the road to becoming a very wealthy man. He smiled to himself. Although he understood little of the Opar language, he knew what was to follow.

"Two of you have been very disobedient!" Calea spoke in her stern-mistress voice. "And you will suffer the consequences for your errant behavior." There was a short, silent pause.

"Elana!" barked out Calea, with the voice of a crusty first sergeant.

Elana quickly scampered out to stand in the same submissive manner in front of her mistress. "Remove your clothes for punishment, and hand them to Old Nanny!" ordered Calea.

Sobbing with tightened lips, the now-respectful slave-girl reached back over her shoulder, untied her breast cloth, and handed it to Old Nanny, herself dressed in a long, plain, dull frock. Next, Elana removed her cloth frock-skirt, followed by her undergarments, handing both to Old Nanny. She maintained her acquiescent posture, nude.

An old, well-worn leather belt was secured around Old Nanny's waist. Calea snapped her fingers. Nanny pulled a length of small cord from her belt, handing it to Calea.

"Hold out your right hand, Elana," directed Calea. Elana complied.

One end of the cord was tied with a noose, and Calea slid the noose over Elana's thumb. She then pulled the cord back under the girl's hand and wrapped it around her fingers. Next, she grasped the end of Elana's fingers with her left hand and slightly bent them back. Elana's thumb was now held securely to the side of her hand while her palm was helplessly exposed. Calea held out her right hand.

With Elana's clothes draped over her arm, Old Nanny now took a strange implement from her belt and handed it to Calea. The simple contrivance was a leather strap secured into an ivory dagger like handle, with a total length about that of a man's forearm, from elbow to wrist. The smooth, thin leather strap was nearly one-half a cubit in length and two fingers wide. The end of the strap was cut, rounded into the shape of a human tongue.

Taking a strong grip on the implement's handle, Calea raised it head-high, then brought the strap down briskly across Elana's soft, uncalloused palm. Elana's face grimaced with the sting, and she closed her eyes. Following three or four hard licks, her palm reddened, causing her to cry and squirm.

After ten hard licks, Calea halted and looked into Elana's face. She was crying hard. Wet tears ran down her red cheeks and onto her neck. "Have you learned a lesson, young, pretty pallake?" asked Calea in her ever-firm voice.

"Yes, Mistress! Yes! Please, no more!" pleaded the sobbing girl.

Calea tucked the ivory handle into her own belt and untied the cord—but she was not yet finished. "Hold out your other hand!" she ordered.

"No, Mistress, please don't. I've learned my lesson."

"Other hand!" demanded a stern Calea.

The distressed Elana obeyed and continued to weep. Calea secured the cord—grasped the hapless girl's finger tips—and lifted the strap from her belt. She delivered another ten solid licks while poor Elana continued her desperate crying. The palm of her hand burned red.

Calea stopped. Again, she fit the strap handle into her belt and untied the cord. She pointed and bayed out another command. "To the corner!" The naked Elana scampered to a corner, holding her punished hands in a tight fist. There she would stand, facing the walls, until Calea had decided she had truly learned a lesson.

Each corner of the room was cleared of furniture and thus utilized as a punishment corner. A wide ceramic krater set in each corner would catch a punished pallake's urine, if necessary. Most punished girls who were forced to corner-stand for at least a turn of the hour glass would need to squat and urinate, adding to their humiliation.

"Felia!" called out Calea. The second nervous girl left her place in the pallake line, sniveling and shaking. She had just cause. The stern penalty was repeated, and soon a crying Felia stood in a corner, rubbing her red, inflamed hands together, hoping to lessen the sting.

Calea returned the tying cord to Old Nanny but slipped the ivory handle of the whipping strap into her own braided belt. She then addressed her remaining row of beauties. "The rest of you may run to the pool and play, swim, and talk. You may touch and kiss, but only from the waist and up. Do you understand?"

"Yes, Mistress," replied all the girls in one voice.

"All right," continued Mistress Calea, "you may go. Nanny Talcrane and Old Nanny will be with you, watching you closely. Nanny Talcrane! You will periodically return, also keeping a sharp eye on these two in the punishment corners."

Nanny Talcrane nodded that she understood while the slave-girls scampered to the pool. The two nannies followed behind. Mistress

Calea walked to a small, tall table with a round, stone top. Taking an hour-glass from the top, she turned it over, setting it back on the table. The red-colored sand began to fall. She looked at the two whimpering beauties in the corners. One was stroking her hands along her thighs, and the other rubbed her hands together. After a distressing hour in the corner, she would have no more trouble from these two. She glanced over to Master Smyth. She had erotic plans for him. Elana and Felia may overhear some of the conversation with her Master but they would understand very little, if any, of the Achaean language. Besides, they were focused on their own difficult situation.

Now she walked to Master Smyth, who remained seated, eating cheese and sipping wine. He held out his hand. Calea withdrew the strap from her belt and took Master Smyth by his fingers. Delicately, she ran the strap tip across his palm, looking into his eyes, wearing a seductive smile. She placed the ivory handle into his palm, then pushed the palm of her hand against his. Master Smyth examined the instrument.

Stepping closer, Calea rubbed her Master's bare shoulders. "It is graciously referred to as the Maiden's Tongue in the Achaean language . . . is it not . . . my Master?"

"Yes, my beauty," he responded softly. "I've spent my whole adult life in the slave market, and yet I have not seen one of these in use. It seems to be very effective on maiden pallakes."

"I have experienced the reason and purpose of its name, *Maiden's Tongue*, my Master, but I have also witnessed its positive effects in other applications."

"Is that so, sweet one? Explain!"

Calea moved closer to Master Smyth's face, intending for him to smell her breath, while she talked. "On the Greenstone Estates, once the Maiden's Tongue has caressed the soft, small penis of a tender slave-boy—the appropriate number of licks—his errant behavior will be drastically altered. With a red face and tears, he will beg his master or mistress for the opportunity to prove his obedience rather than endure another single lick from that dreaded girl's leather tongue."

Chuckling, Master Smyth agreed, "Yes, I can see why that would be true."

Calea rubbed his fat shoulders and tenderly kissed his neck. She smelled him with her nose against his neck, loud enough so that he would know she had done so. His scent was not bad, but he also did not smell good. Not the sweet aroma of her lost husband and certainly not the honey taste of her husband's lips. She quickly put those thoughts aside. "Has the pallake discipline excited your loins . . . my Master?"

"It has. Watching you hand-spank two of my naked beauties has given me the desire for a fokken. But all your talk of slave-boy penis punishment has stirred my cherry desires. Better still, a hot little tea-rose such as yours, Mistress Calea," said Master Smyth giving her an order in a nonchalant manner.

Always maneuvering, sly Calea smiled and whispered, as if keeping a secret just between them. "I have discovered a small alabastron of hyacinth oil, my Master, in the former owner's bedroom. It would seem the previous house master, or his mistress, also had such urges. Imagine how expensive and difficult to obtain the hyacinth oil here in Opar."

Calea now enacted a calculated brief, quiet pause. She offered Master Smyth a sensual smile, then slowly moved, placing her mouth to his ear. She breathed her hot breath on the sensitive area then began to whisper once again.

"With the oil, my Master, your hard phallus will fill me more than ever before. If you allow me, I will be more memorable than any boy you have experienced—tighter by good measure."

Keeping her smile, Calea walked in front of her Master. She took his hand, gently lifting him off his chair. Reaching for the draw strings of her knee-length chiton, she pulled each one over her shoulder, allowing her top to fall to her waistbelt, exposing her breasts. She then reached up—placed her hands on the back of Master Smyth's head—gently pulling him to her bare breasts. He took her shoulders and kissed her breasts and nipples, then sucked her left nipple with heavy breathing and a soft, groaning sound. Calea leaned her head back while her Master continued to hold her shoulders.

When his moist mouth released her nipple, she turned and backed up to him, rubbing her buttocks against his thighs and looking back over her shoulder. Panting, she sighed soft female "Ohs" while she whimpered. Now, keeping his hand, she slowly led him to the master's bedroom, moving her behind in such a manner that no man could resist watching, or in Master Smyth's circumstances . . . following.

"Both of you, step out of the corner, leave your clothing, and run to the pool to join the others," ordered Mistress Calea, entering the central room of the villa. Quickly, the girls did as they were told, and scurried out of the room to the outside gardens and pool, delighted to at last be freed from the penalty corners.

Even though he was moderately small in terms of erection and testicles, Master Smyth had been rather aggressive, using her as he would a boy. The hyacinth oil had most certainly added to their sexual delight. Nonetheless, her nether orifice was sore, motivating her to gingerly make her way across the beautiful gardens to the pool.

Clapping her hands, Calea smiled to herself while she watched the girls scramble, resembling a covey of petite quail finding their places. They were falling into line, although Nanny Talcrane had to encourage one maiden, slow to respond, with a smart slap on the bottom. Calea walked up before her charges, who stood in their respected positions.

"Fall on your knees . . . look up at me . . . and listen carefully!" Calea waited momentarily, looking up and down the line of thirteen girls, who at first stood mystified but quickly obeyed. Once each one was still and looking up at her, she began in a calm, although serious, voice.

"All of us are slaves!" Calea paused, allowing this reality to touch their tender hearts. "Your mother, your sisters, your cousins, and your aunts. Every female of our once-great city will be taken from Opar and sold into slavery. The innocent babies they carried were ripped from their arms . . . killed . . . their little bodies were thrown into a deep ditch. I know you loved some of those helpless infants."

Calea stopped. Tears formed in the young eyes of her maidens. Truth can be a harsh teacher. She continued.

"In the Empire language, a female-slave taken in war is called a *pallake*. There are millions of us across the Empire. There are some male-slaves, but most Achaean Empire slaves are females of all ages. This is the heartbreaking reality we cannot escape." Calea paused, again allowing this painful truth to harden into fact. She continued, keeping a stern voice.

"Nearly all our men, brave warriors and defenders of Opar, have been killed. A few were taken as slaves to live a short, horrible life in stone quarries or mines. Unlike the women of the Achaean Empire, we of Opar do not worship the goddess Asa, although it is said she was born in Opar. Pray to the gods and goddess of Opar that the men of Opar, our warriors—men we loved—did not suffer, although we know, deep in our hearts, that many did, and others will. None of us are excluded. We all ride this harsh, bitter wind. I will mourn the death of my beloved husband and my loving son as long as I live."

"Know this acrimonious, heartbreaking truth. No warrior of Opar is coming to save us. Give thanks to Master Smyth that we, the very lucky few of us, have been chosen by him."

"The god of the sky, of the sun, of war and the goddess of the earth, of the moon, and of love—by their graces, you have been chosen because of your beauty and your health. But make no mistake, you were mostly chosen because you are a virgin, and your hymen remains intact." Calea paused once more, taking in a deep breath, allowing a silent moment to pass.

"Female-slaves of the Achaean Empire are punished by three humiliating practices that are said to be thousands of years old. First and foremost, their bare behinds are beaten by the palm of a man's hand or with a paddle by a woman. The Achaeans call it *spanking* in their language, and the victim is naked and embarrassingly exposed. Also, a leather strap is laid across their naked behinds. They call this a *thrashing* and the slave-girl is usually forced to bend over a pommel horse. More embracing is the harsh Achaean punishment of *figging*."

"A tall, beautiful green plant with bright-red flowers grows throughout the Empire. The root of this plant is harvested, fleshed, and shaped into an object the size and shape of a large man's middle finger. Once wet, it is inserted into a slave-girl's anus, usually after she has been spanked or thrashed. It creates a severe, painful burning sensation."

"After a spanking or thrashing, most female-slaves are gagged and forced to stand on a stool or low bench, placed against the wall, while they suffer a figging. This is to ensure that the rest of the household, especially other slaves, can see what happens to a disobedient slave-girl."

Calea stopped once more to take a short breath. All eyes remained focused on her.

"If not for Master Smyth, all of you most certainly would have been sold as a pallake, a bed-slave or a sex-slave, to a brothel. You would have been forced to have sex with vile, drunken men and forced to kiss them, take them in your mouth, pretending you enjoy doing it, or else suffer the punishments I just described. There would not be delicious food . . . . warm comfortable beds . . . . clean bathing pools in a filthy brothel. You would have lived a horrid, humiliating life. You would not stay young, healthy, or beautiful for very long, and you would know little, if any, happiness.

"Now! Each of you will run to our Master Smyth. Fall on your knees in front of him, and thank him for saving you from that horrible plight." She clapped her hands twice.

It is such a delightful sight and sound, watching thirteen naked maidens scurry across the garden, running in such a manner only young girls can, with the jingle of thirteen slave ankle bracelets, thought Master Smyth, who enjoyed watching and listening to his maidens.

He was walking from the master bed-chamber into the central room when his covey of virgins fell before him, each looking up and thanking him. Beautiful, sweet, young voices speaking the poetic Opar language. He smiled and touched each lovely face, knowing they all belonged to him. He was enjoying this propitious expedition more than any other. The often-heard legends that the women of Opar were blessed with goddess-like beauty, he could now confirm were true. He had never seen so many gorgeous females in one area before, and Calea was certainly worth her weight in gold or silver in more ways than one. But the expedition was, however, far from over, and the long, danger-ous trip from Opar to the Capital City loomed on the horizon. Until his maidens kneeled before the wife of the Emperor's son—before they were each declared *bona fide* virgins—before he held the gold in his hands . . . it was still just a vision . . . a dream . . . a dream yet too far. He knew he must maintain unfailing, auspicious vigilance.

CHAPTER 20

Kaelin: Lord Ravenbourne Saved

FEOHTAN FIGHTERS ENDURED: THEIR LIVES far from easy, but there was no comparison to the dismal existence of a quarry slave or any other male slave, for that matter and their reality was demonstrably better than that of most peasants. Kaelin enjoyed nutritious food, restful sleep, hard training, and occasional sex with a fairly attractive slave-girl. The fighters at the Heart Blood College who obeyed the law, did not attempt escape, and fought well in the arena were not disciplined. They also experienced modest appreciation from the crowd upon killing an opponent, especially if the kill was accomplished in some unusual variety or style, or if the slain Feohtan had managed to gain a reputation.

Master of the Heart Blood College provided his fighters with a feast to celebrate Kaelin's kill of Lood, including a day of rest. Surely, it was enjoyed as if they had attended an aristocratic symposium. Hetaera were hired to provide music, readings of erotic poems, and other expensive delights. Several slender whores were paid to provide sexual favors to the assembly of healthy men, augmenting the slave-girls owned by the Heart Blood College. At Kaelin's request, Coe was also allowed to join, and he ate and talked with Kaelin and Ox. The three friends were happily reunited for a brief period. Death in the arena, however, does not end.

Kaelin's next contest concluded with an easy kill. His opponent hailed from the Lion's Blood College: each of these fighters bore a red tattoo of a lion's paw on the right side of their chests. By reputation, they were lions and, oddly, did not cast their spears. Instead, they fought hand-to-hand.

With the drop of the arena official's crozier, Kaelin's adversary walked toward him with a cold stare of determination, his spear held in a thrusting position. Kaelin took up the same posture.

Staring face-to-face, the Lion's Blood opponent stopped—thrust his weapon toward Kaelin's chest wearing a disfigured face of hatred—and growled loudly, imitating a lion. Unfortunately, the Lion's Blood fighter was slow of reflex, not comparable at all to his namesake feline. Kaelin turned to his side, allowing the spearpoint to pass over his chest, and at that same instant, he thrust his spear into the throat of his hapless adversary. He fell hard to his back—dead when his shoulder blades hit the coarse arena sand.

Another unusual kill brought Kaelin a small notice from the aristocracy. Just as the contest began, his opponent surprisingly turned, running at full speed toward the wall. He then ran parallel to the wall and passed in front of the dais. It appeared his strategy was to cajole his rival into throwing his spear at a difficult, moving target and, of course, miss the mark. Still running, he would then turn, charging full speed toward his now—unarmed foe.

As the opponent ran in front of the dais, his ego obliged him to raise both hands in a salute to the wealthy audience, albeit, not many were present. At that moment, Kaelin launched his bronze-tipped weapon toward the unaware Feohtan and brought him down in front of the dais. The distance was not far; nonetheless, the whole scene amused the red-clad patrons in the dais, and the crowd at large, who rose and applauded. Kaelin left the arena through the notorious, pink exit, taking a modest reputation with him.

By now, Kaelin had walked through the Kunt Gate on more occasions than he cared to remember. It seemed paradoxically laughable to exit the Great Arena at Cappa through the Kunt Gate, and enter the arena of destiny through the other gate. The other option offered to a Feohtan was death, and perhaps a final crowd applause, when his body was carried through the Kunt Gate exit.

"One final word," said the arena official in a tone of warning rather than advice or instruction. "General Y'Sloic attends the fighting today. Aside from the Emperor himself, the Lord of Ravenbourne commands unimaginable power and wealth on the Southern Peninsula, perhaps throughout the whole Achaean Empire." A slight pause of deathly silence followed his words. Kaelin and his opponent rose, called out their names and colleges, and followed the arena official into the great, open stadium.

Kaelin recalled attending the public theater in his beloved Opar and sitting with his family on some instances, his rowdy playmates, or with his girlfriends on other occasions. He had not imagined what it would be like to be an actor or a musician, performing on the floor of the theater, surrounded by the huge crowd of spectators. He also remained amazed at how the same crowd in the arena was both quiet and overwhelmingly loud from one instant to another.

On this occasion, the arena was full but unusually quiet. Kaelin could never predict the crowd noise—when it may be loud—or when it might be deathly silent. It was a beautiful day, the sky as blue as the eyes of a golden-haired maiden . . . smiling . . . ready to be kissed. At least for this brief moment, it was good to be alive.

The trio walked across the coarse sand, when sudden dark flash caught Kaelin's eye. He looked around to see a shadow circling the three men.

It appeared to be the shadow of a bird, a great, soaring bird. Kaelin was careful not to gaze into the sun, shading his eyes with his hand while looking skyward. The bird was a raven, following them in a great, slow loop. It circled them more than once, then suddenly, making a strange, eerie call, it swooped upward so that the sun reflected off its back in a brilliant flash of red. It flew off in a straight path, disappearing over the high arena walls.

They stopped in front of the governor's dais. The crowded pavilion teemed with the aristocracy, delicately adorned in fine clothes, brightly dyed red or trimmed in red—the color of the elite. The upper class also favored the colors of purple and white to announce their wealth. But fine red clothing called out power . . . wealth . . . elite status. A small applause arose from the crowd after the arena official called out Kaelin's name, and the combatants raised their spears in salute. Seemingly, he had garnered a minor reputation.

To both Kaelin's and his opponent's surprise, the official ordered them to face each other and then back-step. It seemed they would fight directly in front of the dais. Kaelin and his adversary faced each other and began to back up, also watching the arena official's staff. They had only taken two or three steps when the arena official stopped and lowered his staff. The official stared up into the dais.

Kaelin heard what would otherwise be interpreted as a disturbance, but it was difficult to discern in the crowed arena. Cautiously, he likewise glanced toward the dais. He could see some sort of fracas, a scuffling. His first thought was that two of the aristocrats, filled with rich cherry wine, had gotten into a physical altercation. To his surprise, however, the arena official turned and walked back toward the entry gate in a hurried pace. Kaelin looked at his would-be opponent, who gazed back. He shrugged his shoulders, offering Kaelin a—who knows—expression, and then following the example of the arena official, he turned to walk toward the Kunt Gate exit with a hurried stride. Kaelin again looked up toward the Governor's dais.

Fighting had broken out. Kaelin could now see that the wealthy aristocrats were under attack. Several men, dressed in plain clothes and armed with swords, assaulted the well-dressed men in the dais who defended themselves as best they could. Kaelin noticed one older man fending off his attackers with a sword in hand. Older, yes, and wrapped in aristocratic attire, he nonetheless knew how to handle a sword and how to fight. He grabbed a footstool or small table and, using it as a shield, knocked down one of his assailants and, at the same moment, engaged a second man. He fell to his knees, and a third attacker now stood over him, sword in hand, with a clear opening for a lethal strike. It flashed through Kaelin's mind that he could save him.

Kaelin could see Capital Guards and other soldiers in armor, with red flowing capes, similar to those of the Ravenbourne Warriors pointed out by Ox on their arrival at Cappa, running toward the scene. They would not arrive and save him. Without warning, that same strange warm wind blew, and Kaelin could feel it on his face and in his hair—the same unexplained susurrus he now felt for the fourth occasion, along with the woman's soft voice.

"Save him, Kaelin!"

Kaelin readied his spear quickly, taking a balancing stance. It would be a long, difficult throw, made trickier by the elevation. It was a risky challenge. He might miss the target, striking a nearby aristocrat or the older man himself. But Kaelin, like all warriors of Opar, did not fear risk. He launched his spear with all the strength and accuracy he could muster.

When he released the spear, he knew his throw was true. It required just a blink of an eye for his javelin to strike the would-be assassin in the back. His blade dropped to his side instead of cutting down on the older man's neck. The attacker first fell to his knees, then dropped the sword from his hand and fell facedown to the floor of the dais—Kaelin's spear protruding from his back.

The older man had quickly glanced at Kaelin. He saw Kaelin cast the spear that saved his life, but the elder aristocrat had no opportunity to ponder the deed. Still battling for his life, he brought his improvised shield down on the leg of an attacker, who threw up his arms in a reaction of pain, providing the opportunity for the older man to plunge his sword into his attacker's midsection. The assassin dropped his blade, staggering backward.

Capital Guards and other red-capped warriors now swarmed the scene, and the remaining assassins were quickly dispatched. The pandemonium began to calm. Other aristocrats were wounded, perhaps killed. Kaelin stood watching.

The older man rose to his feet, his bloodied sword in hand. He looked down into the arena at Kaelin. In an impulsive gesture, Kaelin raised his hand toward the older noble, who knew how to fight and protect himself, but he did not respond. Kaelin calmly turned and walked toward the Kunt Gate exit.

CHAPTER 21

Lord Ravenbourne: Induction

"THERE WERE FOUR ASSASSINS, GENERAL," reported Colonel Cal DuPree, second in command of the Southern Army. "You killed one, the guards killed two, and one was dispatched by a Feohtan spear."

"Too bad about the two attackers the guards killed," replied a disappointed General Y'Sloic. "It would have been beneficial to have taken one or both alive."

"I believe it has always been a mistake, General," continued Colonel DuPree, "not to have any of your Ravenbourne Warrior escorts in the dais with you. I fail to see the logic behind that situation!"

Before Colonel DuPree began to voice his subtle complaint, the Lord of Ravenbourne had placed his thumb under his chin and his forefinger over his top lip, gazing off past Colonel DuPree, deep in thought. He often participated in a conversation and considered some other topic at the same moment. Colonel DuPree stood in silence. When ready, General Y'Sloic spoke, still looking past his patient Colonel.

"Since long before the Great Arena was constructed, Colonel, it has been the Governor's protocol not to include armed guards in the dais, providing a safety measure for all. The aristocrats fear and mistrust each other more than any others. In fact, armed escorts are not actually allowed in the aristocrat section."

"Yes, sir, General, I understand. It still seems to be an unnecessary risk to me."

After a silent pause, his eyes returned to Colonel DuPree. "For the present, the source behind the attack and to what end it was enacted remain a mystery."

"Yes, sir, General," replied Colonel DuPree. "General," he began, then paused, awaiting permission to speak. General Y'Sloic nodded. "Could the Governor have been the target of the assault—not you?"

General Y'Sloic raised his eyebrows as he pondered the question. "Possibly, perhaps us both. They certainly attempted to kill us both. Regardless, the Governor and I will equally make our inquiries. Physician Tomita is investigating each slain assassin . . . I await his findings before deciding my course of action. Meanwhile, Colonel, increase the number of scouts and widen their range, especially to the north."

"Understood, General," replied a cautious Colonel DuPree. "I have increased the scout numbers and included many pairs of long-term scouts who are far reaching and can remain in the field for many days." Colonel DuPree paused momentarily.

"And the one assassin killed by a Feohtan spear, General?"

"Oh, yes," recalled General Y'Sloic. "The daring Feohtan threw his spear from the arena. I saw it very clearly. He saved my life." General Y'Sloic once again gazed off past Colonel DuPree, pondering the audacious incident.

"The arena official announced him as Kaelin from the Heart Blood College, General. Lucky they were positioned close, just in front of the dais."

After a moment of silence, General Y'Sloic's thoughts returned to the present. "Yes, yes, very lucky indeed, as if some deity directed his path. Still, he had to decide on his own to act and have the confidence he possessed the skill to make the throw—a very risky throw. He might have struck someone else, even myself."

"I suppose he believed he could make the throw, General."

"Certainly, Colonel, but therein lies the question." Once more, General Y'Sloic looked past Colonel DuPree, thinking as he spoke, then snapped back to look directly into his subordinate's eyes.

"Buy him from the Heart Blood College, Colonel! I want to test his skill."

Colonel DuPree replied with a voice of apprehension. "I am acquainted with the Master of the Heart Blood College, General. He may . . . I think . . . give you the slave in exchange for a future favor."

The stern General took a deep breath—his face showed a sour expression of antipathy. "By the goddess! Why must everything hide some political motive or advantage?" he bitched in a frustrated tone. "Why not just plain and simple profit and greed?"

Colonel DuPree shook his head. He did not reply, not having an answer. Patiently, he waited.

"Very well, Colonel, pay his price! See to it now! I want to talk with this Feohtan fighter named Kaelin—today—before the sun sets. Take a large unit of soldiers prepared to assault this college compound should the master show any resistance. But pay his price, if he allows you to do so."

"Yes, sir," responded Colonel DuPree. He saluted, then left.

Colonel DuPree led an assault cohort of the Southern Army, complete with a battering ram and a hundred-strong cavalry, to the gates and walls of the Heart Blood College. To add to the gravitas, a squad of Ravenbourne mounted warriors led the cavalry unit. To his surprise, however, the college master gave up his now-infamous Feohtan fighter for an extraordinary sum but neither asked for, nor considered, any political advantage from the Lord of Ravenbourne, now or in the future. He was a common man of greed and profit, not of politics. Lord Ravenbourne would appreciate his motives.

General Y'Sloic ordered a large assembly of the First Legion, two thousand strong, of the Southern Army to "fall in" at the extensive training courtyard located on the edge of the Southern Army Headquarters. The yard was enclosed by a stone wall. A massive stone review stage, constructed on the edge of the yard, was similarly enclosed by a high, trapezoid-shaped stone wall with unusual pillars in each corner. Legend stated that the stage and the trapezoid walls were constructed by ancient men, long before the era of writing, a vestige of heathen sexual rites and human sacrifice to placate prehistoric, pagan gods. Four erotic pillars were constructed in each corner of the trapezoid. The tall, thick stone pillars were shaped in the likeness of an erect phallus, constructed between two large round stones—apparently, corresponding, testicles. The diameter of the round stones measured greater than the height of a man. Large gates were located in the wall on each side of the stage, and a small secret door was cut into the wall behind the stage.

Dressed in parade uniform—white capes trimmed in red—with spears and shields in hand—a squad of Southern Army soldiers escorted Kaelin through a corridor, diverting the First Legion formation to the front of the review stage. On the march from the Heart Blood College, Colonel DuPree had informed Kaelin only that he had been purchased by General Y'Sloic, Lord of Ravenbourne, and was being brought before him. The whole ordeal remained overwhelming to the young warrior of the fallen city of Opar.

General Y'Sloic sat in a large chair on the edge of the stage, surrounded by his high command, entourage, and personal bodyguard corps of Ravenbourne Warriors. The escorts stood aside, and Kaelin—dressed in the attire of the Heart Blood College—stood alone. General Y'Sloic rose. Tumult, commands, and calls of attention spread throughout the legion and assembly, punctuated by thunderous trumpet blasts.

Unexpectedly, a deadly silence fell across the yard. It reminded Kaelin of the silence that befell the Great Arena, after the arena official raised his crosier to initiate a Feohtan contest, or the eerie silence of a whole army just before the command to attack was given.

Lord Ravenbourne looked down on the youthful warrior who, a few days prior, had saved his life. "What is your name?" demanded Lord Ravenbourne in a military tone.

"Kaelin, my Lord. Feohtan fighter of the Heart Blood College."

"How did you become a Feohtan?" continued Lord Ravenbourne.

"I was a warrior of Opar, taken captive at the fall of the city."

The was a slight pause before Lord Ravenbourne asked his next question. "Why were you not killed in battle?"

"I was wounded, Lord, knocked unconscious. After I woke, taken prisoner, I chose to stay alive and endure what fate held for me. To live and fight for Opar on a day . . . yet to come."

"You seem unusually skilled with the Feohtan spear, Kaelin."

"Yes, Lord."

"How skilled are you?"

"I won the Opar City Champion in the javelin throw before I was inducted into the Opar Army."

"As a teenage boy?"

"Yes, Lord."

The Lord of Ravenbourne paused for a moment, looking over the young warrior standing before him. "I offer you another challenge now, Kaelin." He raised his left hand and pointed toward the stage wall. A black silhouette, the shape and size of a man's head and torso, hung on the wall. Kaelin glanced toward the wall, then back to Lord Ravenbourne.

Without taking his eyes off Kaelin, Lord Ravenbourne held out his right hand, and an officer standing next to him handed him a spear. He took the weapon and tossed it down the steps to Kaelin. The spear flew in a perpendicular flight . . . the lethal bronze-tip pointing skyward. Kaelin reached out, catching the spear with little effort.

That action prompted the two Ravenbourne Warriors standing on either side of Lord Ravenbourne to raise their shields and step in front of their Lord. He placed a hand on each shoulder of his protectors, who then sidestepped so that Lord Ravenbourne again faced Kaelin.

"That spear was taken from the body of the would-be-assassin that you slew," Lord Ravenbourne said calmly. "Use it now to strike the target on the wall. A slow death awaits you if you fail."

Kaelin again turned his head to view the target then turned back to gaze into the face of this warrior lord. The soldiers guarding Kaelin stepped away from him.

With fearless motion, unimpeded by the possibility of death, Kaelin aggressively tossed the deadly javelin up into the air so that it fell back to the earth in a horizontal position. He reached up and caught the spear as it fell. Taking a single step, he launched the bronze-tipped wooden staff with lightning speed. The spear flew toward the wall in a flash, with the sun reflecting off the bronze projectile in a ray of light. The fatal point struck the target near the center of the chest with an echoing thud.

All heads turned toward the target in silence, and all heard the thud the spear-point made, penetrating the silhouette. The silence lingered, as if it were a heavy fog. Before any soldier could comment, Kaelin spoke out boldly and loudly.

"Another one!" he shouted, holding out his hand to a nearby Ravenbourne Warrior.

The warrior looked to his lord, who nodded his approval. With ease, the warrior tossed his spear to Kaelin. This was a combat spear. Heavier in design than the Feohtan spear, it was used in a battleline in close-quarters combat. Nonetheless, it could still be cast with lethal accuracy by trained soldiers.

Kaelin caught the spear—turned toward the target—steadied his balance. And even though he took more care in his aim . . . the swiftness he was able to throw the weapon . . . and the speed of the spear's flight caused all eyebrows to raise. The heavy projectile struck the target in the head, creating an echoing thud.

Kaelin remained standing in front of the Lord of Ravenbourne, General of the Southern Army. Lord Ravenbourne turned to his officer on the left. His lord's eyes told him to speak.

"Incredible!" said Lieutenant Colonel T. Rogir, third officer of the Southern Army.

Lord Ravenbourne now turned to the officer on his right. "I've not seen such skill with a spear, my Lord," replied Colonel DuPree. "Never in all my years in the army."

Returning his gaze to Kaelin, Lord Ravenbourne looked hard at the youthful warrior, who stood still, and straight, seemingly unmoved by what had just taken place.

"You saved my life with purpose, Kaelin."

"I did, my Lord."

"What do you want, Kaelin?" called out Lord Ravenbourne in a loud voice, but it was not a shout.

Kaelin raised his hand in a clenched fist and responded as loudly as he could manage. "Freedom!"

He lowered his fist, and spoke again in a normal voice, "Freedom, my Lord."

A quiet calm followed. Lord Ravenbourne raised his hand and pointed to his side without taking his eyes off Kaelin. "My officer holds a document. All I need do is sign it . . . attach my seal . . . and you may walk from here a free man and a citizen of the Empire. I'll throw in a purse of silver coins as well. What will you do with your freedom, Kaelin?"

"Find my mother and sister, who were surely taken as slaves from Opar," answered Kaelin.

"Bring us some water!" ordered Lord Ravenbourne, maintaining eye contact with Kaelin. "Freedom will be yours, Kaelin. You deserve that—and more. But what kind of freedom do you really want?"

Lord Ravenbourne took a deep breath. "Come sit in front of me on the steps, Kaelin, and listen to my offer."

Lord Ravenbourne turned and walked back up the steps toward his chair. "Put the legion and assembly at ease, Colonel DuPree," he ordered as he passed the colonel.

As the command echoed throughout the legion and company, Kaelin walked up the stairs and sat a few steps down from General Y'Sloic, who returned to his chair. Two young, male servants appeared; one carried two mugs of water, and the other held an oinochoe. One servant handed a mug to the General and one to Kaelin. General Y'Sloic drank, and Kaelin followed.

"The great, mythical city of Opar has fallen, Kaelin," began Lord Ravenbourne. "Nearly all the men killed, but a few, as yourself, taken slaves. Most of the women, girls, and children were also taken into slavery. . . babies slain without mercy. Only the very old and very young remain. Soldiers of the Eastern Army occupy the city and surrounding area. It will be repopulated with Achaean citizens of the Empire and become an Empire city. What could wait for you there now, Kaelin?"

Lord Ravenbourne took another long drink. Kaelin followed. He knew the warrior lord was not finished speaking. "Your mother and sister could be anywhere within the Empire, separated or together. How would you ever find them?"

"I don't know, General Y'Sloic. But I must try," answered the calm, stoic Kaelin.

"Yes, Kaelin, you must," answered General Y'Sloic, "but there is more than one way. I offer you enlistment into my Ravenbourne Warrior Corps. A period of four years. Take the oath, and swear allegiance and loyalty to me. Duty and training, food and barracks, prestige and women, unmatched anywhere in the Empire. I offer an enlistment bonus of one hundred silver coins. Half is yours to keep now, and the other half will be deposited into your retirement bank. I will also offer you a very rare Request. If it is prudent and within my power it will be granted once you have been inducted and I have returned to Ravenbourne. A Request is not to be taken at hand but pondered deeply before asking."

Kaelin took a deep breath, as though he was about to speak. Lord Ravenbourne raised his hand. Kaelin continued to remain silent.

"One final offer, Kaelin. The Emperor's administrators and scribes kept records of the slave sales of Opar. How complete—cannot be known. Certainly, a number of slaves passed through the gates of Opar unrecorded, by design or mistake and some records scribed in haste. I will send scholars to the Capital City, and with the Emperor's permission, they will search the records. It remains possible to learn who purchased your mother and sister and thus locate them. It is not a certainty, as it is not certain they were taken slaves or if they were documented. I will make it known that I seek these two female slaves. If they are found, I will buy them and bring them to Ravenbourne. Once your enlistment is up and you are discharged with honor, you, your mother, and your sister will be free."

"You would do that for me, Lord?" inquired Kaelin with humble sincerity.

"I would, to have you enlist in my Ravenbourne Corps," replied Lord Ravenbourne. "And after all, you saved my life."

Kaelin briefly considered informing Lord Ravenbourne that they had met once before. When he was a boy with his mother at the Greenstone Estates near the Capital City. He decided this was not the proper opportunity.

"I accept, Lord, with all my heart," answered Kaelin with a hard swallow.

General Sol Y'Sloic, Lord of Ravenbourne, smiled, and with his hands on the arms of his massive chair, he rose. "Go to the bottom of the steps, Kaelin, and kneel."

As Kaelin complied, Lord Ravenbourne held out his hand to his nearby Ravenbourne Warrior, who pitched his spear to his Lord. He looked at Colonel DuPree. "Call the legion and assembly to attention, Colonel."

Colonel DuPree called out the order. Once again, the order echoed across the massive courtyard, interposed by trumpet blasts. Total silence ensued. Lord Ravenbourne descended the stairs to stand in front of Kaelin, bent on one knee. He laid the spearpoint on Kaelin's left shoulder.

"Do you, Kaelin, swear by your life's blood, on the graves of your ancestors, by any and all the gods and goddesses you may worship, allegiance and loyalty to me, that you will defend the country and estate of Ravenbourne and its villa, its people, the Lady of Ravenbourne and her children, with all your strength, with all your courage, and with your life?"

"I so swear, my Lord," answered Kaelin, looking up into the eyes of Lord Ravenbourne.

Lord Ravenbourne smiled and lifted the spear. "Rise, Spearman Kaelin, Warrior of Ravenbourne."

Once more, the trumpets echoed a resounding blast, and calls arose across the hard-packed field, bouncing off the ancient walls. Suddenly, two thousand men called out a single word in unison. The jubilation was repeated three times. Kaelin rose to his feet.

Tossing the spear to his lefthand, Lord Ravenbourne held out his right to Kaelin, again wearing a smile. Kaelin returned the smile and took his Lord's hand. "Welcome to the Ravenbourne Corps, Kaelin. May you find what you seek."

Lord Ravenbourne looked around at the nearby company of soldiers, who remained in perfect formation. Raising his hand and the spear, he called out, giving an order to the whole assembly: "Congratulate him!"

The formation of the First Legion broke ranks and stepped up to welcome Kaelin into the elite Ravenbourne Warrior Corps. Lord Ravenbourne tossed the spear back to its owner, then ascended the steps of the stone stage. He stopped in front of Ra Machaon, the First Spear of the First Legion.

"First Spear Machaon, introduce yourself to Kaelin and offer any assistance you can before he leaves for Ravenbourne."

In response, First Spear Machaon rapped the end of his spear on the stone stage in salute. "Sir!" he called and turned to ascend the stage.

General Y'Sloic now stepped in front of Colonel DuPree.

"See to it, Colonel, that Spearman Kaelin is escorted to Ravenbourne as soon as is prudent. I want him assigned to the First Company of the First Legion. Take command here and dismiss the legion."

"Yes sir, General!" replied Colonel DuPree. He saluted and turned to the assembly, stepping away to put General Y'Sloic's orders in place.

General Sol Y'Sloic, Commanding General of the Southern Army, turned and walked with a strong pace toward a side gate, then left the ancient stone stage. His entourage followed.

CHAPTER 22

Rohan: Highway to Ravenbourne

WIDELY ACCLAIMED "THE APPETITE OF the World," the Southern Peninsula reigned as the most productive region of the Achaean Empire. Eminent estates such as Ravenbourne, Starfall, and Moonblood and huge farming domains produced grains, cattle, fruits, honey, flax, stone, clay, and timber, providing food, clothing, and shelter for both the wealthy and the poor. High forested mountains; wide, rich river valleys; and broad, flat grasslands each provided a landscape of bounty.

Extending from the northern regions of the Southern Peninsula southward and nearly reaching the coastline, the rugged Mountain of the Goddess bisected the peninsula, providing the birth of all rivers and streams that cascaded, east and west, down the mountain slopes, into the great oceans. Located in the central region of the mountains, the Twin Peaks formed an imposing monument, easily viewed from any location throughout the Peninsula on a clear day. The peaks, always dressed in a pure-white snow cover, were said to be the breasts of the goddess Asa, from which she suckled her twin infants, the male sun and the female moon.

The radiant sun—embodiment of male—hot, predictable, continuously dependable—moved across the sky, bringing warmth and light to the otherwise cold, dark earth below. Conversely, the moon—ever mysterious, ever changing, always unpredictable—the personification of female. Irresistible, she waxed and waned on her own cycle, seeking her own secret motives.

"You're a good horseman," remarked Lieutenant Rin Rohan, second officer of the Ravenbourne Equestrian Guard. "Where did you learn to ride?"

"My father owned a stable in Opar," answered Spearman Kaelin. "I helped, mostly exercising the horses. I also served in the Opar Cavalry."

"Well, if the cavalry was part of the Opar Army, they would have been well trained," offered Lieutenant Rohan, looking back over his shoulder at a trailing party wearing a suspicious face.

The two Ravenbourne Warriors led a military convoy escorting a wagon-load of young Opar pallakes from Cappa to the Ravenbourne Villa . . . a precious cargo to brighten the atmosphere of the luxurious estate. Lieutenant Rohan sported the armor and weapons common to a warrior of the Ravenbourne Equestrian Guard except he did not carry a spear; officers were not required to do so. He kept his helmet tied to his horse's flank on the opposite side of his shield.

Riding without armor or weapons, Kaelin wore only a military tunic—white in color and trimmed with expensive red—the crest of the Ravenbourne Corps was embroidered in black and gold, sewn to the center of his chest. The renowned crest left no question as to the military unit to which this warrior belonged. Attached around his waist was a leather belt; armor and weapons would be issued at Ravenbourne.

The convoy included a company of the Southern Army Cavalry and enough supply wagons for a lengthy journey, commanded by Lieutenant Rohan. The slave-girls rode in a horse-drawn wagon, uniquely designed for passenger comfort. It was pulled by a team of six sturdy draft horses.

"How long were you in the Opar Cavalry, Kaelin?" inquired Lieutenant Rohan, continuing to query his celebrity riding partner. There remained little to do when leading a convoy on the Emperor's Highway other than talk.

"Two years," answered Kaelin.

"Did you see any action?" continued Rohan.

"Heavy action and several engagements," recalled Kaelin. "We were tasked with eliminating the bandits who plagued the countryside and took refuge in the rugged mountains north of the city. Several bands, united under a strong leader, had become more of an army rather than scattered gangs of brigands. The Opar historians called those years the 'Bandit Wars.' One particular engagement, fought at the bandits' stronghold on the Yellowtail River, was bloody and brutal."

"Is that where you acquired those battle scars on your face?" asked Rohan, casually taking another look over his shoulder.

"One of them," answered Kaelin. "The other I wear from the Battle of Opar."

"How did you fare at the Yellowtail River Battle?" asked Rohan.

"We slaughtered every mother's son of the mountain bandits. We freed their hostages and returned them to their families. That ended their army and their threat to peace, leaving only a few scattered gangs."

"Good!" stated Rohan loudly. "Miscreant bandits who take hostages deserve nothing less than death. As for my part, Kaelin, I've not seen action or battle. I do not fear it, nor do I desire it."

Kaelin noticed that Rohan continued to glance over his shoulder. "Wise attitude to take, Lieutenant. I have found no reward in battle, only loss."

The convoy came to a wide section of the road lined with large trees, a frequently used stopover. "Let's rest the horses," the Lieutenant said and reined his mount around, calling out the order. He then guided the company to the road-side, under the trees.

The wagons came to a noisy halt, when suddenly, one of the girls jumped from the passenger wagon, taking off in a run toward the Twin Peaks. "By the goddess!" shouted Rohan. "I've been waiting for that little bitch to try something like this. Kaelin! Go bring her back!"

"Sir!" replied Kaelin—reining his mount—he rode off toward the fleeing girl.

He loped in front of her and halted. She stopped and stood, breathing hard, wearing a distraught face. He dismounted, threw her over his shoulder, and walked his horse back to the caravan, with his attractive cargo kicking and struggling. He set her down in front of the slave wagon.

Wearing a stern scowl, Lieutenant Rohan stood, his hands on his hips. He unfastened the rear gate of the wagon and lowered it down. Reaching out, he took a firm grip on the slave-girl's small wrist. He next sat down on the gate, on his left hip, with his right leg and foot planted firmly on the ground. In one quick jerk, he pulled the surprised beauty over his leg. Reaching down, he took the hem of her frock and roughly pulled it up over her back, exposing her backside.

Showing little tolerance, he administered a fast and furious spanking until he inflamed both buttocks-cheeks while she cried, yelled, and kicked her legs as equally fast and furious. Her slave ankle bracelet and two attached copper bells played a jingling tune, keeping a rhythm with Rohan's swatting hand.

When he stopped, he gripped her narrow waist with both hands and pushed her back into the wagon. Crying, she crawled to the front of the wagon, where she was comforted and snuggled by her companions. They had all watched the punishment in fear—covering their mouth— wringing their hands, with some crying.

"Ask them which one wants to be next, Kaelin," growled Lieutenant Rohan, still slightly out of breath, obviously angered. "Tell her to pull her frock off . . . crawl out of the wagon . . . and lay her honey-sweet little flower over my knee!"

Kaelin delivered the message in the singular language of Opar. The tender pallakes reacted by huddling closer together in the corner of the wagon, a few began to cry; all were frightened and cringing.

Taking a deep breath and letting it out, Rohan calmed himself. "I've tried to talk with them, but I'm not sure if they understand me or not. I know they are just stupid girls, with good reason to be morose, but don't they understand the futility of trying to escape like that. Perhaps I should remove those soft leather shoes. Once their bare feet hit the rough ground and rock, they may reconsider running away."

"Allow me to talk with them," offered Kaelin.

"Certainly," answered Rohan. "If anyone can reason with their silly, little heads, it would be you."

Kaelin stepped in front of the wagon and delivered a stern lecture. They had all heard him speak the Opar language. Now, however, hearing his sincere voice, they listened with intensity. When he finished, they all seemed to answer a yes, with a distinctive change in their emotions. They crawled out of the wagon. Helping each one down, Kaelin continued to speak in a calm, direct voice, pointing to a distant, large tree. To Rohan's surprise, each girl stepped up to Kaelin, placed a small hand on the scar cut into the side of his face, and stood up on their toes to kiss the other side of his face. It seemed to be a sincere kiss of thanks.

They took their blankets and water skins, and while holding hands in pairs, they walked to the base of the large tree. Laying out the blankets, they were soon talking, giggling, and calm.

"A welcomed change in attitude," admitted Rohan, moved by their behavior. "What did you tell them, Kaelin?"

Kaelin smiled at the junior officer. "I told them if any one of them caused any more trouble, such as trying to escape, we would strip them all naked and spank every behind in front of all the soldiers. Then, we would force them to walk, bare naked and red butts showing, all the way to Ravenbourne."

"Well, that may be effective," laughed Lieutenant Rohan out loud.

Now, Kaelin took a more serious tone. "I also told them I had fought as a warrior of Opar against the army of the Empire, outside the walls of our beloved city. I fought with my comrades . . . their fathers . . . brothers . . . and uncles. They were all slaughtered around me. Wounded and unconscious, I was spared by the mercy of the god of war, taken to become a slave of the Empire. I could not escape. There was no place to run to—nowhere to hide—no way to vanish. Disobedience brings only humiliating punishment. I gained my freedom by obeying my master and mistress and pleasing them. I told them that was the only way that they, too, could similarly gain their freedom."

Rohan glanced toward the seven girls, who continued laughing and talking, seemingly calm, gathered under the large shade tree. "Well, your lecture seems to have worked. Thanks, Kaelin. I'll post guards but instruct them to keep a safe distance, giving the girls some privacy."

"Good idea, Lieutenant," replied Kaelin, chuckling. "Given a good view of one stunning behind and the little treasure hidden between her thighs, I surmise any or all of those petite beauties would serve as a comfortable . . . warm . . . bed-slave."

"Bed-slaves and much more, Spearman Kaelin. The Mistress of Ravenbourne will use her unlimited wealth and influence, purchasing the loveliest and healthiest slaves, especially fledgling pallakes, from across the Empire. I am optimistic you will enjoy more than a taste of all the delights of Ravenbourne."

The young officer shaded his eyes with his still-red spanking hand and looked up toward the sun. A lone, dark eagle circled in wide loops and announced its presence with a shrill call. Rohan and Kaelin glanced up at the great bird and lightly smiled at each other. They both seemingly held admiration and envy for the eagle's freedom.

"The day wears on. Follow me, Kaelin! You and I will ride down the line and check the whole caravan before we make camp." Kaelin said nothing as they both walked toward their mounts.

The first night went well. The convoy camped at the fork of the Emperor's Highway and the East Port Road. It was a prepared campground maintained by the Southern Army. Many travelers, convoys, caravans, and itinerant traders along both roads utilized the camp. In addition, the camp also supported one of General Y'Sloic's courier system stations. Any military presence offered a measure of safety for weary civilian travelers. It was, in fact, an enjoyable camp for the whole convoy. Following a hearty meal—camp chores complete—guards posted—most of the company slept well. Even though the convoy was well guarded, Rohan and Kaelin periodically checked their precious cargo. Snug in their wagon with comfortable bedding, the seven girls whispered and tittered for most of the night.

Shortly after day-break, the convoy rolled on its way along the ancient Emperor's Highway; the early dawn provided a peaceful, serene setting. Each day, two squads of soldiers were sent, one forward and one to the rear, to give warning of an ambush or a rear attack by bandits. It was unlikely any band of brigands would dare attack a military convoy on the Emperor's Highway. Nonetheless, Lieutenant Rohan would take no chances with a load of prized cargo bound for Ravenbourne.

This morning, Rohan rode the length of one side of the convoy on his inspection and then rode along the other side, back to the head of the column. He slowed his mount alongside Kaelin.

"Our seven maidens appear to all be asleep," Rohan said with a chuckle. "I think they stayed awake all night talking and chortling. I should order them all out of the wagon and have them walk for a few turns of an hourglass."

"Even though they are pallakes of Ravenbourne, Lieutenant, they are still girls," replied Kaelin. "Let trouble sleep."

"Most assured, Kaelin," replied Rohan.

The caravan rolled along. The slave-girls remained quiet in their wagon, still asleep by midmorning. The two youthful warriors of Lord Ravenbourne grew bored. Lieutenant Rohan responded first.

"With a wagon load of lovely pallakes rolling behind us, Kaelin, the spicy delights of slave-girl sex have roused my curiosity. Your past experiences and the apparent admiration of the tender, young women of Opar tell me that you have had your share of slave-girls, as have I. So would you tell me, as a means of passing today's long ride, who is the sweetest . . . alluring . . . most gorgeous . . . little kunt, you've ever tasted?"

Kaelin lightly laughed. "To find a remedy against boredom, I will tell you about an experience that few men, young or old, have enjoyed."

"Interesting, Kaelin. I'm intrigued. Please continue."

"As a teenage boy, I was lucky enough to win the annual athletic challenge of Opar in the javelin throw."

"A teenage boy?" questioned Rohan.

"At sixteen," replied Kaelin. "The same year I entered military service."

"Impressive, Kaelin. Go on."

"As a reward, the city fathers paid the price for me to spend forty-five days with the most notorious hetaera in Opar. She was a mature woman, some thirty-five to forty seasons, and remarkably stunning. The wealthy and powerful men of Opar paid well for her company and affection. Her name was Salomi. Beautiful, educated, and talented, she rose to become a matron of wealth and property. She spoke with an alluring, unusual accent. I have only recently come to know, she hailed from the coastal country of K'semay. She taught me, a virgin boy, everything a woman could do to a man sexually—and the reverse. She imparted her wisdom on how to arouse a woman so that she would beg me to stop . . . then . . . ask me for more."

Lieutenant Rohan burst out laughing. "Then I'll be sure to query you on female, sexual desire and behavior, Spearman Kaelin, while I have the opportunity during this convoy responsibility. Once you take up your duties at the Ravenbourne Estate, we may never have the opportunity to talk like this again."

"Ask any question," challenged Kaelin.

"I will," pondered Rohan, who thought to himself for a moment then turned to his comrade with a mischievous grin on his face.

"Is it true or not . . . a woman can achieve an orgasmic squirt as though she were a man?"

"It is absolutely true," responded Kaelin. "Properly stimulated, a woman can squirt more than a man does."

Both young men began to laugh so loudly they stirred their sleeping cargo.

CHAPTER 23

Lady Ravenbourne: Secret Courier

GENERAL Y'SLOIC HAD FASHIONED THE most extensive courier systems throughout the Southern Peninsula, which included portions of other regions of the Empire that meshed with the Emperor's system. Every ten to fifteen miles, exchange stations were built. Here, a courier, delivering an important message, could trade his winded mount for a fresh one in a few, short moments. Magnificent horses were specially bred by the Southern Army for speed, endurance, and a calm demeanor. Often, this strain of animals was white in color. Highly sought after by horse breeders across the Achaean Empire, this breed filled the remuda of Lord Ravenbourne's Equestrian Guard and Courier Corps. Hand-selected riders—small, wiry, young men, equally tough—displaying unyielding endurance—completed the singular training. Equipped with an unusually light saddle and riding at breakneck speed, these couriers could cover four hundred miles in three days, often less.

Armed only with a bovine-horn, stamina, and riding skills, the young courier reined his mount in a sharp turn from the Emperor's Highway onto the Ravenbourne Road toward the main gate of the renowned estate. The white stallion recognized the Ravenbourne wall enclosing the villa and instinctively stretched out into a full gallop. Holding his horn to his lips, the courier blew a loud blast to alert the guards, and anyone else, that a running horse was coming through the gates at full gallop.

The Ravenbourne guards hurried to clear the immediate populace to the safety of the roadside and sounded a siren signal of bronze-horn blasts, alerting the entire villa. The courier glided through the gate and continued on the main road toward the villa, repeating blasts of warning on his bovine-horn call.

At the steps to the entrance of the main villa, he reined his heavy-breathing stallion to a halt, jumped from his back, and ran up the steps and down the corridor to the entry of Lady Ravenbourne's private sanctuary. Upon seeing the courier approaching, one of two Ravenbourne guards stationed outside the sanctuary doors pounded with a metal knocker. A female-slave opened a small window cut into one of the large pair of massive wooden doors.

"Send for Lady Ravenbourne! Run, girl! A courier approaches!" The girl closed the small window and hurried with the message.

An "eye of the needle" was constructed adjacent the pair of colossal carved doors that sealed the entryway to the private sanctuary, allowing a single person admission. This door opened, and Lady Ravenbourne, Old Nanny, and the lady's body-guard, Ginal, stepped into the corridor as the courier approached on the run. He went to one knee in front of the Ravenbourne Mistress and handed her the scroll message. She took the scroll with one hand and inspected the seal. She then laid the palm of her other hand on the side of the young man's face. "Thank you, my young man. Arise and wait."

Then she turned to Old Nanny. "Have some honey-water sent."

Old Nanny quickly turned and stepped inside the small door to ensure the order was carried out, as Lady Ravenbourne broke the seal on the message scroll, unrolled it, and read the contents to herself. Meanwhile, the jingle of an ankle bracelet and copper bells could be heard as a naked slave-girl came to the door with a container of water. Old Nanny took it and served it to the thirsty courier.

Rolling the message scroll back up, Lady Ravenbourne stepped and turned to one of her guards. "Call for my escort and send word to Colonel Davis that I request he meet me in the Receiving Hall . . . immediately. Inform him it is most urgent."

"My Lady!" the guard reported. He raised his spear and brought the end down hard on the stone floor—turned—and took off in a run down the corridor.

She now returned to her courier. "See to yourself and your mount. Await further orders at the Courier Station."

"Understood, my Lady!" answered the courier. He saluted, turned, and followed in the steps of the guard down the corridor.

Flanked on one side by Ginal and on the other by the captain of her Ravenbourne Escort, Lady Ravenbourne stepped briskly into the Receiving Hall. Four Ravenbourne Warriors completed her escort and followed behind, two by two. Colonel Davis, the Ravenbourne Corps commander, arrived in the hall from the outside entry. Dressed in full ceremonial attire, his red cloak blew upward with the wind as he entered. He was followed by his entourage and officers.

Lady Ravenbourne stepped away from her escort and walked alone to the far side of the hall, out of voice range. Colonel Davis removed his helmet, handed it to a nearby officer, and walked up to stand in front of the Ravenbourne Mistress. He bowed at attention—the protocol of an elite officer.

Lady Ravenbourne showed the Colonel the message. "You will also receive this message from a secret courier." She took a deep breath and began the urgent news.

"There was a failed attempt on Lord Ravenbourne's life in the dais at the Great Arena. He was unharmed. The four would-be assassins were killed. Interestingly, a Feohtan fighter killed one of the attackers, saving our lord's life with a remarkable spear throw from the floor of the arena. Lord Ravenbourne has inducted him into the Ravenbourne Corps and has sent him by unknown means. I am sure we will soon learn of his arrival."

There was a brief but very silent pause. Lady Ravenbourne then continued, "I would appreciate meeting this daring warrior during our next Receiving Reception before the flax and cherry harvests begin. My field and orchard overseers tell me this year's crops will be abundant and we should expect a large harvest and, accordingly, a substantial gathering at the reception. Do you have any questions, Colonel?"

"No, my lady, you were very clear."

"In addition, Colonel, near the end of this year, we will hold the Hundred Year Celebration of the goddess of Asa. Few of us, if any, have experienced this important gathering. It will be a complex festival and a strain on our resources."

"I understand, my Lady. There is little daylight to waste."

"Well stated, Colonel. There is much to prepare."

Again, the Colonel of the Ravenbourne Corps came to attention—bowed—and left the Receiving Hall through the outside entrance. Likewise, Lady Ravenbourne returned to her escort and her private sanctuary.

The convoy passed a thick, wide hedgerow planted with tall trees extending toward the Twin Peaks on the north side of the road. The tumult clamor of wagons and horses flushed out an enormous flock of black birds which flew in a wide circular pattern, as though inscribing a letter, heading toward the Twin Peaks. The hedgerow opened into a vast field of lofty plants, in bloom with fragrant, blue flowers, stretching to the horizon. The tops of the plants would touch the underbelly of a tall horse. Pleasantly surprised, Kaelin pointed the field out to his riding partner.

"Is that flax, Lieutenant?

"It is, Kaelin. The Ravenbourne Estate cultivates unknown acres of it. Some call it a silver crop because it brings in a substantial price once harvested and sold. The harvest season is a remarkable affair. In fact, the cherry harvest also occurs during the same period. People come from all over the Empire . . . both aristocrats and peasants . . . rich and poor . . . maidens galore. Lord Ravenbourne remains a generous lord. Large fields are set aside that only the poor folks of Ravenbourne may harvest. I understand that most make their own material and thus clothing. And if you are a wine drinker and not tasted the Ravenbourne cherry wine, you're likely to become addicted. It is a luxury item across the Empire. Ravenbourne Warriors patrol the harvesting and camping areas to keep the peace. I'm sure you'll be given the opportunity to undertake the harvest adventure first-hand. Loud, joyous merrymaking occurs every night."

"The harvested flax stems came to Opar by the wagon-load, but the plant did not cultivate in the northern regions. I've not seen it growing." Kaelin spoke as his mount stumbled. He reached out, patting the animal's neck, calming him. The large gelding shook his head in response. "How did you become a Ravenbourne Warrior and officer?" asked Kaelin.

"Not much of a story," answered Rohan. "Certainly not as exciting as your stories of Salomi, but I will tell you if you want. My father has a wealthy friend. A man of some influence who took a shine to me. He has no sons of his own. He paid the entrance fee, which allowed me to enter the Officer Training School at Cappa. Even if my family had somehow raised the tuition money, most certainly, I would not have been accepted. His influence played the major role. I think he hoped, once my education and military career as an officer was complete, I would join his enterprises in the manner a son would." Rohan paused. He looked skyward as though pondering the past events. He then continued.

"Anyway, after my first completed year, I dropped out and enlisted in the army. I was lucky enough to be assigned to the Southern Army. That same wealthy family friend had a prized horse he was very proud of. Again, he used his influence, and I was allowed to ride his horse in the annual racing derby at Cappa. He did have a powerful, puissant horse, and with me astride, we won the obstacle race, the most popular race of the day. General Y'Sloic often attends the races, and he did that day. Apparently, he was impressed. He asked me to join his Ravenbourne Equestrian Guard, and I accepted. Me, a stupid teenage boy, a Ravenbourne Warrior! The years went by. When Aaragon was made captain, Lord Ravenbourne promoted me to lieutenant. Now, here we are. I am the luckiest fokken man in the Empire."

"Fascinating," said Kaelin, "although I would argue you might be the second luckiest man in the Empire and hold the first position for myself." Both men laughed and paused briefly in silent reflection.

Kaelin broke the silence. "If you don't mind my curiosity, Lieutenant, what are your plans after you deliver your—unusual cargo—to the Ravenbourne Corps commander?"

"Not at all," replied Rohan. "I've been granted a thirty-day furlough for my small part in your delivery. Not to mention the Ravenbourne Equestrian Corps rides to the capital. During my years in the army, I have had little opportunity to be on leave at Ravenbourne. Therefore, it will be my purpose to locate a group of Hyacinth Gatherers and offer my services as a warrior guard, escorting them on their journey to Ravenbourne. Many of those groups come to Ravenbourne for the harvest, in addition to selling or trading their urns and alabastrons of that alluring oil. Although I have not tasted one, by reputation, a Hyacinth girl would match your Salomi in all ways any man could conjure up. I intend to discover if a female . . . red headed . . . Hyacinth Gatherer has soft, red hair between her thighs as well."

Laughing, Kaelin queried. "What are Hyacinth Gatherers?"

"Spearman Kaelin," answered Rohan. "I must leave some mystery. I'll allow your orientation sergeant to fill you in on the secrets of a Hyacinth girl. All I'll advise is . . ." He paused forming a smile. "Never pass one up."

Still wearing a slight grin, Kaelin offered another suggestion. "Should we halt early for camp tonight, Rohan? You and I could race these two mounts. Perhaps provide a little evening entertainment for this bored company."

"Good idea, Kaelin. These Ravenbourne horses and those bred for the Courier Corps by General Y'Sloic are the soundest horses on the Southern Peninsula, perhaps in the Empire. The white stallion that Captain Aaragon rides, however, is the most coveted horse in the whole Achaean Empire. I have ridden him on a few occasions. Fastest horse I've ever mounted."

CHAPTER 24

Natasha: Vision Comes to Light

PRIOR TO MELISSA'S ARRIVAL AT the Ravenbourne Village, Natasha had gone alone to the Great Stone Bridge whenever she could. Now that she and Melissa had become good friends—best of friends—they came together on no-work-days and other days when they could get away.

The wonderous bridge was usually quiet and peaceful, but occasionally travelers camped near the bridge because it was easy to water their animals and relatively safe. At the north end stood a military post, one station of General Y'Sloic's courier systems, which included a small garrison of the Southern Army. Her father met her mother when he was stationed at that garrison.

More interesting, the huge bridge was full of unique niches where Natasha and Melissa could sit, talk, and hide. When a caravan passed, it was very exciting to watch. They would watch unseen, *incognito*, as the wagons rolled noisily by, or they would sit on the side of the bridge in plain view—depending on how they felt. As the strong mules and large horses pulled the loud wagons past, the drivers smiled or waved at them, especially if it was an army caravan bringing supplies to Ravenbourne, escorted by mounted soldiers.

"I'm going to miss work today—Natasha . . ." Melissa said with a chuckle and a flirty smile as they left Natasha's house in the morning. "And go with you to the bridge."

"No, you're not, Melissa," scolded a stern-faced Natasha. "You know full well the First Sergeant just took little Malin to the pommel horse a few days ago, and I'm afraid you'll be in trouble as well. Consequently, you are going to march straight to the dining hall. We will enjoy a simultaneous day off soon, and I have another secret place I want to show you."

Melissa looked at her friend with a bright smile. "It's a wonderful location," continued Natasha, "with soft . . . green . . . grass . . . hidden in the forest."

Melissa's eyes grew wide. "Now that sounds mysterious and fun. On our next no-workday, we'll go to your secret, mysterious place and have a private, important talk."

"That will make me very happy, Melissa," said a contented Natasha.

Melissa took Natasha by her shoulders and gave her a firm kiss. She then turned her sideways and laid a solid surprise slap across her behind, taking off in a run.

"Ouch! Melissa, that was hard!"

Melissa was laughing as she ran down the road, then looked back over her shoulder. "A spank's no good, naughty girl, if it's not hard." She blew Natasha a kiss and continued running.

Alone today, Natasha brought her book and found one of her favorite spots on the side of the bridge. She jumped up to stand on top of the sidewall, looking down-river. There were occasions when she could not believe the breathtaking view. The clear, flowing river, its banks lined with gorgeous trees, sparkled in the bright sunlight. Taking a deep breath, she inhaled the aromatic flax, now in bloom. Natasha so enjoyed the harvest; it was full of exciting days. Days of hard work but also celebrations. She could see the tops of a particular grove of trees. That was the location of her secret hiding place. The secret location had she revealed to Melissa as they left the house.

Turning and looking down the road, she could see an approaching caravan still some distance away. She sat down on the bridge sidewall—took out her book—closed her eyes to open it to an unknown page. It didn't matter where she began to read because she had the whole book memorized. Kathleena was one of the main characters in the book. Natasha began to read out loud.

"Kathleena sat on the side of the Great Stone Bridge."

Natasha stopped in disbelief. She looked at the first line again. It had always said, "Kathleena sat on the side of the bridge"—not "the Great Stone Bridge." She was sure—certain. Long ago, she had committed the entire book to memory. On many occasions they had read this book, surely, she and her mother would have noticed if the name of this bridge was mentioned. She looked at the words again, reaching up and gently touching them with her fingers.

She read out loud once more, *"The Great Stone Bridge."*

Closing her book, Natasha stared up into the clear-blue sky. How could this be happening, and why was it happening to her? She thought back to the reflection of the young man in the pool on the morning she had experienced the vision—his vision. Her insides felt funny, but she could not explain the feeling. She was afraid and tempted to run, but what would she be running from? She wished more than ever that her mother was here. She missed her mother. Perhaps she always would.

She was more anxious now than ever before to take Melissa to her secret place and talk. She could not stall any longer. She must talk with Melissa, anywhere they could be alone.

She continued to consider if she might inquire of the priestess at the Sacred Temple of Asa. Natasha laughed at herself, thinking out loud.

"Why would the renowned high priestess talk with me, a nobody? Maybe one of the girls who trained in the temple, one of the acolytes, would talk with me? I

know Melissa would accompany me to the temple and if two girls were asking, it might appear more imperative?"

The most important question remained unasked and unanswered. *"Were these ominous omens a warning of foreboding, or was the young man reflected in the pool somehow an answer?*

Suddenly, the sound of horses' hooves clopping on the surface of the stone bridge caused Natasha to jump, startling her as though she had been in another deep daydream. She looked down to see the caravan rolling onto the bridge. It was a military convoy with a mounted escort. Two lead guards preceded the wagons. They were first onto the stone surface, followed by the clangorous wagons, each one rolling onto the bridge, clamoring toward her.

When Natasha was alone on the bridge, the mounted soldiers and drivers often waved, whistled, or cat called as they passed by. Sometimes, Natasha would wave back at the "gentlemen," usually the drivers, who just smiled and waved. Conversely, she frequently offered an impolite sign to those who whistled or cat called, usually the mounted soldiers. More often than not, however, she just sat motionless, watching. Now days, coming to the bridge with Melissa had been more exciting. She was never certain what naughty gesture Melissa might do and how she might expose herself. Melissa was always a surprise, and daring, when it came to men.

Natasha recognized one of the lead mounted soldiers, a youthful officer, a Ravenbourne Warrior. It was always thrilling to see a Ravenbourne Warrior, especially on horseback. He passed by closely and kissed his fingers blowing her a kiss. She stuck her tongue out at him, causing him to laugh. He pulled up on his horse and turned it around, heading back down the length of the convoy, exposing the other rider.

The second rider wore only an army tunic, without armor or weapons, but the tunic bore the magnificent Ravenbourne crest, perhaps a new recruit for the Ravenbourne Corps. He was well built, with muscular arms. When he passed, he smiled, offering her a salute with two fingers.

Natasha froze with an open mouth when she saw his face. She could not believe it. How could this be happening to her? It was him—the beardless man in the pool's reflection. There could be no doubt—he passed by so close. His hair, his eyes, the scars—it was the same man. Natasha sat motionless. She did not see the other wagons and soldiers passing by, although in the background of her thoughts, she could occasionally hear a whistle or call, but as though far off in the distance. She sat—again in a daydream consciousness—deep in perplexing thought.

Abruptly looking up, Natasha could see that the caravan was long past, and she could no longer hear the horse hooves or the creaking wagons. She was not afraid, instead, bewildered or confused. These strange events had all been real, but what did they mean? Were they messages from the goddess Asa? Were they an answer to her prayer, or an ominous warning? And what did this young stranger have to do with it all? She put her book back into her bag and jumped off the side of the bridge onto the roadbed, heading back to the village.

These questions were now implacable and could wait no longer. She must talk with Melissa—she must—as soon as possible. Even though her dear friend was well versed in matters concerning men and sex, she was surely unlearned in these types of phenomena. But that did not matter. She knew Melissa, her loyal friend, would help her.

She wished her aunt would come. Natasha's aunt often came and stayed during those lengthy periods when her father was sent away on military duty. Her aunt taught both her and her mother. She wished she was not so impious. Perhaps then she could also go to the Sacred Temple of Asa and ask. She remained afraid to do so. And why would they listen to her? She once more reminded herself and reiterated her status—a nobody!

Natasha suddenly remembered Melissa's aunt, Ymir. She had always been friendly, even before Melissa came to Ravenbourne. When Natasha and her mother went past her house, they frequently stopped and Ymir and her mother chatted.

"I know Melissa and I could talk with her," Natasha, said out loud. "I think she is a follower of the goddess Asa. Surely, she would help me?"

Calea: Susanna's Blue Dots

"MASTER, I'VE BEEN CONTEMPLATING OUR virgin presentation to Princess Alexandria Ocaesio." Sitting at a small table, Master Smyth took a small slice of fruit from a serving bowl and tossed it into his mouth. He nodded for Calea to continue.

"I recommend we use a luxurious sheer apron design, one piece in front and one in back. They should be bare-breasted, but perhaps breast artwork and flowers. I will also need to consider other, seemingly small details, such as hair, jewelry, and footwear. I am guessing the Princess will not be easily impressed."

"I leave their apparel in your hands, Calea," responded Master Smyth. "We have two nannies, and there is no need for you to constantly watch our covey of maidens."

"Thank you, Master." Speaking softly, Calea smiled, slightly tilting her head—manipulating him with humble charm.

She then continued. "The former mistress of our villa, Master, maintained an elegant *boudoir*. I looked through it briefly, finding the attire I wore when meeting you. She stored a large selection of clothing and fabric, including elegant sheer material of *mauve* color, violet in Achaean, my Master."

Calea paused briefly while Master Smith proceeded to enjoy the succulent fruit and drink wine, but he still listened. *He seems to eat most of the day,* she thought. She continued.

"I am hoping to take one of the girls and go through the *boudoir,* examining the sheer material. Next, I'll prepare one complete costume for your inspection and approval. I also suggest, Master, we complete all the girls' costumes here at this villa before we embark on the caravan trip to Capital City. We could hardly create costumes on the road, if at all. More importantly, you will want the girls ready for presentation upon arrival, not spending those days in preparation."

Calea took a deep breath and sighed. "I don't believe I have talked so much in several full moons."

Master Smyth chuckled as he drank wine, and Calea resumed. "One more suggestion, Master." He nodded his approval.

"Once our *glacé* virgins are nestled in bed and Old Nanny is with them, ensuring they are peaceful . . ." Calea walked slow and elegantly toward Master Smyth while she talked. Softly taking his shoulders, she spoke close to his face so that he would inhale her breath, knowing this action usually motivated him to an erection.

"Nanny Talcrane and myself could visit your bedroom, Master, with the intention of exploring the delights of a *ménage 'a trois.* I believe you would be stimulated, watching two nude women embracing in your bed, knowing you would be next to share the honied touch of their lips."

Master Smyth couldn't care less concerning Opar words adopted into the Achaean language; *albeit,* he was familiar with this sexual phrase *ménage 'a trois.* "I look forward to that erotic encounter . . . my sweet," confessed a smiling Master Smyth, his attention drawn away from his fruit and wine.

Reaching down between his legs, Calea grasped his erection, applying a generous squeeze. "As do I and Nanny Talcrane, my Master."

Susanna followed her mother up the stairs to the former mistress's *boudoir*. The two nannies supervised the other twelve virgins at the pool and enjoyed a midday swim with the maidens as well. Master Smyth lumbered about in the large courtyard where the soldiers stayed at bivouac. Horses and wagons were kept there as well. The rest of household and the the slaves were preparing the next meal in the kitchen or entertaining soldiers in their courtyard tents. Consequently, they could remain alone and undisturbed, just as Calea had planned.

Located on the second floor, the *boudoir* appeared as a citadel rather than a higher floor. Here, Susanna and Calea could talk alone, undisturbed, for a considerable period. Walking into the room, young Susanna wondered what could compare to living in such a luxurious bedroom. Variegated in color, the walls were decorated with delightful paintings—some were erotic—causing her to quietly giggle to herself. Additionally, elegant tapestries hung by the bed, adding to its splendor.

Searching through the mistress's material, Calea brought out several pallets of the fine, sheer fabric, mostly white but with a limited example of other colors, especially *mauve*. She laid them on the bed. She brought out other stylish clothing of the female aristocracy, chitons and peplos, some dyed in red. Rarely seen in Opar, red-dyed material was not only expensive but also difficult to acquire. Opar did not trade with the primitive Dye Traders from the other side of the Hindu-Cush. To the city fathers, bronze was far too valuable for the protection of the city to use to appease aristocracy egos.

Susanna also went through the mistress's wardrobe—her breath taken by the beauty and expense of such elegant clothing. Such finery both delighted and saddened. She would never own one article of such rich attire, much less enjoy a full, large wardrobe. She was a pallake of the royal family of the Achaean Empire. Most likely, she would serve nude for the rest of her life. Her mother's voice caused her to look up, but she hid her melancholy mood.

"I don't think we will be disturbed for a considerable period, sweet love," said Calea as she carried an armful of clothing and laid the articles on the bed. "If we are, we will pretend we are trying on and looking through this material to make the presentation costumes. Which we will eventually do."

As they sat on the grand bed, Susanna began to cry. Her mother knew why. Calea took her daughter's face in her hands and tenderly kissed her. "I know, my sweet. It is not the life we envisioned— dreadfully unfair—terribly wrong. But look around us. The kitchen girls working, sweating every day in the hot kitchen. Soldiers take them by the hair and drag them out to the backyard, bend them over a table, pull their frocks up, and have their way with them. The other pallakes must entertain all the soldiers daily in those tents or face severe reprimand. We have watched together, in tears, the lines of naked Opar women, ropes tied around their necks and tied to the back of wagons, struggling as they began the torturous walk to the Capital City. All those poor females, many we knew. It could have been us, my love."

"I know Mother. I'm so thankful you saved us. But I still can't help but be forlorn when I think of the happiness we lost, our home, Kaelin, and Father."

Calea hugged and comforted Susanna. Her mother's embrace did ease her fears. "We saved each other, my love, and it's not over yet. We play a very serious game . . . one we cannot lose. To that end, I have something very important to tell you, love. This is why I have brought you here to be alone. What I'm going to tell you, this knowledge, will save your life and perhaps save mine as well. Do you understand?"

Susanna wiped her eyes with her finger tips. "Yes, Mother. . .." She said with a hard swallow. "I will be attentive and hope I can recall what you're saying."

Pleased, Calea once more kissed her daughter's beautiful face. "I am going to tell you an unbelievable tale—a deep hidden, secret—listen and remember."

"Lord Philemon, general of the Western Army of the Achaean Empire, came to Opar on business with the Opar Army. He saw me, an orphan girl, alone on the streets of Opar. He felt compassion for me and took me in. I returned with him to his villa, the Greenstone Estates. It was a magnificent villa, on the coast of the Inner Sea, to the west of the Capital City. Lord Philemon once said it would be a sin to leave such a beautiful child in the streets."

"The gracious Lord and his wonderful wife, Lady Baucis, raised me. They were very kind to an orphan of Opar, and I was treated more like a daughter rather than a servant. I cared for the younger children of the Lord and was their nanny, but I was also educated along with them. I was offered all the benefits any daughter of the Achaean aristocracy would receive."

"I am also not ashamed to tell you, my darling, I was Lord Philemon and Lady Baucis's lover. I slept with both on many a wonderful night. No one else within the estate was allowed to touch me . . . man or woman. Additionally, Lady Baucis wanted to keep my virginity and did not want me impregnated; therefore, those precautions were strictly enforced."

"One day, when I became of age, a contingency of the Military High Command of Opar arrived at the Lord's villa for an extended stay. With them was a new, handsome, and notoriously arrogant escort guard . . . your father."

Susanna smiled at the thought of her father. She could see him, a young, arrogant soldier. Just like Kaelin.

"He quickly learned I, too, was from Opar," continued Calea. "We fell in love, and I returned with him to Opar with Lord Philemon and Lady Baucis's blessing."

"We struggled for several years on a soldier's pay. Still, we were newlywed, in love, and very happy. It is strangely common for people of means to look back on their youth, when they were poor, having very little, and see those years as enjoyable days."

Susanna sighed and tried not to appear bored. Calea smiled— reached out to catch a lost tendril of her daughter's hair—combed it back—over the tender girl's ear. "I know this first part is boring, but I want to give you some context. What I must tell you is very important."

"I know, Mother. I'm listening."

"Yes, my girl. I know you are. Accordingly, before you were born, when Kaelin was just a boy, your father went off to war for Opar. We had very little during those days, only a rental apartment. Consequently, I decided to return to the home of my youth. Your father approved; in fact, it was his idea. Lord Philemon welcomed Kaelin and me with open arms, and so did his whole family. Even though I worried and fretted for your father's safety, it was nonetheless a wonderful period. I once again taught my Lord's children, along with Kaelin, who became fluent in the Empire's language during our stay."

"On one bright, sunny day, the Lord of Ravenbourne came to the villa. It seems my beloved Lord Philemon and Lord Ravenbourne's father were good friends. He had known the Lord of War from the mystical land of Ravenbourne since he was a boy. Well, the whole household burst with excitement. I cannot explain how thrilling it was watching Lord Ravenbourne lead his corps of mounted Ravenbourne Warriors into the courtyard. Every female, young and old, in the villa ran to a window, a door, or outside to watch."

"Most certainly, I was not a bashful maiden. A married woman, and Kaelin about ten or eleven summers of age. Nonetheless, Lord

Ravenbourne took a shine to me and requested me. I was told to keep him company and to tend to all his needs. Lord Ravenbourne asked one of his Ravenbourne Warriors to give warrior and fighting lessons to Kaelin. They trained every day with weapons. Kaelin was delighted."

Calea paused. She then continued with a soft yet sincere voice. "I slept with him, my sweet, and would not dare refuse him. The goddess was or was not with me, depending on one's interpretation. I was between the moons-of-fertility, and I should have been safe—nonetheless. ..." Calea hesitated and looked into Susanna's face. "I became pregnant, my darling."

Susanna now became frightened and sucked in her breath. She began to fear what she was about to hear. So fearful, she began to whimper. "Oh, Mother."

Reaching out and cupping her daughter's face, Calea gently pulled her to her breast. "Listen, my sweet love. Through no fault of your own, you are the daughter of the Lord of Ravenbourne." Calea held her daughter—petting her hair—allowing such frightening words to sink in.

"Powerful men, my love, the lords of the Empire, could care less if a servant girl becomes pregnant or not. I also remain confident, my sweet, Lord Ravenbourne did not know I was an orphan of Opar . . . nor did he ask or care. It was not important to him or my Lord Philemon, consequently, my origin was never discussed. But you are a special daughter of the Lord of Ravenbourne, and it might be a blessing or a curse. But let me finish so that you know it all, and we can decide our best course of action."

Continuing to pet Susanna's hair, Calea kissed her head. "All right, my love?"

"Yes, Mother," whimpered a frightened but attentive Susanna.

"On the small of your back, just above your buttocks, there are two blue dots, one on each side of your spinal cord."

"Yes, Mother, you told me they were birthmarks."

"They are, Susanna. You were born with the dots, but they are a special mark of the goddess Asa, identifying you to be a daughter of Lord Ravenbourne. The worship of Asa is prominent among women of the Achaean Empire but not of Opar, though the myth tells that the goddess was born in or near Opar. Accordingly, my sweet, knowledge of the worship and the secret rituals and beliefs is kept secret and difficult for a woman of Opar to learn. The priestesses and other women in the higher echelons of authority use a secret language. But this is what I was able to acquire."

Pausing for a moment, Calea caught her breath. She now wished she had brought a skin of water. She continued, "The kingdom of the goddess Asa is the mystical land of Ravenbourne, on the Southern Peninsula of the Achaean Empire. The land she created. Every city of any size throughout the kingdom will maintain a temple. Accordingly, the temple may be extensive and wealthy or small and humble. Every temple has a priestess, but the high priestess resides in the temple at Ravenbourne, the holy center of their worship."

"Every hundred years, daughters are sired by the Lord of Ravenbourne for some special purpose. I do not know that purpose or how many girls are born. I am certain; however, it is not sinister. The girls are not, say, sacrificed or kept as slaves but rather, held in high regard."

Unable to help herself, Susanna began to cry softly. She continued to lay her head against her mother's soft, comforting breast. Calea tenderly kissed her daughter's head and proceeded.

"While we lived in Opar, very few would ever witness the blue dots, outside our family. Those few who might would make no connections to the worship of Asa. Within the Empire, any man who might see the dots would be far more interested in your beautiful behind than any unusual birthmarks. But now we are slaves of the Achaean Empire.

Empire women who might see you nude and see the blue dots will know. Perhaps not in detail, but they will know that you are an important phenomenon to the goddess Asa and to her worship."

"I was torn whether to tell you or not. If you had no understanding, you could offer no information. Eventually, they would come to me. But we may be separated once we reach the Capital City. I fear Master Smyth will want to keep me, and he may be allowed. You, most certainly, will stay with Princess Alexandria in the royal palace. Once you are discovered, and you will be discovered, my love, they will question you."

Calea now took Susanna by the shoulders and looked sincerely into her eyes. She spoke with certainty. "It may be stressful . . . my love . . . but not painful. I do not believe they will hurt you. When you must, reveal this story. They will certainly come and question me, as well. Always—always keep this in mind—my dearest. You are the daughter of Lord Ravenbourne, perhaps the most powerful lord of the Achaean Empire, and you bear the mark of goddess Asa. Those two facts may well be your road to freedom and it may, perhaps, be mine."

Stroking Susanna's hair, Calea allowed this information to sink in and Susanna to regain a level of calmness. Calea had not, however, revealed all. A moment of truth—no—more than a moment—an episode from her past. An ominous secret, she had kept completely to herself for just over two decades. She had known Lord Ravenbourne some eleven years prior to the encounter she had just described to Susanna, when the Lord of War first became an army general.

Lord Ravenbourne had come to Greenstone on an official visit with Lord Philemon, who once was an army general. Early in his stay a regretful slave-woman had some how slighted the Lord of War from the mystical land of Ravenbourne, and she paid the painful penalty over Lord Philemon's knee. A small household crowd watched, and Lord Ravenbourne stood beside Calea. He had taken a liking to her.

After finishing his task, Lord Philemon ordered her off his lap and to go beg forgiveness from his powerful guest. When she scampered to him, her breasts jiggled in syncopated unison with her ankle bracelets. She fell to her knees—kissed his feet—taking hold of his knee with both hands, then looked up, her face red and wet with anguish.

The repentant slave-woman begged for forgiveness, and Lord Ravenbourne gave it, lifting her to her feet. She then scurried away, the wiggle in her well-formed buttocks, now glowing bright red and blue, would entice any man.

Lord Philemon approached and took Calea by her shoulders. "This virgin beauty is named Calea," he announced to his powerful friend. "She is several seasons past budding but remains a maiden. She is very clever."

He next looked around and nearly shouted in an angry voice.

"And she's better behaved than nearly all the women in my villa!" The crowd, mostly female servants and slaves, quickly dispersed to resume their daily tasks.

"I would enjoy a taste of her," stated Lord Ravenbourne, and Lord Philemon nodded in agreement. The commanding Lord took Calea's slender neck with both hands and brought her to him. The power overwhelmed her.

Although a virgin, she was not novel to passion. She slept with the Lord and Lady of the villa, and Lady Baucis taught her how to kiss and please a man. She took him by the waist with both hands, stepping against him. Looking up, she closed her eyes and opened her mouth. The embrace was warm and wonderful. The Lord from the land of Ravenbourne was well versed in *l'art de l'amour*.

After the kiss ended Lord Ravenbourne continued to cup Calea's neck, gazing into her young eyes. She was left breathless. "Sweeter than the cheery wine of Ravenbourne, Lord Philemon. . .." Lord Ravenbourne smiled. "I look forward to more."

The powerful men laughed and walked away. Both remained in a pleasant mood, talking while they moved along. Calea's origin, an orphan child from Opar, was not mentioned by Lord Philemon. After so many seasons had past, it was not important to him and he did not consider it anymore. Calea followed behind, her heart fluttering.

"We must keep this very secret, my love; no one must know." Lifting her head from her breast, Calea wiped the tears from her daughter's beautiful eyes, prompting her to a slight smile.

"Now, let us look over this wonderful material. It will be a shame to leave this elegant wardrobe and cloth." Susanna nodded in agreement and tried her best to smile.

CHAPTER 26

Lady Ravenbourne: Preparation

WOMEN OF THE TAOLIAN RACE held the reputation of exotic beauty. Even so, Ginal remained a remarkable example, blessed by the goddess with a stunning female shape. She was tall—as tall as a man—lithely slender, muscular, with small, flat, yet attractive firm breasts. Her narrow waist rested on top of muscular thighs, shapely hips, and gorgeous round buttocks that, when she passed by, no man could resist watching. All mortals could see her strength in her walk.

Her facial features were equally stunning. She generally wore a pleasant but serious expression. Her violet eyes were deep, dark, and mysterious, narrow but clear—the wonderous eye color of all her race. Her full lips were more than inviting. Legend held that if a Taolian woman reached out and cupped your face or neck—gently pulled you toward her—no mortal, man or woman, could help but surrender. None could resist, and all would come to her for the warm embrace of her kiss. There remained no doubt, Ginal was an exceptional Taolian beauty—but likewise a chameleon.

Trained from a budding youth by the Ravenbourne Warriors of Lord Ravenbourne's elite corps, Ginal was transformed into a skilled, lethal warrior. By official design, she served as personal bodyguard to Ann Y'Sloic, Lady of Ravenbourne, but in reality, she was much more—exceptionally more. Only on very rare occasions did she leave Lady Ravenbourne's side. Every other day, she took a half day's leave from Lady Ravenbourne to exercise and train with the Ravenbourne Corps. Occasionally, in the presence of and thus so ordered by Lord Ravenbourne, she might be excused. Otherwise, she ate and slept with her Mistress, day and night. Indeed, Ginal served as Lady Ravenbourne's bodyguard, but she was also her companion, her friend, and her lover. They loved each other but also knew each other's roles.

Ginal was all personalities to Ann Y'Sloic, androgynous, both man and woman. She was forever unyielding, loyal, and obedient. On the one side, she bore the gentle, soothing hand of a lover, but on the other side, if so requested, she could become the strong, hard hand of discipline. She was skilled in all weapons but best with sword and shield. She was the only female Ravenbourne Warrior to have ever existed.

Nearly every morning, the Ravenbourne Mistress completed a tour of her sanctuary in whole or in part. Busy females toiled throughout the wall-enclosed grounds. The majority were young, especially the slave-girls and pallakes, but a wide spectrum of ages were represented—some slave—some free. Slaves were unclothed, but free women dressed in accordance with their tasks. The contingent of skilled gardeners, for instance, usually wore thick pants and shirts similar in dress to the Hyacinth Gatherers. Conversely, artists and musicians were adorned as any middle-class woman of Cappa.

Ginal walked along on the right side, slightly behind her Mistress. Her Ravenbourne Warrior tunic was cut and sewn to fit her female form. She bore armor only on the outside of the sanctuary but always carried a sword and dagger. Old Nanny occupied the left side of Lady Ravenbourne, while the three hand-maidens followed behind. Occasionally, Old Nanny would drop to the rear of the procession to ensure the girls kept up and did not fall behind.

As Lady Ravenbourne approached, all slaves were required to fall to both knees with bowed heads. Their Mistress might or might not address them. If she did, she lifted their heads with her finger-tips and spoke, smiling into their faces. Ginal stood by, ready to correct and discipline any female-slave, if necessary.

The lady approached a middle-aged gardener who stood with bowed head. Behind her, three small pallakes went to their knees and likewise lowered their heads. Lady Ravenbourne spoke to the gardener, who then raised her head.

"Good morning, Agatha."

"Good morning. my Lady."

"Oh, wonderful. The purple blossoms are beautiful this year. Congratulations!" praised Lady Ravenbourne.

"Thank you, my Lady. We've been blessed by the goddess with a bountiful crop this season," replied Agatha.

"We will require several wreaths this morning for the receiving," stated Lady Ravenbourne. She reached down and picked up a green-leaved vine plant adorned with purple flowers and brought the blossom to her nose.

"Understood, my Lady. My girls have been working since dawn, and we have three large baskets full now."

"Splendid, Agatha. We will need the wreaths at the Receiving Hall after prayers. Keep a close eye on your girls, Agatha. We don't want them wandering off or becoming lost outside the sanctuary."

"Understood, my Lady. There is only one with trouble on her mind."

"Oh yes, I know . . ." Lady Ravenbourne sighed. "Little KatNip, yet our Lord continues to protect her. Well, do your best, Agatha. I can't help, but have confidence she'll find some mischief. One day, Lord

Ravenbourne will lift his protection—I will cook her adorable little bottom for her."

Agatha laughed out loud. "Yes, my Lady.

We will keep a close watch on her while we're in the Receiving Hall. We shouldn't be there long."

Artist Mar-Hellen approached Lady Ravenbourne in the central area of the sanctuary. Her servant followed behind. A wooden box, held in place over the nude girl's shoulder with a leather strap, contained the paint, brushes, and other tools of an artist's trade.

Fully clothed, Mar-Helen was a free woman who, in the distant past, had signed a contract to work for Lady Ravenbourne and live in the sanctuary. The length of the contract expired years ago, but she discovered she enjoyed the company of women and remained. Last year, she once again considered returning to the outside world. Lady Ravenbourne, offered her a young, attractive pallake to be her helper and possible trainee. The slave-girl turned out to be eagerly affection-ate and enthusiastic to learn the artist trade. Consequently, Mar-Helen continued life in the sanctuary.

As the artist approached, Mistress Ravenbourne's three handmaids jumped up and down, clapping their hands and laughing, causing the bells on their ankles to chime in unison. Breast and body painting found popularity with young female-slaves and pallakes across the Empire, who were usually required to appear bare-breasted. The opportunity to wear clothes and the adventure of leaving the private sanctuary with their Mistress to visit the Receiving Hall made them all giddy. Although body painting was a simple task for the experienced artist, it was equally a pleasure for Mar-Helen to decorate the near perfect-figures of each adorable handmaiden. She initiated the task with Kasena. Beginning at her navel, she created two green vines, with attached miniature leaves, that gracefully spiraled up her stomach—around her ribs—culminating at each petite nipple. Her small breasts were transformed into two bright-red flowers. Each nipple became the center bud of the flower. Finally, a pink tea-rose was added, just below her breasts.

After Mar-Helen had completed Kasena, she continued to create the same beautiful flower designs on Malia and Aleah. The three girls laughed, joked, and teased each other during the whole process. This was, however, just the beginning of their preparations. Old Nanny assisted each handmaiden in dressing.

A belt of lace and gold adorned each slender waist just below the navel. A narrow piece of rare translucent cloth material, trimmed with cerise lace, hung from the belts down to their knees, partially concealing their flowering innocence in front and the valley of the buttocks' cheeks in the back. Each girl wore dazzling earrings of gold with an attached crystal stone, and gold arm-bands adorned each left arm while a gold bracelet wrapped each left wrist. To complete the attire, a wreath of purple flowers sat on top of the three pretty heads.

Prompted by Old Nanny's instruction and hand clapping, the three handmaidens ran to find Ginal's armor. They enjoyed helping to fit the leather and bronze onto Ginal's large, commanding figure. They each rubbed their hands over the shiny bronze shield and the beautiful Ravenbourne symbol. It required two girls to carry her shield.

"Be careful now—be careful . . .!" called out the stern Old Nanny. "Don't drop that heavy bronze on your feet." Eventually, Ginal was outfitted in full armor. She held the shield in her left hand. She did not carry a spear, leaving her right hand free to assist her Mistress, but she could draw the sword in the blink of an eye.

Lady Ravenbourne looked over her three beauties, and she was pleased. "Beautiful . . . elegant . . . and revealing . . . but also discreet. Are we ready?" she asked with a smile.

Kasena, Malia, and Aleah all replied, "Yes, Mistress." Each girl also wore a beautiful smile.

Suddenly, Ginal drew her sword, seen only as a flash. The swift action caused the three slave-girls to drop their smiles, cover their mouths with small hands, and quickly step back, frightened, and back up against Old Nanny. Lady Ravenbourne and Old Nanny, accustomed to warrior habits, only chuckled at the timid slave-girls' behavior.

Holding her bronze sword up in front of her, Ginal offered a military salute. "My Lady!" she said in a serious, military tone.

Lady Ravenbourne acknowledged Ginal's salute, turned, and walked toward the doors of her private sanctuary. The others followed in their usual places.

CHAPTER 27

Kaelin: Receiving Hall

A FIRST-TIME VISITOR TO THE enchanting Ravenbourne Estate was always left breathless. The entry road to the main gate, paved with white, flat stones provided by the estate's quarry and lined with enormous, ancient trees, gave one a sense of entering a numinous, ancient realm—a dominion—not belonging to this world. The road crossed a clear, sparkling creek spanned by a wonderous arch bridge constructed, to incorporate an ancient lava flow and white quarry stone. Molten rock had once flowed over the creek and several large boulders forming a natural black lava rock bridge. The current bridge was constructed over this natural lava formation. Ravenbourne Warriors patrolled the road and saluted all visitors, which gave them a feeling of welcome but also informed them that no one approached the Ravenbourne Estate unnoticed. If the entry road did not fill a guest with enchantment—the main entry gate would.

A large black lava tube formed the Main Gate. The entry wall appeared as an expanding high lava flow, stacked with white stones. Gates of tall wooden beams, held together by thick bronze bands, barred the entry and exit to the lava tube, reaching some eight cubits in height.

Ravenbourne Warriors stood guard at the gate and inquired of each visitor. Certainly, village residents, who worked on the estate and frequent merchants, came and went each day without ceremony. Conversely, a visiting dignitary or members of the aristocracy required

269

an official inquiry. Once it was known who they were and their business—and most certainly if they bore an official document requesting their presence—they were provided with a formal warrior escort, both mounted and on foot. Once inside, all visitors were astonished, having stepped into an enchanted world they could not believe nor describe.

Dignitaries were escorted down paved roads and paths through enchanted gardens of exotic plants and birds brought from all over the Achaean world. They would be taken over bridges that spanned lavabed pools of hot, steaming water, flowing from deep inside the world's core. And finally, they would walk along spring banks of clear, cold water that flowed into an adjacent hot pool of water. All the natural wonders were, most certainly, created by the goddess Asa. The entry road and paths ended at the Receiving Hall.

Anywhere else in the known world, the Receiving Hall would have been described as a temple, dedicated to some powerful god or goddess. Common with many Ravenbourne features, it was constructed around and incorporated with the natural black-lava. The flooring was paved in white flagstone and ceramic tiles. Tall pillars of white stone lined the circular gallery. At one end, a white stone stage had been built on top of a lava flow. Steps lined the length of the stage, and large, bright tapestries hung on the back wall. Two regal chairs rested on the sunlit stage—magnificent seats for the Lord and Lady of Ravenbourne. In another country, the chairs would have been called thrones, but only the Emperor sat on a throne in the Capital City of the Achaean Empire.

A score of female serving-slaves gracefully maneuvered throughout the Receiving Hall, bearing oinochoes of drink and trays of bread and feta. Following the Ravenbourne custom, each was elegantly attired in identical, albeit meager dress. Snuggly fitted red undergarments were partially concealed by sheer, white aprons falling from each slender waist to just above the knees. Each narrow pinafore was held in place by a soft, black-rope belt. A bright red flower was embroidered in the appropriate spot on the front of each delicate apron. Small bare feet quietly stepped and glided on the white, polished floor. Around each right ankle, a thin gold-gilded chain linked with an identification band and two attached copper bells clinked and jingled, creating a distinctive chiming with every right-footed step.

Commonly referred to as "flower maidens" by frequent guests these female-slaves did not speak unless addressed but offered a delightful smile to all. They were bare from the waist up, although a painting of two green vines with small leaves gracefully extended from each navel upward, then circled each breast, ending with a small pink tea-rose just below their breasts. Artist Mar-Helen had completed the artwork, similar to the style she had decorated Lady Ravenbourne's three hand-maidens. A purple flower wreath, set on top of each pretty head, was provided by Agatha and her female crew.

A long table was placed against the side of the hall in front of the tall pillars. It was covered with a lengthy, red tablecloth, stylishly trimmed. The table offered a generous display of drinking mugs—oinochoes of water and beer—and the celebrated Ravenbourne cherry wine, including large plates of bread and feta. Three flower maidens stood behind the table, assisting patrons.

The receiving steward greeted arrivals, especially visiting dignitaries and other aristocrats. After an exchange of pleasantries, he would wave a flower maiden over, who promptly stepped up with a refreshment tray and a smile. The steward also ensured that the Master of Ceremonies was aware of anyone of position, such as a lord or a lady.

Lieutenant Rohan presented Spearman Kaelin to the Ravenbourne Corps commander, Colonel Davis, with orders sealed and signed by Lord Ravenbourne. The youthful warriors shook hands, and Kaelin wished him luck. Rohan then departed to complete his delivery of the new slave-girls and the final disposition of the convoy. After that, he would be off on his thirty-day furlough and his personal mission of locating an agreeable group of Hyacinth Gatherers.

Authorized a pack horse and supplies, Rohan inquired of the quarter master, whom he had known for years. "Sergeant Yazen, who should I ask to obtain information concerning Hyacinth Gatherers?"

"That's easy, Lieutenant . . . First Spear Thoas. Lives in the village. Married to a Hyacinth girl . . . fair beauty she was. They say he met her when he guarded a Hyacinth group. He's a good story-teller and, he'll talk with you. Take a few pouches of beer."

"I've heard of him, Sergeant, a renowned warrior, but that is all I know. How would I find him?" asked Rohan.

"That's also easy, Lieutenant," replied Sergeant Yazen. "Ask anyone in the village . . . they'll know where he lives. Saw him earlier today. He stopped by to talk about ash spear shafts. Said he was going to the Receiving. After that, he'll be in the village somewhere."

"By the way, Lieutenant," continued Sergeant Yazen. "You should stay on here at Ravenbourne a few days . . . enjoy a taste of local women. You won't find prettier slave-girls, brothel whores, or free-women anywhere in the Empire. Slave-girls won't say no to Ravenbourne Warrior."

"Thanks, Sergeant Yazen! That's a splendid idea. I may just do that," said Rohan as he turned and walked away.

"Good luck, Lieutenant! Don't come back married."

Lieutenant Rohan raised his hand over his head and waved as he made his way toward his waiting mount and pack horse.

"Spearman Kaelin," said Colonel Davis, dressed in full ceremonial uniform. "I have received your orders from Lord Ravenbourne, and it is my pleasure to welcome you to the Ravenbourne Corps. We have been anxious for your arrival."

"It all remains overwhelming for me, Colonel Davis," answered Kaelin, "but I am grateful to be here and likewise anxious to begin my duties."

"Excellent! Your first ten days will be an indoctrination period," continued Colonel Davis. "You'll spend it with Sergeant Lutas here."

Kaelin looked over to see a mature soldier standing to the side, also dressed in ceremonial uniform. He nodded. Kaelin likewise responded.

"Each full moon cycle," instructed Colonel Davis, "Lord and Lady Ravenbourne hold a formal 'Receiving' where anyone from throughout Ravenbourne having justified concerns may come and address them. It is an important, formal event. Lady Ravenbourne has requested that she meet and greet you at this Receiving. It is in the process of beginning. Sergeant Lutas will take you there. I will meet up with you at the Receiving Hall. That is all I have for now."

Understanding his meaning, both Sergeant Lutas and Kaelin saluted. They turned and left the Ravenbourne Corps Headquarters.

"Magical and fokken overwhelming—is it not?" offered Sergeant Lutas, voicing both a statement and a question as he and Kaelin made their way from the Ravenbourne Fortress, through the North Gate, and into the dream-like world of the Ravenbourne Villa.

"Not in my wildest dreams have I imagined such a place existed." Kaelin was unsure he believed all that he saw.

"Oh! I understand. Was the same myself. Just like seeing a fresh little kunt for your first taste," laughed Sergeant Lutas. The rustic Sergeant abruptly hacked—turned his head—and spit.

"Everyone is overwhelmed when they first see Ravenbourne. Legends say that the village, the buildings, the walls, and gates were built by Lord Ravenbourne's ancestor . . .but the land was created by the goddess Asa. At least, that's what they say."

Sergeant Lutas stopped, and Kaelin followed suit. "Well, Spearman Kaelin, as Colonel Davis said, you'll spend ten days with me, an induction period . . . and well. All new recruits do it."

"Understood," replied the recruit, continuing to look around. Kaelin saw a dream like world of magnificent gardens surrounded by tall, thick walls. A breathtaking landscape composed of a strange combination of black lava flows—running water—unique vegetation—and white stone.

"Well, where to start?" asked Sergeant Lutas, unmoved by the indescribable landscape. "The quarter master will take your measurements; your armor should be ready in a few days. For now, your tunic, sandals, sword, and dagger are all you need."

"The armor you wore in the Opar Army won't be much different than here," continued Sergeant Lucas, "but I might as well point it out while I'm dressed in full armor." Lucas reached up and removed his helmet.

"Bronze helmet with a colored plume to identify rank. Red for officers, green for sergeants and 9th men, and spearmen wear white. The leather jerkin covers the torso, with this bronze Ravenbourne symbol clamped to the center of the chest." He reached up and pointed to the symbol. "Underneath, a white tunic, just like the one you're wearing now."

Kaelin continued to listen to Sergeant Lucas while they walked on. The sergeant cleared his sinuses—spit on the ground—and began to chuckle. "They say women make a fortune sewing these Ravenbourne symbols on our tunics. If you ever see a woman wearing a Ravenbourne tunic . . .." He paused. "Never mind. I'll tell you about that later."

"I didn't carry my shield and spear because I weren't part of the ceremony. We have the best bronze shields in the army. They also have the same Ravenbourne symbol, only painted black in the center of the shield. Bronze greaves, lined with soft cloth . . . leather wrist-guard on the right wrist . . . and a spear in hand. Well, you know the rest."

Sergeant Lucas paused again for a moment, then remembered something. "Oh yeah! The red capes. Those are worn only in ceremony. We won't wear them very much, but they are something. Women also love those capes. I've always wondered how much one of them capes cost—must be a fortune."

Kaelin noted that the guards posted at the North Gate and on the wall wore full armor and carried a spear but did not have on a red cape.

"I'll just keep tellin' you what you need to know," said the Sergeant Lutas in a rough, nearly hoarse voice, "no certain order. Lord Ravenbourne spares no expenses for the Ravenbourne Corps, armor, weapons, horses, food. We even have the best wagons in the army. And wait 'til you see the horses the Equestrian Corps and the courier's ride."

"Let's see now," continued the veteran warrior. "Warriors on guard duty . . . ah, such as at the North Gate we came through back there. We all do it. Usually boring but not always. Let's say you have to break up two slave-girls in a scuffle and teach them a lesson in behavior. Can be fun—always exciting. Unusual, but things happen. Anyways, guards are not at attention. They are alert to what's going on around them and respond when they need to. We talk with all the people and answer questions . . . but we are not there to talk story."

"Well, this is the Receiving Hall," reported Sergeant Lutas. "We'll meet up with Colonel Davis here. This will be an eye-opener for you, Kaelin. And. . . ." Sergeant Lutas chuckled. "I've only been at one or two of these myself. Should be fun."

The Master of Ceremonies waited patiently outside the prodigious doors to the sanctuary with Lady Ravenbourne's warrior escort, all formally attired in ceremony uniforms. Their graceful red capes fell from their shoulders down their backs, reaching their knees and calves. By order of Lord Ravenbourne, her escort was comprised of five Ravenbourne Warriors—a captain in the lead, followed by two sergeants and two spearmen. Lord Ravenbourne's Law stated that on any occasion that Lady Ravenbourne left her sanctuary, she must be accompanied by her escort.

The eye of the needle opened. The Mistress of Ravenbourne walked through, followed by her company. A bright cerise peplos of fine woven mousseline fell from her slender shoulders, reaching nearly to her ankles, and spoke of both wealth and elegance. Finley trimmed in white cotton—painstakingly embroidered with small pink tea-roses—the exquisite dress would most certainly lift the eyebrows of any aristocratic female. Gold clasps anchored the peplos at her shoulders, adorned with precious stones. A lace belt was fitted around her narrow waist, kept snug by a golden buckle. It was decorated with the Ravenbourne symbol, the same found on each Ravenbourne Warrior's shield.

The ends of her shimmering auburn hair brushed against her calves and gently swayed with the rhythm of her hips with each step of her gold-trimmed sandals as she led her escort through the corridor and onto the Receiving Hall stage. She stopped, standing in front of her throne-like chair—adjacent the seat of Lord Ravenbourne.

The lady's trailing entourage took their appointed places on the stage. Her three handmaids reclined on the floor around her chair on thin pillows, one in front and one on each side. Ginal stood on her right side, while Old Nanny placed herself several paces behind her Mistress. The escort commander took position on her left. The two sergeants stopped near the front edge of the stage at the left and right ends, while the two spearmen stopped at the back of the stage, behind the sergeants.

There was no need for the Master of Ceremonies to announce Lady Ravenbourne's arrival. All the guests who filled the Receiving Hall were drawn to the stage and now stood in front of her ceremonial chair—waiting in silence.

"I welcome all of you to our Receiving Hall," said Lady Ravenbourne in a commanding yet sophisticated voice that carried throughout the hall. "We have much to cover this morning. We shall proceed." Low voices were heard across the hall as she took her chair.

The Master of Ceremonies, stood to the far right on a wide step, three steps down from the top of the stage. When Lady Ravenbourne was settled, he struck the end of his crosier on the step with three counts, in the same manner a soldier would salute with his spear. Once more, a hush fell over the Receiving Hall.

He called out in a lurid voice, as if giving orders to soldiers under his command.

"Spearman Kaelin . . . Ravenbourne Warrior . . . Step forward!"

Standing at the back of the hall, near the entryway, between Colonel Davis and Sergeant Lutas, Kaelin began to walk toward the stage and the seated Lady of Ravenbourne. A loud applause broke out as the crowd divided, clearing a path that he followed to stand at the foot of the stage at attention. Lady Ravenbourne stood, and a hush fell upon the crowd. All this had taken Kaelin by surprise, although he did not show it, keeping a solemn face.

"Welcome to Ravenbourne, Kaelin," she said with a smile and sincere voice. "I am pleased you are here and pleased you have joined the proudest soldiers in the Achaean Empire and beyond—the Ravenbourne Warrior Corps."

Again, loud applause erupted, but on this occasion, it was quelled by the crosier of the Master of Ceremonies. Kaelin nodded slightly, looking up into her face. As with all men upon first seeing Lady Ravenbourne, he was somewhat taken aback by her. He was not prepared for how beautiful she was.

"All of Ravenbourne," continued Lady Ravenbourne, "is grateful to you, Kaelin. You have saved the life of our great Lord. I know that Lord Ravenbourne questioned you at length, although I am uninformed of what he asked or how you answered. Therefore, grant me the audacity to ask you: why did you save our Lord?"

"I answered that question when asked by Lord Ravenbourne, my Lady, and my answer remains the same," said Kaelin respectfully. "I did not know the senior man under attack in the dais, except the obvious. That he was an important aristocrat but not a typical man of wealth. I could see he was a skilled warrior fighting for his life, unafraid. It did not seem right that he should meet his fate in such a manner. I was a slave . . . I sought freedom . . . I still do. And perhaps the gods had provided me an open gate to freedom. I took it."

"Might not your spear have struck my Lord as well as the brazen assassin?" asked Lady Ravenbourne, keeping her sincere tone.

"No, my Lady!" replied a confident Kaelin. "Little or no chance. My spear strikes at that which I aim. Even if so, my Lady, the Lord of Ravenbourne would have wanted me to take that risk—small or great. It was his only chance for life."

Once more, the crowd in the great hall erupted with an emotional outburst of applause and cheer. Kaelin remained stoic and seemingly unaffected. Lady Ravenbourne looked up and around the room, smiling, but the Master of Ceremonies would have none of this. Again, he quieted the hall with raps of his crosier on the stone steps.

"I believe you Kaelin," confessed Lady Ravenbourne, retaining her impressive and erudite voice, heard throughout the hall. "I offer you a gift to convey my gratitude. In the future, you may approach me with a Request. If it is prudent and within my power, it will be granted, realizing Lord Ravenbourne rules Ravenbourne. . . ." She paused briefly. "Not I."

Kaelin slowly drew his sword, allowing her soldiers to see he was not hostile, and holding it up and out in front of himself, he went down to one knee. He looked up at Lady Ravenbourne's alluring face and called out in a loud voice.

"My Lady! My sword, my spear, my heart, and my life are yours— from now—until the end of my days!"

The hall remained in an eerie hush as Lady Ravenbourne descended the stage in graceful steps, able to look down at Kaelin and not her feet. She stepped up to Kaelin, who continued to hold out his sword. She reached out her hand—placed her fingertips under his chin—gently raising him up.

"Rise, Spearman Kaelin . . . Ravenbourne Warrior!" she called out in a clear, loud voice. "Come, all, and welcome him."

Once more, the hall broke out in cheer and applause. Lady Ravenbourne turned around and walked back up the steps, gracefully lifting the hem of her peplos. Kaelin sheathed his sword, with the crowd gathering around him to do as the Lady had spoken. All present wanted to shake his hand, pat his shoulders, or simply just touch him. He made his way through the crowd, somewhat awkwardly, to return to Colonel Davis and Sergeant Lutas, who likewise congratulated him.

The three Ravenbourne Warriors then made their way toward the Receiving Hall entry. They suddenly stopped while Colonel Davis stepped away to have a brief discussion with retired First Spear Thoas. He returned, and the three Ravenbourne Warriors continued and out through the elaborate entry while the crosier of the Master of Ceremonies once more struck the steps of the stage. They walked along a path, reaching a distance so that the noise of the Receiving Hall dissipated. They stopped, and Colonel Davis turned to Kaelin.

"A new life begins for you, Spearman Kaelin. Young men and boys from across the whole Empire dream of becoming a Ravenbourne Warrior. And here you are . . . once a slave . . . now a free man. I leave you in good hands." He spoke as if giving an order.

Kaelin responded with a salute and so did Sergeant Lutas. Colonel Davis returned their salutes, turned, and made his way toward the Ravenbourne Corps Headquarters. Kaelin and Lutas continued walking—Kaelin looked at Lutas with a serious expression.

"Free from slavery, Sergeant, but not a free man. Not yet."

CHAPTER 28

Melissa: Dragon's Tongue

HOLDING AN EMPTY BEER OINOCHOE, Natasha stood by the front entry to the kitchen. She looked about the large dining hall, wondering where Melissa could be. Nearly all the men were seated and eating. "If she's late, she'll likely be in trouble again," she said softly to herself. Earlier, she overheard the First Sergeant state that there was a new recruit; consequently, all the help, especially the servers, would be expected to be prompt.

Suddenly, to her surprise, First Sergeant Klause stormed out from the rear kitchen exit with Melissa at his side. He held her by the neck and marched her down the wall, past Natasha, and up the steps onto the platform.

"Commander!" called out the First Sergeant in his loud, imposing voice.

The commander looked up from his meal as a shroud of silence fell over the hall.

"I caught this girl stealing from the kitchen—again! I've warned her on a handful of instances that if she was caught once more, it would cost her ten licks over the pommel."

Melissa stood shaking while the First Sergeant tightened his grip on her neck. The company of soldiers stirred with surprise—chatted among themselves—then fell once more into silence.

Natasha was now very worried. Although she could only see Melissa's back, she could see she was shaking. This was going to be real trouble Melissa might not escape from.

"Might that be too austere, First Sergeant?" responded the commander. "After all, she's just a girl."

"Obedience is learned through severity, Sir!"

The commander took in his breath and swallowed. "Is the girl married?" queried the commander.

"No, commander. She is single," answered the First Sergeant.

"Well, then, does she have a father we could report her to, recommending he give serious thought to her need for discipline?" continued the commander.

"No, Sir, she does not," growled Sergeant Klause.

"Does a Ravenbourne Warrior protect her?"

"No, Sir, commander," echoed the implacable First Sergeant. "If we do not correct her, no one will. Once before, I applied the strap to her, but it appears it was not enough licks to change her childish behavior."

The commander looked around at the faces of his top command, seated at his table. No objection was raised. "All right, do your duty, First Sergeant," ordered the commander.

Melissa's hands went to her mouth. "No! No! Please, First Sergeant! Please!" she pleaded—her hands now folded in front of her distraught face.

Stepping in front of the frightened Melissa, the stern First Sergeant reached up, roughly pulling the drawstrings at the neckline of her frock. With experienced hands, he unfastened her leather belt and lifted it and her sheathed dagger, letting them fall to the wooden floor. The hall remained a caustic quiet as the belt and dagger echoed a rare sound, colliding with the smooth wood surface.

"Arms up!" he ordered as he pulled her flaxen frock up and over her head, revealing a stunning young figure of round hips . . . narrow, flat waist . . . and firm, full breasts. Low catcalls and whispers filled the stone walls of the hall as the First Sergeant dropped her frock. It floated silently down, quietly covering her belt and dagger.

In a desperate attempt to intercede, Natasha set the empty oinochoe down against the wall and hurriedly ran up the steps, falling on her knees in front of the resolute soldier. "Please First Sergeant, please! Give her another opportunity. She does not mean to be impudent, and I know she can change her ways. I'll watch her to ensure she changes and never steals again. I promise!"

The First Sergeant, wearing a rare smile, reached down and lifted Natasha's chin with his fingers. "You're a loyal friend, girl, but Melissa has had too many chances. Her day of reckoning has come."

Releasing Natasha's chin, Sergeant Klause turned to pull the drawstrings of Melissa's tan, cotton undergarments and, slipping his fingers inside, relieved her of her last stitch of clothing, except for her soft leather shoes. He dropped her undergarments letting them fall on top of her frock. Melissa now began to cry in earnest as a quiet calm—chuckling—and "ahs" rose from the warriors' tables in response to the frightened girl—now completely exposed. With heavy steps, the First Sergeant walked to the wall and took down the terrifying Dragon's Tongue. Although nearly in tears, Natasha remained silent as she rose to her feet.

Suddenly, an unexpected loud voice called out.

"I'll take her punishment, First Sergeant!"

A warrior seated at the first table stood up. A mysterious hush fell across the hall. Only Melissa's quiet whimpering could be detected—she stood with her left arm crossed over her breasts—her right hand covering her flower of innocence—as best she could.

The commander now rose, bringing an abrupt hush to his warriors. "Our new recruit, Spearman Kaelin!" he called out. "You will endure the Dragon Tongue's burning caress for this girl?"

"I will. Commander," echoed Spearman Kaelin.

"You come to us with an admirable reputation, Kaelin," called out the commander. "An Opar soldier taken captive at the fall Opar. You saved our Lord Ravenbourne from assassination as a Feohtan fighter with a spear throw from the arena at Cappa. Spearman Kaelin. . .." He hesitated. "You need not prove yourself here."

"I'll take her place. Commander," Kaelin called out again.

There was a momentary pause as the hall remained silent. The commander again looked around at those seated at his table. No objection was raised. "A test of pain and courage," stated the commander, now looking out over his whole command. The silence continued.

He turned his eyes to the First Sergeant. "What say you, Sergeant Klause?"

Taking a deep breath, the First Sergeant bellowed in a low, loud voice. "If he will take the tongue in the same manner as this girl would . . . naked and bent over the pommel. I say, why not . . .commander? Why not?"

The dining hall erupted as nearly a hundred Ravenbourne Warriors shouted out in unison—a strange, high-pitched call . . . pounding their fists and beer mugs on the table tops.

"You heard the conditions, Spearman Kaelin. Advance forward," ordered the commander. He then sat back down. Kaelin turned and walked over to the steps, descending to the platform.

Natasha hurried over and reached her arm around Melissa's bare waist. She stood in front of her to conceal her embarrassment as best she could. Melissa folded her arms over her breasts.

The neoteric Spearman approached; Natasha now had the opportunity to look into the face of the heroic warrior named Kaelin. She was taken aback and gasped. She opened her mouth and sucked in a mouth full of air, then swallowed it hard. Had she been anywhere else, she would have cried out loud. It was him. The same handsome, scarred face she had seen in the pool on that faithful, still—unexplained day. The same new warrior she had witnessed arriving with the slave escort on the Tyner Bridge. The same striking, wounded, young face.

He offered her and Melissa a casual, beautiful smile, seemingly undisturbed by his circumstances. Meanwhile, Melissa trembled. Bewildered, Natasha held her tightly, hoping to calm them both.

The confident Kaelin made his way to the edge of the platform, facing the hall. He unbuckled his belt and Ravenbourne dagger and dropped them to the floor. He pulled his Ravenbourne tunic over his head. Natasha now moved Melissa across the platform to the other side to be out of the way. His tunic fell to the floor.

A stone monument stood just inside the Main Gate to the Ravenbourne Villa. On it was carved the Oath of the Ravenbourne Warriors. Poised on top of the monument stood a beautiful sculpture, in pure white stone, of a naked, striking warrior holding a spear and shield. It was the most handsome young man Natasha had ever seen. She fell in love with the striking figure, as did many innocent girls of Ravenbourne. They dreamed that somehow the figure could come alive and carry them off to an unknown mystical land and marry them. There they would live a long, happy life together. In Natasha's mind, that perfect sculpture had now come to life in the form of Kaelin. She remained bewildered.

Kaelin now untied his loin-cloth. Dropping it to the floor on top of his tunic, he stood nude and exposed in front of the whole company unashamed, unafraid, unembarrassed. Natasha could see painful whip scars across his back and an ugly wound on his left side. Glancing down, she sucked in her breath at the horrible whip scars laid across his round buttocks.

She thought to herself. *What cruelty could do such horrendous acts to such a stunning young man?*

Returning to the showmanship he displayed at the great arena of Cappa, Kaelin raised his arms to the company. Once again, they cried out the same one-syllable shout, followed by fists, palms, and beer mugs soundly laid on the table. The whole Ravenbourne Warrior company rendered a loud, if short, appreciation.

Kaelin turned and walked toward the pommel horse, his manhood, pillar and stones, swinging with his steps. He approached the pommel as a stallion might approach the rump of a waiting mare—her head lowered—looking back over her shoulder. This awaiting horse appeared common, similar to many others. Constructed of sturdy wood, it resembled a narrow barrel. It was padded with leather and reached nearly one-half the length of a man. Strong brass handles were fastened to the top at each end to facilitate movement. Kaelin grasped each handle and moved his waist against the pommel.

Normally, a female rider was forced to put her arms in front of her, bending all the way over the horse and lifting her feet off the ground, spreading her legs. This exposed her womanhood to a laughing male audience, adding to her humiliation.

Kaelin, however, with legs spread, bent only slightly over, looking straight ahead. No objection was raised by the company. In fact, they preferred to see his shoulders and face and thus his reaction to each impending lick. His manhood nestled between the top of his thighs and the bottom of his rump.

First Sergeant Klause took his place with the Dragon's Tongue in hand. His arm . . . extended at his side . . . the tip of the tongue just reaching the floor. Natasha and naked Melissa held each other in fearful anticipation. Natasha rubbed Melissa's bare shoulder to help ease her trembling. From where they stood, they were witness to Kaelin's whole backside and the side of his face.

Following protocol, the First Sergeant swung the tongue with its tip just missing the floor, creating that fearful hissing sound as it cut through the air. He took a careful stance, firmly planting his army sandals on the floor. He then raised his arm back—and swung.

The hissing sound of the leather strap in flight was only heard for the twinkling of an eye. The impacting slap, when the tongue's end licked Kaelin's right buttocks cheek, echoed off the stone walls of the silent hall, louder than a strong man could clap. The sound of leather on flesh is a din unique to itself, frequently heard after wagon drivers snap the leather reins on the rumps of mules or horses; nonetheless, it often goes unnoticed. This noise, however, was heard by all within the hall as the tongue left its ardent red brand on Kaelin's cheek.

Natasha and Melissa pulled each other closer together in an anxious embrace, closed their eyes, and whimpered. All other eyes and ears focused on Kaelin. He did not move, did not flinch—he did not blink—and he most certainly made no sound. He remained still as the statue of the Ravenbourne Warrior standing on guard at the Main Gate, and true to that solemn oath, he stood frozen, a solid rock.

First Sergeant Klause, skilled in this type of punishment, laid the next lick adjacent to the first but not on top of it. All reactions to the first thrash remained the same, including Kaelin's. He did not move.

Raising his hand, the First Sergeant pointed toward Melissa. "Count your licks!" he ordered in his rough, deep voice.

"Yes . . . First Sergeant! Two . . . First Sergeant!" Melissa called out, as loud as her sobbing voice allowed, but it seemed to be sufficient. Though they could hear the frightful sound of each horrible lick, Melissa and Natasha now kept their eyes open.

The third lick was laid on Kaelin, and duplicating the first two, the First Sergeant was able to avoid laying one burning brand on top of the other. He would not always be able to do so. Eventually, the buttock cheeks would be covered, and he would be forced to lay one thrash on top of another.

Melissa now called out five, her soft voice quivering. The Ravenbourne company, all brave men, watched first Kaelin's buttocks and then his shoulders and face. Yet still, he did not move—not a single flinch. Those who were observant or close enough to see would have noticed Kaelin's arm muscles contract as he gripped the brass handles on the end of the pommel.

The sixth fell on Kaelin's left cheek. The only change in reaction by all within in the dining hall was that Natasha and Melissa were crying harder and louder, pulling together tighter still. No objection was raised.

On the eighth, Natasha looked up to the ceiling, tears rolling down her face, off her chin, and onto her neck. "Please, Goddess, please," she whispered. "Please give him strength. Please be with him. I'll do anything you ask of me. Please!"

Unexpectedly, a warm, soft breeze came to Natasha's ear. A breeze that might have gently blown across the extensive estate fields of tall flax in bloom with beautiful, blue flowers. It felt like some mysterious lover was blowing and whispering into her ear. The soft, tender voice of a woman spoke, but she spoke in the secret language of the Hyacinth Gatherers.

"Fear not, my sweet girl. I am with him!"

Natasha sucked in her breath. She held it and then swallowed. And suddenly, she was not afraid anymore. Her eyes remained wet with tears and she softly mewled, but she stopped crying.

"Ten, First Sergeant!" Melissa was just able to choke out the final number.

An unusual, eerie hush fell upon the dining hall, seldom experienced, if ever before. No breathing could be heard. The soft whimpering and crying from the two serving maids on the platform ceased. Perhaps all held their breath.

Suddenly, resembling a loud clash of thunder, the clamor arose, loud enough to crack the huge wooden dining hall beams. The noise erupted with the high-pitched unison call of the warriors, followed by their fists and beer mugs pounding on the tabletops. The clamor reached a high pitch and slowly began to ease.

To the amazement of all, Spearman Kaelin remained at the pommel, as if he were a stone statue. His muscular arms remained stretched out, still attached to the brass handles. Motionless, he called out in a thundering voice, "I want an urn of honey!"

Once more, the short-lived silence was followed by a clamor of eruption. Melissa's legs buckled. Natasha held on to her, attempting to keep her upright, but then went to the floor with her. Melissa collapsed to her knees—her folded hands to her breast. She cried out in a desperate, pleading voice.

"No, Kaelin! No! Please don't. . . ." She hesitated, taking a deep breath. "I don't want any honey. Please . . . no more Kaelin!"

The commander once more rose—the hall came to 'at-ease.' "What do you think, First Sergeant?"

Holding the tongue in his straight arm, the crusty sergeant looked to the commander and then across the warriors in the hall. "If he wants a jar of honey, let him earn it with the usual price." He wiped the sweat from his forehead with his arm.

"Done!" ordered the commander, returning to his chair. The hall once more erupted in applause as Melissa covered her face with her hands and wept. Natasha held onto Melissa as tight as she could. She was no longer in tears.

Stepping to Kaelin's side, First Sergeant Klause spoke in a low yet commanding voice, "I won't hurt you, Spearman. Stand erect!"

Kaelin complied. Reaching in front of Kaelin, the sergeant lifted Kaelin's balls. "Put your legs together and return to position," he ordered. Once more, Kaelin complied.

Returning to his place, Sergeant Klause steadied his feet to gain balance. Reaching back his arm, with a tight grip on the Dragon Tongue's handle, he delivered another thrashing blow. This solid lick struck the back of Kaelin's thighs. Natasha now saw that the savvy sergeant had spared Kaelin's buttocks more punishment and protected his manhood, making sure the tip of the tongue did not strike his testicles. He looked over to Melissa and Natasha on the floor, awaiting the count. The lamenting Melissa, however, could not speak.

"Eleven, First Sergeant!" called out Natasha in the loudest voice she could muster.

The sergeant was appeased and continued. Twelve and thirteen were laid across Kaelin's thighs, just below his buttocks. Natasha called out those numbers with the brassiest voice she could.

The whole company could see the handiwork of the tongue. Natasha choked back a gasp. She nearly burst into tears again, because his buttocks were so painful to look at. The center was marked blue, nearly purple, surrounded by red, tormented flesh, well-nigh to erupt with blood. The rest of the area, including his thighs, was inflamed.

Kaelin remained in position, solid as stone, his muscular arms flexed, gripping the pommel's brass handles. He had not flinched—moved a single muscle—uttered a single sound, and even though his face was flushed-red, it seemed he had not even blinked.

What kind of a very remarkable man could this be? thought Natasha. *It takes a singular kind of courage to stand there naked in front of the whole company . . . bend over the pomme . . . endure thirteen hard, trashing licks . . . and never flinch—never move—or call out.*

Kaelin now rose and turned around. He raised his arms up, and for the first occasion, he smiled. Then, to all's surprise, he called out that signature, one-syllable shout, loud as a lion's roar, that all the Ravenbourne Warriors seem to know. And in unison, all the company responded in kind with that strange salute and the hall, once more, erupted to a pandemonium.

Clever Natasha realized this was her opportunity to act. She helped Melissa to her feet. "Come, Melissa. You must dress."

Melissa swayed but could stand. Natasha pulled Melissa's frock over her arms and adjusted it in place. Next, she grabbed Melissa's belt with attached dagger and buckled it around her waist. Seeing Melissa's undergarment on the floor, she whisked it up and stuck it in her own belt.

Rising again, and following suit with his men, the commander pounded his fist on the tabletop. Meanwhile, First Sergeant Klause congratulated Kaelin, patting him on his shoulder. He walked to the wall and returned the wicked Dragon's Tongue to its perch.

The commander raised his hand over his head and waved it back and forth. The company became still, as ordered. "Now that is how a warrior takes punishment. We salute you, Kaelin." Again, the hall erupted while Kaelin, barely able to stand, once more raised his arms to return their salute.

When the company began to still, the commander called out an order directed at Natasha and Melissa. "You two girls take Spearman Kaelin to a side guest room. Alert the kitchen to bring food and water."

"Beer!" called out Kaelin, bringing a laugh from the commander and the whole company.

"Take them what they want. Food, beer, wine. . .." Shouted the commander. "And order the physician to report immediately to see to Kaelin!"

A relaxed atmosphere began to fall over the hall, although the excitement remained. Still standing, the commander was not finished. "Sergeant Lutas," he called.

The veteran warrior stood up at attention and responded. "Sir!"

"Keep an eye on Kaelin for the next few days, and when he has recovered, initiate your ten-day indoctrination."

"Yes, Sir," replied Lutas, raising his hand in a clenched fist as though he held a spear. The commander likewise saluted, and returned to his seat.

Meanwhile, Natasha took Melissa by the shoulders. "Now you must take a hold of yourself. Understand?"

"Yes, love," replied a recovering but still shaky Melissa.

"We must take Kaelin to a guest room," she ordered. "Come now. All are watching."

Natasha scampered and retrieved Kaelin's discarded apparel. She quickly wrapped and tied his loin cloth around her waist and managed to tuck his dagger and belt inside her belt. She grabbed up his tunic and hurriedly stepped to him. The First Sergeant was standing next to Kaelin, with his strong arm around his waist. Kaelin rested his forearm on the sergeant's shoulder to maintain balance. Standing in front of him, Natasha held his tunic, ready to pull it over his arms and head.

"Good," said the old sergeant.

He released Kaelin and walked toward the steps. Natasha pulled Kaelin's tunic over him and threw her arm around his waist. He reached his right hand up and took her shoulder. He could nearly stand alone and used her more for balance than support. She looked up at him, her head nearly under his armpit. She now gained a new awareness of how large and heavy he was. She also took in a hint of his male aroma. It was exciting. She looked back over her shoulder and called out to Melissa, who now ran up and likewise took hold of their handsome patient. They slowly made their way across the platform—down the steps—toward the guest rooms, located along the side wall of the large dining hall.

They entered a guest room that held three beds and managed to help Kaelin lie down on the center bed on his stomach. The First Sergeant and Sergeant Lutas entered the room.

"Melissa, you take over and stay with Kaelin a day or two and help him recover," ordered First Sergeant Klause. Sergeant Lutas will be nearby if something is needed." He then looked at Natasha. "I appreciate your help, girl. I'm giving you three days of leave with pay. You're dismissed!"

"Yes, First Sergeant," replied Natasha.

Natasha took the items from her belt and laid them on a table, then left through the door. A kitchen boy and another server hurried past her and entered the room. As she made her way to the dining hall door, she saw a physician with a shoulder bag walking toward the guest room at a hurried pace.

CHAPTER 29

Sergeant Lutas: Indoctrination

ROUGH, DIRT ROADS, WORN DEEP with wagon-wheel furrows, crosshatched most villages and poor country shires throughout the Achaean Empire. All were continually dusty in dry weather or muddy in wet. The main road through the Ravenbourne Village, however, was paved with stone and interconnected with the Southern Peninsula Road system and with the Emperor's Highway. Although not paved, other roads throughout the village were graveled with debris from the local quarry and packed with clay and limestone, forming a solid road surface. The Ravenbourne villagers, especially those whose homes and shops lined the roads, were grateful to the Lord of Ravenbourne, who maintained the village road system, lifting the burden and discomfort of dust and mud of a mired dirt road.

Their military leather sandals knocked hard on the solid surface of the Ravenbourne Village Road as Lutas and Kaelin stepped briskly through the busy village. Sergeant Lutas had quickly taken a liking to the newest Ravenbourne Warrior, Spearman Kaelin. He came to the 1st Company, bearing an impressive background, with a certain degree of celebrity status. His Dragon's Tongue ordeal in the dining hall only heightened that standing.

Although he was a 9th man in rank, everyone called Lutas "Sergeant," and he soon realized that age could be a camouflage of deception. This

295

young recruit was also an experienced soldier and war veteran who had experienced several battles. He should not have been surprised, however, knowing full well only warriors of exceptional skill were recruited into the Ravenbourne Corps regardless of age. A segment of Sergeant Lutas's indoctrination—a special articulation of his own invention—included a harmless incursion to the Ravenbourne Village and an investigation of the local houses of pleasure.

Lutas and Kaelin wore their army tunics displaying the Ravenbourne crest, embroidered in red and black on the center of the chest. Tailor-made from the finest linen and dyed white, the tunics of the Ravenbourne Corps displayed the highest quality and superior work of craftsmen and seamstresses. Lord Ravenbourne encouraged his warriors to wear their army tunics as civilian attire. He believed it would demonstrate to both the military and civilian populations that the warriors of the Ravenbourne Corps were not only the most skilled but also the best equipped. Such fine clothing was envious to all, including the wealthy aristocracy.

A bronze sword and dagger were attached to the leather belts buckled about their waists. No finer weapons in all the Empire. The Ravenbourne daggers, however, were most coveted. Every mortal, man and woman, would look upon a Ravenbourne dagger with desire and cupidity to own one. So revered, the daggers were incorporated into the common language and elevated to a mythological status. As they walked along, Lutas freely shared his vast experience as a warrior of the Ravenbourne Corps, especially concerning protocol and of course women.

"Being stationed at one of the greatest villas in the whole fokken Achaean Empire sure does have advantages," explained a jovial Sergeant Lutas. "Only the palaces of the Emperor outshine the Ravenbourne Estates. Now, all this splendor allows us, the Ravenbourne Warriors, to choose between buying the favors of the village whores or taking our pleasure from villa slaves and pallakes alike. Neither should be taken lightly."

Lutas paused to allow those statements to sink in. Then he snorted, cleared his throat, and continued. "Every warrior at Ravenbourne takes a slave-girl now and then. If you can manage to get one alone, they usually won't refuse a Ravenbourne Warrior. Now, it's not always a good fokken, unless you got the skill to calm a scared slave-girl down, especially a pallake. But, not all them slave-girls are afraid. They know Ravenbourne Warriors won't hurt'em. They also know a Ravenbourne Warrior could help and protect them—help them to freedom—could even marry'em."

Lutas chuckled to himself at the thought of marriage. "By comparison, now, a local whore might be a better fokken, but Ravenbourne slave-girls are much prettier. But some of them whores working in a brothel . . ."

Lutas stopped and held up a finger, making a point. "Better say a 'house of pleasure.' I know one thing, Kaelin. You'll have the chance to fokken more prettier girls here at Ravenbourne than you will ever have again in your whole fokken life. And at your age, you best ought to take advantage of it." Lutas paused for a moment, smiling.

"By the way, did you manage to taste that naughty little Melissa's kunt?" asked the jovial Lutas.

"I didn't have the opportunity," explained Kaelin. "She rubbed a fragrant oil on me that the physician gave her. A miracle ointment, it stopped nearly all the pain. I think she fingered me as well."

Lutas looked at Kaelin. He let out an abrupt snort . . . "Humph!" It was a snort though his nose and saying "hmm" at the same moment. He often used this snort, generally as a dismissive reply. In this instance, however, he smiled at Kaelin.

"Oh yeah," exclaimed Lutas. "That's Melissa!"

"I drank a potion," continued Kaelin, "also from the physician. It put me to sleep all day and night. Perhaps longer. When I woke, you were there. She bathed and fed me, and I left with you. If any fokken occurred, I don't know about it."

Sergeant Lutas laughed, slapping Kaelin on the back. "Well, after what you did for her, I'd say Melissa would pull her frock over her head and hand you her undergarments whenever you want."

"I intend to keep that in mind," said Kaelin with a slight smile. "And while we are discussing Melissa . . . there was another girl with her."

"Oh yeah," replied Lutas. "Natasha! Saltiest virgin in the whole village, but the prettiest little kunt there is. She's only worked in the dining hall a few days, but born here in the village. Melissa's best friend. Her mother went to the other side not long ago. A beauty herself—a Hyacinth Gatherer."

"I should learn who these Hyacinth Gatherers are," stated Kaelin. "They are frequently discussed."

"Don't rush it," answered Lutas. "You'll learn. Most Hyacinth girls have bright-red hair . . . same as Natasha. Anyway, Natasha's father is a village Elder and was a renowned soldier. He was First Spear of the Thirteenth Legion—earned the Empire's highest decoration. The Emperor himself awarded it to him. She gets away with more mischief, her and Melissa, because of her father. Keep that in mind. Also know she is a rare filly that just needs a little taming. I would go after that ride if I was your age." Lutas paused, looked around on the ground for a likely place to inelegantly spit, and did so.

"There must be relationships between Ravenbourne Warriors and free village girls?" asked Kaelin.

"Sure are," Lutas said with a laugh. "Most village girls, and their moms, have hot, little kunts for Ravenbourne Warriors. But that risk, not to be taken lightly. A girl belongs to her father. He says who she can fokken and who not. Did you have a girl in Opar, Kaelin?"

Kaelin stopped and looked at Lutas with a smile. "I did."

"Well, the same thing here. Just keep the girl's family in mind—that's all."

Kaelin nodded that he understood. They walked on. Inquisitive Kalin remained full of questions.

"Tell me more about Ravenbourne slaves," inquired the novice Kaelin.

"Ask away," said Lutas.

"Are all Ravenbourne slaves attractive?"

Sergeant Lutas chuckled. "Well, I'll tell you this. Lady Ravenbourne spares no coin when she buys slaves, and she will buy the healthiest and prettiest slaves she can. You won't see an ugly slave, woman or girl—boy, for that matter—here at Ravenbourne."

Sergeant Lutas stopped and looked at Kaelin with an unusual, stern expression. "Take heed and remember, new recruit Spearman Kaelin, Lord Ravenbourne's Law." Lutas paused and continued to gaze into Kaelin's eyes telling him the seriousness of what he was about to say.

"Slaves will not be raped or beaten. I can't say it in a smart language like others can, but here it is. Know the difference between spanking a naughty slave-girl and beating her. And the difference between sweet-talkin' an unwilling slave-girl, into giving you her little kunt and raping her. A Ravenbourne Warrior will not beat or rape a Ravenbourne slave, girl or boy. Such a foolish soldier would certainly face Lord Ravenbourne's justice—most likely soon meet his fokken ancestors. If you have to discipline a slave-girl, spank her little butt with the palm of your hand. Any girl, for that matter. It's more fun anyway, and you got her butt cheeks and everything between them in your hands." Sergeant Lutas turned his head, coughed, and spit on the ground, wiping his mouth with the back of his hand.

Kaelin was reminded of the ancient Opar term *fokken* used by nearly all Empire soldiers and lower-class men. He was tempted to smile at the use of the word but remained stoic, listening to his mentor.

Lutas continued in a stern tone, "Remember, Spearman Kaelin, only a bastard would fokken a slave-girl and not reward her. Only a real bastard, not worthy to be a Ravenbourne Warrior."

"In what manner could one reward a slave?" asked Kaelin.

"Well, it's a delicate matter," continued Lutas, returning to his usual jovial manner while they continued to walk. "I'm glad you're asking. A Ravenbourne Warrior can't give slave-girls items he would usually give to other women, such as clothes or jewelry and other female belongings. It would be hard, if not impossible, for a slave-girl to hide and keep such things. Money can be good and a better choice, small gold or silver coins. Many slaves hide money, hoping to buy their freedom or to build a cache just in case they try to escape. Lord Ravenbourne's Law, Kaelin, 'Slaves may buy their freedom without deceit.' Now let's say if a slave-girl is smart and has somehow managed to save enough coins to buy her freedom . . . well, she'll go to her master or mistress with someone, a friend, but not a slave. A Ravenbourne Warrior is her best choice. Say, as a witness. The slave owner will fill out a paper, with the name and price of the slave, then sign it. The Ravenbourne Warrior will also sign it with the mark of Lord Ravenbourne. No one will disagree with it. It's even better for her if the Ravenbourne Warrior is her Protector. Otherwise, a scumbag-cheating bastard of a master or especially a bitch mistress may take her money and say she never had any. But no one, even the lowest bitch, would dare break Lord Ravenbourne's Law in front of a Ravenbourne Warrior."

"What did you mean when you said 'if the Ravenbourne Warrior is her Protector'?" asked Kaelin.

"Glad you brought it up. You should know about the Protector, a long-standing Ravenbourne tradition, not hard to understand. Just what it sounds like. A Ravenbourne Warrior and a woman, a slave-girl, like each other. Maybe love, and they would marry, but he can't because of his tour of duty. He might become her Protector. Sure, he protects her when they're together, but if anyone assaults her, he will take revenge on them. She will wear something so all will know a Ravenbourne Warrior protects her. Say, his dagger or the Ravenbourne crest from our tunic. Some women sew a frock from a Ravenbourne tunic; then there's no question—she is protected. I've seen some wearing our red capes."

"Do all soldiers of the Achaean Empire hold with this tradition?" asked Kaelin.

"Well, the Southern Army does, but I don't know about the others. But that's not all, Kaelin. Lord Ravenbourne's Law plays a part here. The Warrior-Protector also protects the female from herself. He is the one who disciplines her if she does not behave or if she breaks Lord Ravenbourne's Law. He becomes both her father and husband, and he is the hand of discipline."

Lutas cleared his throat and turned his head to spit on the ground. "It's not to be taken lightly or agreed with too fast. Some girls, especially slaves in a pleasure house, will want a Ravenbourne Warrior's protection so they can get away with something. Make sure the female understands the rules. It's a serious duty not to be agreed to too fast."

Kaelin nodded in agreement. "Along with small, valuable coins, how else can I reward a slave- girl?"

"Now that's an easy one, Kaelin. Often as not, slave-women will want foodstuffs they usually aren't served, especially sweets or salts. They relish cake . . . honey . . . and salt."

Lutas laughed. "Women are funny. Aristocrat or poor, slave or free, they all seem to enjoy one extreme or the other. They want sweet or salt, or they love you or hate you, no in between. Anyway, it just depends on the slave-girl."

Again, Lutas spit, then continued. "There are these certain small clay containers with a stopper top. The men are constantly sneaking these into the dining hall and filling them with dining hall honey . . ."

Sergeant Lutas paused, smiled, and slapped Kaelin on the back.

"What the fokken is the matter with me? Old age, maybe. You know all about these little pots, Kaelin. You took three Dragon's Tongue licks for one."

"Not with certainty," admitted Kaelin. "I heard the soldiers sitting at the table talking about the urns, and thought I would throw that out. Women call the urns alabastrons. I wasn't sure of the outcome when I said that."

"What?" asked Lutas. "Al-la-bass-troon. Did you learn them kinds of words in Opar?" He shook his head, laughing. "You're a constant surprise, Spearman Kaelin," said Sergeant Lutas with a sincere tone. Kaelin made no response.

"Anyway, the Ravenbourne Warriors exchange them honey pots for a fokken with slave-girls who delight in these small pots filled with honey. A sweet little honey pot, traded for a sweeter little honey pot," laughed Lutas, seemingly pleased with his play on words.

"I know one particular slave-woman in the bakery. Now . . . she will fokken you for a jug of beer. She's not a great beauty, but she is not bad-looking, either, and she keeps herself as clean as she can. Now . . . she will bend over . . . spread her legs . . . fokken on the spot for a jug of beer. She'll drink it while you pound against her butt. I'll show her to you sometime. She can be a blessing from the goddess if a man is broke and hungry for a little kunt."

Lutas spit again, and wiped his mouth with the back of his hand before continuing. "All this talk about fokken beer has made me thirsty. I'm about to die for one." He laughed with a friendly gesture, taking Kaelin by the shoulder.

"Sergeant Lutas," said Kaelin with a firm but not angry voice. "I don't want to offend you, Sergeant, and I know you are sincere. But I don't appreciate being grasped or slapped on the back or shoulder."

"Why didn't you say something, Kaelin?" asked a sincere Sergeant Lutas.

"Because I believe we are going to be friends, Sergeant, and I have no friends here in Ravenbourne."

"Friends tell each other the truth, Kaelin, without offense," concluded an honest Lutas. "If you say or do something that bothers me, I'll say so. And you do the same."

Sergeant Lutas held out his hand. "A warrior and a friend's handshake."

Kaelin took Lutas's hand. "You are a rough-talking man, Sergeant, but a man of wisdom."

Sergeant Lutas laughed. "Only about women and beer, Kaelin."

"Tell me more," requested Kaelin with a rare smile.

"Well, Kaelin, a slave, woman or girl, wants their freedom. You were a slave, so you understand that. If they can strike up a relationship with a Ravenbourne Warrior, many will, hoping the soldier will want to marry them and buy their freedom. A Ravenbourne Warrior can buy a slave girl from Lord Ravenbourne for a year's pay. Of course, all slaves aren't for sale, except that all slaves can always buy their own freedom. Anyways, Lord Ravenbourne is relaxed on the matter. If a Ravenbourne Warrior is willing to give up a year's pay to marry a slave-girl, Lord Ravenbourne will go along with it. He will give her to the soldier as wife, and she will have her freedom also. Lady Ravenbourne, on the other hand, is a harder choice. She will first talk with the slave-girl and wife-to-be. Oh, the year's pay seems to be a standard price, but she will ask for something more from the Ravenbourne Warrior. She will take some type of actions to make sure the wife is protected. I am not sure just what, because it depends on their situation."

Kaelin noticed, while they walked along, how clean and well-kept the Ravenbourne Village was. There were no rotting garbage piles, dilapidated huts, or cur dogs infested with sores running through the roads. He'd also heard that an underground sewer system ran throughout the village, and there was safe drinking water from well systems.

"How do you know if a house is a whorehouse?" asked the inexperienced Kaelin.

Lutas chuckled. "A man just learns, over time, but normally, the whores are at the windows or the doors, and usually they sit out front of the house on benches. Some houses have balconies. By village law, they are not allowed to work or go after customers outside of the house or at least away from the house. They go and fetch water from the wells like all women, but if whores are caught out on the road, asking for customers, they could be whipped in front of the whole village. That's Lord Ravenbourne's Law."

"Have you ever seen a whore whipped in public?"

"Well, no, *whipped* isn't the right word. Village women and girls are not whipped or flogged. Men are, but not women. But I did once see a filly-whore get her pretty, little butt tanned good and hard with a stiff leather strap. Some call the strap a Dragon's Ton..."

Lutas stopped himself in mid-sentence. "Well, I guess we both know a lot about that, don't we?"

In a rare moment, Kaelin laughed out loud. "Yes, we do, Sergeant Lutas. There was a quiet pause. "What ever happened to the tanned whore?"

"Oh yeah!" continued Luas. "Well, she stayed inside the whorehouse for a long while after that. I'm not sure what ever happened to her," he admitted scratching his chin and gazing upward. "She was sort of pretty and more than a first-rate fokken. Anyway, asking for customers out in public. Well, it's hard to enforce that law, but it can happen."

Fearless, Kaelin became bold with his questions. "Why do they call you sergeant, 9th Man Lutas?"

Once more, Sergeant Lutas snorted an abrupt. "Humph!" He smiled at Kaelin. "I was a first sergeant in the Southern Army and had a strong disagreement with a green lieutenant. I hit him, knocked him flat. I was flogged—reduced to a spearman—doomed to be discharged before accumulating enough years to retire."

He turned his head for a quick spit. "And next, to the whole army's surprise, General Y'Sloic asked me if I wanted to join his Ravenbourne Guard. He promised me, if I completed my quota of years required for retirement, he would retire me on first sergeant's pay. In return, he demanded absolute loyalty to him . . . Lady Ravenbourne . . . and the Ravenbourne Estate. So here I am!"

"Do you have enough years to retire?" asked a sincere Kaelin.

"Oh yeah, but I would rather keep working. I'm not ready to hang up my armor just yet. I still got plenty of fighting years left in me. Besides, the food is too good to pass up, and I have become addicted to beautiful, tender slave-girls and village whores. Like I said, young Kaelin, Ann Y'Sloic makes a gritty effort to buy only good-looking female-slaves. She has several fortunes to spend on slaves, and she does. Won't see ugly ones at Ravenbourne and every slave I've known, young or old, is always a good fokken."

"I came to Ravenbourne from Cappa," added Kaelin in a friendly tone, "escorting a military caravan with a wagon-load of seven slave-girls from Opar, bought by Lady Ravenbourne. And Sergeant Lutas. . .." He hesitated. "They were all adorable . . . mesmeric."

Sergeant Lutas shook his head, laughed, but did not reply.

"Are women in the whorehouses free or slave?" asked a still-curious Kaelin.

"Both—some free—some slaves." Sergeant Lutas paused momentarily. He rubbed his cheek with his fingers, spit, and continued. "One of the best houses of pleasure is called Virgin Cheeks and Thighs. A man owns the Virgin Cheeks and Thighs. Mostly he goes unnoticed, stays in the background, so his wife operates the house. They say he's strict, fast with the strap. She uses him to keep the girls in line."

"Most whores in a whore-house are slaves, but some are professional ladies of pleasure. They are trained and skilled in music, dancing, and talking poetry. Usually for aristocrats and wealthy men. Not sure what they're called." Lutas paused, scratching his chin.

"Hetaera," said Kaelin. "I think the term is *hetaera*."

"Yeah! Think your right, Kaelin. Did you go to schools in Opar, Kaelin?" inquired Lutas.

"No, but my mother was a teacher. She taught me the Empire language."

"Well, she did a good job because you speak it good. Anyway, there's not many aristocrat whores here in the Ravenbourne Village."

"Now understand, it's not an easy life, Kaelin. Some whores will freely fokken an animal for a few coins, but others are forced to have sex with the most foul, drunken men. Rules in a whorehouse are strict, and punishment comes fast. Most whores will have their backsides strapped or be hand-spanked every so many days, even those who are free and serve wealthy men. But still, it's only wrong when a poor drunken father sells his daughter to a whorehouse, to be a slave or an indebt-servant."

"But no one has ever said there was fairness in this mortal world. You know, a whore, even a slave whore, lives better than most other female-slaves, especially those few agricultural female-slaves, and certainly better than poor peasant girls in the villages around Cappa or the Empire Capital City. But you won't see poverty like that here at Ravenbourne."

"Ah, here we are at my favorite whorehouse! The Virgin Cheeks and Thighs."

CHAPTER 30

Bistre: Brown Eyed Girl

KAELIN AND SERGEANT LUTAS STOPPED in front of a large brick house. A hefty arched doorway in the front and a roof balcony, sided with a wooden post railing, gave the structure a wealthy, villa-like presence. It appeared, at least on the outside, to be clean and well kept.

"My favorite whorehouse and one of the best in Ravenbourne," bragged a smiling Lutas. "I'll wager a month's pay it will also be yours," he boasted. "Now I've heard plenty of soldiers argue over which whore-house is the best—one has prettier or cleaner girls than another. The truth is, they're all about the same, but I just seem to like this one. By the way, Kaelin. Women at a whorehouse like us to say a 'house of pleasure' and not *whorehouse* and they are 'women or girls of pleasure,' not *whores*."

"Humph!" The rustic sergeant grunted, spitting to make his point.

A woman walked out onto the balcony, prompting Kaelin and Lutas to look up. Kaelin saw that she wore facial coloring—her cheeks and lips colored red—blue shading around her eyes.

"Good morning, Sergeant Lutas," said the painted woman, leaning over the railing.

"And a good morning to you, Beath," replied a cheerful Lutas. "You're as lovely as the dawn itself."

Beath blushed with a girlish laugh. "Who is your handsome, young friend?"

"This is Spearman Kaelin, new Ravenbourne recruit. He was a soldier from Opar."

"Oh my," smiled Beath, "I've heard that men of Opar are as good of lovers as they are warriors. Is that true, young Kaelin?"

"Yes, it is," replied Kaelin. "Some say even better."

Beath laughed a noticeably pretend laugh. Kaelin noticed that she wore a strange, revealing frock. The neckline was cut low, illuminating the tops of her breasts. Tailored to a tight fit, the garment sported shoulder straps rather than sleeves. The material was expensive cotton, dyed white. Kaelin also noticed she was mature and certainly not a gamine youngster, yet still an attractive woman. She would be more attractive without the facial coloring, he thought.

"Come in, Sergeant Lutas. If you have an itch, I will scratch it with my tongue." Beath smiled, slowly licking her lips.

Sergeant Lutas clapped his hands together—rubbing them. "Let us go in and inspect this stable of fine, fresh fillies, Kaelin." Together, they entered the house.

Inside, Kaelin saw that the house was larger than it appeared on the outside. They stood in a sizeable front or end room. To his surprise, the room was empty, Kaelin and Lutas the only patrons. He expected there would be a morning clientele. Kaelin also noticed the floor was fitted with large tiles. Padded benches, seats, and small tables lined the walls of the room, leaving the center open. A hallway was oddly constructed down the center of the building. He could see several doors on one side of the hallway wall and thus concluded there were small rooms on either side of the hall. The first two end rooms, however, were open and appeared to be a kitchen and a beer serving room, both with a serving bar.

Brightly painted walls added a cheerful mood to the room, including erotic illustrations of nude women and playful, puerile lovers. Several rows of pegs were also attached to the walls for hanging various items.

Kaelin especially noticed three leather straps with ivory handles, hung side by side, one large and two smaller. A leather-padded pommel, set out from the wall, stood in front of the three strange straps. Kaelin was very familiar with this leather arrangement. He smiled to himself.

"Ladies!" called out Beath in a tone reflecting an order rather than an introduction. "We have guests—Ravenbourne Warriors!"

Kaelin heard movement . . . shuffling, padded bare feet, and female giggles and squeals. Suddenly, three young women seemed to appear from nowhere and scurried to stand in a line with Beath, all three ready to be inspected. One was completely nude—one wore a frock similar to Beath's—the third wore only a white female undergarment and a fitted breast cloth. Sergeant Lutas looked at Kaelin, wearing a mischievous smile and exclaimed. "Humph!"

Possessing not one drop of bashfulness Lutas, stepped right up to inspect the line of girls while Kaelin leisurely strode toward the wall to sit at one of the tables. The nearly naked girl on the end, wearing only, undergarment and breast cloth, was young, with resplendent, brown hair. While Lutas inspected her, she remained motionless, staring off past him. He gently grasped her shoulders and her waist, looking her over from head to foot.

"Yes, yes, very nice," he opined, certainly an experienced buyer. He turned her around, running his hands down her back and her hips. He gave her buttocks several light but loud swats on each cheek, turning her again to face him. All the while, her face remained stoic, without expression. She gazed off past him, seemingly in a hypnotic state. Lutas went on to examine the other two girls, who were older than the one in white undergarments, and stopped in front of Beath.

"You know, Beath, I've fokkened every girl in your house, including them three new ones. They are . . . each one . . . sweet, young, and pretty. I especially love that brown-haired beauty in white, and if I was to retire and marry, I'd buy her from you for a wife. But some days,

I just want to come back to you, Beath." Smiling, Beath reached out, taking his hand.

"Don't be bashful, young Kaelin," encouraged Beath. "Examine the girls; see which one stirs your fancy. There are others, if you desire a larger selection. We have ample beer—the first flask is free. Enjoy a taste of good-morning beer and talk with the girls."

Smiling, Beath led Lutas away by the hand but called out over her shoulder, "Enjoy yourself, Kaelin!"

A youthful woman approached bearing two flasks of beer and set them down on the table. She appeared unglamorous—freckled face— yet attractive. She smiled at Kaelin and watched him for a moment. Then, with a daring approach, she put her hands on her hips and shifted her weight from one foot to the other, slowly moving her hips in a se- ductive manner. To his surprise, she leisurely ran her hand down the front of her dress and cupped her groin between her thighs.

"Oh! Oh! Oh!" she groaned in a slow whisper, with each "Oh" a little louder than the first, as she clamped her thighs against her own hand, massaging herself. She next grasped the sides of her frock and, pulling it tight, turned around, bending her knees. She looked back over her shoulder at Kaelin, smiling as she wiggled her near-perfect buttocks at him. Quickly, she stood upright and, without looking back, walked away in a seductive female stride—her enticing hips careening in a gentle sway.

Kaelin was thus far impressed and becoming sexually aroused. He studied the minx, nearly naked, brown-haired beauty. The strings of her elegant, triangular-shaped undergarment were tied in a bowknot at each curved, graceful hip. Her breast cloth was likewise triangular- shaped, covering most of her small breasts with the strings tied behind her neck and in the back—also in long bowknots.

Kaelin recalled a childhood poem his mother would read to him about a gamine, little girl with lush, bistre hair and deep-brown eyes.

She often misbehaved but could always talk her way out of chastisement by placing a little finger on her lips; looking up with those big, beautiful, sad eyes, squirming; side to side; and whimpering in a sad, soft little voice, "I'm sorry. I'm sorry." The gorgeous specimen before him now must certainly be that girl.

Her bistre-brown hair was cropped short in common slave fashion but appeared thick and full, giving her an appealing, boyish appearance. But she seemed to be in some type of shock or a trance, whether real or acting. There was something mysteriously desirable about her. Kaelin rose and walked to her.

She continued to gaze intently, straight ahead, to avoid looking up into his face, instead staring at his chest, seemingly lost in her own world. Walking behind her, Kaelin noticed she bore several leather strap marks across the back of her shapely legs. The welts were old and faded to a pale-yellow and bluish color, rather than the blistering cerise shade—recently laid.

He stepped back in front of her. She was more than attractive. He noticed a small mole on her right cheek, but it was not displeasing. In fact, it added a sense of mystery to her stunning face. He now noticed her white undergarments were trimmed with a narrow strip of ruffled material the same color as her very kissable lips. He must have a taste of her.

Leaning into her, Kaelin smelled her neck. Her scent was pleasing, very pleasing. He then took her small chin in his fingers and pushed down, compelling her to open her mouth. Her unemotional gaze continued, locked straight ahead. He leaned into her, his nose touching her lips, and smelled her breath. The aroma of her breath was also pleasing, and he found himself achieving an erection. He kissed her open mouth, and she returned his kiss. This was not her first, and her tongue and wetted lips were deliciously enticing. She remained, however, motionless.

Strangely, she moved her lips as though speaking, but she made no sound. Kaelin looked into her face and into her eyes—beautiful, large, brown eyes. She had the eyes of a doe, a frightened, small doe. Yet again, she moved her lips, as in speech, but absent any sound. Kaelin now understood. He put his ear to her mouth, and she whispered—a mysterious whisper.

"Will you . . . take me . . . without . . . hurting me?"

Kaelin moved back, somewhat taken. Once more, he moved his ear to her mouth to hear her whisper. It was the same.

"Will you . . . take me . . . without . . . hurting me?"

"Yes," Kaelin answered.

Suddenly, without warning, Kaelin scooped her up in his powerful arms and instinctively carried her toward the hallway. She threw her arms around his neck, laying her head against his chest. Kaelin carried his light female burden down the hallway and stopped at an open door. The room was unoccupied. He carried her inside. Small, sparsely furnished, the room contained only a bed; a small, sturdy table against the wall; and a diminutive table by the bed. Nonetheless, it was warmly painted and decorated with, paintings, flowers, and a variety of vases—hydria, amphora, aryballos, and krater scattered about the room. A white stamnos chamber pot occupied the far corner. The bed was pushed against the wall, adjacent to an open window, and was also lined with large pillows. A colorful headboard, painted on the wall, displayed flamboyant designs. The hydria was filled with water and sat on the table against the wall with the large, deep krater, creating a small washing area. Towels and washing cloths hung from pegs above the table. The room reminded Kaelin of a small, comfortable room in his parent's house in Opar with a bright, cheerful window. It was his mother's favorite, and she often used the peaceful room for reading.

Kaelin carried her to the bed and gently laid her down. Along with the pillows, the bed was well dressed with bright blankets and sheets.

He stepped to close the door and returned to the bed, where the girl was up on her knees. She smiled at him and reached behind her neck, pulling the drawstrings and removing her breast cloth. Her breasts were firm, petite, and perfectly shaped, with small, delicious nipples. Kaelin unbuckled his sword and dagger belt.

"Kaelin, may I. . . ." She finally spoke. Her voice was a soft, pleasing whisper. "My I touch your dagger?"

Taken aback by her request, Kaelin looked at her to see a strange but pleasant expression. With a little smirk, he withdrew his dagger from its sheath and handed it to her. Smiling, she took it. She examined the legendary weapon, glancing back to Kaelin. She was now all smiles. She looked at herself in the blade's polished reflection. She grasped the point of the dagger with two fingers and, holding the handle, attempted to bend the blade. She glanced up at Kaelin's face.

"Women say the manhood of a Ravenbourne Warrior's erection is as hard as his dagger." Her voice remained pleasant as she handed the dagger back to Kaelin. He slipped it back into the sheath, then laid the belt, sword, and dagger at the foot of the bed. He pulled his Ravenbourne tunic over his head.

Smiling a beautiful, mischievous smile that a naiad would wear to tempt her man, she pulled the bow knots on each side of her white undergarment and slipped it off with her fingertips. Casually, she let it fall to the bed—her brown eyes never leaving Kaelin. Completely naked, she patted the bed with the palm of her hand.

"Foot here," she requested, using a tone that a mother would when undressing a small child.

Kaelin raised his foot and placed it on the bed. Quickly, she unbuckled his sandal straps, lifted it from his foot, and let it drop to the floor. He returned his bare foot to the floor.

Again, she patted the bed. "Other one," she said softly in the same motherly tone.

Once more, Kaelin elevated his foot to the bed, and the girl quickly unfastened his sandal, likewise letting it fall to the floor. Now, she reached up and took his hand. She smiled at him—another beautiful, yet mischievous smile.

"My mother would spank my younger brother's behind with a hard, wooden hairbrush, redder than two ripe cherries, if she caught him standing on our bed with his sandals on."

She paused. "But then, she would find better things to do with you," she whispered, gently pulling Kaelin to her.

She took Kaelin into her arms and kissed him. He responded, softly massaging her delicate, small flower—soft and warm with dew. She tenderly took his erection, spread her legs, and lay back, gently pulling him to her.

"I can't wait to have you in me. I'm wet enough."

She maneuvered her hips and his erection to her female entrance and released him to grasp his hips. She pulled him into her, raising her hips off the bed.

Kaelin slowly but surely slid into her, making certain he did not hurt her . . . keeping his promise. The girl moaned and groaned in a deep whisper, pulling him into her. She whined and whimpered in the delicate, soft voice of a young girl.

Kaelin jaunted his brown-mane filly with a smooth, even gait. She wrapped her strong legs around him, her arms around his neck, and rode with him, making high-pitched groans each moment his groin rubbed against hers. Headlong they rode, perspiration rolling down their naked bodies, as though they rode through the rain. She held to him—he pressed into her full and deep—but not painful . . . floating. If she released him, she would fall. Panting, Kaelin could see the green meadows outside the walls of Opar where he took the horses from his father's stable for exercise and fresh green grass. He could sense a slight breeze and smell the fresh air—or did he feel her panting—smelling her warm, sweet breath?

Suddenly, the brown-eyed filly's voice changed, and she called out in a high-pitched tone.

"Oh! Oh! Oh, my fokken goddess! Oh, my fokken goddess! I'm going to spray, Kaelin! I can't believe it; I'm going to spray!"

She pulled Kaelin's face as close as she could to hers, whispering and shouting at the same moment. "Give me all your milk . . . Kaelin! Give me all your milk!"

She slid her hands down Kaelin's wet back, grasping his buttocks, digging her nails into him. She squeezed and pulled him into her with all her strength. He emptied himself into her, gasping in long, drawn-out moans.

Calm—quiet—Kaelin could hear birds singing outside. The brilliant sun peeked through the window, brightening up the whole charming, small room. The lovers lay in each other's arms, smiling into each other's faces, peaceful and content. Every so often they kissed, or the brown-eyed beauty would lean into Kaelin and rub the side of his mouth with the side of her mouth, in the same manner a small female cat in heat will rub her large tom. Abruptly, they heard a loud voice from outside the door, interrupting their serene moment.

"Hurry up in there, Bistre! Get him off, girl, and send him out!"

"It's Beath," whispered the doe-eyed beauty. "Please, hurry and go out, before I'm in trouble."

"I'll pay for a turn of the hour-glass with her!" called out Kaelin, rising to rest his weight on one hand.

"Very well," Beath replied. "May we bring you something?"

"Beer, water, and food!"

"I'll have one of the girls bring your refreshments." Beath shook her head and chuckled to herself, returning to the front room. "Men are so easy . . . easy to please . . . .." She mused. "All a girl need do is show up naked, bring food, and they will be content."

"Bistre—is that your name?" asked Kaelin in a low voice.

"Yes," answered Bistre in a whisper.

"A pretty name for a very pretty girl."

"Kaelin," replied Bistre, blushing.

Kaelin leaned down and gently kissed her while she rubbed his arm. He rose, stepping to the far corner. He removed the lid from the white stamnos chamber pot and urinated, long and hard.

"Oh my," whispered Bistre, turning on her side to watch him. She thought to herself.

He reminds me of a half-wild stallion, peeing on the muddy ground just after he has fokkened one of his bashful fillies.

Kaelin walked to his clothes and fumbled with them. Bistre's eyes followed him with a smile. She suddenly put her hands to her mouth to remain quiet when she saw the scars on his back and buttocks. Evil whipping scars and other dreadful wounds. To her surprise, she certainly recognized the blue and yellow bruises on his buttocks, the telltale colors of a recent Dragon's Tongue thrashing.

How strange, she thought, *for a man to have his buttocks punished with a Dragon's Tongue. I would like to hear that story . . . but maybe another day.*

She quickly dropped her hands and smiled when he turned around and returned to bed.

He made himself comfortable, and she kissed his cheek and whispered in his ear.

"I must go pee, too, so don't peek. Promise?"

Kaelin chuckled loudly. "I won't look. I promise!"

Bistre slid out of bed and quickly stepped to the far corner, holding herself, resembling a little girl. As she scampered to the chamber pot, the bells on her ankle jingled with each step. Removing the lid, she squatted over the pot. She looked up to see Kaelin had turned his back, patiently waiting. She finished and dried herself with a dry cloth hanging on a nearby peg. Scampering back to bed, she climbed in and snuggled up to her new, and pleasantly warm, bedmate.

"I could easily lie here with you the rest of the day," said Kaelin quietly, smiling while he looked into her eyes.

"Me too," answered Bistre in a soft whisper.

He gently took her hand and opened it. She smiled a childish grin, thinking they might play a game. To her surprise, however, he placed a silver coin in her hand. Her large brown eyes grew even larger, and her mouth opened wide.

"For me?" she asked in a high-pitched voice.

"Yes," replied Kaelin.

"I may have this for my own?" she asked. Unable to control herself, she began to cry.

"Yes," replied Kaelin, "an inducement. Hide it, keep it, save it, and with more, buy your freedom. The most precious thing you can own, is . . . freedom."

She took the coin in both hands and pulled them to her breast. Kaelin again noticed what beautiful breasts she had. Impossible not to kiss and caress.

"I've never had any money before." Tears softly rolled down her cheeks and over that unique, small, umber mole. "Oh, thank you, Kaelin, thank you. . .!" She hesitated and swallowed hard. "I will! I will! I'm not sure how, but I will."

Kaelin cupped her face and neck, kissing each wet doe eye while she continued her quiet crying. "This I learned today. Lord Ravenbourne's Law—slaves may purchase their freedom without deceit. Your mistress cannot cheat you. You gain your freedom by being wise, obedient, and cunning. Your quest for freedom will be won by stealth, not strength. Soldiers and other men will offer you coin on the side if you treat them the way you were with me—pert but affectionate—warm—always innocent. Once you have saved the price, approach your mistress, and purchase your freedom, but not alone. Have a friend, a witness at your side, especially a Ravenbourne Warrior. Have your mistress sign a paper, and the Ravenbourne Warrior must also sign. He will place the mark of Lord Ravenbourne on the paper, and no one will dispute it. Freedom will then be yours."

"Will you be my witness, Kaelin? Will you help me?" her young voice was soft and tearful.

"I will, most certainly."

Reaching out, Kaelin took the back of her neck. He pulled her to him for another kiss. She quickly went to him; her clenched fist held her silver coin. She returned his kiss with gentle affection.

A quiet knock and easy voice interrupted their kiss. "Refreshment!"

"It's Carla," said Bistre in a whisper.

Kaelin rose —walked to the door—and opened it. Meanwhile, Bistre slid under the cover, still sitting up, and pulled it up under her chin. Carla held a tray with food and drink. Kaelin took it from her. He smiled but did not speak.

"Oh my," said Carla reaching in and pulling the door closed.

"Carla!" scoffed Bistre. "She acts like she's never seen a naked man before."

Kaelin set the tray down on the small table adjacent to the bed. He handed Bistre the water jug. He then picked up the flask of beer and sat on the bed. They drank together, smiling, as might two innocent youngsters—just after love's first encounter.

With the beer flask empty, Kaelin returned it to the tray. Bistre handed him her water jug, and he likewise placed it on the tray. Kaelin climbed onto the bed and sat with his back against wall, supported by a large pillow. Sliding to him, Bistre quickly snuggled up next to Kaelin, feeling both affection and passion.

"Thank you, Kaelin." Bistre smiled, looking up at his face. She moved close to him and spoke in a faint voice with her lips close to his.

"You know, you can take all of me if you want, Kaelin. Affection is all I have to give you. I can use my mouth and hand on you, better than any girl you've ever had," she whispered while she tenderly kissed him, sliding her hand to gently massage his stones. "I have Hyacinth oil I keep secret for special men like you. If you want to, boy . . . take . . . me." There was a brief, still pause.

Bistre slowly moved up on her knees. With her back toward Kaelin, she looked over her shoulder with an impish smile. She placed her hands on the soft bed and stretched out with her arms in front of her—fingers gripping the bed—as if sharp claws. She arched her lower spine and pushed her bottom back. Bistre exposed herself, becoming an eager feline in heat, enticing her mate to wrap his paws around her narrow waist—clamp the back of her neck with deadly jaws—keeping her still, preparing her for deep penetration.

Kaelin moved from the decorated wall headboard and came up on his knees behind Bistre. Her sienna-pink tea-rose and the moist folds of her vagina flower were exposed. He gripped her hips with both hands, his stiff erection pulsating. He pulled her toward him, and she easily slid into a position he preferred. Bistre reached her right hand back to Kaelin, which held a small alabastron vase that women used to store perfume or oil.

Kaelin took the vase from her. He pulled off the snug stopper and poured a driblet of the luxurious attar onto his index finger. He replaced the stopper top, then set the miniature urn on the bed.

Tenderly, he applied the Hyacinth oil to her private, tiny tea-rose. Taking himself in hand, he carefully found her delicate opening—slowly easing his male hardness into her—once again gripping her curved hips with both hands.

Kaelin closed the door to Bistre's small, comfortable room and walked down the hall into the main first room, which was now occupied by several customers. A few men sat at a table, drinking and talking, while one examined a girl near the center of the room, one of the girls who had lined up for Kaelin and Lutas. Another man dandled a girl on his lap, who gripped his shoulders with both hands. She leaned over and whispered something in his ear, provoking a laugh. Beath sat at the large table by the window, drinking a mug of beer. She looked up when Kaelin approached.

"Now, I presume that was a good fokken, Spearman Kaelin. But on occasion, that can be a problem with young men like yourself. After you pull a girl's undergarments down and bend her over the end of a bed, you always want to squirt your milk twice. I'm glad you offered to pay for the additional attention."

Kaelin did not reply. He fished a coin from his pouch, walked over to Beath, and set it down on the table. She looked at the money and grinned.

"Now that's a generous payment."

Again, Kaelin did not answer but instead walked over to the pommel horse and the three odd straps hanging on the wall. Beath reached across the table and picked up the coin. Curious, she rose and walked up to Kaelin. He turned and placed his hand on the leather-covered horse and spoke without looking at her.

"The pommel horse is used to train soldiers to mount a horse while wearing armor," he stated as he rubbed the horse and gave it a few pats.

'Oh," answered Beath. "Really? I did not know that. We use it for a more adventurous purpose here."

Kaelin took a few steps to examine the larger of the three leather straps.

"It's called a Dragon's Tongue," stated Beath.

"Yes, I have heard," replied Kaelin.

"Remove your belt, tunic, and loin-cloth, new-arrival Kaelin . . . bend over the horse . . . and I'll demonstrate how it is applied!"

Kaelin looked at her and smiled. "I'll use my imagination to experience the Dragon's Tongue application." He next took the smaller strap from the wall.

"That one is called the Maiden's Tongue," offered Beath, using a teaching voice. "It is pragmatically employed when less severe learning is required, in particular—more immature offenders. I've heard it said that when an ill-mannered, stripling's penis has been reddened by enough licks of the Maiden's Tongue, he will obey his mistress's every word for a long spell to come."

Kaelin chuckled to himself, returning the Maiden's Tongue to its proper peg, and took down the third instrument. The ends of the strap were split to form two sharp, adjacent points. He strapped the palm of his hand three or four swipes measuring its sting.

"That unique item is lovingly called a Serpent's Tongue, and you see why," said Beath with a perky smile. "It licks the most secret and tender of places." Again, Kaelin chuckled to himself—returned the odd strap to its peg—and walked back to the table. Beath followed. Kaelin now looked seriously at Beath and spoke with no hint of humor.

"I will propose a deal, Beath,"

"Speak on, Kaelin," she said in a relaxed manner and casually sat back down at the table, grasping the beer mug.

"I prefer smooth skin without blemish. A soft, round butt and long, slender legs, that are void of strap marks remain very appealing to me. On the next occasion I see Bistre, I would prefer to have her butt and legs in that condition. Do you understand?"

Beath paused. Although he was a new recruit and only held the rank of spearman, she suddenly realized that, nonetheless, he was a Ravenbourne Warrior. She could ascertain from his manner that he was deadly serious. The same warriors who vowed to protect the innocent were equally lethal. A hint of fear crept into her heart. She knew now to proceed with caution. Besides, all she needed was for a Ravenbourne Warrior to offer protection to one of her girls. She would never be able to keep that girl in line. It would not put her out of business, but it would make things harder than they already were.

Beath smiled as best she could, though it was a smile born of fear. "Yes, Spearman Kaelin, I understand. But if Bistre or any of my girls are disobedient or misbehave, they need to be corrected, and the Dragon's Tongue, or similar application from the Maiden's Tongue, is the best form of correction. Naughty and unruly slave-girls . . . bed-slaves . . . and pal-lakes have been spanked for thousands of years, Kaelin, slave-boys as well. That's why it was invented. A humiliating, painful punishment that does not cause any real damage, such as whipping, caning, or flogging would. That is why parents employ spanking on unruly children. This is a brothel, Kaelin, and she is my slave. It is not an aristocrat's seminary for girls."

Beath paused and took another healthy drink of beer, then wiped her mouth with the back of her hand. "It could be worse. Most other brothel slaves are punished with figging, in addition to the Dragon's Tongue. My husband and I have never used figging on our girls."

"You have not offered a solution," stated Kaelin, holding his stern expression.

Beath cleared her throat. "All right!" She paused and took another long drink while looking at Kaelin. She set the ceramic mug back on the table before continuing.

"Perhaps I have an idea." Beath cleared her throat and swallowed. "I'll promise not to punish her. I will keep an accurate account of her behavior. I will keep it in writing. When you return to my house, I will inform you of her recorded behavior. You may punish her yourself, or not, depending on what you think she deserves. But we must ensure Bistre understands our agreement, and most importantly to me, she is not free. Her price will be paid. Is that a deal?"

Kaelin looked into Beath's eyes. His cold stare continued to send fear into her heart. She put her hands together under the table because she trembled.

"It is," he responded. He casually looked around, hoping he might see Sergeant Lutas.

"Your companion will be in the room most of the afternoon, Kaelin, until nearly dark." Beath punctuated her statement with a fake laugh. "Sit down and have a beer on the house."

Just then, the brown-haired, doe-eyed beauty walked briskly into the room, dressed in her alluring, white under garments. Kaelin did not respond to Beath but instead walked to Bistre, taking her in his arms and kissing her. She returned his kiss with soft affection and a hint of passion.

He took her chin with his fingers and said in a solemn voice. "Beath and I have an arrangement. She will explain it to you in detail. She will not punish you. But if you misbehave, I will discipline you on my return in the manner slave-girls have been chastised for thousands of years . . . or so I have been told. Do you understand?"

Bistre looked first at Beath and back to Kaelin. She nodded her head and stood up on her toes to whisper in his ear allowing only he would hear her. "Yes, I understand, but maybe I want you to spank me."

Kaelin took her shoulders and was tempted to give her a shake. Instead, he gave her a stern look and emphasized in a firm voice.

"I am very serious. You be on your best behavior until I return."

He then spoke softly into her ear. "Remember, honey earns more coin than vinegar. Honey marks the road to freedom."

"I will. Kaelin. . . ." She whispered. "I understand, and I will."

Kaelin gave Bistre a tender kiss, which she returned, taking his face in both her hands. The kiss ended, and they smiled warmly at each other. Kaelin turned and walked to the door.

CHAPTER 31

Kaelin: Village Girl Rescue

STANDING OUTSIDE OF THE VIRGIN Cheeks and Thighs, Kaelin looked up and down the roadway. He began to walk down the paved village road, having no destination, just exploring. He had not felt this good in a long while. That soft, lovable, brown-eyed delight was the sweetest diversion he could ask for. She reminded him of the passionate nights he spent with Salome, the hetaera he stayed with when an inexperienced youth in Opar. Bistre's passion reminded him of her.

He drew his right hand up to his nose and breathed in. Her scent lingered on his fingers—the aroma delightful. He would not wash his hand for a while, and most certainly he would return—after all, he had promised. More than a promise, it was now an obligation. Soon, he passed another whorehouse. A woman lay on a bench outside the house. She sat up as he approached her.

"Hello there, Ravenbourne Warrior." She smiled an attractive smile. Kaelin drew near. He stopped but did not answer.

"I see in your face you are fledgling but equally experienced. If you allow me, I believe I can persuade your maleness to give me your secret male fluid in all three of my female folds of pleasure, in exchange for that Ravenbourne dagger. Hmmm—have you ever ejaculated three in a row? Once in my mouth, once in my flower, and once in my tight, little cherry."

Kaelin still did not reply but smiled and walked on. The woman shrugged her shoulders and reclined back on the bench. He continued on, turning onto several side roads to eventually come to the edge of the village. Suddenly, he heard a loud voice calling out.

"Warrior! Warrior!" Kaelin turned to see an elderly man with thick grey hair and beard walking toward him with a hurried gait. In one hand, he held a walking stick supporting his limp, and in the other, a spear. The old man called out again, prompting Kaelin to advance toward him.

"Run step, warrior . . . run step!" The old man called out a military order in a desperate voice and Kaelin complied. When he neared the old man, Kaelin saw that he wore what seemed to be an aged military tunic—an old army belt about his waist—holding an army dagger. The elderly man was obviously ex-army. He was breathing hard and wore a desperate look on his face, but his words were clear.

"Warrior, three men have abducted a young girl and have carried her off behind that abandoned hut!" He pointed as he spoke in a clear, direct voice. "Go to her aid. Surely they intend to rape her . . . and . . . probably kill her."

The old man tossed Kaelin his spear. He grasped it in midair. He recognized the feel. It was the same type of weapon used in the Feohtan arena.

"I'll follow behind you as fast as I can!" called out the old soldier.

Kaelin nodded, turned, and ran toward the hut. It did not take long for him to reach the apparently abandoned house. He approached the front, ran to the side, then to the back of the dilapidated building, stopping some twenty paces from the heinous violation in progress.

The helpless, young victim lay on her back on an old wooden work table, her frock ripped open in front, exposing her. Her three attackers had tied a gag around her small mouth to muffle her desperate cries for help. One assailant stood at the corner of the table and held her right arm, pinning it down on the table. The second did the same, at the other corner, securing her left arm on the table. The third nefarious brigand stood with his back and side to Kaelin, between her spread, kicking legs. He had lifted his tunic and was holding his erection, preparing to penetrate her innocence.

Lifting the spear, Kaelin twirled it in his hand, preparing to throw. All three were close, easy targets. He quickly plotted a strategy. If the spear hit the man in the middle, the one about to rape the helpless girl, it might pass all the way through him, with the point protruding out his chest on the other side. He would most likely fall forward on top of the girl, perhaps stabbing her with the spear point. Consequently, one of the other rapists would be his first target. Kaelin chose the brigand on the left—extended back his arm—balanced his stance—and cast the lethal, bronze projectile.

Surprisingly, his target looked up to see the flash of the spear speeding toward him, but for only a moment. Just enough pause to widen his eyes with an expression of terror as the point struck near the center of his chest with a strange, nearly silent thud. Along with a stream of blood, it protruded out his back. He managed a gargling cry of pain, grasping the spear shaft. Blood flowed from his open mouth, as though escaping from a spewing fountain. Falling backward, he alerted the other two rapists, who were momentarily stunned

The dog holding the girl's other arm released her but stood silent, seemingly immobile. He gawked at Kaelin with his mouth open wide. He looked to the ground, at his speared partner, and back to Kaelin, all the while with a gaping mouth, continuing to gawk at Kaelin in shock and disbelief.

The third cur, who had been about to assault the helpless child, reached over, pulling his sword from his belted scabbard, which he had removed and laid next to him on the ground. With his sword in hand, he stepped forward.

The instant Kaelin released his spear, he, too, drew his sword, and now ran toward the two brigands. He came face to face with the third thug, who awkwardly swung his sword in a great arc at Kaelin's head. So common with thugs and criminals—Kaelin knew they were prepared and eager to harm the innocent but were essentially poorly trained in combat skills. He would take great pleasure in ending this worthless life.

Kaelin easily ducked his adversary's hacking sword and, at the same moment, brought his own sword in a deadly, slashing swipe across his challenger's stomach, making sure he did not strike the man's ribs, which might break his sword. The surprised wounded man called out in pain, while blood soaked through his tunic and his warm, bloody organs slipped through the wound. In that same instant, Kaelin sliced his sword in a backhand swing, striking the side of the coward's neck.

Holding his left hand to his bleeding stomach—his guts seeped out into his hand—dropping onto the ground in slimy, bloody entrails. The wounded man fell to his knees. He looked up at Kaelin in shock and disbelief, then fell over onto his back. Kaelin stepped on the brigand's right wrist, pinning his right hand and sword, to the ground. Swiftly, with the point of his sword, Kaelin pierced his victim under his chin, pushing his sword deep into his cranium. It was a bit of bloody overkill that Kaelin thoroughly enjoyed. The brutal coward cried out, a final desperate cry, muffled with blood. He kicked his legs in violent reflex, releasing his foul soul to eternal fate.

Meanwhile, the third brigand had now responded and taken flight. Kaelin knew he could run down the fleeing coward, but the muffled cries of the girl turned his attention. He quickly wiped the blood from his sword on his slain victim's tunic, returned it to its scabbard, and approached the girl. She lay curled up on her side, weeping desperately.

"It's all right, child. It's all right. They won't harm you now." He spoke gently and as calmly as he could.

She looked up at Kaelin with an anxious, terror-stricken expression. He saw his own sister in her frightened, innocent face. Slowly, he held out the palms of his hands. He could not help but feel misting tears in his own eyes.

"I am a Ravenbourne Warrior, child, and I will protect you. Those evil men are gone," he said, speaking in the tenderest voice he could find.

"They are gone. And. . . ." He paused taking a silent breath. "They will never return." When Kaelin gently touched her shoulder, she came to him, and he cradled her against his chest.

"You're alright now—you're alright," he said in a calming voice, while he untied the gag, thus completely releasing her from her attackers. She put her arms around him, holding on to him as tight as she could, crying with her head against his chest. Kaelin petted and stroked her hair, comforting her. "Have no fear now; those evil men will never hurt you again."

"Bravo, warrior, bravo! No doubt you are a Ravenbourne Warrior!"

Kaelin heard the voice of the veteran soldier. He looked up to see the old man approaching with a broad smile shining through his grey beard.

"I believe you can still run that fleeing coward down," declared the old soldier.

Kaelin glanced in the direction the running brigand had taken, and turned back to the old man. "No, let us tend to the girl. I know what the bastard looks like, and I'll kill him the next we meet."

"Good," lauded the old man. He reached down and patted the girl's leg. "You'll be fine now, child. Don't fret." Recognizing the seasoned warrior, the girl seemed somewhat relieved. "I don't know the girl's name, but I know her family. Let's take her to them."

Kaelin nodded in agreement. He picked the girl up, cradling her in his arms. The grey-headed veteran directed their path toward her family's hut, which was situated on the opposite side of the village. Although calmed, the girl still whimpered, clinging to Kaelin's tunic—her face against his chest.

Moving along the main road, curious villagers approached the old man to inquire. "This brave Ravenbourne Warrior saved this girl from rape by brigands," he lauded. "He killed two of them! The village Elders will meet to discuss this attack. So will the whole village."

The aged soldier spoke with some authority. *Perhaps he is a village Elder*, thought Kaelin. The apparent Elder continued with this same announcement while they made their way along the main road of the village.

To Kaelin's sudden surprise, a young girl, about the same age as the one he carried, came running up. "Grandpa! Grandpa!" she called out. She stopped in front of them, and they also halted. The girl took the old man's hand.

"I know this girl, Grandpa." She looked up at her. "Are you alright, Jenny? Are you alright?"

The girl reached her hand up, and Jenny, the girl Kaelin carried, responded in kind. They did not speak but exchanged teary-eyed smiles, holding hands. Jenny then released the girl's hand, reached her arm around Kaelin's neck, and returned her head to his chest. They continued on the road, with a small group of villagers following.

"The girl and her family are from Mysia," offered the apparent village Elder. "The mother has a strange, although pleasant, way of talking, but the girl grew up here at Ravenbourne. The father was a soldier. He was killed at Opar.

"Many good soldiers were killed at Opar," added Kaelin. "Including my father."

The elder soldier did not respond as they stopped in front of a well lived-in hut. He called out. A woman came running from inside the hut. Kaelin let the girl down, and she ran to her mother, who got down on her knees to embrace her child. While the aged soldier told the tale, the girl found more tears. The mother comforted her daughter while she listened, and she was driven to tears by the story's end.

The teary-eyed mother looked at Kaelin. She got up and stepped toward him. The daughter followed, keeping her arm around her mother's waist. Reaching out, she took Kaelin's hand.

"Thank you, Warrior, thank you," she said, speaking and crying at the same moment. Kaelin only nodded.

"What is your name?" asked the mother. Kaelin replied. Again, the mother smiled, touching her fingers to her lips to say thank you.

"We will always be grateful for what you did, Kaelin," confessed the tearful mother.

Humbly, Kaelin nodded. "I must go and report to my sergeant and officers."

"Most certainly, Spearman Kaelin of the Ravenbourne Warriors," replied the elder soldier. "There is much more to be decided about this attack," he said, again speaking with a voice of authority, looking around at the small following, who all nodded and mumbled with approval.

Kaelin allowed a final nod and left to find Sergeant Lutas. Departing, he heard the granddaughter say, "Grandpa, Momma says I'm to bring you home for dinner."

"That sounds a wonderful idea to me, child. Lead on."

Kaelin found his older comrade still at the Virgin Cheeks and Thighs, sitting out in front of the house on a bench, enjoying a mug of beer. Lutas smiled, lifting his container. Kaelin approached, stopping by the bench.

"You know, Kaelin, I got to tell you something. I've tasted every little kunt this old whorehouse has had, for many seasons now. And though I follow that old Beath, that brown-haired Bistre is the sweetest girl I've ever had. If I was to ever buy a slave-girl for a wife, she would sure be the one. Not that I would ever have that kind of money."

Lutas took another drink and spit. "There is some sort of commotion. I wonder what it is?"

"I know," replied Kaelin, looking at Lutas. "I killed two men, preventing them from raping a girl. A third attacker ran away. An aged soldier with a limp was witness to it all. In fact, he directed me to the location where the three brigands had taken the girl."

Lutas looked up at Kaelin without expression. He didn't seem in the least bit excited or troubled by the news. "Yeah, that would be Old Torrhen, retired army sergeant and village Elder," he replied.

He took another mouthful of beer, then again spit it out on the ground. "Come and show me the two bodies. After that, we best report to our sergeant." Kaelin agreed.

"Want of mug of beer before we go? It's free."

Kaelin smiled, shaking his head no. Lutas stood up, taking another long drink from the mug before setting it on the bench. "Sure not very good—watered down—but free."

He looked at Kaelin with a big grin. "Excitement just seems to follow you, Spearman Kaelin. I hope we end up together on duty. It won't be boring—that's for sure."

Shrugging his shoulders, Kaelin, offered a halfhearted, nonchalant smile. Lutas turned his head for a concluding spit, and the two Ravenbourne Warriors walked off toward the attack scene.

The whole village remained in a stir, with everyone talking about the abduction and attempted rape of the village girl named Jenny by brigands from the mountains. The talk, however, seemed to focus on the new Ravenbourne Warrior who saved Jenny named Kaelin. News spread with a snail's pace across the Southern Peninsula; nonetheless, the villagers learned more about this warrior from the fallen Opar. That he had endured a torturous slave march and saved Lord Ravenbourne's life in the Great Arena at Cappa as a Feohtan fighter. He quickly became a local hero.

Melissa and Natasha sat on the sides of the village well, listening to the other young village women gossip about this now-notorious event—but mostly about Kaelin. Many were servants and slaves. It remained the daily task of the unimportant women of the household to carry water from the well. Although none had actually seen him, most of their discussion centered on how handsome he might be, presuming he was attractive at all.

Natasha whispered to her best friend.

"This is fun, Melissa. No one of this girl-gaggle is aware we know all about him. We've seen him baby-bird naked."

Melissa covered her mouth, laughing. "I know! What if we were to tell them how large and heavy his pillar and stones are?"

"We could also describe to them how large and hard his erection was, even though I didn't see," continued Natasha, joking and whispering.

"I didn't either, Nati," murmured Melissa, trying not to laugh out loud. "You know, Sweetie, he mostly lay asleep on his stomach when I was there in the guest room. And when he woke, he talked with Sergeant Lutas, not me. And I sure didn't see his erection."

"I would love to inform them that he is the most handsome man I have ever seen," added Natasha. Both friends continued to laugh, trying not to be noticed.

Soon, the atmosphere around the well quieted down. Some of the girls remarked that they had tarried too long and could be in trouble. Others picked up their full hydria jugs and hurriedly returned to their households.

"I have a serious question for you, Melissa," proposed Natasha, her expression now a frown.

Wearing a simper on her face, Melissa reached up and pinched

Natasha's cheek. "Don't be so serious, Nati. You have the sweetest smile of all the village girls, so let me see it!"

Natasha blushed. And she could not help but smile. She was lucky to have such a good friend as Melissa.

"Should we inform my father about Kaelin's Dragon's Tongue strapping in the dining hall?" A solemn pause followed. "You know the two village Elders are meeting with my father at our house, and the village meeting is today at high noon."

"I don't think so, Sweetie," answered Melissa, although she continued to ponder the question. "I've heard the warriors say that what happens in the company should stay in the company. And even though we aren't warriors, of course, we are still part of the company. If word leaks out, then it does, but it won't come from us. Your father and the other two Elders are all veterans. I think they would tell us to keep it to ourselves."

"I think you're correct Melissa," said Natasha with a sigh. She then leaned over and gave her best friend a quick kiss on her lips.

Melissa patted Natasha's cheek. "Let's carry the water back to your house, Nati!"

Both girls picked up their hydria jugs and brought them to their shoulders. "Can you carry a hydria of water on your head without using your hands, Nati?" asked a laughing Melissa.

"No!" answered a smiling Natasha. "Not at all."

"My Aunt Ymir can," admitted Melissa. "But I'm not sure I even want to learn."

The village council consisted of three Elders, all retired military: Old Torrhen, Army Sergeant; Natasha's father Thoas, First Spear of the 13th Legion; and a third army veteran named Ned Coxen. They had discussed the matter at the house of First Spear Thoas. The solution was not difficult.

At high noon, the village residents gathered at the town square. A small but sturdy wooden platform stood on the edge of the village road, near the village well. The three Elders took to the platform, seated on three small chairs.

The village men gathered around the platform to hear the Elders' solution to this problem and discuss that solution or a course of action. Women and children were also present, but stood on the perimeter of the assembly. Most of the young village girls, including Melissa and Natasha, sat on or near the well. Because they visited the well nearly daily, it had somehow become their female area. Very little was actually discussed. The solution was clear and quickly decided. The three Elders requested a meeting with the commander of the Ravenbourne Corps, who most certainly would agree without hesitation.

The small meeting hall at the Ravenbourne Corps headquarters was filled with military men—young—old—retired and since they were meeting to discuss a military matter, it seemed fitting. They gathered around a large table of rough-hewn wood; some of them sat, mostly the elderly, while others stood. Colonel Davis, commander of the Ravenbourne Corps, sat at the end of the table. He stood and glanced around the room to initiate the proceedings.

"The village council of three Elders," began Colonel Davis, "are here representing the voice of the villagers. Old Torrhen, retired Army Sergeant . . . First Spear Thoas of the 13th Legion . . . and also retired Army Sergeant—Ned Coxen."

Pausing for a moment, he then continued. "Spearman Kaelin,

Ravenbourne Warrior, will describe the events of that day to the best of his recollection."

Kaelin rose and related the narrative of the attack, short and to the point, which was his manner. Old Torrhen, somewhat more vocal, likewise added his part. In the end, the solution was simple. The Elders requested that a permanent patrol be assigned to the village. Colonel Davis agreed.

"It wasn't that many years ago the village was included in our regular patrols. I'm not sure why that ended," he explained. The Elders also requested that Kaelin command the patrols. He had become a village hero, and he certainly had the experience for such an assignment. Again, Colonel Davis concurred.

"Yes! Spearman Kaelin is the best choice to command this village patrol." Colonel Davis looked over to a civilian member of his staff, a scribe. He was seated next to the Colonel, with pen and parchment in front of him. He had been recording the notes of the meeting all along.

"Take these instructions!" ordered Colonel Davis.

The scribe quickly looked to his employer. He politely nodded. Pulling out a new sheet of parchment, he prepared to write.

Standing up tall and erect, Colonel Davis looked to Kaelin. "Spearman Kaelin!"

Kaelin promptly stepped out to stand alone at attention. A hush fell on the assembly, as they all knew what was about to occur. Colonel Davis spoke his orders in a loud, stern voice.

"You are promoted to the rank of lieutenant. You will take command of two squads of Ravenbourne Warriors, ten in each squad, and initiate a patrol of the Ravenbourne Village. Your patrol will protect the village residents. Bring law and order to the village. Enforce Lord Ravenbourne's law. Maintain good rapport with the villagers."

A small applause followed. The three village Elders knocked their fists, two or three raps on the table, to show their approval. Colonel

Davis thus knew the Elders were in agreement. He now looked over to Lutas. "Ninth Man Lutas!"

Lutas followed Kaelin's example and stepped out from the assembly to stand alone. Once more, the assembly became still, and once more, Colonel Davis issued an order.

"Ninth Man Lutas: you are promoted to First Sergeant of the Village Patrol. I trust you can avoid knocking your commanding officer to the ground . . . First Sergeant?"

"Yes, Sir," answered Lutas, standing tall and straight, yet wearing a playful grin. "I'll do my best, Sir!"

The assembly was mildly entertained by Colonel Davis's humor. He continued with instructions. "I will send the engineers to construct a long-term bivouac, Lieutenant. Locate a suitable location as soon as possible. More importantly, secure a site for a permanent station. Headquarters, barracks, kitchen, dining hall, and other buildings will be required. I'll place a request into the Southern Army Command. Slaves and civilian employees will also be residing at the station. I'm sure the fast experiences of First Sergeant Lutas will be a valuable asset in the selection of female-slaves and kitchen help."

Once more, lighthearted laughter rolled around the assembly. "Yes, Sir! Lieutenant Kaelin can count on me, Sir." offered Sergeant Lutas.

"Lieutenant Kaelin!" continued Colonel Davis. "You will remain under the command of Captain Tydeus. You and your men will form with the 1ˢᵗ Company."

Colonel Davis now looked around the meeting hall. It was obvious he was ready to conclude. "Any questions or suggestions?" he asked.

"Sir!" inquired Captain Tydeus. "I suggest Lieutenant Kaelin ask first for volunteers, then recruit, if necessary, to fill the Village Patrol force."

"Agreed!" responded Colonel Davis. He paused and again surveyed the room. "This meeting is concluded!"

Natasha: Sharing Her Vision

Early in the morning, before most villagers had awoken, Natasha took Melissa to her secret place. With bags of goods and a blanket across their shoulders, they slipped away from the village, with Natasha leading Melissa along her usual out-of-sight paths to the Great Stone Bridge. The hideout was located just downstream from the Great Stone Bridge on the Tyner River. It lay hidden from view by a small grove of trees, which stood in a strange spherical formation around a patch of thick, soft grass.

Natasha pointed, maintaining serious enthusiasm. "There, Melissa . . . do you see that clump of trees?"

Melissa looked and answered, "Yes, I see them!"

"That is our destination. That is my secret place."

Natasha took Melissa's hand, tugging on her to follow. They scampered around the end of the bridge and the Emperor's Highway, following a path down the embankment to the river.

"Let's hurry, Melissa," called out Natasha in an adorable, nearly childlike voice.

"I can't run as fast as you can, Natasha. Slow down!"

They followed the river to Natasha's secret place. Once there, Natasha stood in the middle of the soft grass—holding out her arms— twirling in a circle. "Do you like my secret hideaway, Melissa?"

"Oh yes," she replied with a broad smile, looking around. "It's beautiful. The circle of trees makes it look magical."

"I know," agreed Natasha. "I have often wondered if the trees were planted by unknown ancient mortals, long ago, for some unexplained purpose. Also, I have explored most of the area around the Ravenbourne Villa and the village, and this is the only location where I have ever noticed this type of exotic grass. It's very comforting to lie in the soft grass, rolling over its dark, brilliant blue-green color while taking in deep breaths of its piquant, almost alluring fragrance. I like to imagine that perhaps the women who worshipped long ago in the ancient temple used this location. Or better still, the grass originated from some nameless, distant land, brought here by ancient travelers. They sowed the seeds and planted the trees for a now—long—forgotten, mysterious reason. And Melissa. . .." Natasha hesitated. "Perhaps it was for a surreptitious purpose."

Melissa had to smile at her dear friend's words. "Maybe it was created by the goddess Asa, Nati."

Natasha formed a surprised but pleased expression. "I had not thought of that. Yes, Melissa. Maybe so?"

Adding to the privacy and allure of the hideaway, short, thorny shrubs grew around the base of the trees and along the edge of the grassy patch. In the spring, large, fragrant flowers bloomed on the shrubs.

"Look at all of the beautiful flowers that grow on the shrubs around the edge of the grass, Melissa. Their fragrance is simply wonderful," exclaimed an excited Natasha.

Melissa took a deep breath. "Oh yes, Natasha. They're beautiful and very romantic."

"Because the shrubs are thick," continued Natasha, "colorful birds often nest in the protected undergrowth. On many relaxing days, I lay on the soft grass, reading, thinking, sometimes napping, hidden from view, even from the height of the tall bridge." Natasha pointed to the huge bridge.

"The angle and line of sight from the bridge are such that my hide-away remains hidden by anyone crossing the bridge, so we can remain out of sight, watching the travelers crossing the bridge, although they, too, are partially obscured by the sides of the bridge."

They laid out the blanket on the soft grass and made themselves comfortable. Natasha was extremely happy to share her secret place with her best friend. She also knew, however, that she must explain her vision to Melissa and its connection to the appearance of the new Ravenbourne Warrior, Kaelin. And, it was more complicated now that he had endured Melissa's punishment in front of the whole company. But first, she just needed to begin talking, knowing no one could hear . . . so she did. Melissa, her patient and true friend, listened.

"I'm not all that ebullient about working as a server in the 1st Company dining hall," admitted Natasha. "Even though I only work one day every three days. It's not necessarily easy but not hard either, albeit working with you is fun. And my father told me I could keep all the pay for myself, and that is wonderful. My father is often too stern, but he is also very generous."

"I wish I had a father like yours Nati," confessed Melissa. "Maybe your father will adopt me?"

"He will Melissa. We are the same as sisters now, especially when you are staying with us. But you know he is very strict," cautioned Natasha. "He might proffer your bottom a skelping if he catches you do-ing some of the activities, I know you engage in. But you know I won't tell on you."

"Well, he sure can't be any worse than mean old First Sergeant Klause," complained Melissa—rubbing her behind—making a face—and pretending to cry as loud as she could. Both girls lay back, laughing out loud and rolling around on the soft grass.

"I hoped I could save up enough money to buy a book, but I also know that wish remains unrealistic," conceded Natasha.

"Even so, Nati!" challenged Melissa. "You could still save enough money for a dagger, maybe an army dagger, or perhaps a hairbrush. Something like those things that you've always wanted."

"Well, maybe you're right, Melissa. But I must admit, it is exciting to be around such a large number of Ravenbourne Warriors," confessed Natasha, "and even a little more so to be with the elite warriors of the 1st Company of the Ravenbourne Corps. But I think the men are copious in teasing me."

"What does that mean, Sweetie?" asked Melissa.

"Oh! It means they tease me a lot," answered Natasha.

"You should be pleased, Nati," responded Melissa. "They tease you because you're so pretty. Enjoy it while you can. Take advantage of it."

"Well, I guess I don't mind all that much, but occasionally it's embarrassing," answered Natasha.

"Of course, it's embarrassing Sweetie, that's what makes it fun. And you could get lots of urns of honey if you wanted. Slave-girls trade sex for urns of honey and sometimes for silver coins." Melissa looked at her with a big, mischievous smile. "Remember my silver coin from Sergeant Derick?"

"You know I've not indulged in sex, Melissa. I'm afraid," said Natasha with a serious face.

"Yes, I know. And there is nothing wrong with being afraid. It's normal to be. And I'm going to help you on that journey that all girls take." Melissa reached up and cupped Natasha's face.

"I'm going to help you just like a big sister or your mother would, even your aunt. Follow your heart, Nati. You'll be ready when you're ready, but I also know a Ravenbourne dagger might be yours just for a little ride with a Ravenbourne Warrior."

Melissa again cupped Natasha's face. She slowly leaned forward—kissed her forehead—both her eyes—and finally, a long kiss on her mouth. She then patted her checks and smiled.

"All right! I'll consider it," replied Natasha with a swallow.

There was a short silence. Melissa could tell Natasha was thinking of something. She waited with patience.

"Melissa?" began Natasha in an asking voice.

"Yes, Sweetheart?" she replied as an older sister might.

"I want to tell you something very private, but you know I've been afraid to!"

"Oh, Nati! Sweetheart." Melissa reached up and again cupped Natasha's face, tenderly kissing each tearful eye. She then wrapped both her arms around her and gently embraced her.

"Don't ever be afraid to tell me anything Nati . . ." she softy scolded. "We are best friends and sisters. We can share all our secrets with each other and we can always trust each other."

Natasha snuggled into Melissa and rested her head on her shoulder, as Melissa petted her head. "I will," promised Natasha who was now comforted, relaxed, and cuddled into Melissa. She began her confession.

"Nearly two moons had passed since my mother died and you had arrived at Ravenbourne Village. I was so unhappy, nearly distraught. One morning I followed the creek to that wide pool all the village children play in. It was early, and I was the only one there. I prayed to the goddess, saying that I didn't want to have a village life. I wanted to somehow have adventure and maybe see wonderful things, or go to other places, the same as you and my father. I don't know what I really want, but I do not want to be a village girl and wake up and discover one day that I'm an old village woman, still here in the village."

Natasha paused, breathing hard, and whimpering. "It's all well, sweet love," said Melissa in a comforting voice once again petting her head. "Go on when you're ready."

Natasha swallowed hard and continued, "I offered a gift to Asa in the pool. And when I looked into the pool, the reflection was not mine. By some strange magic I don't understand, it was Kaelin, and I was terribly afraid"

"What?" interrupted Melissa. "Are you sure, my sweet?"

"Oh yes!" replied Natasha in earnest. "No mistake! All the villagers heard he saved Lord Ravenbourne's life, and subsequently, he came here as a Ravenbourne Warrior. I was on the big bridge the day he arrived with a wagon-load of Opar pallakes for Lady Ravenbourne. I saw him for the first occasion on the bridge."

Natasha now began to cry. "And now he took your punishment in the dining hall. He displayed such enormous bravery. He didn't move or flinch during that horrible beating. I was terribly distraught. We both were. I prayed to the goddess and asked her to give him strength—to be with him. I also said I would do anything she asked. Suddenly, a strange wind blew into my ear. How could there be wind in the dining hall? A soft female voice spoke to me in a whisper. She spoke the language of the Hyacinth Gatherers, and she said. *'Fear not, my sweet girl. I am with him!'* I don't know what it all means, and I don't know what to do."

Melissa also began to cry sympathetically. She wrapped her arms around her friend in warm embrace—kissing her cheek—and the side of her head. "Don't cry, my sweet. . . ." She whispered into Natasha's ear. "We will figure this out together. We will ask an older, wiser woman. Maybe my aunt or even the temple priestess."

"I had thought the same, but why would the priestess talk to me—a nobody?" asked a sniveling Natasha.

"The priestesses at all the temples," answered Melissa, trying to speak and end her own crying, "talk to all women, my sweet love, especially the young women. Remember, you are a Hyacinth Gatherer and those people are special to the goddess Asa. We will figure something out. I promise you we will." Melissa then kissed Natasha's forehead and petted her mystical, red hair.

Constructed on the far end of a one-acre plot, First Spear Thoas's house was somewhat isolated from most of the village but still situated on the main road. Natasha and Melissa walked hand in hand down the main road, having now recovered from their anxious discussion and attempting to appear pleasant. They each found a friendly greeting with other villagers they met. Thoas and his two veteran partners were working on a wagon, which they would use when they made their journey to the mountains to harvest their ash tree plantation for spear shafts.

Approaching, Natasha and Melissa both waved, and Natasha called out. "Father!"

Thoas looked up and returned their wave with his own. He laid his tools down and stood with some difficulty, using the wagon as a brace. Then he approached the two girls with his stiff-legged walk.

Wrapping his arms around both girls, Thoas kissed each one on the forehead. Over the past several full moons, he had become a surrogate father to Melissa, and she completely enjoyed the comfort of having a concerned—caring—albeit stern father. "I have some good news for you," he said in a cheerful voice.

"Oh, some good news would be wonderful, Father," confessed Natasha. Smiling, Melissa nodded her head in agreement.

"I attended the last full-moon Receiving Reception," began First Spear Thoas, "as myself and not representing the village. I asked Lady Ravenbourne if she could assist my sister, her former matron Elbe, to return to Ravenbourne in the light of my wife's recent passing."

Thoas looked at this daughter and continued. "She replied, that she would indeed and that I should consider it already accomplished."

"A courier was dispatched to Lord Ravenbourne. He will inform Matron Elbe that she is requested to come to Ravenbourne. Lord Ravenbourne will provide escort."

"All that lengthy clarification," explained Thoas, "means my sister . . . your Aunt Be . . . is on her way here, but it will take a few more days of travel for her to arrive from Capital City."

Natasha and Melissa clapped their hands and cried with joy. They both hugged Natasha's father while laughing at the wonderous news.

CHAPTER 33

Aunt Elbe: Arrival

P ULLED BY TWO DRAFT HORSES, a lightweight wheeled cart turned east from the Emperor's Highway toward the Twin Peaks, and rolled up the scenic Ravenbourne Road toward the Ravenbourne Villa. The sides of the wagon bore the crest of the Southern Army. A youthful Ravenbourne Warrior drove the wagon while another mounted warrior rode alongside. A second horse was haltered with a lead rope to the back of the wagon.

A mature woman sat next to the driver, laughing and talking with the young warrior, who responded with familiar smiles and conversation. She was attractive. Her hair was full and long, and the grey blended in with the flaxen color, forming a pleasing combination. She wore a well-sewn, expensive, but plain green frock and a matching palla. Seeming to enjoy the early-morning ride, she pointed to the primeval forest and the ancient ruins while the wagon turned off onto the Ravenbourne Village Road and soon clopped along the paved, main village road.

At the northern edge of the village, the wagon stopped at an isolated, well-constructed house. The woman lifted the palla from her arms and, using the driver's shoulders for balance, stood, and called out in a cheerful, loud voice;

"Thoas! Brother Thoas! Come out! Your favorite sister has arrived!"

The rider dismounted and secured his horse to the wagon, stepping to the front. He reached up and took the woman by her waist. She placed her hands on his shoulders and jumped. He lifted her up—set her on the ground—laughing. It was obvious they were well rehearsed in this wagon dismount.

At the door appeared First Spear Thoas. Smiling, he walked through the door with a limp, his right leg stiff and straight. "You are not only my favorite little sister, Elbe, but my only sister. Father and Mother wanted to have more children, but they were stuck with us."

"Thoas!" she called out, running to his arms and kissing his cheeks. He wrapped his arms around her waist and lifted her from the ground in an awkward, stiff-legged twirl. After he sat her down, she took his hands, stepped back, and inspected him, looking up and down.

"You look well, brother. How do you feel?"

"I'm well, Elbe, and glad you have come," answered Thoas.

There was a moment of silence, and then Elbe spoke. "I'm so, so sorry, Thoas," whispered his sister, tears forming in her eyes.

Thoas embraced her, which stopped her from speaking. He took her by her shoulders. "I'm not going to talk about her, Elbe. I've mourned her passing all I'm going to."

"I have equally so, brother," said Elbe, trying to smile and rubbing her eyes. "I loved her as a student and sister, but I'm still a woman, and I'm emotional." She took a loud, clearing sniff. "So now . . . how is Natasha?"

"It's been very hard on her," answered Thoas. "She tries to hide it, but she still mourns."

"Yes, she would," responded Elbe. "They were very close. More than mother and daughter, they were also best friends."

Elbe looked around. "Where is our beautiful Hyacinth girl?"

Thoas responded with a hearty laugh. "She works at the 1st Company dining hall with her best friend, Melissa. That girl is into more mischief than any youngster in the Southern Peninsula, but she is a good friend to Natasha. If they stay out of trouble, which they find difficult to do, they should be home soon."

"My word!" replied Elbe, completely surprised. "Now that is a remarkable change."

"Let's have you unloaded!" called out First Spear Thoas; in a voice he might use in commanding a squad of soldiers; "and send these warriors on to other duties!"

He paused, looking at his sister. "Unless you are staying in the private sanctuary of Lady Ravenbourne?"

Elbe laughed. "I certainly intend to see her and visit my former lady and her sanctuary, but I'm not going to stay there."

The wagon driver stood, saluted, and called out; "First Spear Thoas!" The older warrior standing by the wagon repeated the salute and recognition.

"I appreciate your salute, Warriors!" said First Spear Thoas, but he did not return their salute. The driver jumped down and secured the draft horses. Both warriors began to unload Elbe's boxes and carry them into the house.

"It was a long, hard, exciting journey, Thoas, all the way from Capital City with two handsome Ravenbourne Warriors—any woman's dream. The Inner Sea coastline remains rugged and treacherously beautiful."

"I vividly recall that coastal road, Elbe, rugged and treacherous undeniably," replied Thoas, "but my memory fails on the beautiful part."

"That is because one must be a romantic . . . brother," Elbe said smiling, "not a soldier, to see its . . . wild—untouched—beauty."

Not quite crying; but at least misty-eyed; Elbe bid a passionate farewell to her two Ravenbourne Warrior escorts. Anyone watching would presume their relationship during the long journey was more than casual.

"I normally do not kiss and tell," Elbe said chortling, "but I'm going to tell every woman I talk with about you two. And I. . . ." She hesitated wearing a smile. Hope it makes them jealous."

Both warriors laughed. "We don't care!" called out the senior warrior, securing his mount to the back of the wagon, adjacent to the other horse. "Tell all the women, Elbe, and let them come and find us." They both climbed into the driver's seat, waving.

"Warriors!" called out Thoas. "I appreciate your escort of my sister, and you have my thanks."

"First Spear Thoas!" acknowledged the older warrior. "It was our honor, as well as our duty, Sir!"

"Where do you report?" continued First Spear Thoas.

"First to the Ravenbourne Corps headquarters and then we return to the Ravenbourne Equestrian Guard at the Emperor's palace. Additional Warriors will join us."

"Good luck and safe journey, Warriors!" called First Spear Thoas, and on this occasion, he waved his hand over his head. The two Ravenbourne Warrior escorts returned his wave. The driver snapped the horses forward and turned the team around, heading on to the Ravenbourne Corps headquarters.

Meanwhile, Melissa and Natasha strolled happily down the village road, hand in hand, singing a happy song and trying to harmonize, laughing when the harmony went flat. They waved and called out, "Hello! Hello!" as the military wagon went by. The warriors returned their waves and greeting. Surprising all, Melissa raised up her frock to reveal her undergarments and moved her hips from side to side, prompting the warriors to whistle and catcall.

Natasha began to scold her but instead looked down the road to see two figures out in front of their house. She recognized the woman immediately. "It's my aunt!" called out Natasha, "my aunt Be!"

She took Melissa's hand and pulled. "Hurry, Melissa! Hurry! Let's run!" Holding hands, the two excited girls ran up the road toward the house—Natasha in the lead—pulling her friend most of the way.

Still holding hands, the two girls approached as the always-emotional Natasha began to cry. Aunt Be, also in tears, opened her arms wide. "Oh, Natasha! My sweet girl!" Natasha threw herself against her aunt, and the two embraced, both shedding emotional tears.

Aunt Be took Natasha by the face with both hands and tenderly kissed her mouth, in the fashion of Hyacinth Gatherer females, and proceeded to kiss the rest of her face. Natasha wrapped her arms around her aunt's waist, feeling the warmth and security with her head against her breasts.

Continuing to laugh and cry at the same moment, Natasha and Aunt Be both looked to Melissa, who stood by, hands folded in front. "And who is this pretty girl?" asked Aunt Be in a warm, motherly voice.

"This is Melissa, Aunt Be," responded Natasha with her head still snuggled against her aunt's full breast. "She is my very best friend."

"Well!" responded Aunt Be, drawing the word out. She reached her right arm out. "Come, sweet girl. Come say hello." Melissa gladly stepped into Aunt Be's arms.

"I'm so glad to meet you," Melissa said in a soft, puerile voice. "Nati talks about you all day long."

Aunt Be kissed Melissa's forehead and cradled the two girls, who smiled into each other's faces. The domineering yet loving aunt held each of the two friends as though they were two nursing toddlers. They were both calmed and comforted.

Natasha's father and his two veteran partners continued to pursue their venture for the ash tree harvest, still intending to take advantage of the warm mountain weather. The two village Elders, First Spear Thoas and Sergeant Ned Coxen, were joined by retired Ravenbourne Warrior Daron. To Melissa and Natasha's surprise, Melissa's aunt, Ymir, also joined the three men in the preparations and would accompany the party as cook when they left for the mountains. Ymir enjoyed a long, romantic relationship with Ned Coxen, and the two girls were amazed to learn of a more adventurous background than they would have imagined. When Ymir was a young woman, she had endured several similar expeditions and could handle a team of mules. She was also an accomplished rider since childhood. The four senior adventurers spent most nights together at Ned Coxen's or Daron's house, primarily repairing and preparing their wagons. Consequently, Natasha, Melissa, and Aunt Be stayed together at Natasha's house.

That evening, as they huddled together on comfortable blankets around a small campfire, Aunt Be listened attentively to Natasha's story. First and foremost, she explained her vision of Kaelin in the pool, without question sent by the goddess Asa. Next, she described how Kaelin, as a Feohtan fighter had saved Lord Ravenbourne's life and had come here to be a Ravenbourne Warrior. Subsequently, he saved a village girl from an assault, and he now led the village patrol. Natasha also expressed her belief this could not have all happened by chance.

She correspondingly recited how the goddess Asa had spoken to her during Kaelin's cruel strapping, after she prayed to the goddess to help him, and how the goddess Asa told her not to fear for Kaelin because she was with him. Before Natasha had completed her oral narrative, both she and Melissa were in tears. Natasha, however, was once more deeply distressed.

Finding a woman with a loftier education than Aunt Be would no doubt be stressfully difficult—perhaps impossible. When she was a teacher in Lady Ravenbourne's sanctuary, she had taught Natasha's mother to read and provided her with an education most Hyacinth girls dare not conceive of, much less hope to achieve. She was also a personal friend of both Lady Ravenbourne and the high priestess of the temple. Finally, as a follower of the goddess Asa, she understood the cult and religion of the goddess. She once more took Natasha into her arms to comfort her.

"The solution is quite simple, my sweet girl, and I am confident you also know the answer. You must approach Kaelin . . . and being alone . . . tell him of these occurrences."

"I know, Aunt Be," admitted a fearful Natasha. "And although I had my arm around him in the dining hall after he was punished, I remain completely afraid!"

"I'll go with you, Nati," offered Melissa. "Then you won't be all that afraid."

"I know you want to help your friend, Melissa," cautioned Aunt Be, "but Natasha must accomplish this alone, and by any means possible. But I do not think it will be all that difficult, Natasha. I think all you need do is to walk up to him and ask to speak with him. Nonetheless, whatever it takes, you must do. There is no other alternative or solution."

After a pause Aunt Be continued in a serious teacher voice, "And that is not all. You must also ask him to go with you to see the temple high priestess. Reveal your vision to her, and ask for her advice."

"I'm too afraid to go and see the priestess, Aunt Be," cried Natasha. "I'm just a nobody. What if she turns me away? Then it will be worse!"

Once again, the warmhearted aunt took her distraught niece into her arms. "Sweet child. That portion will be easy. Kaelin is not a nobody. And if, for some unknown reason, she will not see you, I will make a request. If necessary, Lady Ravenbourne will ask the priestess. She would not refuse her."

"Lady Ravenbourne would do that for me?" asked Natasha with

a surprised voice and eyes wide open. "Me, a nobody girl from the village?"

Aunt Be took a slow breath. "I'm going to tell you something, Natasha, but I cannot tell you all that I would like to. You are not a nobody. You are much more than you know. Lady Ravenbourne will make certain that you and Kaelin are able to talk with the high priestess of the temple. Most assuredly, my sweet."

Natasha and Melissa looked at each other with wide-eyed expressions. "I've only seen Lady Ravenbourne on one singular occasion," remarked Natasha, "and that was only because I was with Father. And I have certainly never talked with her."

"Set that part aside, Natasha, and cross the first bridge first," asserted Aunt Be. "You must initially talk with Kaelin, and you must do so alone. This is not the occasion for surreptitious behavior. You must do what you must do—whatsoever required—sardonically if necessary. Take off all your clothes! Throw rocks at him! Slap him in the face! Any action that will serve the purpose. Understand?"

Aunt Be's confidence and wisdom were comforting. Melissa and Natasha both solemnly nodded to Natasha's aunt, that they understood then looked at each other, now smiling. "You're so beautiful, Nati," boasted Melissa. "I say you take off all your clothes. And if he sees you naked, he won't be able to resist you. You can be with him alone all day long, but he won't want to do any talking. He'll have something else he will want to do to you!" All three women embraced again, laughing.

CHAPTER 34

Lord Ravenbourne: Aftermath

THEO TOMITA, PERSONAL PHYSICIAN OF General Y'Sloic, steadily made his way across the open courtyard. He was headed toward the headquarters complex of the Southern Army, located outside the city of Cappa. All passing soldiers saluted him, although technically, he was a civilian.

"Good afternoon, young man, good afternoon." He smiled and acknowledged each salute. As he walked, he adjusted a leather strap stretched over his shoulder and attached to a well-worn leather pouch, which carried his papers and reports. His thick white hair and beard were cropped short in military manner, and his long white tunic, trimmed in aristocratic red, fell to just below his knees.

The tunics of young and middle-aged men were short, reaching their thighs. The thin knees of elderly men, however, always seemed to be chilled, regardless of the weather, and ached to be covered. He also wore the distinctive red cloak of a Ravenbourne Warrior and the prestigious embroidered Ravenbourne crest on his tunic. The clasp securing the cloak around his neck identified him as a member of General Y'Sloic's personal staff. A gold chain and medallion acknowledged him as a member of the Company of Healers.

The Emperor himself certified this prominent fraternity. To earn acceptance into this elite order, Tomita attended the University of the Northwest Region, a long four years. Upon graduation, he was accepted

355

into the prestigious University of the Capital City, where he studied anatomy, drugs, potions, and herbs. Finally, he completed a four-year apprenticeship under another physician, who likewise belonged to the esteemed organization.

Physician Tomita had devoted nearly all his adult life to the Y'Sloic family. First as a soldier and Ravenbourne Warrior—followed by a sponsored university student—and finally as physician to General Y'Sloic's father. He had served General Y'Sloic as his personal physician, since the General was a boy, both at the Ravenbourne Estate and now at the headquarters of the Southern Army at Cappa.

Holding such a prestigious position and having close familiarity, Physician Tomita required neither invitation nor announcement to see the General. Slowly, he climbed the steps into the Great Hall and passed the sprawling administrative sector, where soldiers, civilians, and slaves busied themselves with keeping the Southern Army fed, armed, clothed, and paid. He noticed Ravenbourne Warriors of General Y'Sloic's personal Equestrian Guard posted with the usual duty guards throughout the complex. Physician Tomita did not recall ever seeing Ravenbourne Warriors in the headquarters complex. It would seem the failed attempt on General Y'Sloic's life had induced some concern.

Continuing his slow but steady journey, he approached the doors at the back of the complex. Two guards acknowledged him, and opened the doors to allow him to pass. He quietly offered his appreciation and followed the empty halls to General Y'Sloic's private, elegant quarters. He pushed open two massive wooden doors. Physician Tomita had always marveled at the ease with which the heavy doors swung open. He entered the room and closed the doors. General Y'Sloic stood outside on the balcony, leaning with both hands on the stone banister, gazing out across the back courtyard.

"Lord Ravenbourne!" called out Physician Tomita.

General Y'Sloic turned. His face brightened as he walked toward his trusted physician. "Theo, come in, come in. Allow me to pour you some refreshment."

"Oh yes, Sol! Water would be a welcomed respite."

Lord Ravenbourne poured two glasses of water, handing one to Physician Tomita. The senior doctor was one of only a handful of people with the status to address the Lord of Ravenbourne by his first name.

"Thank you, Sol, thank you."

"Take a seat, Theo." General Y'Sloic gestured with his hand.

"Ah, yes," said Physician Tomita, more to himself rather than a reply. He sat down, making himself comfortable, taking a taste of water. General Y'Sloic took a seat across from his trusted physician and waited for him to speak.

"I have thoroughly examined the bodies of the four would-be assassins. And what I offer you now, Sol, must be kept in strict confidence."

General Y'Sloic raised his eyebrows, somewhat surprised. He nodded his head yes, took a sip of water, and listened intently.

"The four deceased men were young, healthy, and appeared strong," began Physician Tomita. "Their scars tell me they were men of arms, such as Feohtans, or common criminals injured in street fights, perhaps brigands. My experience, however, tells me they were soldiers, wounded in battle. They displayed no tattoos or other marks to indicate any exotic origin. I found no clues or evidence that might identify any of the four or link them to any interest." He paused, taking a sip of water.

"It is unfortunate none of the four were taken alive. Under torture, they may have revealed an associated importance," remarked General Y'Sloic with tightened lips.

"We would not have gained any benefit, Sol, had any or all of the four been taken alive. They would have all departed this world before sunset," stated Physician Tomita in a matter-of-fact tone.

General Y'Sloic paused. He looked to the elderly physician with a stern expression. "What do you mean, Theo?"

Physician Tomita took a slow breath through his nose—another sip of water—and answered. "Each assassin had consumed a rare, exotic poison with extremely lethal properties. All would have died, not long after the attack, from the excruciating, albeit short-lived, painful effects of the toxin. The stench of their breath and the color of their tongues provided the clues for my findings."

After taking a short recess and a silent, long breath to collect his thoughts, Physician Tomita continued; "When I was a student at the University of the Capital City, one of my masters presented a lecture on just such a poison. He stated that it was of such extreme rarity, its origin was not exactly known, and it was generally presumed the toxin was manufactured from an exotic plant originating outside of the Empire's realm. He believed the origin resided on the other side of the Hindu-Cush, in the land of the Nak'la-Sat Dye Traders . . . brought into the Achaean Empire by the Dye Traders."

"Did your university master have any of the poison, Theo?"

"He did, Sol, a very small sample. But more germane, he had a drawing of the plant, obviously drawn by a man of science, not an artist. At that lecture so long ago, I don't know exactly why, but I drew a copy of the plant drawing, along with another young student. I do not currently recall his name, but I eventually will."

Physician Tomita reached down to retrieve his leather pouch—fumbling through it—withdrew the drawing. "Note that the plant has a distinctive 'three-leaf' configuration," he said, pointing to the drawing. "You will want copies, and I have them here for you."

"Where did your master obtain the sample?" asked General Y'Sloic.

"He did not say exactly, although he did mention the sample had passed through one or two hands before coming to him. One of those prior owners was an Imperial Master of Nature who studied the strange dye kernels."

Concluding his sagacious narration, Physician Tomita took another sip of water and cleared his throat. "Will you allow me to present what this suggests . . . my Lord?"

His lifelong friend and employee to his family was wise and trusted, perhaps more than any other man. General Y'Sloic nodded yes.

"The assassination attempt, Sol, holds a deeper plot and purpose. The Empire remains replete with men of power who could hire four daring brigands to assassinate, in public, another man of authority. Someone such as yourself, for instance. But to bring a rare, exotic plant, such as this one, over the Hindu-Cush would require an individual of enormous power and wealth. An individual with enough influence, such as a lord or a lady, perhaps the general of an army, as yourself."

"A member of the royal family," posited General Y'Sloic.

"Perhaps, Sol. A member of the royal family would certainly have such power and influence at their disposal, but Emperor Y'Capis would not seek your demise. You are, perhaps, the only general he can trust."

Physician Tomita took a deep breath. "I believe we are talking about a rebellion, Sol. Taking over the Achaean Empire, in whole or in part. The Southern Peninsula could be formed into a prosperous country. After all, history records that it was an independent nation in the ancient past."

"I fear you are correct, Theo," admitted General Y'Sloic. "And I further fear a dark history will now be recorded. A pejorative, treacherous history of civil war."

"What do you intend to do . . . Sol?" asked the concerned physician.

"I can't move against a suspected rebel, such as the general of an army, without proof. If I did, I would be the one who initiated a war. Perhaps exactly what a disloyal dissident wants. No, I must take a wiser approach. I have heard rumors, just in passing, that the Emperor intends to take over the dye trade. I've paid no attention to this palace gossip, and he has not consulted me. But now, this will be my purpose."

Tossing his head of thick white hair back, the gentleman physician chuckled out loud. "Exceptional thinking, Sol. I told your father you were ingenious when you were a small boy. . . ." He hesitated and chuckled under his breath. "Now you're on the right path."

"I intend to take over the dye trade, Theo," avowed General Y'Sloic. "The Achaean Empire will send our own caravans over the Hindu-Cush, and we will set the price, the amount of the bronze and red dye to be exchanged, and when. I will send my own men over that frozen pass into that Stone Age, heathen world. Perhaps they can discover the rebel—who brought that noxious plant—more deadly than the vainest dagger—into the Empire."

Without speaking, Physician Tomita raised his glass of water. General Y'Sloic followed, picking up his glass and toasting with Theo. The high-pitched, clinking sound of the glasses seemed to fill the large, luxurious sanctuary. The two old friends smiled as they swallowed.

"I will go and speak with Emperor Kaius Y'Capis before making any final decisions on how to proceed."

"This must be kept very secret, Sol," cautioned Tomita. "I advise we speak with no one else, save the Emperor Y'Capis. And Sol. . . ." He hesitated. "This includes Lady Ravenbourne. She would never reveal the secret: nonetheless, a message sent to her could be confiscated."

"Absolutely, Theo," answered General Y'Sloic, "absolutely. I will send a message informing her I leave for the Capital City, but no more."

"Such an undertaking has the makings of a great adventure, Sol."

The elder physician spoke with a sparkle in his eyes. "It is possible there are worlds on the other side of those majestic mountains that could fill our imaginations. Worlds . . . lands . . . oceans . . . environs, and cultures, stretching endless to the horizons."

General Y'Sloic laughed out loud. "You are a hopeless romantic, my old friend. A scholar and a poet."

Smiling as he finished his water, Physician Theo Tomita walked to General Sol Y'Sloic, and they embraced. Reaching down, he took his worn leather pouch and lifted it over his shoulder. "I remain at your call, Sol. Always." He made his way to the doors.

Following orders to report, Captain Aaragon, commander of the Equestrian Guard; Colonel Lycus, commander of the First Strike Force; and Colonel DuPree, second officer of the Southern Army, were waiting in the headquarters when General Y'Sloic entered. He addressed his High Command.

"In two days, at dawn, I leave for the Capital City to meet with the Emperor. I will take the Equestrian Guard and the First Strike Force, which is why you are here. You have what is left of this day and tomorrow to prepare for departure." He looked at Captain Aaragon and Colonel Lycus. "That is all." The two soldiers saluted, turned, and left. He turned to his remaining officer.

"Colonel DuPree, as we have already discussed, you will take command here. Send for my courier to the Emperor, Sergeant Jori, and another for Lady Ravenbourne. I also want a secret courier sent to the commander of the Ravenbourne Corps." Colonel DuPree saluted and left.

"I hand-picked and trained you, Sergeant Jori, to be a special courier to the Emperor, although you are still a teenage boy." Young Sergeant Jori stood erect, holding the halter reins of his mount, knowing his general and lord was not finished.

"You traveled with me to the Capital City, on one of my rare visits, to meet the Emperor to ensure the ruler of the Achaean Empire would recognize you as the special courier from me. This precaution was added to provide an extra level of security—any message I would send to Emperor Kaius Y'Capis—would be of an urgent nature. That occasion is upon us!"

Sergeant Jori had held a stern face but now smiled. He touched the leather pouch strapped across his left shoulder and then his sounding horn, secured in like manner over his right. The pouch carried the all-important sealed communication scroll, and the horn would announce his arrival at the several courier stations along the route to prepare a fresh mount.

He turned and mounted one of the fine white courier horses from the Cappa courier station. It was his favorite. A large mare, some ten seasons in age. She stood alone, without a colt. Suddenly, to General Y'Sloic's surprise, the white mare reared up on her hind legs—her front legs pawed the air. Jori raised his right hand in a clenched-fist salute and called out, "Lord Ravenbourne!" He turned the sleek mare and headed off in a dead run, beginning the difficult ride along the Emperor's Highway to the Capital City, following the coast of the Inner Sea.

Lord Ravenbourne chuckled to himself. *I often wish I was a teenage boy again. Maybe all men my age do? A substantial period has passed since I last saw the Capital City, the Emperor Y'Capis, and his luxurious palace. Too bad this trip will not be a visit for pleasure.*

CHAPTER 35

Calea: Departing Opar

AN ADDITIONAL COMPANY OF IMPERIAL soldiers joined Master Smyth's enterprise, including twenty-five cavalry, twenty-five mounted scouts, and supplementary supply wagons in support. The impressive number of soldiers, including mounted forces, would be enough to deter even the largest band of brigands—if the waving flags and banners of the Royal Army—did not.

Master Smyth compelled an Imperial administrator and scribe to come to his headquarters at the villa, where they would accept the slave payment and complete the documents and written receipts. He did not want this lengthy and complex transaction to occur at the Main Gate of Opar while his convoy waited. His thirteen virgin pallakes would be stressed enough under the best of circumstances. Security was also an issue.

Normally, Imperial administrators and scribes would not agree to such a meeting, but once it was learned, however, this was a transaction with the royal family, the chief administrator, two of his underlings, two scribes, and an armed escort of Eastern Army soldiers arrived at the villa. A considerable period was required to complete the slave inspection, transaction, and documentation. The name, sex, age, and price of each slave were recorded, including the buyer. The documents listed: thirteen virgins, two nannies, four female cooks, six kitchen girls, fifteen female bed-slaves, one kitchen boy, and Calea. The total number reached forty-two. The total sum Master Smyth paid to the chief administrator was more than the total amount he had ever earned in his whole life. If the thirteen virgins were somehow lost in transport, he could never recover the lost amount. Death would be his only recourse. Conversely, once Princess Alexandria paid him for the wagon load of virgins and the other slaves as well, he would be wealthy beyond his wildest visions. One of the wealthiest men in the Capital City.

Commerce moved along the road between Opar and the Capital City. Thus, it had been to the benefit of each polity to maintain the highway in a reasonably good condition. Aligned west from Opar, the highway, commonly called the 'Opar Road,' crossed a wilderness of unsettled terrain until it intersected with the Emperor's Highway. A rustic explorer or the romantic poet might consider travel across the wild landscape an inspiring journey; conversely, those transporting market material and merchandise knew it as a dangerous trip. A sudden attack by brigands or mounted outlaws remained a constant threat.

Anticipating a flow of slaves and material wealth from Opar, the Emperor had directed the general of the Northern Army to establish military posts and patrols necessary to protect commerce along the western section of the Opar Road. The general of the Eastern Army provided protection along the eastern segment. Opar now belonged to the Empire, and settlement of that untamed wilderness was long overdue.

"I have made the trip between Opar and the Greenstone Estates near the Capital City on four separate occasions," (recounted Calea to her thirteen charges) while they discussed the journey, sitting in the soft grass adjacent to the pool on the day before departure. "On each trip, I was attended by a military escort. The first trip, I was a child with Lord Philemon. During those days, he was General Philemon of the Western Army. The second trip I returned to Opar as a new bride with my beloved husband and his contingency of Opar warriors. Next, on the third trip, I returned to Greenstone with my dear ten-year-old son, Kaelin, again in the company of Opar warriors. And finally, I returned to Opar with my son, escorted by Imperial soldiers of the Empire."

Throughout the day, Calea answered questions from her charges, and as well as the other pallakes, especially the younger fifteen bed-slaves. Late in the afternoon, they returned to the villa. That evening, the whole household of slaves ate together in the banquet hall, with Master Smyth at the head table. It was an enjoyable meal. It was Master Smyth's idea. He knew there would be few enjoyable meals in the female slaves' future.

With the clamor of a small army, the Imperial convoy made its way through the main gates of the fallen city of Opar on the following day. On this early, sunny morning, the convoy carried its exotic cargo, more valuable than bronze weapons—more desirable than red dye or fine red material—thirteen virgin pallakes now owned by Master Smyth—destined for the royal family.

Aristocratic families purchased elaborate wagons designed for comfort to transport their family members or other precious cargo, such as expensive pallakes or other slaves. Two such wagons, owned by the royal family, were included in the convoy, each drawn by four impressive draft horses. The Imperial family spared no expense. Each coach was elaborately decorated, inside and out, and served as a comfortable riding wagon during the day and a tranquil bedroom at night.

Twenty-five Imperial, cavalry soldiers led the procession, with the Imperial banners and flags in the lead, followed by one company of soldiers afoot. The first wagon of virgins followed. The driver's seat had been specially modified, and Master Smyth and Calea sat with the driver. Inside, safe and sound, rode six maidens, one slave-boy, and Nanny Talcrane. The next virgin wagon accommodated seven tender fillies and Old Nanny, followed by four sturdy wagons loaded with the remaining female slaves. One-half of the second company marched behind the four sturdy wagons, and they were followed by the long line of supply wagons. Fifty soldiers of the second company protected the rear.

The twenty-five mounted scouts patrolled the front, the rear, and both flanks of the convoy. In the first turn of the hour-glass, an incident was reported. An Imperial scout rode upon two brigands spying on the convoy—most certainly they would report back to their outlaw band with information about potential opportunities to attack. Upon seeing the scout, the spies mounted and fled, pursued by the scout. Astride a superior mount, the scout caught up to the fleeing spies. He launched his spear, striking one in the back, who managed to stay mounted and rode on. The scout came along-side the second spy and struck him in the neck with his sword. He fell to the ground, but his horse continued, following the first wounded rider. The scout then returned to the convoy and reported to his commander.

"Good!" shouted the commander with a loud, rough voice. "Hope the two horses return to the outlaw camp and the one rider with a spear stuck in his back lives long enough to report to the outlaw leader. Give him something to. . .." He turned his head and spit. "Something to gnaw on before he attacks this caravan."

Late in the afternoon, Master Smyth allowed the convoy to stop and the forty-two pallake-slaves to unload from their wagons. They stood together to say goodbye to fallen Opar before their city, their home, and a lost way of life sank below the horizon and out of sight. Calea addressed the group in the beautiful, romantic language of Opar, which most likely would fall from use and memory in the next generation or two. She spoke in a soft, sincere voice. No one, including her daughter, Susanna, was ever witness to her weeping, but while she spoke, warm tears ran down her face to gently fall from her chin.

"Most of us will never see our beloved city again, and those who might will see an Achaean City, not our cherished Opar. Nearly all the men we have known and loved have been killed. And even if a few that might still live . . . will not survive for very long . . . and they, too, will follow to the other side. We know that all our men, young and old, died bravely. We pray they did not suffer."

"We will all be slaves to the royal family, perhaps for the rest of our lives. Yet we remain better off than most of the poor women of Opar. How many did we see led away, naked, wearing only painful strap marks on their hips and thighs—ropes and collars fastened to their necks— tied to the back of wagons? How many helpless babies did we see ripped from their mother's arms and slaughtered . . .?" Calea stopped. She took a deep breath before she continued.

"For better or for worse, this convoy will roll through the gates of the Capital City of the Achaean Empire. Yes, we will serve as slaves, but always remember, it is through faithful service that each of us will gain freedom. Know that! Tomorrow is promised to no one. Not even to the royal family. And no one—no one—knows what tomorrow will bring."

Calea took another deep breath. She smiled a teary-eyed smile, slowly looking over the quiet group, most likewise weeping. She then wiped the tears from her eyes with her hands as best she could, turned, and silently walked toward the waiting wagons and anxious soldiers. The forty-two pallakes, some old but most very young—all women save but one boy—followed Calea to the wagons—all remained in silence.

CHAPTER 36

High Priestess Ish-Bel: Final Right

LOOKING OUT OVER THE OPEN Cave Hall of the Sacred Temple of Asa, High Priestess Ish-Bel stood erect and somber behind the huge temple table, uniquely created by the hand of the goddess. The bottom portion of the table was an exceptional lava flow, forming a low arc and topped by a wide, flat surface. Attached to the top of the lava surface lay a large, thick slab of polished wood, taken from a majestic tree named Maladarwin. This redwood giant had stood as the oldest living creature in the Achaean Empire. It was named after the legend of a man bearing the same name, said to have lived for one thousand years. Once felled, the perishing, colossal tree was determined by foresters and men of science to be seven thousand years old. The precious slab was a generous gift to the temple from Lord Ravenbourne's father, DeMond Y'Sloic.

Two thick volumes of the Books of the Temple rested on top of the massive table. The First and Last Volumes—both large, heavy tomes— lay side by side. High Priestess Ish-Bel carefully opened the First Volume to a marked section. She began to read out loud.

"The goddess Asa and her worship are elucidated throughout the Books of the Temple. Read . . . Learn . . . Remember . . . Rejoice! Asa was born from the goddess of the sea and the god of the heavens in the land of Zhana, near the coastal area that will become the city of Opar. It would be, however, the lands of Ravenbourne that were favored by the goddess and held sacred to her."

"If ever seen by mortal woman, the goddess herself will be wearing a long, black peplos of a fine material made from hummingbird nests called silk—spun and woven by humming-birds. The most skilled of mortal seamstresses could not cut and stitch the material. Thus, the fine silk material clings to her curved figure as though it were painted on. Around her waist, she wears a thin leather belt, which secures a fine dagger. The sharp, polished blade is set in a handle of ivory and so brightly reflects the sun it causes any mortals around her to close and shield their eyes. Nearby perches her pet raven, which she will send out, to return with all manner of knowledge. Humming-birds, similarly, take information back to the goddess with remarkable speed."

"Since ancient times, well beyond generations of mortal memory, the vast holdings of the Y'Sloic family are believed by pious followers to be the honored domain of the goddess Asa. Akin to the goddess Asa, Ravenbourne lands remain beautifully and breathtaking—shrouded and mysterious—inspiring awe—yet also lingering trepidation."

"The wondrous hot-water springs, pools, and streams remain inexplicable—heated by the warm breath of the goddess herself. More mystifying, the hot water flows and collects in pools adjacent to clear, cool springs and pools—the purest drinking water in the entire world. A world that will become the Achaean Empire. The goddess once bathed in numinous hot pools, where she relaxed and lounged, occasionally reaching her hand over to an adjacent pool of sweet, cool water—taking a handful to quench her thirst."

"The followers of Asa are taught that 'female' is personified by water . . . the endless seas . . . and the moon because each female is ever changing, cold, and moody. 'Male' is experienced in terra firma and the sun, both of which continue unchanging, rugged, warm, and stable. The land remains firm, year after year, life after life, generation after generation. The sun, as it moves across the open heavens, remains full—predictable—always rising, always setting. By combining the two, water is female, although hot, flowing water is male."

"Born deep inside the male earth, heated by the breath of the goddess, hot-water springs spew out replicating hot male sperm, his fluid milk. In as much as the hot springs flow to the womb of the sea: Surely Conception Is Inevitable."

"Female orgasm—pleasurable to the goddess—desired by women—is equally beneficial for gestation. A woman's orgasm—squirting feminine wetness with the male's hardness inside her—The Path To Conception."

"Where hot water surges from underground, forming warm, soothing pools, and continues to flow and empty into the ocean, such pools are held sacred by Asa. Because here, hot male water, becoming warm sperm, gushes out and flows into and thus impregnates the sea—the womb of the goddess."

"Many sacred locations of the goddess may be found along the seacoast. Indicative of such places are small, isolated coves, suffused by black lava, blessed with pools of hot, steaming springs, uniquely formed adjacent pools of sweet, cold drinking water—delicious and pure. "Temples and shrines will be erected at such locations in honor of the goddess Asa. Here, women followers will gather each year on the day of the first full moon following the longest day of the year to Celebrate . . . Feast . . . Commune . . . Dance . . . Sing . . . Worship. Girls who have reached their first menstruation are, accordingly, allowed to attend. The observances last all day and into the night, allowing the brightness of the full moon to illuminate the fête."

"The moon, ever mysterious—ever changing—appearing as the personification of womanhood, waxes and wanes on her own cycle. Accordingly, the fuller the moon during the activities, the more fulfilling the experience."

"Devout women will continue to worship throughout the night and into the morning. The first rays of the male-sun, striking the sacred site, will bring the ceremonies to a close. Every tenth year will be especially honored, and every cult follower is encouraged to attend at least one ten-year celebration in her life."

"Moreover, and more importantly, attending a Hundred Year Celebration is a unique opportunity for those fortunate enough to be alive during the end of a hundred-year cycle and the beginning of another. It is the most important event for the followers of the goddess Asa that can occur in a woman's life, second only to marriage and childbirth."

After reading the passages, High Priestess Ish-Bel carefully closed the First Volume of the Books of the Temple and slid it aside. She moved the Last Volume in front of her and opened it to a marked passage. Once more, she read.

"Seven daughters will be born at the Century of the Raven, each one marked, the same as all before them, with my teardrops, the color of the sky—two at the base of each spine—all sired by the Lord of Ravenbourne:

A maiden from those who gather my sacred plant.
A virgin slave of Opar.
A poor slave abused and raped of K'semay.
A virgin of the Vratzan.
A virgin of the Taolian.
A maiden of the Mysia.
A child of the priestess of the Estoria Temple."

Carefully closing the ancient volume, Ish-Bel looked out toward a prepared funeral pyre, erected in the center of the hall, beneath a natural opening in the roof of the Cave Hall. The precious wood of the hyacinth tree was carefully stacked as the pyre fuel. A small assembly of temple acolytes attended the pyre. The High Priestess motioned to the small group of young women to begin.

The acolytes of the Sacred Temple began to carefully pour hyacinth oil on a small, thin, ancient body. With loving care, they rubbed the precious ointment down her back, gently massaging the two small dots at the base of her spine, the color of the blue sky. They looked up when they completed, and with an approving nod from the High Priestess, they cautiously turned the anachronous priestess over. They prudently anointed her front with the hyacinth attar. Completing the anointment, they covered the ancient figure, wrinkled and thin, with a sheer, black shroud and quietly joined the group of their sister attendants, standing nearby in formation.

Stepping out and walking away from the temple table, High Priestess Ish-Bel took a torch from its floor base in hand and held it high. The assembly of sister acolytes began to cantillate a melodious prayer in beautiful voices, tears gently forming in their youthful eyes. The high priestess offered a solemn prayer to the goddess Asa, her voice unwavering.

"We send you the Ancient High Priestess having no name. She was the last of your daughters from the previous Century of the Dragon. She served you well . . . all her life. We seek hope in your daughters of the new and beginning Century of the Raven."

Walking forward to the funeral pyre, Ish-Bel inserted the torch, and stepped back to a safe distance. The fire rapidly burned with a colorful blue flame, nearly reaching the opening in the temple roof. It quickly consumed the remains of the Ancient High Priestess having no name.

With a raise of Ish-Bel's hand, the harmonious voices of the acolyte choir stilled. The high priestess cupped her hands to her breast. The faint crackling of the low fire continued as she spoke.

"Once the fire has cooled, we will gather any remaining bones and crush them into powder. Along with prayers, the powder will be dropped into hot alter pools, thus leaving no remains of the last daughter of Asa from the Century of the Dragon. Her spirit now dwells in the spirit world of the goddess. Remember her in prayer."

Ancient trees grew along the paved path interconnecting the Sacred Temple and the Ravenbourne Villa, appearing the same to those growing along the Ravenbourne Road. Low hedges of colorful tea-rose also lined the path, filling the wind with their sweet, aromatic fragrance. Tall and erect as one of those ancient trees, High Priestess Ish-Bel walked from the Sacred Temple toward the Ravenbourne Villa. In both hands in front of her, she held a bronze container with a latched top. Two temple acolytes, dressed in long, white-cotton frocks, followed respectfully behind. Normally, temple acolytes dressed in common frocks of pale-yellow flax . . . these two, however, held significant positions and were thus so attired.

Woven from fine cotton, the priestess' black chiton fit tight around her waist and hips, revealing her elegant female figure. Her sun-colored hair was expertly braided—hanging long—far down her back. Shining in the morning light, it gently swung back and forth, keeping pace with each agile step. A magnificent red cape, the cape of the Ravenbourne Warriors, fell from her shoulders, nearly reaching the ground. The Ravenbourne crest was embroidered in black on the back. The beautiful cape would announce a dire warning to all citizens that this woman was protected by Lord Ravenbourne, and hence the Ravenbourne Corps. Only a foolish mad-man would dare confront her.

Ish-Bel came to the Sacred Temple while still a child and truly adored the temple life. She also, however, enjoyed excursions from the temple and walks across the enchanting grounds of Ravenbourne. More importantly, she loved visits with Ann Y' Sloic and came to her sanctuary when she could.

She approached a Ravenbourne Warrior. He offered her due respect and stepped aside, giving her the path. He bowed slightly when she passed. She looked into his face, smiling.

"Thank you, my love." She spoke with true sincerity. She called all the Ravenbourne Warriors her "love," and in many respects, they were.

Approaching the Main Gate of the sanctuary, the guards promptly opened the eye of the needle and bowed at attention. Thanking her two loves, she walked into another closed world exclusively populated by women—save one man—the Lord of Ravenbourne.

The first woman she met was mature and clothed. She stopped upon seeing the high priestess. "Please run, my sweet, and inform your mistress that I am here." Without a reply, the woman turned and left in a scamper.

Soon, Ann Y'Sloic appeared, followed by her party. Upon seeing the priestess, Ann walked briskly toward her. Ish-Bel turned and handed the bronze container to an acolyte behind her. She promptly stepped to meet Ann Y'Sloic with open arms. They embraced and shared a long kiss, nearly one of passion. They were delighted to see and greet each other.

"It pleases my heart to see you, Ish-Bel," said Ann Y'Sloic, nearly in tears, grasping the High Priestess' hands.

"Yes, my darling Lady," replied the High Priestess, I dearly miss you. But I must tell you, my visit is not one of good news."

Noticing the bronze container, Lady Ravenbourne knew the reason for the visit. Taking the High Priestess' hand, she began to walk with her. "Let us go to my small retreat, where we may talk in private."

Ann turned to Ginal and Old Nanny. "Allow my handmaidens to entertain our two temple guests."

They both responded with, "Yes, my Lady!"

Stepping to Ginal, the High Priestess reached up and touched her chin with her fingertips. "Thank you, my love," she whispered.

Ginal responded in the fashion of all Ravenbourne Warriors. First, she came to attention. She did not have a spear but instead grasped the handle of her sword. Then she respectfully bowed.

Closing the door to her private, small retreat, the two friends once again embraced—kissed—and held hands. Lady Ravenbourne spoke first. "It is not such heartbreaking news, my dear Ish-Bel. The end to such a long, wonderful life, few women could ever enjoy. I know. . . ."

She paused and squeezed Ish-Bel's hands. "She longed to go to the goddess . . . to meet again the friends and loves . . . from her youth."

"I agree, my love. But I must tell you, I now worry. The days grow short, and the Hundred Years Celebration approaches. If our Lord Ravenbourne had touched on any insight, he would have told you. Two of the daughters remain unknown, and I fear we have no answer. But I must also tell you of a remarkable happening." She paused, taking a deep breath.

"The moment before the Ancient High Priestess passed, Asa spoke through her. It was a wonderful experience, Ann," recounted the High Priestess. "It felt as if I was in the presence of the goddess. And perhaps, in one understanding, I was."

"Oh yes, Ish-Bel," exclaimed a delighted Ann Y' Sloic, "you must tell me what was revealed."

"It makes no sense to me," said Ish-Bel, "but this is what the goddess spoke through the Ancient High Priestess.

"I send you a young warrior of Opar. He will protect my daughters and lead you to the missing two. He is more than you know. It will be revealed in the aftermath of a great upheaval."

"Is it helpful?" asked Ish-Bel.

Smiling—more than smiling—glowing, Lady Ravenbourne reached out and once more took the High Priestess' hand. "The second part, I, too, do not understand. But the first part is very helpful, Ish-Bel. Very helpful indeed. The goddess has revealed how to find her two lost daughters."

CHAPTER 37

Kaelin and Natasha: Desperate Encounter

ON A STILL, EARLY MORNING with First Sergeant Lutas at his side, Lieutenant Kaelin led his dual squads of twenty men through and around the Ravenbourne Village, assessing the layout and possible patrol routes, with the aim of eventually selecting a site for the patrol headquarters. He also wanted to acquaint the villagers that armed Ravenbourne Warriors patrolling the village would now be an everyday occurrence. Although he was mildly aware that he held at least an obscure reputation, he still wanted the villagers to see the new Ravenbourne officer out on patrol.

"It feels somewhat awkward, First Sergeant Lutas," admitted Lieutenant Kaelin, "to not carry a spear."

"Hmmm!" replied Lutas turning his head to spit on the ground. "Do officers carry spears in the Opar Army?"

"They do, Sergeant," answered Kaelin. "All warriors carry spears, regardless of age or rank."

"Well, you'll get use to it Sir, but I want you to know one thing . . . for sure. We find ourselves in a skirmish with brigands, I'm tossing you my spear, so be ready for it. I haven't hit the fokken target during spear practice for, say, two or three years now."

Kaelin formed a rare smile. He had only visited the village on the singular occasion of the morning of the attempted rape of the village girl. His First Sergeant Lutas, however, was well acquainted with the roads and paths and remained on friendly terms with many of the village residents. He was particularly popular with the female population, especially the professional women from the pleasure houses. Occasionally, a village woman called out his name and waved, and a few ran to the roadside, waving, while the fully armed patrol made its way along the main road in a route-step march.

The villagers looked on while the Ravenbourne Warriors filed by—the bright, morning sun reflecting off their bronze helmets, shields, and greaves—their scarlet red cloaks blowing freely in the fresh breeze. Then, after the warriors passed by, they nonchalantly returned to their morning tasks. All were aware of the plans to patrol the village. Kaelin believed any rancor would be minor, in fact, most villagers favored the idea. Nonetheless, he allowed that a few might dislike the proposal. The heavy footsteps of the patrol—echoed through the otherwise serene, quiet morning—amid the pleasant background sounds of crowing roosters, the laughter of playing children, and an occasional barking dog.

Suddenly, to Kaelin's surprise, two girls ran to the roadside, seemingly from out of nowhere, giggling and waving. "Hello, Kaelin! Hello!" they called out in cheerful voices.

Kaelin smiled and returned their greetings with a friendly wave. He immediately recognized Old Torrhen's granddaughter and Jenny, the girl he had saved. Jenny wore a frock with the Ravenbourne crest embroidered on the front. Unbeknownst to all, including Sergeant Lutas, Kaelin had managed to offer a Ravenbourne tunic to Jenny's mother who resewed the material into a beautiful frock to fit a slender girl. He hoped the frock would offer some comfort to Jenny and her family, knowing she was now under his protection. And likewise, a dire warning to any brigand, who might consider assaulting her. Kaelin felt good in his heart to see Jenny playing and laughing. Removing his helmet, Kaelin returned their waves with a friendly smile.

Then, to his amazement, both girls kissed the palms of their hands and threw him a kiss. He was reminded of the girls he saw throwing kisses to the mounted Ravenbourne Warriors when he rode in the Feohtan wagon with Ox and Coe through the streets of Cappa on their way to the Heart Blood College. Following those Ravenbourne Warriors' actions, but not completely, he pretended to catch their kisses—brought his fingers to his lips, then raised the palm of his hand—smiling a wide grin. The girls clapped their hands, laughing, filled with excitement, then turned and ran giggling and swiftly disappeared.

Standing in silence and sporting a grin, Sergeant Lutas glanced around at the other soldiers, who likewise wore a silent grin. "One of the girls is Old Torrhen's granddaughter . . .," announced Sergeant Lutas, "and the other . . . wearing our Ravenbourne crest is Jenny . . . the girl Kaelin saved."

Lutas recalled that Kaelin did not appreciated being touched. Nonetheless, the veteran sergeant placed a hand on Kaelin's shoulder. "You're a remarkable man Kaelin." Removing his hand, he once again looked around at the rest of the patrol.

"We've all been ordered by the high command to maintain rapport with the villagers!" quipped Lutas. "And throwing kisses to village girls is a good start." The whole patrol, including Kaelin, found a little humor in Sergeant Lutas's wit. They continued their patrol.

This beautiful morning found Natasha alone. Her father and his ash tree harvest crew, including Melissa's adventurous Aunt Ymir, were spending the next few days at Ned Coxen's house, who lived on the other side of the village. They continued preparing for their departure to the mountains. Melissa was working at the dining hall, and her Aunt Be had gone to see Lady Ravenbourne. She wondered how it would be to presume one could just go and see a wealthy aristocrat such as Lady Ravenbourne, the wife of a great lord. Her aunt must certainly hold a place of significant influence.

Consequently, she was working unaccompanied in their poor, neglected garden, and now, she and Melissa would be responsible for Aunt Ymir's garden and her house as well. Her and Melissa's responsibilities would be endless. But a more important matter weighed heavily on her conscience—Kaelin.

She must confront him—talk with him—alone. She couldn't avoid him, even if she wanted to, now that he was stationed here in the village. They might construct the patrol station adjacent to her father's house, and accordingly, she would see him daily. But the more important question remained: Why did she fear talking to him? Did she fear her own destiny? She had prayed to the goddess for an alternate fate, a destiny different from a village life. Additionally, she had offered a sacrifice to the goddess. Perhaps destiny was now being offered to her, so why her trepidation? Suddenly—unexpectedly—without warning—Destiny comes nigh.

She heard the footsteps of soldiers approaching and looked up. The new village patrol was advancing up the road. They wore their beautiful red capes. She had a good idea concerning the red dye and the material used for one of those capes, but more pertinent, she knew they only wore them for special occasions. Accordingly, this particular patrol must be singular to them. The leading officer was surely Kaelin, and the sergeant next to him had to be Sergeant Lutas. Suddenly, without explanation, fear stabbed into her heart. Nearly the same anxiety she felt while she watched First Sergeant Klause deliver a hard skelping to poor little Malin and when he approached her. She had feared he was about to drag her to the dreaded pommel. This was the same fear she experienced then. Unexpectedly, the patrol stopped in front of her father's house.

"The north or south perimeters of the village, Lieutenant, would be the best places to locate the patrol station," explained First Sergeant Lutas. He pointed northward. "Not far in that direction is a large, deep hot-springs pool, and as you can see, we are close to the village creek." He now pointed toward the Twin Peaks.

"I like it, Sergeant!" admitted Kaelin in a positive tone. "Nonetheless, I will want to inspect the pool area before I make my final decision."

"Good idea, Lieutenant," exclaimed Lutas, clearing his throat and spitting on the ground.

The whole squad was standing in front of Natasha's father's house, seemingly taking a rest. She watched them pulling off their helmets. Lieutenant Kaelin wiped his sweaty forehead with his arm, and glanced over to Natasha. Natasha's mouth opened. She froze. She had to do something—but what?

"Sergeant Lutas!" called Kaelin. "That girl over there. Is she who I think she is?"

Lutas looked over at Natasha. "Absolutely right Sir!" Lutas said chuckling. "That is Natasha, daughter of First Spear Thoas. She works in the First Company dining hall, if you recall."

"Oh yes!" reminisced Kaelin. "I believe we all know her!"

"Prettiest little kunt in the whole fokken village," blurted out Lutas, prompting the whole patrol to respond with snickers and belly laughs, "and the saltiest. But it shouldn't take much to tame that Thoroughbred filly! Maybe all a man would need is a few urns of honey to sweeten those pretty . . . little . . . bitter . . . lips!"

"I'll see to her later," promised Lieutenant Kaelin. "We'll finish this first patrol, and you and I will return to inspect the pool area and the river."

"Oh no! Oh no! They're going to march on!" Natasha did not know if she was speaking out loud or to herself. "Oh, goddess! Help me! I must do something! I can't allow him to walk away! I can't!" Her aunt's advice soared through her mind and into her heart.

Suddenly, not certain if she was thinking clearly, Natasha picked up a rock and, with a boy's accuracy, threw it at the patrol. Kaelin saw the rock in flight speeding toward him and, with little effort, moved his shield to block the stone. Natasha watched it strike the black Ravenbourne symbol then ricochet off his bronze disc with a loud clank. All the Ravenbourne Warriors in the patrol saw Natasha throw the rock, and they responded with an outburst of uncommon joviality.

"Don't you dare walk away, Lieutenant Jackanapes!" barked out Natasha as loud as she could, similar to a name-calling child. Kaelin looked at his laughing men and smiled along with them.

"What the fokken does that mean?" asked an amused Lutas.

"It could mean she loves me, Sergeant, or maybe it means she hates me." Kaelin's voice was amused and he chortled. "Perhaps both are true." Kaelin glanced at Natasha and back toward Lutas. "I wonder why she is angry with me?"

"When you figure out why women think the way they do," called out a loud, jovial Sergeant Lutas, "just let me know. Along with the honey, I'd say all the pretty dove needs would be a good tail-feather tanning, followed by a good, hard fokken. Or maybe she needs a fokken first and next a tanning—one she won't never forget."

All the warriors continued to look at each other and at Natasha, smirking and laughing. A few struck their shields together. "Did you happen to bring some honey, Lieutenant?" joked Sergeant Derick, first squad leader.

Before Kaelin could respond, another stone came flying toward him, and again he blocked it with his shield, striking the Ravenbourne symbol. Once more, the warriors broke into loud laughter, all of them entertained. Kaelin likewise chuckled while he handed his shield to

First Sergeant Lutas and his helmet to Sergeant Jarried, second squad leader.

"Take over, Sergeant Lutas!" ordered Kaelin. "Continue the assessment and the march-through. I have an important extra duty to accomplish here."

Lutas handed his spear to an adjacent warrior, taking Kaelin's shield. "Good luck, Lieutenant!" called out Lutas. The warriors refitted their armor, and Lutas led the patrol away.

Kaelin looked at the rebellious Natasha with a very serious expression, though not with anger, and quickly walked toward her with determined steps. Natasha reached down—picked up another stone—threw it at him, as hard as she could—just when he reached the garden fence gate. Seemingly with little effort, however, he tilted his head to one side and dodged the projectile while it whispered past his ear. He continued, halting a pace in front of her, glaring at her with a stern expression, although he was laughing inside.

"It's a crime to assault a Ravenbourne Warrior, punishable by a public whipping!" growled Kaelin in a strict, military voice, not yet in anger but sincere determination. "You work for the First Company dining hall! Your father is a village Elder and war hero! And yet you dare break Lord Ravenbourne's Law?"

Defiantly, Natasha stood with her hands on her hips—feet spread— her chin raised high. But inside, her youthful heart pounded. She may have been more afraid now than ever before. *Please help me, Goddess*, she thought to herself—or perhaps she whispered it out loud. She was not sure.

Natasha remained rebellious, glaring back at Kaelin, holding a stern facial expression, seemingly unafraid. Kaelin had paid little, if any, attention to her in the dining hall, even though she had placed her arm around his waist and helped him to the guest room.

Such a beautiful little attacker, thought Kaelin. *Lutas was right—she is a little nymph of the goddess and a Hyacinth Gatherer with bright red-hair.*

Her long, red hair was cut short across her forehead and tied in the back, resembling a horse's tail, with long tendrils falling on the side of her face and over her ears. The afternoon sun reflected off her hair's beautiful fire-red color and made all the more beautiful because her hair was also streaked with brilliant yellow strands, as though the goddess had taken hold of wisps of her hair, changing them into gold. Although glaring a hole through him, her sparkling eyes reflected a deep-green hue—deep and clear as any mystical pool. Her snarled mouth prompted Kaelin to find a small grin. Her lush lips were a very kissable reddish-pink color and appeared to be soft and warm.

"I'm tempted," he threatened in a rough voice, "to take you by the sides of your face . . . pull you to me . . . and kiss you with intense passion, right here. . . ." He paused and smiled. "Perhaps your first adult kiss."

Kaelin stood more than a head taller than Natasha. She stared angrily up at him, the top of her head just reaching the center of his chest. "I'll give you a kiss!" she snarled.

Suddenly, without warning or even a change in her expression, she swung her open right hand at him, as hard as she could, in an attempt to slap his face. To her surprise, however, he quickly moved his left hand up to parry her slap. Her hand made a loud slapping sound when it struck the back of Kaelin's hand. Startled—Natasha's eyes grew large. She stood astonished that his reflexes were so fast that he could move to block her slap. She continued to glare at his face and into his gorgeous brown eyes. She now saw a hint of anger in his eyes and stern determination, with a slight smirk on his lips.

He is extraordinarily handsome, she thought to herself. *Exciting . . . fearfully handsome.*

Natasha did not change her defiant expression but now considered, if she was in trouble—big trouble? She was not sure why, but her slapping hand remained in the air, touching the back of his hand. She did not draw it back. She swallowed hard, hoping Kaelin did not notice it and thus realize her inward anxiety.

Kaelin moved his hand and firmly grasped Natasha's wrists. She heard his strident intake of breath and could now feel his ire splashing over her like a large wave on the coast of the Outer Ocean. She could likewise hear anger in his voice when he spoke.

"You now attempt to strike a Ravenbourne Warrior? You desperately need to learn a disobedient little girl's hard lesson."

He quickly looked around, noticing the nearby wooded stream. Turning, he pulled her across the garden, through the gate, and along the path leading toward the wooded creek. Natasha struggled to break free of his grip, but he held her fast. She was amazed—and now frightened—by his strength. She pulled with all her might but could not break his grip. His large, powerful hand held her as would bands of bronze, and his palms felt tree bark rough.

"Release me immediately! Let me go, you ribald brute!" called out Kaelin's fuming captive.

"If you fall, I'll drag you," warned Kaelin, pulling the struggling Natasha down the path toward the stream.

"I demand you release me!" growled Natasha in the meanest voice she could muster. "When I pull free, I am going to skelp you so hard, it will knock you down—you ignorant *teratoid*."

Although angry, Kaelin managed to appear amused at her childish insults, noting her educated vocabulary, rather remarkable for a village girl. He was not sure of the meaning of skelp, but *teratoid* was a graceful word of his own poetic language of Opar, borrowed and incorporated into the brutish language of the Empire. It seemed rare that a common village girl would know any Opar words. They were moving too slowly to suit him.

Suddenly, Kaelin stopped. He turned to Natasha and, in one strong motion, bent his knees and pulled her over his left shoulder—his strong left arm encircling her knees. He gave her butt a hard swat with his right hand. It nearly knocked the breath out of her. He continued toward the stream with his beautiful burden thrown over his shoulder.

Natasha struggled. She pounded his buttocks with her fist and called out a few more chosen obscenities. She was helpless, however, to free herself. It did not take long for them to reach the wooded stream.

Natasha now realized the futility of struggling and calling him names. If anything, it would have a pejorative effect, fanning the flames of his already fiery anger. No wondering remained. She knew she was in trouble, and she feared to discover what he meant by . . . "a little girl's hard lesson," because deep down, she knew what he planned to do to her.

Kaelin saw a recently fallen large tree on the edge of the stream. He carried Natasha down the stream's steep terrace and behind the hefty tree. The embankment and tree concealed them. He saw a large limb that paralleled the ground, about knee-high, and he placed his sandaled foot on the limb, pushing his weight against it. The limb held solid. "Good," he remarked out loud, "this will be satisfactory!"

Without ceremony, Kaelin lifted Natasha from his shoulder and laid her over his knee, forcing her head down. Her hands grasped the same tree limb Kaelin rested his foot on. So sudden and abrupt, the move surprised her—lifting her up and around—the same manner he would if she were a sack of goose feathers.

"What are you doing?" she growled in a voice so deep, it irritated her throat. "Let me up immediately, you . . . you louse-ridden bully!"

Grabbing the hem of her plain frock, he pulled it up. Using both hands and a little effort, he slipped it over her hips, exposing her from the waist down. She wore the familiar female bow-tied undergarment, but to his surprise, hers was dyed a striking red color. Kaelin marveled to himself. *How is it a common village girl could afford red-dyed material?*

Kaelin's fingers found the drawstrings of the bow on the right side of her very expensive undergarment and pulled it to release the knot. He slipped his fingers inside the waist, and with three hard pulls, he yanked it down to her knees, exposing her well-shaped, perhaps slightly chubby but unquestionably gorgeous buttocks.

He now rubbed his hand over her smooth pastel skin, which was remarkably void of blemish, except for two strange blue dots at the top of each beautiful cheek, near the spine. Two side-by-side blue dots, each about the size of a raindrop. Kaelin vigorously rubbed each dot, expecting the two marks to wipe off, but his scrubs had no effect.

How odd, he thought. *Birth marks?* Suddenly, he remembered he had encountered these strange blue dots before, on more than one occasion. He was too busy now to search his memory, but he would later. Now, he must attend to the task at hand.

Kaelin did not scold, lecture, or describe what she was about to endure. He took a deep breath to relax any anger—raised his right hand high over his head—and brought his palm down hard on her right bottom cheek. He repeated the slap four or five counts, landing on the exact same spot. He marveled at how her lovely, light skin turned to a pinkish glow, and yet he could also see white-colored fingerprint marks. He applied an equal number of cuffs to her left cheek.

Natasha cried out, "Oh! Oh! You're not hurting me. . . ." She paused to take a deep breath. "I'm just mad. You arrogant bully!" She punctuated *bully* with a loud shout. To the contrary, however, the slaps did hurt, creating both an awful burning and stinging pain simultaneously. Additionally, because the skelping did hurt, it drove her to more anxiety. She could not believe that Kaelin was actually giving her a child's spanking chastisement. She struggled, to no avail. His strong left hand and fingers gripped her hair, tied in a horse's tail, at the back of her neck, holding her in place, while the palm of his hard right hand fell solid on her vulnerable behind.

Then suddenly, without warning, a mystical wind blew through Natasha's hair, lifting the tendrils on the side of her face as if the wind whispered to her. Mysteriously, Natasha began to feel her awareness changing. She grasped the tree limb hard in both hands. The reality of *moment* was slowly being lost. She began to move in a vision.

She was bent over Kaelin's knee, but was it for just a brief period, or was it continuing—without end? She could hear the loud, hard slaps—feel the burning sting—sense her helpless struggle. And yet, the wind whispered in her ear, and her cognizance floated—wandered—mimicking the drifting mist gently rising from the stream, glistening in the early-morning sun. Similar to the mist, her consciousness likewise floated, as though she were moving in and through a dream.

In like manner, Natasha began to feel a burning sensation flowing through her blood. She had never experienced this strange conscious-ness, combining both yearning and anxiety in the same moment. She could feel her blood begin to flow warm, heated from the burning dis-comfort of her bottom. She wanted it to stop, but equally, in an ironic paradox, she also wanted it to continue.

Suddenly, the scorching on her skin spread from her buttocks into her blood and then throughout her whole body, arousing her. It spread to her groin. For the first occasion in her young life, Natasha experi-enced a warm, moist sensation in her groin. It flowed inside the folds of her flower, her womanhood. The sensation felt good—wondrous—she wanted more.

Natasha began to rub her naked groin against Kaelin's leg. She reached, grasping his ankle below the bronze greave of his sandaled foot—planted firmly on the tree limb. Compelled, she must call out, "Oh. . . . Kaelin." At first, she whispered. "Oh. . . . Kaelin." Now she moaned. "Oh. . . . Kaelin!" She cried out loud, calling out to the goddess.

While Kaelin chastised his exposed, beautiful quarry, an unexpected morning breeze gently blew from the misty river. He had paid little attention to the breezes, minding his task at hand, but when this slight wind touched his face, he heard a soft voice of a woman speak into his ear. It was the same enchanted, goddess-like voice he had heard on the three other unexplained but important occasions: first on the battlefield of Opar—second during the slave march—and third in the Great Arena of Cappa. On each mystical occasion, upon following the voice's advice, he was saved. But on this singular instance, the enchantment loomed even greater, if that was possible, because two voices now spoke to him simultaneously in the erudite language of Opar. Along with the woman's elegant speech, Kaelin could also hear his father's deep voice speaking into his ear, offering the advice and wisdom his father had quoted to him on more than one occasion.

"When you must discipline, Kaelin, remain prudent. Do not strike in anger. Do so because it is warranted and just. And above all, always remember—never break the spirit of a Thoroughbred—only tame her."

Kaelin stopped. Natasha's inflamed buttocks tightened, and she flinched, expecting the next spank. He did not count the number of slaps he delivered, but it was more than enough. Natasha's hot blood raced beneath her skin, causing her lush buttocks to glow a fiery red—redder than two delicious apples buffed and shined to a glow by an apple maid, ready for market. He rubbed his handiwork, smiling—hotter than a burning ember, but he had been careful not to bruise her.

Youthful Natasha heard herself softly puling and whimpering in the thin voice of a child. She could feel the burning discomfort but was also aware Kaelin had stopped. Suddenly, inexplicably and frighteningly, once more in a dream, she could again see Kaelin's face in the clear, deep pool of her vision. His eyes and his expression revealed that he was dissatisfied—angry. Not only could she see his face, but she could also feel or sense his being—that he was deadly, deadly lethal, and yet she was not afraid of him. She sensed he had passion—a deep passion for her.

Now she saw his face when he passed her that day on the Great Stone Bridge, with his cocky yet pleasant smile. She could feel joy in him—joy, fun, and adventure. Her blood continued to stir—to heat. Was this the goddess Asa continuing to move within her?

Another breeze abruptly blew from the misty river. Natasha could feel it touch her legs, move over her backside, and gently flow into her ears. It felt warm, as though it may have been heated from her ardent buttocks. Without explanation or warning, the breeze suddenly became the fevered, soft voice of a woman, speaking in the tongue of the Hyacinth Gatherers. She could not explain why, nor did she understand how, but she knew it must be the goddess Asa.

Kaelin is your providence, my sweet love, and your future. I have sent him to you. Accept your fate and endure your discipline. Kaelin leads you to your destiny.

Instead of chastising, Kaelin's rough hand now gently rubbed her flaming buttocks, hot to his touch. He kneaded each cheek, not with a firm squeeze but with a tender, soft caress. Again, his index finger rubbed each small blue dot at the top of her backside, but just as before, they did not rub off. Taking a liberty, he leaned over slightly to gaze between her thighs, and although her ankles were crossed, he could see the beautiful folds of her female innocence—wet—glistening—swollen.

Kaelin delighted in this exquisite vision, but it was not enough. He wanted to see more—he wanted to see all of her. He brought his left hand from her horse's tail hair to her buttocks and spread her cheeks apart to reveal her maiden opening, waiting to be entered, and slightly above was her nether orifice—her cerise-pink, delicate tea-rose, the size of his thumbnail.

Exposed to the air, Natasha whimpered and instinctively flexed, tightening her secret, delicate treasure hidden between her cheeks. Kaelin marveled at the subtle movement. He brought his two middle fingers to his mouth, wet them, and gently slid both between her cheeks, to touch her dew-moistened flower. Gently, he caressed the folds of her maiden opening but did not insert his fingers. Sliding his wet fingers forward, he found her sensitive female organ and tenderly, ever so gently, massaged her secret treasure. It swelled, growing rigid.

The feeling of Kaelin's gentle caress was more wondrous than Natasha could have ever imagined. For an instant, or perhaps an eternity, she again became lost in the paradox and in the unseen, mystical world of the goddess Asa. The power of the goddess moved in her. Her hot, youthful blood continued to flow from her burning buttocks, throughout her entire body and to her pulsating, feminine flower. Her heart pounded, and her hard breathing, through her nose and mouth, sounded in a syncopated chorus. Her hands once more gripped Kaelin's ankle, below his greave and around his sandal. Her ankles, knees, and thighs tightened together. Her moist flower swelled and throbbed. Finally, and suddenly, her rigid female organ contracted. Natasha moaned loudly in a high pitch. Kaelin stopped massaging her organ and instead gripped it between his fingers. It seemed to burst. Every muscle in her body flexed, especially her pelvis and buttocks. She thought she might urinate—her whole body became more rigid than an excited man's stiff erection.

Without warning, it all relaxed. Natasha panted but calmed to some measure. She could not believe she—or any female—could experience such a wondrous feeling. Kaelin slowly withdrew his hand but continued to massage her buttocks.

Natasha felt beyond description—wonderful, breathtaking, and spectacular—she could think of metaphors unendingly. Now she knew what all the excitement was about—and she wanted more.

"Oh, yes! Blessed goddess," she said out loud, but under her breath. She wanted much, much more.

Kaelin pulled Natasha to her feet to stand in front of him and lifted his sandaled foot from the limb, planting it firmly on the ground. He held her by her shoulders as she gazed up at his face. She swallowed hard, panting. Stepping to him, she gently laid her head against the bronze symbol of the Ravenbourne crest, fixed to his leather jerkin, and wrapped her arms tautly around his waist. Her arduous breathing inhaled the aroma of his leather armor, mixed with his male scent.

Moving one hand lightly on the side of her head, Kaelin placed the other on the small of her back. They both softly panted. After a moment he slowly brought his head down until his lips found hers, then kissed her with a warming tenderness. Moving her head just slightly up, Natasha returned his kiss. Such a kiss she had not before experienced. A kiss the poets could not describe—the first kiss of love.

Tilting her head back, Natasha gazed up to his face and into his deep, brown eyes. She still panted lightly and whispered faint, delicate "Oh" sounds. Kaelin's expression was serious, but he also wore a slight smile. He remained a continuing paradox. Silence filled all the air around them. Natasha could hear her own breathing and heard herself speak.

"Kaelin! Are you going to make love to me?" she asked in a childlike voice:

"Yes," he whispered, moving close so that his lips just brushed against hers and she could feel his soft touch and smell his ardent, sweet breath. "And when I am finished, you will belong to me."

Kaelin's hands cupped Natasha's face and neck. His index fingers lay along her jaw while his thumbs gently caressed the corners of her mouth. His right palm felt hot—Natasha opened her mouth—lifting both her hands to the back of his neck. With sultry, passionate breath, their warm, open mouths met, and he kissed her again with both unyielding strength and a craving passion.

Suddenly, Natasha could no longer stand. She felt herself collapsing. Kaelin caught her and swept her off her feet . . . and into his arms.

Appendix: Characters

Ravenbourne Villa Estates
  Sol Y'Sloic, Lord of Ravenbourne (general of the Southern Army)
  Ann Y'Sloic, Lady of Ravenbourne
  Old Nanny, lifelong nanny to Lady Ravenbourne
  Ginal, female Taolian, personal bodyguard of Lady Ravenbourne
  Kasena, handmaid to Lady Ravenbourne
  Malia, handmaid to Lady Ravenbourne
  Aleah, handmaid to Lady Ravenbourne
  Ish-Bel, high priestess of the Sacred Temple of Asa

Ravenbourne Warrior Corps
  Commander, Colonel Davis
  Lieutenant Ginal, personal bodyguard of Lady Ravenbourne

  First Company
  Commander, Captain Tydeus
  First Sergeant, Klause

  Equestrian Guard
  Commander, Captain Aaragon
  Second Officer, Lieutenant Rin Rohan
  First Sergeant, Twilsua

Village Patrol
>   Commander, Lieutenant Kaelin, soldier of fallen Opar
>   First Sergeant Lutas
>   Sergeant Derick, first squad leader
>   Sergeant Jarried, second squad leader

Ravenbourne Villagers
>   Natasha, village girl
>   Melissa, Natasha's friend
>   Thoas, village Elder, Natasha's father
>   Old Torrhen, village Elder
>   Ned Coxen, village Elder
>   Aunt Elbe, Natasha's aunt
>   Aunt Ymir, Melissa's aunt

Starfall Villa Estates
>   Lizabeth Y'Liory, Lady of Starfall
>   LinDar, Nefarian Slave-girl

Dragonstone Villa Estates
>   Baron Dardanus, Lord of Dragonstone, father of Lizabeth Y'Liory

Dragonfire Villa Estates
>   Drako de Camp, Duke of Dragonfire (general of the Eastern Army)

Greenstone Villa Estates
>   Lord Philemon
>   Lady Baucis

Southern Army
    Commander, General Sol Y'Sloic, Lord of Ravenbourne
    Second-in-Command, Colonel Cal duPree
    Third-in-Command, Lieutenant Colonel T. Rogir
    First Strike Force
    Commander, Colonel Lycus

Eastern Army
    Commander, General Drako de Camp, Duke of Dragonfire

Royal Family and Court
    Emperor, Kaius Y'Capis
    Prince, Thadious Y'Capis (Emperor's son)
    Princess, Alexandria Ocaesio Y'Capis (wife of prince)
    Imperial Physician/Master of History, Caysil Abeta

Opar Slave Buyers
    Master Smyth, royal family slave buyer
    Calea, Master Smyth's interpreter, Kaelin's mother
    Susanna, virgin pallake of Master Smyth, Calea's daughter
    Old Nanny
    Nanny Talcrane

Others
    Ox, Feohtan of the Heart Blood College, Kaelin's friend
    Coe, bed-slave of the Heart Blood College, Kaelin's friend
    Theo Tomita, personal physician of General Y'Sloic, Lord of
    Ravenbourne

And don't miss the next installment of the
Ravenbourne Trilogy: Book II

Ravenbourne Searching

By

Benjamin H. Barnette

Previews

Lord Ravenbourne marches to Capital City with his personal Equestrian Guard and the First Strike Force, to meet privately with Emperor Kaius Y'Capis. Does the attack on his life mean there is a plot of a rebellion—if so—who? He learns the Emperor has already decided to take over the dye trade from the Nak'la-Sat traders and wants him to command that effort. The General of the Southern also experiences the intrigue, mystery, and noir atmosphere of the Royal Palace including the Emperor's rare Nefarian slave-girl.

Captain Aaragon and First Sergeant Twilsua are assigned by Lord Ravenbourne to travel to the Dye Trader camp and join the next caravan across the Hindu-Cush. Lord Ravenbourne and the Emperor hope it will be the first of many Imperial caravans taking over the caravan trade from the Nak'la-Sat. The two Ravenbourne Warriors are also tasked to learn what they might of the deadly plant consumed by Lord Ravenbourne's attackers and what they can of the secretive dye kernels. They are likewise introduced to the mysterious Nak'la-Sat, in particular, one numinous, young servant girl with an irresistible allure.

Calea also travels with Master Smyth and an Imperial caravan to Capital City, the first part of her destiny complete—she and Susanna are slaves of the Royal family—rather than a miserable brothel or some other horrid establishment. But what of their future? Will she stay with Susanna and the Royal Family or Master Smyth? She is yet not sure. And Susanna now knows she is one of the rare seven daughters of the goddess Asa. Surely the women of the palace or the Princess herself will discover that secret. And more importantly, will that discovery give her and Susanna freedom or condemn Calea and her daughter forever in slavery?

Lady Ravenbourne, along with high priestess Ish-Bell and Natasha's aunt Elbe, have now learned the identity of the two missing Daughters of Asa—through Kaelin. Even so, it does not mean they know where they might be found. And Natasha, is seemingly one of the seven Daughters of Asa, the Hyacinth Gatherer, as she bears the strange blue dots. Apparently, however, she is unaware of her preponderate circumstances. The quest of the three Ravenbourne women of power becomes more complex and equally mysterious. Surely, they must now confront Kaelin and Natasha—together—or separately.

The destinies of Kaelin and Natasha have now been ostensibly united, but love remains a dichotomy—it can both unite and separate. Kaelin still seeks complete freedom and the whereabouts of his mother and sister. Natasha continues to yearn for a better future—more than a village life. And when it is learned that Natasha and Susanna are both Daughters of Asa—sired by Lord Ravenbourne the complexity, intensity, adventure, bloodshed, and passionate sexual desire can only build.

Also by Benjamin H. Barnette

"Fans of Ice Age prehistoric fiction settings ala Jean Auel's 'Earth's Children' series will relish the setting and events in *Winds Across Beringia*, which is set in the last Ice Age on a narrow channel connecting Alaska with Siberia.

—*Midwest Book Review*

Diane Donovan, Senior Reviewer

Author Biography

Benjamin H. Barnette was born in Muskogee, Oklahoma and holds a Ph.D. from the University of Nebraska-Lincoln. He has been a working "field archeologist" for over 35 years with his professional focus on North American prehistory. He has completed wide-ranging fieldwork in the states of: Nevada—Alaska—Oregon—Arizona—Oklahoma—California—and Hawaii. Although he has not accomplished work in Classical or Bronze Age archeology he has completed, extensive research in Bronze Age, Mediterranean cultures.

Photograph by Evan Smith, Grass Valley, California 2016.

A Vietnam veteran, Barnette spent four years in the active Air Force serving in Guam and Thailand in 1968 and 1969. He later enlisted in the Army and Air National Guard serving a total of 20 years. He retired in 2007. He is a proud member of the Muscogee (Creek) Nation of Oklahoma.

Ravenbourne Slavery is the first Book of the Ravenbourne Trilogy and his second novel. His first, *Winds Across Beringia*, was published in 2020 and a Historic Fiction epic about mammoth hunters, living on the Bering Sea land bridge called Beringia. He currently resides in Tahlequah, Oklahoma.

BENJAMINHBARNETTE.COM

BENJAMINHBARNETTE ON FACEBOOK